Leabharlann Shont

MORTAL
ALLIES

Also by Brian Haig

Secret Sanction

MORTAL ALLIES

BRIAN HAIG

ORION

First published in Great Britain in 2002 by Orion Books
an imprint of The Orion Publishing Group
Orion House, 5 Upper St Martin's Lane, London WC2H 9EA

A CIP catalogue record for this book is available
from the British Library

ISBN (hardback) 0 75284 664 7
ISBN (trade paperback) 0 75284 665 5

Printed and bound in Great Britain by
Clays Ltd, St Ives plc

To Lisa,
Brian, Pat, Donnie, and Anne

Acknowledgments

No book is an author's alone. Some individuals help conjure the images, like General (ret.) Robert W. RisCassi, who commanded the alliance in Korea for three years and did more to improve our common security than anyone will possibly know. And did more to inspire my imagination—as well as many others—about the true meaning of great leadership and personal character than he will ever know. Or Pete Kinney and Chuck Wardell, two former soldiers who help shape the picture of Sean Drummond.

Or Luke Janklow, my agent, friend, and advocate. And all the rest of the team at Janklow & Nesbitt, who really are the best in the business.

Or Rick Horgan, the kind of editor every novice writer dreams about: demanding, thoughtful, experienced, and on the mark.

Or Mari Okuda and Roland Ottewell, who did the copyediting and, to my everlasting chagrin, corrected more mistakes than I can count. And all the rest of the folks at Warner Books, from Larry Kirshbaum down, who make the book business seem like a circle of friends just having a great time.

I owe them all my appreciation.

As I do to the men and women of our Armed Forces, who keep us safe.

MORTAL
ALLIES

CHAPTER
1
★ ★ ★

There are two things about Korea you never forget.

The first is the roiling mishmash of stinks. That May, there was the bitter stench of tear gas, an essence of spring and fall, since Korean students are what you might term fair-weather protesters. There was the ripened aroma of kimchi, a spiced and aged cabbage that makes your nostrils think your upper lip's plagued with gangrene. On top of that was the acrid odor of garlic, the lifeblood of every Korean. Finally, there were all the smells of careless progress: smog, construction, and human sweat.

The second thing you never forget is exactly how miserably steamy a Korean late spring day can be. My shirt was pasted to my back before I got halfway across the tarmac to the flight building of Osan Air Base.

I dashed straight through the entry and shoved aside a sputtering Army captain who was rooted like a potted plant waiting to meet and greet me.

"Major Drummond, I, ooof—" was all he could manage before he crashed up against the wall. Then I heard him skittering along behind me.

I moved my stiff legs as fast as I could, till I spied the door I so desperately sought. I lunged through hard enough to blow it off the hinges; the captain scurried right behind me. At the urinal I got my zipper down not a moment too soon. Another millisecond and the jig would've been up.

My escort propped himself against the sink and studied me with an awed expression. "Jeez, you should see your face."

"You got no idea."

"Long flight, huh?"

I put my left hand against the wall. "Long ain't the half of it. Know whose neck I'd like to wring? The miserable bastard who broke the only toilet in the C-141. I've had my legs crossed since the Alaskan border."

"Well, you're finally here," he consoled, grinning like a fool.

"I guess I am."

A full, awkward thirty seconds passed before he nervously tapped his leg. "My name's Chuck Wilson. I, uh, I've been told to pick you up and escort you to Seoul."

"Hey, that's great, Chuck. Why?"

"Huh?"

"*Why* are you taking me to Seoul? *Why* am I in Korea in the first place?"

An exquisitely befuddled look popped onto his face. "I got no idea, sir. Why *are* you here?"

The stream of urine flooding out of my body had not abated one bit. I got worried. Has anybody ever pissed himself to death?

I didn't ask *him* that, though. I said, "If I knew that, why the hell would I be asking you?"

He glanced down at his watch and said, "You okay, Major? It's been over a minute."

"No, I'm not okay," I complained. "My hand's tired. This damn thing's so big and heavy. Can you come over here and hold it for me?"

We both chuckled a little too emphatically, like real men do whenever any topic arises even remotely touching on homosexuality.

"Sheeit," he drawled in a deep, manly way, "some things a man's gotta do hisself."

"Damn right," I firmly pronounced.

He averted his eyes while I gave Ol' Humungo a manly shake, reholstered, and got my zipper back up. "Okay," I said, moving to the sinks and splashing some water on my hands and face, "let's find my bags and get outta here."

"Forget the bags," he said. "My driver's getting 'em."

We went out, and a husky young corporal named Vasquez was standing proudly beside a spanking-new black Kia sedan with lots of gleaming chrome. I made him open the trunk so I could peek in, and sure enough there sat my duffel bag and oversize lawyer's briefcase. Then Wilson and I climbed into the backseat.

"Well, ain't this the plush life," I remarked, running an admiring hand across the leather upholstery. "I figured you'd get me in a nasty old humvee."

"Not unless I got an armed escort."

"Armed escort?"

He gave me a curious look. "Haven't you been reading the papers?"

I said, "Hey, Chuck, see these shorts and this ratty T-shirt I'm wearing?"

"Yes sir."

"This is what's called formal attire in Bermuda. See, that's where I was until, uh, oh"—I looked at my watch—"until about twenty-eight hours ago. Know what's so great about Bermuda? No? Let me tell you: No newspapers. No TVs. No cares in the world but which beach has the skimpiest bikinis and which bar's having a two-for-one special at happy hour."

He nodded right along. "Yeah, well, things aren't so blasé over here. We're drowning in anti-American riots. It's gotten so bad we're restricted to our bases. No civilian cars with U.S. plates and no unescorted military vehicles are allowed outside the gates."

"That why we're in this Kia?"

"It's less noticeable. And it took a two-star general to sign off on letting me come get you. I asked for a helicopter, but, no offense intended, they said you just weren't that damned important."

"A helicopter?" I asked, beginning to think this captain was a lit-

tle over the edge. This was South Korea. These people were our allies, not our enemies.

Sounding not the least bit contrite, he said, "I know it sounds
crazy, but, hey, the American embassy got firebombed two days ago.
The ambassador actually got beat up. Bad, too. He had to be mede-
vaced to Hawaii."

With the worldly resignation of one who has spent some time
in Korea, I said, "Look, anti-American riots are a popular local sport.
You must be new. Trust me, Chuck, you'll get used to it."

Three seconds later, I ate my words.

We'd just crested a long, steep hill, and the back gate of the air
base loomed only twenty yards ahead. The roof of our car suddenly
sounded like it was exploding. The sound came from a shower of
rocks that struck like pistol shots. I looked through the front windshield and saw three Molotov cocktails come sailing, end over end,
through the air. Two exploded on the tarmac directly ahead. The
third grazed off the trunk of our car and erupted right behind us.
Two dozen military policemen were careening through the gate,
flailing hopelessly with their nightsticks, shoving backward, and
being chased by a huge mob of Koreans.

I'm no expert on riots, but I've seen a few. I once watched a
bunch of Somali provocateurs trying to get a rise out of some
American peacekeepers. That was a taunting kind of riot, not really
meant to harm the peacekeepers; in fact intended to achieve the
opposite: to get the peacekeepers so riled up they'd do something
harmful to the crowd and end up looking like bad guys. The idea
was to provoke an atrocity.

And as someone who lived through the Vietnam era, I witnessed my share of antiwar riots. Those "riots" were actually more
like big frat parties with lots of kids showing up for the free dope
and to get laid. Those kinds of riots, everybody walks on eggshells,
and they do it in a real fretful way, because both sides are praying
the other doesn't do anything stupid. Atrocities are the last thing
anybody wants.

The mob bearing down on us looked to be the third kind of
riot: the bad kind of riot. The folks in this crowd had menace in

their eyes and mayhem on their minds. Their faces were snarled with anger and hatred, and a lot of them were carrying bats, or Molotov cocktails, or throwing big stones. By the guardshack, two MPs were down, and several Koreans were gathered around kicking and beating them like they were snare drums.

Corporal Vasquez, the driver, jammed down hard on the brakes. He rubbernecked around to face us. "Hey, Captain, what do ya want me to do?"

Wilson craned forward and peered through the windshield. He rubbed his jaw thoughtfully and studied the situation, and looked more thoughtful. His prolonged thoughtfulness made me nervous.

"Gun it!" I yelled.

"Huh?" Vasquez asked.

"Go!" I yelled.

Vasquez turned out to be my favorite kind of soldier: the hair-trigger obedient type. He spun back around, downshifted into neutral, jammed the gas pedal to the floor, then shifted into gear. The car nearly leaped off the ground. The tires screamed as they got traction, and Vasquez wisely shoved down hard on the horn, adding to the racket.

All of a sudden the mob focused on the big, noisy black sedan bearing down on them. That look of the maddened crowd evaporated. I guess they realized there's a fundamental difference between chasing a group of outnumbered, scared MPs and eating the front bumper of a speeding car.

Rioters dove all over the place. We raced through the narrow gate, then Vasquez took a hard right turn, with more squealing tires, and drove madly through a bunch of skinny twisted streets with tightly packed shops on both sides. It took about three minutes before we cleared the village of Osan and made it to a country road that led to the Seoul-Pusan highway.

Captain Wilson's fingers had a death grip on the back of Vasquez's seat. His face was chalky white. "You shouldn't have done that," he moaned. "That was a real bad idea."

"How come?" I asked.

He shook his head and gave me an exasperated look. "'Cause

we're gonna get an official complaint. No doubt about it. You coulda hurt some of those people."

"Hey Chucky, you got things backward. They wanted to hurt *us*. Besides, Osan Air Base is military territory. We have an agreement with the South Koreans. Those people were trespassers. If we'd hit one, it would've been perfectly legal. Trust me."

He gave me a dubious look. "What makes you so damn sure of yourself?"

"I ought to be," I told him. "I'm a lawyer."

"A lawyer?" he asked, like he'd just discovered a big gob of smelly dog doo on the sole of his shoe.

"Yeah, you know. A JAG officer. One of those guys with a license to practice law."

His face got this very pained expression. "You mean . . . you mean, I went through this shit to get a *JAG* officer?"

With the tension and all, he just blurted that out. I didn't take offense, though. See, in the Army, JAG officers aren't real high on anybody's be-sure-to-invite-to-the-party lists. We're regarded as geeky, bookish, wimpy types without a lot of redeeming virtues. Lawyers aren't all that popular in the civilian world, either, but at least they inspire envy with the money they earn.

Military lawyers, nobody envies us. We shave our heads and dress somewhat funny, and our pay's only a hairsbreadth away from minimum wage.

I leaned back into my seat and crossed my recently tanned legs. "So what's got the natives up in arms this time?"

Wilson let loose his grip on Vasquez's seat and drifted back also. "What happened was that three American soldiers raped and murdered a South Korean."

"That's too bad," I said in a casually offhanded way. "Regrettable, I'm sure, but that kind of thing's happened over here plenty of times. Anything special about this one?"

"I'd say."

"What?"

"It was a fag rape."

I nodded, but "Umm-hmm" was all I said.

"That's not the least of it, either. The kid they raped and murdered was a Katusa."

I nodded and umm-hmm'd some more. Katusas are South Korean soldiers assigned to American units. The term actually stands for "Korean Augmentees to the U.S. Army"—more proof that the military can convolute anything into an acronym. Katusas are almost all highly educated college graduates who speak English if not fluently, at least with some degree of proficiency. Most Korean kids consider Katusa duty to be the most agreeable way to perform mandatory military service.

With good reason, too, because the Korean Army is a brown-shoe affair, much like the American Army back in the thirties, where a common soldier's lot is fairly spartan. The pay stinks, the barracks are rustic and unheated, the food's just enough to keep you from starving, and Korean sergeants believe fervently that if you spare the rod, you spoil the child. Hazing and beatings are fairly common.

The American military, on the other hand, is inarguably the world's most spoiled and pampered. Barracks are like college dorms, food's . . . well, at least ample, and if a sergeant so much as raises an open hand in the direction of a private, he's going to need a good defense counsel, like me.

Naturally, any Korean kid with an iota of sense wants to be a Katusa. And just as naturally, any Korean kid with rich or powerful parents usually gets his way.

I looked at Chuck. "I can see where that would be ugly."

"You don't know the half of it," he replied, sighing very visibly. "The Katusa's name was Lee No Tae. Of course, since nearly everybody who lives here's named Lee or Kim, I don't expect you to see the significance of that. His father is Lee Jung Kim. Ever heard of him?"

"Nope."

"He's the defense minister of the South Korean armed forces."

I felt a sudden wrenching in my gut. I mean, here I am, a JAG officer, and I get this panicky call from the Judge Advocate General, the two-star general in charge of the entire Army's JAG Corps, ordering me to terminate my vacation and haul my butt up to Andrews Air Force Base to catch the next military flight to South Korea. Worse, he wouldn't say why. He just said I'd find out when I got there.

It was my turn to squeeze the back of the seat in front of me. "Has this got anything to do with why I've been brought over here?"

It was a rhetorical question, of course.

"No sir," he said, sounding completely resolute. "Not a thing."

"Yeah? How do you know?"

"'Cause, according to the papers, the Organization for Gay Military Members—some group back in the States—hired a bunch of civilian attorneys to come over here and represent the accused."

A relieved sigh escaped from my lungs. I don't mean to sound squeamish, but in my eight years as an Army lawyer, I'd managed to never once be involved with a court case related to homosexuality. There aren't a lot of experienced military lawyers who can say that. I could, though. I was damned glad of it, too.

The thing about flying twelve hours with my bladder pumped full of coffee and that six-pack of Molson I now sorely regretted having smuggled aboard was that I couldn't sleep for fear I'd awaken with a big wet spot in my lap. I smelled foul and was wrung out, so I told Captain Wilson to wake me up when we got to Seoul.

CHAPTER
2
★ ★ ★

Corporal Vasquez flapped his arms and chewed on his lips as he inspected the big pockmarks on the car's roof, and I felt sorry for him as I yanked my gear out of the trunk. He was no doubt scared witless about how he was going to explain those ugly dimples to the motor pool sergeant who'd loaned him the car. If you know anything about Army sergeants, you'll understand.

I walked through the entry into the Dragon Hill Lodge, a military-owned and -run hotel located smack in the middle of Yongsan Garrison, the military base located in the heart of downtown Seoul. This is where the big cheese headquarters is located.

Captain Wilson, being a good sport, followed me across the cavernous, marble-floored lobby and waited while I checked in. The girl at the desk found my reservation, traded my Visa for a magnetic key, then peered intently into her computer screen and informed me I had a message.

A message already? Wasn't I the popular guy?

"Kam sam ni da," I charmingly said, tossing out one of the few Korean phrases from my sparse inventory.

She handed an envelope to me and I tore it open with a finger. The message said I had an appointment to be in the office of the Commander in Chief of the United Nations Command and the Combined Forces Command, at exactly 1500 hours. This was the big cheese himself, a four-star named Martin Spears whom I'd never met, but who was known for being frighteningly smart and painfully demanding.

Fifteen hundred hours is three o'clock to those who don't talk military, and the word "exactly" was harshly underlined three times, like if I came one minute late, well . . . there'd be this firing squad thing.

My watch said ten minutes till one. No problem. That left two hours to take a long, relaxing shower, scrub the whiskers off my chin, and get changed out of my plaid Bermuda shorts and sweaty T-shirt and into a fresh uniform. That's when I remembered my watch was on Bermuda time. I glanced at the clock on the wall: ten minutes till three.

I turned to Wilson. "This note says you're supposed to have me in the Commander in Chief's office in ten minutes, or else. I don't mean to worry you, Chuck, but I sure hope you can get me there in . . . oops, look! Only nine minutes."

Poor Wilson's eyes went wide and his face quivered with fear. He grabbed my duffel, threw it over the counter, clutched my arm, and began tugging me back across the lobby.

We got all the way out the doors before he realized we'd released Vasquez and the sedan. Wilson's head spun around like a madman's until he saw a guy climbing into a black taxi about ten yards down. He sprinted over, grabbed the shoulder of the poor soul, and flung him backward.

"Military necessity!" he yelled.

I climbed into the back right behind him and listened patiently as he screamed at the driver to spare no gas. We were down to eight minutes. The hack punched the pedal and we sped out of the parking lot.

The Yongsan Military Garrison is divided into two halves. The side we were on contains mostly housing and support facilities—the hospital, the veterinarian, the grocery store, and such. The two halves are divided by a major intracity artery, and the headquarters for all the military forces in the Korean alliance is located guess where? On the other side, of course.

We got to the gate and could look across the road to the entrance of the other half of Yongsan; only this was where things suddenly looked hopeless. The road was choked with Korean protesters holding up signs, some of which were in English and said pretty despicable things, and some of which were in Hangul, which is the Korean script, and who cared what they said, because what you don't know don't hurt you.

Captain Wilson gave me a nice grin as he yelled at the driver, "Gun it! Drive through them!"

"What?" the driver screamed.

Wilson lurched forward and screamed in his ear. "Go! Honk your horn! Drive! Get us across this damn road!"

The driver punched his horn, hit the gas, and we sprang forward through a crowd of Koreans frantically diving every which way.

Somehow, almost miraculously, we made it across without killing anybody. At least, I don't think we killed anybody, because there were none of those awful crunching sounds you hear when you run something over. I heard three or four bodies slam loudly against the side of the taxi, but hopefully all they got were bruises for their trouble.

I said, "I really wish you hadn't done that."

"Huh?"

"*That,*" I replied, pointing through the rear window. "*That* was a really bad idea."

"But you did it. Back at Osan."

"Where it was entirely different," I informed him. "We were on military property. This highway belongs to the city of Seoul. Also, those were peaceful protesters, not blood-crazed rioters flinging rocks and Molotov cocktails."

His eyes got watery. "You mean, I screwed up?"

"You screwed up bad," I assured him, just as we pulled up to the front entry of the big headquarters building.

As I climbed out, I bent over, looked into his downcast eyes, and said, "Look, you get in trouble, give me a call. I'll serve as your attorney. Okay? Don't worry, I hardly ever lose."

He suddenly grabbed my arm and shook my hand, and was still mumbling pleading things at my back as I walked through the grand entrance of the headquarters. Infantry officers might not have a real high regard for lawyers, but they kiss your ass pretty good when they think they need you.

The full colonel who was obviously the general's gatekeeper looked up from his desk when I barged in and gave me an instantly disapproving glare. He looked down at my sandals, paused at my plaid shorts, then dwelled speculatively on the letters on the front of my T-shirt, which read "Go Navy, Beat Army." Poor choice on my part, I suppose. He must've been a West Pointer, because that's when his eyes really caught fire.

"Who the hell are you?" he demanded.

"Major Sean Drummond," I said. "I just got to the hotel and there was a note at the desk that said if I wasn't here at 1500 hours, I'd get castrated."

I grinned stupidly. My wisecrack was supposed to soften the mood, show I was one of the guys, elicit a sympathetic smirk.

Oops. He leaped up and said, "You've made it all the way to major and never learned to salute when you report to a senior officer?"

He definitely was a West Pointer, because you can't ever salute or say "sir" enough to the bully boys from the Hudson.

I whipped off a humdinger of a salute. "Major Sean Drummond, reporting as ordered, sir."

This seemed to mollify him somewhat. Not a lot; only somewhat. He returned my salute, and hot damn, if it wasn't more of a humdinger than mine. You could almost hear the air crackle, his hand sliced through it so fast.

"You're the lawyer, right?" he asked.

"I am *a* lawyer, sir," I dutifully confirmed.

"Your co-counsel is already in General Spears's office."

"My co-counsel?"

"That's right," he said, glancing down at his watch. "Unlike you, she arrived right on time."

"She?"

"What are you waiting for?" he barked, pointing a long, stern finger at a hand-carved wooden door.

I got the message. I walked over, knocked gently, and entered the office of General Martin Spears, Commander in Chief of every military thing south of the 38th Parallel.

The first thing I saw was the back of the woman who was standing in front of the general's desk. There was a shock of gleaming dark hair that hung like a shimmering flag all the way to her rump. She was short and slender with wide shoulders. She wore the traditional garb of a female lawyer: a dark blue pinstriped pantsuit cut to look neither sexy nor nonsexy. It didn't seem compatible with her long hair. She looked like a tiny ballerina who'd gotten her wardrobe mixed up.

Something was disturbingly familiar about her.

Spears tore his piercing eyes off her and targeted them at me. He was a thin, late-middle-aged man with sparse, graying hair, a face like a bloodthirsty Mohawk, and eyes that looked menacing enough to shoot tank rounds at you.

I swiftly marched forward, his eyebrows making me painfully aware how shabbily and inappropriately I was dressed. I hoped that if I did this just right, he might, maybe, hopefully, please God, ignore my attire. I stopped in front of his desk and, inspired by the example of the colonel in the general's outer sanctum, rocketed my right hand to my right brow so hard I nearly punched a dent in my forehead.

"Major Sean Drummond, reporting as ordered, sir."

He nodded and then glumly murmured to the woman, "Your co-counsel has arrived."

She slowly turned her head and I nearly fell out of my chair. Actually, I wasn't sitting in a chair. But you get the point.

Katherine Carlson had been in my class at Georgetown law school eight years before. Actually, not just in my class, she was first in my class. She was the smartest damn thing anybody ever saw: summa cum laude as an undergrad at Harvard, full scholarship to law school, editor of law review, and—please believe me when I say this—a royal pain in the ass.

If you've heard the phrase "made sparks fly," that understated what happened anytime Katherine and I got within spitting distance of each other. We made trees explode into flames. The law professors hated us. The other students hated us. Hell, even the janitors hated us. They didn't hate me personally. Or her personally. They hated *us*.

The whole point of law school is to study, dissect, and discuss issues of the law. Well, that's what Katherine Carlson and I did. The problems came when we got to that "discuss" part because she and I never, not once, saw eye-to-eye on anything. If you want to know what it was like, think about what kind of philosophical discussion the Easter Bunny and Attila the Hun might have if they sat down to compare lifestyles. Katherine would be the bunny, of course. I wasn't really Attila, though that's what she spitefully called me whenever she wanted to get a rise out of me. And when I wanted to taunt her, I called her Moonbeam, because she was so damned liberal she'd fallen off the left edge of the earth.

By the second year of law school, it got so bad the dean actually decreed that Carlson and I weren't allowed to take any more classes together. Then we weren't allowed to eat in the school cafeteria together. Then we weren't allowed to be in the same hallway, then the library, or even the same building together. I heard through the grapevine that halfway through our third year, the faculty committee was making arrangements for one of us to be forcefully transferred to another law school—one far away, like maybe Europe or Asia, where nobody could hear us screaming at each other.

We weren't just different; we were wildly, inconsolably, antagonistically different. Carlson wasn't even her real last name. Can you imagine that? It was some half-assed moniker she chose for herself, since her parents weren't actually married. At least, not married in any traditional sense, like having stood in front of a preacher or a local magistrate. That's because Katherine's family thought names, and organized religions, and governments, and laws, were all useless anachronisms. Her parents were sixties flower children who never recovered, who still, to the day we were in law school, lived in one of those preposterous rustic communes in the mountains of Colorado. The name of the commune, I'd once learned, was Carlson. See why I taunted her with the nickname Moonbeam?

I, on the other hand, was sired by a United States Army colonel who slapped his name on my birth certificate the day I was born and made me keep it. He was a career soldier, a shoo-in to make general until he was forced to medically retire after he got shot with a crossbow in the Vietnam War. Where he got shot is something of a delicate subject, but if you really want to know, it was square, dead center, right in the ass. And as for his politics, suffice it to say my father would've been a John Bircher except the Birchers are a bit too wimpy and undisciplined for his liking. Plus, my father was never a bigot. That not-a-bigot thing, that was the only thread of liberalism in his entire being.

Spears was now looking at me inquisitively, I guess because my bottom lip was quivering and my eyes were bulging out of my sockets. "Major, I assume you and Miss Carlson are acquainted."

I somehow choked out, "Uh . . . we, uh, we know each other."

She calmly said, "Yes, Martin. I actually went to law school with Attila here."

My ears winced, not because she'd called me Attila, but because she hadn't called him General, or General Spears, or sir. She'd called him Martin. When you make your living in the Army, like I do, you can't imagine generals have first names, except as distinguishing appendages to use on their signature blocks, just in case there is more than one of them and you can't tell precisely which General Spears you're dealing with.

Of course, a woman like Katherine Carlson would find military ranks absurd, a loathsome badge of an Orwellian, tyrannical society. That's the kind of person she was. Please believe me about that.

Spears leaned back in his chair and I could see him staring at the two of us, struggling to sort through what might be happening here.

"Miss Carlson, this is the officer you requested, isn't it?"

"He definitely is," she assured him.

"Good. I was hoping we didn't make a mistake and get the wrong damned Drummond."

"No, he's the right damned Drummond," she mocked.

Then Spears bent forward and his eyes, which were menacing even when they were relaxed, stopped relaxing. "Major, is there a reason you're dressed that way?"

"Uh, yes sir. Actually, I was in Bermuda, on leave, when I got called by the Pentagon and was ordered to get myself immediately to Andrews Air Force Base to catch a C-141."

"And you couldn't change into a uniform between Bermuda and here?"

"Uh, actually, sir, no. See, I didn't bring any uniforms with me. To Bermuda, that is. Not to worry, though. My legal assistant pre-loaded a duffel bag in the cargo bay of the C-141. So I've got uniforms. Now I do, anyway. I, uh, I just didn't have time to change."

I was blabbering like a fool, because my composure had taken a leave of absence a few seconds ago. He sat back and absorbed my words, no doubt thinking I was some remarkably rare variety of idiot.

"Do you know why you're here?" he asked in a very simple-minded tone, the way parents talk to small tots.

"No sir. Except what I just heard you and Miss Carlson discussing. I guess she's requested me as co-counsel," I said, trying without much success to mask my disbelief.

"Your guess is correct."

"Might I be so bold as to ask the general: co-counsel for what?"

Spears began playing with the knuckles of his right hand. I heard one or two crack loudly, almost as though he'd just sundered the bone. "Have you been following the Lee No Tae case?"

Something in the pit of my stomach rumbled in a very ugly way. "I've heard about it," I admitted. "Something about a Katusa soldier who was raped and murdered?"

"Right case," the general said, "but wrong order. First he was raped, then murdered." His mouth twitched with disgust. "Then he was raped again."

Katherine said, "I've been retained by OGMM, the Organization for Gay Military Members, to represent one of the accused. Since military courts require civilian attorneys to have a JAG co-counsel, I requested you."

I nearly choked with surprise. See, an accused in the military has the right, if he or she so desires, to be defended by a civilian attorney in lieu of a uniformed barrister, provided they're willing to pick up the tab themselves. However, the Uniform Code of Military Justice, or UCMJ, which is the code of laws Congress passed especially for the Armed Forces, has some striking differences from your ordinary, run-of-the-mill civilian law. And since civilian attorneys aren't expected to know the peculiarities of the UCMJ, or the ins and outs of court-martial procedures, they *must* have a qualified JAG officer by their side to advise them. That way, if the accused loses, he or she can't appeal on the basis that their civilian lawyer didn't know the difference between a 105mm round and a buck sergeant.

Spears's hawklike face suddenly got real intimidating. He was glaring nastily at us both. "All right, listen up. The reason I asked you here is because I want to pass on a few warnings." He then very pointedly looked at me. "I can't begin to describe how sensitive or explosive this case is. Lee No Tae was the son of Lee Jung Kim. Minister Lee is not only my close personal friend, he is a man of legendary stature in this country. This story has been on the front page of every newspaper on this peninsula for the past three weeks. We have ninety-five American military bases here, and at this moment every single one of them is ringed with protesters and rioters. It's been this way ever since we arrested and charged the three soldiers involved with this crime."

I glanced at Katherine; she appeared to be absently paying attention, sort of half listening, half not.

The general couldn't miss her studied indifference, but he went on anyway. "We've been on this peninsula since 1945, and frankly, the list of crimes our troops have committed against Korean citizens could fill libraries. They're tired of it. They have a right to be. Murders, rapes, robberies, child molesting—you name it, we've done it. And more likely than not, we've done it at least a few hundred times. It's bad enough when a Korean commits a crime against another Korean. It's doubly bad when an American does it. We're foreigners for one thing, and it contains a hint of racism for another. But this crime, murder, then raping a corpse . . . Christ, it would turn anybody's stomach. It's inflamed the Korean people like nothing I've ever seen. Do you understand what I'm saying?"

Katherine shifted her weight from her left foot to her right. She began studying her fingernails, as though to say, Couldn't he just get this over with, because she did have this very urgent appointment for a manicure.

"No, Martin," she said, "I don't understand. Exactly what are you saying?"

If I hadn't just been appointed co-counsel for one of the accused, I would've weighed in right then to warn Spears to be painstakingly careful with the next words to come out of his lips. He could not appear to be predisposed or prejudiced on the guilt or innocence of the accused. This *was* the Army, and if Katherine could prove he'd in any way used his four stars to prejudice or influence the fate of her client, she'd get this case thrown out of court in a New York second. The larger thing, though, was that Katherine Carlson was a thirty-three-year-old woman with an angelic babyface and a pair of wide, seemingly gullible emerald green eyes that made her appear hardly old enough to be out of law school.

What that serene camouflage masked was the most ruthless and vindictive legal mind I'd ever encountered.

He blinked once or twice, and chewed on something in the back of his throat. Sounding strained, he said, "What I'm warning you, Miss Carlson, is to be damned careful. Things are very flammable here. I won't have anyone running around recklessly playing with matches."

She looked up at the ceiling for a few seconds, like she was gazing at the stars, except the only stars in the room were the four on this gentleman's shoulder, which she was making a point of openly ignoring.

I wasn't, though. I wasn't at all.

She said, "Are you telling me I can't represent my client to the fullest extent of my legal resources?"

"I'm not saying any such thing," he protested, although truth be known, I didn't detect the slightest hint of conviction in his tone.

"Then what exactly are you saying, Martin?"

"I'm saying I don't want any attempts to try this case in the media. It's a crime that involves homosexuality, and we all know what that means. But you better recognize it's also got damned serious diplomatic consequences. Say the wrong things and you'll spark riots. People can get badly hurt. Don't make a circus out of this."

Katherine bent over and put her hands on the front of the general's desk. She leaned forward till her face was inches from his.

In frigidly cold language, she said, "Now, I'm going to make myself perfectly clear. My client is accused of murder, necrophilia, rape, and a long list of lesser charges. He faces the death penalty. I will do everything in my legal power to protect him. I'll be watching you and every other tinpot dictator in uniform like a hawk. Do one thing, just one thing, to impair my ability to defend my client, and I'll get this case thrown out faster than you can spit. Then you'll have to explain to the Korean people how my client walked free because you screwed up."

She straightened back up to her full five feet two inches of height and glared down at him. "Martin, do you understand everything I just said?"

Poor General Spears just got his first whiff of what I had to put up with during three years at Georgetown Law. Only this was just a half dose of what Katherine Carlson had to offer. Maybe a quarter dose. She really was a royal pain in the ass—you *have* to believe me on this point.

His face got real red, and his fists got tight, because he certainly wasn't accustomed to being talked to this way. And besides, he was justifiably worried about the safety of the thirty thousand Americans under his command and about maintaining the military alliance, which could possibly get ripped asunder by this case. I sympathized with him terribly.

My lips were just parting to assure him we'd be good and damned careful, and responsible, too, when Katherine suddenly whirled and faced me.

"Keep your mouth shut," she hissed. "Not a word. You're my co-counsel, but I'm in charge of this defense. You'll follow my lead or I'll file a complaint and have you disbarred for malpractice."

I felt blood rush to my face and I gulped once or twice. I looked down at General Spears. He was staring back up at me. It was not a pretty look. What his eyes were saying was that I better get control over Katherine Carlson, and I better do it fast, or he'd hang my gonads on his Christmas tree.

CHAPTER
3
★ ★ ★

I sulked the whole way to my room in the Dragon Hill Lodge. The other three people in the hotel elevator even edged away from me, because my eyes were glowing murderously. I sulk in a very nasty way.

I don't like being publicly dressed down, especially by a civilian, and even more especially by a civilian woman in the presence of a four-star general. But most especially of all, I don't like being dressed down by Katherine Carlson. Call me petty, but there it is.

I was well aware of what she'd been up to the past eight years. For one thing, Georgetown University, despite its Catholic heritage, was inexplicably proud of her. Any number of fawning articles had been written about her in the alumni magazines I got in the mail every quarter. For a second thing, her name frequently got mentioned in *TIME* and *Newsweek,* not to mention every other prominent magazine or newspaper you could name. This happened almost anytime there was a big military case involving a gay soldier, or a soldier accused of being gay.

See, Katherine Carlson was the legal attack dog of America's gay culture against the Armed Forces. The "Apostle of Gayness," she'd been nastily labeled by one right-wing journal that was outraged by her brutal tactics and unswerving persistence. More friendly journals called her "William Kunstler in drag." She'd han-

dled many dozens of cases, and her trademarks were there for
everybody to see. She terrorized the judges and opposing attorneys. She lambasted the military profession. She burned down the
courthouses. She didn't win a lot of cases, because the laws were
written against her, so she was a legal Sisyphus, fiercely rolling that
big rock up that long hill, again and again. That was okay with her,
though. She didn't really intend to win. She just wanted to make
damned sure that every time the military won, it was a bloody,
Pyrrhic victory. She was a brilliant theoretician and a canny tacti-
cian. She slashed and burned in court, and she tried her cases in
the press, and America's journalistic corps loved her for it.

To Katherine, this was war. She was a single-issue acolyte. She
treated the defense of gays like a religious calling, only you have to
think once or twice about the issue she glommed on to. I mean,
there're lots of good, worthy liberal causes a lady with her fiercely
anarchic bent could pick from. She could've been a tree hugger, or
a save-the-whaler, or a defender of the homeless, or even an ASPCA
freak. Those are all reputable lefty causes, right? But no; she chose
gay rights. Now I hate to draw hasty conclusions, but real, meat-
eating heterosexuals just don't get too worked up about gay rights.
There's a certain amount of self-interest in all of us, and she sure as
hell wasn't being paid a fortune to handle those cases. In fact, it
was public interest law, so she was making about half what I was.
And I wasn't making much, believe me.

I therefore naturally, inevitably concluded that Katherine Carlson was a lesbian—though don't think I'm so hasty and narrow-
minded that I drew that conclusion merely on the basis of the
cause she so ferociously represented. The fact is, I never once saw
her with a boyfriend back at Georgetown. Her being angelically
beautiful and actually quite sexy in an oddly chaste sort of way,
guys talk about those things. Nobody else ever saw her with a
boyfriend, either. Think about it. I mean, there're lots of guys who
could care less how grating a girl is—and please believe me,
Katherine is grating as hell—as long as she looks great and puts
out.

Carlson sure as hell looked great, but there wasn't a guy in that law school who could work up a smug smirk and say she put out. She was always surrounded by other girls, and most of them looked pretty masculine to me.

I threw my clothes on the bed and stepped into the bathroom for a long-overdue shower. After I finished shaving, I wrapped a towel around my waist and lay down. I was damned tired and still hadn't adjusted to being yanked out of the lethargic, unhurried pace of Bermuda. I closed my eyes and was just at that point of drifting off when the phone rang.

"Hello," I mumbled, or grumbled, or something.

"Attila, I'm having a defense meeting in ten minutes. Be here. And be on time."

Then she hung up. She hadn't said where she was having her meeting. She hadn't said where she was staying. She hadn't said who else was going to be there. I wanted to strangle her.

I called the front desk and asked if she had a room here at the Dragon Hill Lodge. I was lucky. She did. In fact, only two floors down. I slipped on my battle dress, speedlaced my boots, and actually was standing at the door to room 430 on time.

I knocked, the door opened, and an amazon stared down at me. I'm not exaggerating, either. She was staring *down* at me. She was easily six foot three, a lanky, stretched-out lady, with a long, narrow face, a huge, parrotlike nose, and spiky hair. She was wearing a flowered dress that hung down to her bony knees, but nothing was going to make this woman look anything close to feminine.

I stared up at her a long moment. How could I not? I'm only five foot ten, and she'd moved up real close, like she wanted to accentuate her advantage.

I nearly screamed in fright, only I'm too tough for that.

"Who're you?" she demanded in a gruff voice.

"Drummond, Sean, Major, one each. Reporting as ordered," I said in my most wiseass tone. When I'm scared out my wits, I get like that—blustery to the point of being obnoxious.

She turned around and yelled, "Katherine, you expectin' some runt in a uniform?"

"Does he look sort of Neanderthalish and ignorant?" a voice yelled back.

"Uh-huh," she grunted.

"That's just Drummond. Let him in."

The amazon stepped aside and I warily circled past her. There were two other people in addition to Katherine and the amazon. One guy and one girl.

The guy was improbably handsome. He was a few years younger than me, blond with sea blue eyes, perfectly white teeth, a slender build, and facial features that presumptive writers might describe as sculpted. Maybe I was predisposed, but I had the impression of a guy who was naturally good-looking who went to some lengths to be even better-looking; an effort that makes many manly guys somewhat squeamish and mistrustful, if you know what I mean.

The other woman had short-cropped brunette hair that accentuated her delicate, almost tiny features. She was actually an inch or two shorter than Katherine, and was so slight of build that she was what my mother would call dainty. Like Katherine, she was dressed in a fancy silk pantsuit and would have been quite pretty if it weren't for the gloomy frown on her face. I thought she seemed feminine in a kittenish way, but that got cleared up real quick when the amazon lumbered past me, jumped on the same bed, and threw an extraordinarily long arm around her neck. To say they were an unlikely-looking couple would be to put too fine an edge on it. They looked like a distorted version of a Disney tale—a teeny beauty and a gangly beast.

It's important at this point to understand that I grew up on military bases and spent my entire professional life in the Army. You become accustomed to the military culture, which has a fairly masculine ambiance and a distinctly conservative bent. Anything that's divergently different makes your hair stand up. And that's what was happening at this instant. I literally reached up and patted down the top of my head, so it wasn't too obvious.

"Hey, everybody," I said, with this painfully awkward smile.

Katherine said, "Attila, you look like you're about to faint. Excuse him, everybody. I warned you he'd be a big disappointment."

"Heh-heh," I laughed, just to show them I was a good sport.

Nobody else laughed, I noticed.

The amazon said, "I'm Alice. I like Allie, though."

"Pleased to meet you, Allie," I incoherently mumbled, since it wasn't strictly correct. I wasn't the least bit pleased to meet her.

"I'm Keith," the guy said, bouncing off the bed with his left hand hanging from a very limp wrist. "Keith Merritt, if you want my full name."

His handshake was so quick and light, you wondered if it actually happened.

The other woman stayed on the bed, frowned, and complained, "I'm Maria."

"Hi," I said, smiling. She didn't smile back.

"Okay, everybody's met," Katherine said. "Get seated and let's get started."

I looked around for a moment and wondered where I should sit. Allie the amazon stayed on the bed right next to Maria the grump. Keith patted a spot on the mattress he was stretched out on.

I rolled my eyes and audibly groaned, then went over and sat on the floor in the corner, as far from everybody as I could belligerently get. The rest of them giggled, like my discomfort was just the funniest damn thing in the whole damn world.

Katherine studied us all in a businesslike way.

"We've got a court date," she announced. "It's set for two weeks from today. They're bringing in a judge from Washington. Attila, have you ever heard of a Colonel Carruthers?"

"Barry Carruthers?" I asked, and she nodded. There's actually a fairly small corps of military judges, and lawyers are inveterately gossipy, and if there's one thing lawyers love to share, it's stories about judges.

"I've heard of him," I admitted. "I've never tried anything before him, but I know his rep."

"And what's his rep?" she asked.

"A prosecutor's dream date. Loose on rules of evidence, murder on theatrics, and he'll kill you if you deal with the press."

"Uh-huh," she said, apparently unimpressed.

She should've been impressed as all get out. Barry Carruthers loved to dance with defense attorneys, only it was a very ugly kind of dance, because he always took the lead, he stepped on your toes, and he whirled you around so hard that you fell on your ass a lot. Just hearing he was assigned to a case was enough to make some defense attorneys bawl like babies. The stories about him were legion. He'd once suspended a trial for two months because a defense lawyer raised an objection that so thoroughly aggravated him, he actually threw the attorney in the slammer. It did not escape my notice that the Army was bringing in the most notoriously antidefense judge on its rolls.

I raised my hand like a schoolchild. "Could I ask a question?"

"What?" Katherine barked.

"I'm sorry. I don't mean to get too technical at this early stage, but who's our client?"

The other four in the room all looked at one another like I'd just asked the stupidest question there ever was. I didn't think it was stupid.

Katherine said, "Captain Thomas Whitehall."

She started to open her lips to say something else, and I raised my hand again.

"What?" she said, even more agitated.

"Hey, I apologize if I'm getting ahead of myself here. What's he accused of?"

Katherine shook her head and looked around at the others in exasperation. "I'm sorry," she explained, very nastily, "I know this case has been plastered for weeks on the front page of every newspaper in the U.S. and Korea, but Attila here doesn't know how to read. Keith, would you quickly summarize the case for our token Army lawyer?"

Keith turned to me and smiled. "Three American soldiers, a first sergeant named Carl Moran, a private named Everett Jackson, and our client were all seen entering an apartment building in the

Itaewon section of Seoul. This was around nine o'clock on the
night of May 2. Three different witnesses observed them. There was
a fourth party with them, a Korean soldier wearing an American
Army uniform. His name was Lee No Tae. The witnesses also testi-
fied they heard sounds of a loud party that lasted past midnight."

"The witnesses," I asked, "they were all South Koreans?"

His smile broadened. "Oh, Sean, how wonderfully clever of you.
Anyway, the four soldiers were all in Apartment 13C. It had a living
room, a kitchen, three bedrooms, and was leased by Captain Whitehall. About five-thirty in the morning, First Sergeant Moran entered
the bedroom where Captain Whitehall was sleeping and discovered him on a sleeping mat beside Lee No Tae. Lee had been strangled with a belt. An autopsy was done and revealed that his anus
contained two different specimens of semen. One was traced to
First Sergeant Moran, the other to Captain Whitehall. The autopsy
also revealed that at least one case of anal penetration had been inflicted after the victim was dead. Since corpses can't willingly consent, that leads to charges of murder, necrophilia, and rape."

"Uh-huh," I said. "And aside from the fact the victim was lying
beside him, what evidence is there that Captain Whitehall did the
crime?"

"Lee was strangled with an Army-issue belt that turned out to
be Whitehall's. Also First Sergeant Moran and Private Jackson are
both turning evidence against Whitehall. Finally, one of the two
semen specimens was traced to Whitehall, and he was the last
known partner Lee slept with."

"This is not good," I said, which was so ridiculously obvious
that everyone else chuckled.

"No, it's worse than that," Keith went on. "You know about Lee's
father?"

"The defense minister, right?"

"Also a living legend. He was a big war hero in one of the two
army divisions the Koreans sent to Vietnam back in the sixties.
When he returned home, he became disgusted with the military
dictatorship here, resigned from the army, and became a demo-
cratic activist. He was imprisoned a number of times. He was

beaten, tortured, and nearly executed, but he never broke. Every time he got out of prison, he went right back to the barricades. Once democracy finally came, he could've run for president and easily won. But he never did. He refused to take any rewards, until Kim Dae Jung, the current president, begged him to take the post of defense minister. The reason he begged him is because the Defense Ministry is so rife with corruption that the past three ministers have all ended up in prison. President Kim hoped that Minister Lee would lend his own good name to restore some public confidence in an institution known for being completely rotten."

I said, "So that makes it bad from a public relations standpoint, but what does it have to do with this case?"

"Well, Lee No Tae was *supposedly* lured to the apartment without any foreknowledge that the three American soldiers were gay. *Supposedly*, Lee No Tae just thought he was being given the chance to party with some friendly Americans, one of whom was a high-ranking noncom, and another of whom was an officer. If you accept that, then he was raped twice, once by Moran and once by Whitehall."

"So that gives the prosecution something to hang over Moran's head? Is that your point?"

"Oh, Sean, you *are* clever. But there's one other point: Nobody in the American Army wants to insult Minister Lee by impugning his son's sexuality. Like adding insult to injury, if you get my meaning."

"And what have Moran and Jackson said?"

"We reviewed the statements they gave CID. They say Lee was straight, that he was just there to party, a lot of booze was being imbibed, and things got a little carried away."

"Anything else?" I asked, noting with some dubiousness how Katherine's team all seemed to believe the murdered man, Private Lee, was gay, despite what the witnesses were saying.

Katherine said, "Moran refused to confess he had intercourse with Lee. For obvious reasons, of course. He said the last time he saw Lee was when Lee and Whitehall entered the bedroom together, sometime around one in the morning. He said he heard them arguing angrily in the bedroom, but couldn't tell what the argument was about. Jackson says pretty much the same thing."

Katherine then began pointing her tiny fingers and handing out assignments to her coterie of cronies, while I stewed and moped in my corner.

I'd never given much thought to the topic of homosexuality, I guess because I'd never had to. I know damn well which sex I want to go home with when the cocktail party's over, and that's that. And the thing with the Army is, if you're gay, you can't tell anybody, or act like it, so to the best of my knowledge I didn't even have any gay friends or acquaintances.

But I'd spent my whole life listening to jokes about gays. Eventually that seeps in, so you get to think of gays, at least the male ones, as whimsical, capricious, odd little creatures. Not all of them, though, because there's another type. There's the Rock Hudson variety that can completely fool you. I mean, he and Doris Day did manage to pull off some pretty steamy scenes. To this day, all lurid disclosures aside, I still wonder about the Rock. Anyway, his kind of gay doesn't bother anybody in the least, because after all, what you don't know don't hurt you.

I stared at the floor and wished I was anywhere but here. There're some cases you don't mind defending, some you're uncomfortable defending, and some that make you want to leap off a cliff—the kind that make you ashamed to be a lawyer.

Murder, necrophilia, rape: Katherine must've plotted her sweet revenge against me for eight long years.

She finally finished passing out instructions, and it didn't escape my notice that no chores fell my way. The other three went eagerly dashing out of the room. I sat perfectly still in my corner till they were gone. Katherine acted like she took no notice of my still sitting there, till I finally stood up and walked over. I got right in her face, which made it damned hard to pretend I was a piece of furniture.

She broke into an impish grin. "Isn't this exciting?" she asked. In all seriousness, too.

"No, it's not exciting. See, exciting is a vacation in Bermuda, living in a cottage only a ten-minute walk from Horseshoe Bay. Exciting is lying on a beach and having no cares in the world. Exciting is wondering which girl's skimpy bikini top is gonna get washed off by the next big wave. Those were all things I was doing until thirty hours ago."

"What would you call this, then?"

"May I be candid?"

"Within limits," she carefully replied. Like I said earlier, the woman wasn't dumb.

"Completely absurd. You've got a client who's probably guilty as hell. You've got a political agenda that never was popular, and your client has probably set it back a few centuries. And you've got an axe to grind with me."

The grin left her face and she turned around and went over to sit in a chair by the window. It struck me she was buying time to think about how to address all that. Then she spun and looked out the window at all the twinkling lights off in the distance.

She lightly said, "You've got two out of three correct."

"Which two? The guilty client? The political agenda? Or the axe to grind?"

She ignored my question. "Lighten up, Attila. When I got here ten days ago, they assigned a local as my co-counsel. I didn't like him, so I fired him and asked for you."

"What didn't you like about him?"

"He was a homophobic bigot, for one thing, so my assistants didn't trust him. He was dumb, for a second thing. Third, he was the kind of spit-shined, pants-pressed, salute-himself-in-the-mirror type your JAG Corps has in too great abundance. This is going to be a tough case. I can't afford an unthinking automaton on my team."

"Why me?" I asked. "To say it charitably, you and I never hit it off too good."

I was still looking at the back of her head.

"At least I know you," she said.

"Then what? Is this one of those 'devil you know' things?"

She nodded. "If you want to put it that way."

"Well, I've got a few problems that have to be ironed out or this isn't going to work. Actually it won't work anyway, but here it is. First, don't you ever dress me down in public again. You have a problem with me, muzzle it till we're in private. This isn't the law school library, and I'm a professional officer. Two, I'm no token. You want a token, I'll get on the phone right now and have the Army send you one."

She slowly twisted around in her chair and faced me. There was an odd glint in her eye. It didn't fit right with somebody who was being told where to get off. I should've wondered about that. I was just too pumped up on my own vinegar to stop myself.

"If you're not a token, what are you?"

"I carry my weight. I get jobs just like the rest of your team. Only I'm different. I've got a law degree and eight years of court-room experience under my belt. Also, I'm an expert at military law."

The corners of her lips cracked upward a tiny bit. "And what gives you the impression the others aren't attorneys?"

"You mean—"

"Keith was third in his class at Yale Law. Maria and Allie attended UVA Law together. They weren't top of their class, but they're no slouches."

Rather than choke on my own tongue, which was what I felt like doing, I saw an opportunity here. "Then you don't have any paralegals or legal assistants?"

"Not yet," she admitted. "But OGMM's working to rectify that as we speak."

"Tell 'em to stop."

"No, I won't tell them to stop. We've got only two weeks till court. We've got work and motions backing up. I can't afford to have Keith or Allie or Maria wasting any more of their time on simple clerical chores."

"I'll handle it."

"And how will you do that?"

"I've got the perfect legal aide who'll handpick three or four of the best assistants in the business."

"Look, Attila, no offense, but I've seen the quality of legal work your uniformed stooges perform. I can't afford that. Not on this case."

"You owe me," I said, literally stamping my foot like a three-year-old, suddenly desperate to win this argument.

"I don't owe you shit. I asked for you, but that doesn't mean I owe you any damned thing."

"Wrong there," I said, pushing an accusatory finger at her face. "You ruined my Bermuda vacation. You got any idea how hard it is to get a beach bungalow in May?"

She started to say something, so I took a step toward her, forcing her to lean back. "Also, I'd just met this very fetching Swedish stewardess. And things were going real well, too, if you get my thrust. You got any idea how hard it is to find a real live Swedish stewardess in Bermuda?"

A disgusted look came to her face, because she obviously didn't want to hear about my sex life. That is, unless my Swedish stewardess happened to be bisexual, in which case, well, maybe an exception could be made.

"And another thing," I threw in, before she could say no. "This is an Army base in Korea, seven thousand miles from home. It's not like cases you might've tried back in the States, where the moment you step outside the gates you're on your own turf. You're stranded here. You're going to need someone who knows their way around the Army. It's the simple things like getting a car from the motor pool, getting copiers, making travel arrangements."

She was getting tired of listening to me, but I was speaking so emphatically she just knew I'd keep quarreling all night if I didn't get my way.

"When can you have him here?" she asked, not yet committed, but giving a little ground.

"Probably within twenty-four hours."

"Twenty-four hours, huh?" she asked, looking suddenly thoughtful. Then her expression changed to a threatening snarl. "If I agree to this, he better be damned good."

"She. And she's fantastic, trust me."

She said okay, and I left relishing my one small victory. If I had to endure Katherine's legal freak show, I'd at least have a few trusted aides by my side. Allies. Normal folks. Well, normal compared to what OGMM was likely to provide, and after one good look at Katherine's crack attorney team, I didn't want to even hypothesize what OGMM's paralegals and legal assistants might be like.

I got all the way back to my room and was still feeling smug and self-congratulatory when it hit me. I wanted to kick myself in the ass, only I'm not double-jointed enough. Katherine had just picked my pocket. She'd picked it clean, too.

That's why she'd been goading and ridiculing me from that opening moment in Spears's office. Being her co-counsel, I could just go along for the ride. All I was legally obligated to do was offer her timely advice when it was called for, advice limited essentially to the peculiarities of military law. A token was what she'd called it. Well, to be perfectly precise, that's exactly what I was being paid to be.

And frankly, it was a safe harbor, as sailors are wont to say. It would keep me out of the way of the political crossfire, which, frankly, wouldn't hurt my career any. I had this lurking suspicion the Army wasn't apt to be real grateful toward any officer who threw his heart and soul into defending Captain Whitehall.

What she'd just managed to pull off was to get me to commit myself to her team. She knew from past experience exactly how to twist my noodles, and she'd adroitly done just that. I'd been sucker-punched.

The intriguing question was why she thought she needed me. She was the one with eight years' experience in gay cases. She should know every devilish twist and turn on the subject. And the same with that trio she'd brought along with her. But maybe they lacked experience with murder cases. Maybe that's why she needed me. Or maybe she knew her defense was hopeless and was grabbing at straws, any straw, even me.

Well, anyway, retribution was on the way. In less than twenty-four hours, Sergeant First Class Imelda Pepperfield was going to climb off an airplane and stomp her way into town. Just wait till she got a look at Katherine and her crew. The thought almost made me drool. This was the same Imelda Pepperfield who could shatter bricks with her tiny, beady eyes. She'd have them all spit-shining their shoes and begging for mercy. Hell, she'd probably get them all to turn straight.

I immediately got on the phone and called the Pentagon. An ice-cold voice answered, "General Clapper's office."

"Major Drummond here," I said. "Could I speak with General Clapper, please?"

"Hold for a moment," came the stiff reply.

I twiddled my thumbs for nearly five minutes before a warm, friendly voice said, "Sean, Sean, how are you?"

The voice was too friendly by half. Slick try, but I wasn't born yesterday.

"Why'd you do this to me?" I moaned as pitifully as I could, because the central motive of this call was to load so much guilt on Clapper's shoulders that he'd do anything for me.

"It wasn't me, Sean. You were requested. By name."

"Do you have any idea what you've gotten me into? I'm one of five co-counsels. You should see the others."

He chuckled. "I've seen photos of Carlson. She doesn't look so bad."

"Don't be fooled by her exterior. Her interior belongs in the crocodile pond, except the other crocs won't have her."

He chuckled some more. It was one of those phony, don't-tell-me-your-problems, I've-got-enough-of-my-own chuckles. "Look, Sean, I needed to put a good man in there anyway. Someone tough, someone who can handle themselves under fierce pressure. When she asked for you, it made perfect sense."

Now I was getting the old muzzle-him-with-compliments act. Clapper wasn't pulling any punches today.

"Look, General, I'll admit I'm just coming up to speed, but this thing's dynamite. Spears did a tap dance on my ass this afternoon. I've already waded through two riots over here."

"Believe me, I'm aware of the situation over there. It's nearly as bad over here."

"How's that?" I asked, since I still hadn't glanced at a newspaper in three weeks and therefore hadn't the foggiest notion what was happening.

"The Republicans are pushing a bill through Congress to overturn the 'don't ask, don't tell' policy. They're saying Whitehall, Moran, and Jackson prove it doesn't work. You know who asked them to push the bill?"

"Who?"

"South Korea's ambassador. Publicly, too. It was couched like this: Get the homosexuals out of your military or we'll throw your troops out of Korea."

"You think they mean it?"

"We *know* they mean it. Go review a few weeks of newspaper and magazine articles. Once you get current, then call me back."

This was a very polished brush-off, only I wasn't done with my business. I quickly said, "I, uh, I need a favor."

"Favor?" he asked in a very halfhearted tone. Not "Gee, Sean, considering the nasty briar patch I've thrown you into, whatever you want." I should've realized right then that I was swimming in quicksand.

"I want Sergeant First Class Imelda Pepperfield flown over here right away. And I want her to bring her pick of assistants."

There was this fairly long pause; this long, nauseating pause.

"That, uh . . . I'm afraid that's not really a very good idea."

"How come?" I dumbly asked.

"It really isn't a good idea to militarize the defense team. Whitehall made a deliberate choice to rely on civilian attorneys and, frankly, it was astonishingly convenient. You get my meaning here, don't you?"

Yeah, I sure as hell did get his meaning, didn't I. The Army was exceedingly pleased to be relieved of the distasteful responsibility of defending Whitehall. Win, lose, or draw, there weren't going to be any happy endings here, and it was vastly preferable to have some wild-eyed civilian lefties arguing on his behalf. You didn't have to look under the table to get the message being sent to me, either: stay well-hidden behind Carlson's skirts.

So I lied. "Look, General, I'm just a messenger boy. Carlson ordered me to pass this request. She said to tell you to either get Pepperfield over here, or she'll call some of her press buddies and say you're trying to sandbag her defense."

"Bullshit. She's never heard of Pepperfield."

"Well, I, uh, I let the cat out of the bag. Of course, I had no idea until a second ago that you didn't want to green up the defense team."

He said okay, or he snarled okay, or he shot the word out from his lips like a bullet. Then he hung up, much harder than was necessary. Not that he had more right to be peeved than I did, since I now had a pretty clear inkling where I stood.

I was working for a lesbian who had rotten memories of me, not to mention a satchelcase packed with hidden agendas on how she intended to employ me. The chief of the JAG Corps who'd assigned me to this case wanted me to sandbag my co-counsel, and thereby my client, whom I'd never met—although given the crime he'd apparently committed, I didn't want to meet him.

All in all, a vile situation.

Fortunately, though, I'm afflicted with a short attention span. I lay down on the bed and got comfortable. I thought of Bermuda and that Swedish stewardess; although from a strictly technical standpoint, she hadn't really been Swedish, since she was from the Bronx and had one of those Italian names. And she wasn't really a stewardess, either, but a secretary at some advertising agency, out prowling for a good time. Well, I'm a good time. In fact, I'm a damned good time. And if you could ignore her Bronx twang, and the big, puffy hairdo, you could force yourself to believe she had some Swedish blood in her. I mean, those Europeans were always invading one another, weren't they? Who knows how much cross-breeding occurred?

Okay, it's a stretch, but sometimes when it comes to the opposite sex you have to let your imagination paper over the rough spots.

I dozed off with a happy smile.

CHAPTER
4
★ ★ ★

The phone rang at 6:00 A.M. I lifted it up and Katherine said, "Get down here right away. We've got a big problem."

I spitefully took a nice long shower, shaved in languorous slow motion, took forever to put on my uniform and tie my boots, then watched TV for ten leisurely minutes. The thing about life is, you've got to take your cheap victories where you find them.

Allie the amazon answered the door again, only this time it was just her and Katherine and Maria in the room. Maria again had a pouty frown on her face.

"Hey, what's happening?" I said to Allie, trying to sound hip, because she was really hard to look at early in the morning, and it was either act hip or vomit all over the floor.

She looked down at me like I was the one who was tall and gangly. "Hey, Katherine, he's back."

I smiled nicely and tried to think up a wisecrack but nothing particular came to mind. Or actually, lots of particular things came to mind, only I didn't want to create any irreparable rifts this early in the game.

"Attila, what took you so long?" Katherine barked from across the room.

"What's going on?" I yelled back, spitefully refusing to answer.

Katherine walked across the room until she was right in front

of me. "I've just been notified the South Koreans are taking jurisdiction over our case. They want Whitehall turned over to their custody."

"Who notified you?"

"Spears's legal adviser."

"He would know," I drolly observed.

"Can they do it?"

"This is South Korea. They can do any damned thing they want.
Do they have the legal basis? Well, that's another story."

I smelled the aroma of coffee and my nostrils twitched. Katherine pointed at an urn in the corner. I went and got a cup, using the
time to think.

"Look," I said, "here's how it works. When we have troops stationed on foreign soil, we first sign something called a Status of
Forces Agreement, or SOFA, as we commonly call it, that sets up
how these things are supposed to be handled. Of course, we have
a SOFA agreement with the government of South Korea. What it
stipulates is that anytime an American soldier commits a crime, we
get to try them."

"So they can't do this?" she announced, or asked, or prayed.

"Well, here's where it gets itchy. The crime was committed off
base in Itaewon. The victim was a South Korean citizen. He was
wearing an American Army uniform and was serving in an American unit, because he was a Katusa. But he was still South Korean.
And it was a particularly nasty crime and the Korean people are obviously very annoyed."

"So what? Tough shit," Allie said. "A diplomatic agreement's a
legal document, right?"

"True, but the SOFA agreement has been a source of great ag-
gravation and controversy over here. It even had to be amended a
few years ago, because the South Koreans are fed up with all the
crimes American soldiers have committed over the past four or five
decades."

"Amended how?"

"We still have the right to try the accused. However, the issue
of pretrial confinement is now negotiable. Also, once there's a con-

viction, we now have to bargain with the South Korean Ministry of Justice over who gets to punish the criminal."

Allie said, "So I was right, then. They have no right to try Whitehall."

"Partly right. The South Koreans don't like our legal system one bit. They think we give way too much leeway and protection to the accused. They think we're too procedural. To their way of logic, it's incomprehensible that a criminal could get off just because somebody failed to read him his rights, or some piece of evidence got contaminated, or someone on the jury had a bellyache and voted impulsively. They apparently don't want those risks in this case."

Katherine stroked her chin. "So what's their legal system like?"

"From a defense perspective, Dante's inferno. A system designed by victims, for victims. To them, a trial is a search for truth and justice. And sometimes they go about finding it in some pretty ugly ways. South Korean gendarmes and prosecutors can get pretty rough, if you get my meaning. There's this hilarious joke about the Korean who really wanted to sign the confession, only he couldn't, because all his fingers were broken. But you probably don't want to hear that joke right now."

Allie's big nose stuck out about two inches. "We'll just tell them to blow it out their ass. We've got this SOFA shit on our side, right? They can't have him. It's that simple."

I replied, "Very eloquently stated, but it's not that easy. It's their country, so like it or not, we're walking on eggshells."

Katherine began pacing across the room. She took small, measured, deliberate steps, because it wasn't a real big room, but also because she was that way. Very calculating, very shrewd.

"Do you have any suggestions?" she finally asked me.

"Sure. Arrange an immediate meeting with Spears's legal adviser and the ambassador. Except, if I heard right, the ambassador's in a hospital in Hawaii. So maybe the embassy chargé instead."

"What for?"

"Mainly to hear what they've got to say."

"Anything else we should do?" Katherine asked.

"Yeah."

"What?"

"Have a big breakfast. It's going to be a long day."

She and Allie and Maria didn't want to eat a big breakfast, or any breakfast, which I can't say displeased me all that much. I therefore went downstairs and ate alone. I stopped in the convenience shop first and picked up the newspapers for the past two days. These were issues of the *Stars and Stripes,* an overseas military newspaper that included excerpts from stateside Associated Press stories and lots of local news articles written by a regional staff based in Japan.

Updates on the Lee murder case filled the front pages of both days' papers. As Clapper had warned, the case was every bit as much a lightning rod in Washington as in Seoul. Not only were the Republicans trying to usher through a bill to overturn the "don't ask, don't tell" compromise, but a consortium of angry Southern Baptist fundamentalists were mustering a march on Washington to protest the godless policies of the President who had opened up the military to gays.

I was just finishing my second cup of coffee when Katherine and Keith swooped down. Keith looked handsomer than ever in a superbly tailored worsted gray flannel suit, with a silk handkerchief stuck out of his coat pocket that perfectly matched his necktie. He looked like one of the models you see in all those catchy men's fashion magazines Army guys don't subscribe to. Our fashion world is prescribed in tedious detail by something called a regulation that doesn't leave you the least bit curious about what lapel cuts or tie widths are in vogue this year.

Katherine looked frantic. "We've got an appointment at the embassy in thirty minutes."

"Have fun," I mumbled, whipping the paper back up in front of my face.

She and Keith kept standing there, and I knew damn well what was going through Katherine's mind. She wasn't about to beg me to come along, but hey, she was way over her head on this.

I wasn't over my head. I was swimming in my own métier, as

the saying has it. But I also wasn't about to come along—unless, that is, she did beg me. I can be real churlish that way.

She said, "Attila, I wouldn't mind if you wanted to tag along."

"Uh-huh," I murmured, hibernating behind my paper.

"You know, this might be a fairly interesting session."

"Bet so," I idly mumbled.

"Come on, Attila. You coming?"

"I haven't done the crossword yet," I remarked indifferently.

Another moment passed. I heard Keith whisper something in her ear.

"Attila, *please* come," she said.

"Hey, Moonbeam, my name's not Attila," I replied, pointing down at my nametag. Keith's eyebrow shot up in the air at that one. He looked questionably at Katherine as though to say, Moonbeam? Then he smiled, because really, as monikers go, it fit.

She ignored him and said, "Okay, Major . . . Major Drummond . . . Sean. Please come."

I put down my paper with an exaggerated sigh. "Be happy to. If you think I would be helpful, that is." I looked up into her beautiful face and could see this was getting excruciatingly painful for her.

Her big green eyes got narrow and pointy, and her cute little lips shrank. "It could be helpful," she said, with no effort to disguise her resentment.

"I'm sorry. Was that *could* be helpful? Or *would* be helpful?"

"It, uh . . . it *would* be helpful. Okay?"

I could tell I'd extracted about as much humility from her as I was likely to get. On this round, anyway.

"And how were you planning to get to the embassy?" I asked.

"I thought we'd take a taxi."

"Won't work," I told her.

"And why not?"

"Because we'd never get there. Just a minute."

I went to a phone by the hostess's table. I dialed the operator and asked her to immediately put me through to the MP station. A desk sergeant with a brusque, uncompromising voice answered. I told him to connect me to the shift commander.

An only slightly more reasonable voice came on the line. "Captain Bittlesby."

"Bittlesby, this is Major Drummond, co-counsel for Captain Whitehall."

"Yes sir."

"My other two co-counsels and I need to be transported and escorted to the American embassy. Immediately."

"Is this trip authorized?" he wearily asked.

"Authorized by who?"

"By Major General Conley, General Spears's chief of staff."

"This just came up. There isn't time for that."

Sounding a little too happy, he said, "Too bad, then. Without Conley's signature, nobody leaves base."

I said, "Listen, Captain, we've got an appointment in twenty-eight minutes to meet with the acting ambassador. You could take that for authorization. Or, if you'd like, I'll tell the ambassador, 'Gee, I'm sorry, Captain Bittlesby says we can't come.' Then I'll call the *New York Times* and tell 'em some captain named Bittlesby is trying to sabotage Whitehall's defense."

The thing with the Army is that a little bit of the right kind of coercion goes a long way. Soldiers don't like to get crossways with diplomats. What they like even less is having to explain to their prickly bosses how they made it onto the front page of a nationally read newspaper in a distinctly unfavorable light.

Bittlesby said, "You wouldn't really do that, would you?" He wasn't really asking. He was taking the first grudging step in a full-scale retreat.

"Twenty-seven minutes, Captain."

"Where are you?"

"We'll be at the front entry of the Dragon Hill Lodge in thirty seconds."

Half a minute later, Katherine, Keith, and I stood at the hotel's entrance as three humvees with flashing yellow lights careened around the corner. Katherine looked at me and I shrugged nicely.

It was the kind of taunting gesture meant to say, "Pretty cool, huh? Think you could've pulled it off?"

The first and last humvees were loaded to the gills with military policemen in riot gear. The middle one contained only a driver, also in riot gear.

I swiftly moved to the rear door of the middle humvee, yanked it open, and held it for Katherine. They don't call us officers and gentlemen for nothing. But before I could react, Keith swiftly walked over and climbed in, brushing my arm softly and saying, "Thanks, sweetie."

Katherine chuckled and climbed in the front seat. That left me to join Keith in the back. I could've strangled her.

By the time we got to the gate, it seemed apparent that the MPs had radioed ahead, because a platoon of South Korean riot police in blue uniforms were already shoving and hammering protesters aside to make a path for our convoy to get through.

Lots of angry, sullen faces glared at us as we passed through the crowd. It didn't leave you with the impression you were among friends.

The ride to the embassy took just shy of thirty-five minutes. At the gate, once again, a platoon of South Korean troops in blue uniforms with riot shields and batons were beating a wedge through more protesters.

We dismounted at the front entrance and the young lieutenant in charge of the convoy came over. I told him to wait till we were done, and with excruciating politeness he said he would. Bittlesby must've warned him I was a righteous prick.

After a security check we took an elevator to the fourth floor and walked into the ambassador's outer office. The secretary had a long, droopy face and a long, narrow nose, and she looked at us like we were stray dogs who'd come to crap on her lawn. She lifted the receiver, pushed a button, and announced we were here. Then with a dismissive wave, she signaled us to enter the door to the left of her desk.

Two men were seated on gold silk couches in the corner of the regal-looking office. They stood as we entered. I might've been imagining things, but their faces looked vaguely guilty, or slightly embarrassed, or mildly entertained, or maybe all three.

One had the eagle of a full colonel on his collar. "Janson" was written on his nametag. He was in his mid-fifties, with short, tightly cropped gray stubble on his head, tough, distrustful eyes, and lips that were too big and wide for his narrow face. Like the lips on a piranha. He wore JAG brass on his other collar, of course, since he was the legal adviser to General Spears. He didn't look like a lawyer, though. He had the aspect of a high school disciplinarian who accidentally got a law degree and still resented it.

The other guy looked exactly like what he was supposed to be: a diplomat—a particular kind of diplomat, though. I mean, they're not all vanilla ice cream, and he was the type I guessed I wasn't going to like a lot. Maybe late forties, with black hair that was blow-dried back in the currently fashionable style, and that should've had at least a few wisps of gray but mysteriously didn't. He had a chiseled, lined face, dark, piercing eyes, and an imperious curl on his lips. There was a gold Harvard ring on his left hand, but no wedding band. He was either single or advertising his availability.

"Welcome," he announced, acting falsely warm as his eyes took our measure. They skipped past me in a millisecond, paused briefly to envy the cut of Keith's suit, then feasted for a long, lusty moment on Katherine. Heh-heh, little did he know. He'd have better luck with Keith.

"I'm Arthur Brandewaite, the acting ambassador. This is Colonel Mack Janson, General Spears's legal adviser. Please," he said, with a smooth flourish of his arm in the direction of the two couches. That flourish-of-the-arm thing was so profusely elegant I figured he must practice it in front of the mirror.

We all trooped over. Brandewaite and Janson sat back down on their couch, and the three of us scrunched up together and faced them.

"So," Brandewaite said, "Colonel Janson tells me you've already gotten the news. We're all so terribly sorry about this, but . . ." He brought up his hands in a helpless gesture.

Katherine, with a very belligerent motion of her own, said,

"Why are you sorry? We're not turning my client over. Period! End of statement! He won't be tried in a Korean court."

Brandewaite glanced at Janson, an impatient, testy glance, like, What's this? Did you fail to deliver the full text of the message?

Then he turned back to Katherine and started shaking his head in contrived consternation. "Miss Carlson, it seems there's some kind of mistake here. The South Korean government didn't *ask* us to turn over Whitehall. They *demanded* he be turned over by close of business today. We are, after all, guests in their country."

Katherine said, "I don't care. My client has rights and you have a Status of Forces Agreement that obligates you to ensure he's tried in an American military court. In case you've forgotten, he's not only a soldier, he's a taxpayer and therefore your employer. He's not being turned over."

Janson was glaring spitefully at me, because obviously someone had explained that inconvenient little Status of Forces Agreement thing to Katherine. And, uh . . . well, I guess I did appear to be the most likely candidate.

"Miss Carlson," Brandewaite said with a tone of condescending patience, "I certainly understand your position. I even share your sympathies. However," he continued, making that "however" sound deeper and wider than the Grand Canyon, "when one international party says it will no longer honor a diplomatic agreement, there's nothing we can do."

Katherine bent forward fiercely. "Bullshit. You force them to abide by it. For Chrissakes, we're the ones defending them from the bad guys, aren't we? That's called leverage."

"It doesn't work like that," Brandewaite insisted.

"Then *make* it work like that," Katherine demanded.

"I couldn't . . . even if I wanted to. My position has been approved by both the State Department and the National Security Council. The situation is already radicalized enough. We don't want to do anything that will stoke the fires. Whitehall will be turned over to the Koreans at five o'clock today."

"No, he won't! I'll file a motion and get this blocked," Katherine threatened.

"With who?" Brandewaite asked, barely concealing a smile.

"What do you mean, with who?"

The acting ambassador leaned back into the couch and crossed his legs. He ran pinched fingers along the creases on his worsted wool trousers and admired the shine on his fancy shoes. "Who will you file the motion with? This is Korea, not the United States. File it with a military court, and I guarantee you it will be overturned by noon. File it with the Koreans and they'll laugh at you."

Janson was vigorously nodding his head, and since he was the military adviser to the Commander in Chief, that made it a fair bet Brandewaite wasn't blowing smoke.

Katherine looked inquisitively at Keith, who shrugged, and only then did she turn her big green eyes beseechingly in my direction.

I could and probably should've ignored her.

Instead, I said, "Mr. Brandewaite, exactly what is your agreement with the South Korean government? Who's it with and how much have you conceded?"

Brandewaite nodded at Janson to take over.

"We've already agreed to turn Whitehall over for pretrial confinement. In about an hour, General Spears is going to meet with Chun Moon Song, the minister of justice, to inform the Koreans we also formally relinquish the right to try Whitehall."

"Only Whitehall? What about Moran? What about Jackson?"

"Uh, no. Only Whitehall. The South Koreans haven't requested the other two. Their crimes were reprehensible, though clearly not as heinous."

"Have we ever ceded the right to try before?"

"This is a unique case. You know how the law works, Major. Precedents are guides, but they aren't binding. Every case is decided on its own merits."

"Is this a reciprocal agreement?"

Janson's expression was perfectly innocuous. "What do you mean?"

"Is there a quid pro quo? You turn over Whitehall, and in return other prisoners remain under our military jurisdictional courts. Are we trading flesh for flesh here?"

Brandewaite quickly placed a hand on Janson's leg. "Major, you know that diplomatic discussions between the U.S. government and the government of the Republic of Korea are strictly confidential. We simply can't disclose what we've discussed."

"No?"

"No," he replied, very firmly.

"Can you at least disclose who's been negotiating with the South Koreans?"

"Of course. I have. And Colonel Janson has very kindly served as my co-interlocutor."

Co-interlocutor? Where the hell did they find these guys?

But I didn't ask that. Instead, I asked, "So, it was just you and Colonel Janson here, huh?"

Janson started to open his lips, but Brandewaite shut him off with a quick chopping motion. A bad mistake on his part.

"That's right, Major. There were some notetakers, but the colonel and I spearheaded this effort."

"Good, that keeps it nice and clean."

"Keeps what nice and clean?"

"Who we cite."

"Who you cite for what?"

"For obstructing justice and engaging in a criminal conspiracy to defraud our client of his legal rights. And the civil suit we'll file for violating the constitutional rights of our client."

A look of ugly shock registered on Brandewaite's face. He patted his puffy, oddly nongrayed hair and stared at me. "Drummond, I am an acting ambassador and you're a low-ranking military officer. If you dare threaten me, I'll speak with General Spears and have you court-martialed."

I looked instantly abashed. "Mr. Brandewaite, you'll have to excuse me. Please. I don't know what came over me," I said, and that brought a slight twitch to the corners of his mouth. Not quite a smile, but it was moving in that direction before I said, "The problem we've got is mistaken identities. I'm not just any Army officer, I'm an attorney. Besides, there's a big difference between a threat and a promise. Sometimes you have to listen close, but that wasn't a threat. Right, Miss Carlson?"

"Goddamn right," she said with perfect timing. "I'd call it a favor, Brandewaite. He's giving you the chance to warn your public affairs officer about the announcement I'm going to make at the press conference I'm going to convene as soon as we depart your office."

"I will not be bullied," Brandewaite said, glaring at her, at Keith, at me, then at Janson, whose only real offense was being a lawyer like the rest of us. Guilt by association, I guess.

"That's right. We will not be bullied," Janson loudly and indignantly echoed, trying to work himself back into the diplomat's good graces. "Besides, you're bluffing. You can't sue a functionary acting in the best interests of the U.S. government."

Then, to my immense surprise, Keith said, "Counselor, my field of expertise is suing federal officials. It's how I make my living. Let me add, I make a good living. What I particularly like about this case is that not only will I win a great deal of money from both of you, but I'll also get to cite you for criminal behavior. You said it yourself. You must be acting in the best interests of the U.S. government."

"We are," Janson insisted.

"You're not. You're conspiring with a foreign government to deprive an American soldier of his most fundamental rights. Open and shut. You've now been personally advised of such, which deprives you of any defense based on legal ignorance." Keith leaned hungrily forward and awarded them a sly grin. "The facts being what they are, defending our client was going to be an uphill battle anyway. What were our chances of winning, right? This at least allows us to salvage something. An officer suspected of being gay makes legal history by being the first soldier turned over to the South Koreans for trial. It's too bad about Whitehall being martyred and all that, but wasn't it Robespierre who said you can't make an omelet without breaking a few eggs?"

I wasn't all that pleased that he'd broadened the issue from the fate of our client to the overall cause, but before I could think about it further, Katherine caught on to his thrust. She also leaned forward. "We're going to make you two very famous."

And the truth was, they were right. They *would* make mincemeat out of them, and Janson, the trained lawyer, was the first to figure this out, because he was the first one to turn so apoplectic I thought blood might start leaking out his ears.

"Look, lady"—he pointed a finger at Katherine's face—"we're not flying by the seat of our pants on this thing. This action was approved by the National Security Council."

Katherine smiled. "I don't care if Santa Claus gave you permission, asshole. You're the two government officials we looked in the eye and warned. Turn over Captain Whitehall and we'll publicly fry you."

After that, we probably could've sat there and spit more screwyous at one another, but what would be the point? We'd gotten our message across, so we all got up and trooped for the door. And I had nearly made it out when Janson grabbed my sleeve and yanked me backward.

He whispered something short and pungent, and then let go and backed away.

What he said was, "I don't like you, Drummond. I'll fuck you for this."

Subtlety didn't seem to be his forte.

None of us said anything the whole ride back because there was an MP in the front seat and confidentiality was critical at this point. Besides, I was too infuriated to talk. I was furious at Katherine for roping me into this. I was mad at the Army and at General Clapper for conceding my services. I was mad at Keith for shifting the discussion away from Whitehall and his rights and enlarging it to the gay cause.

Know who I was maddest at? The guy with the really big mouth.

Why did I have to threaten the acting ambassador? Why did I have to jump out in front and stuff my stupid head into the lion's mouth? I knew the answer to those questions, and I wasn't real proud about it.

I was trying to impress little Miss Number One in the Class, who'd goaded and ridiculed me for three straight years. I was trying to prove I could outmuscle her as a legal brawler.

Well, I'd showed her.

CHAPTER
5
★ ★ ★

We went straight to Katherine's room, only nobody was there, just a message telling us a big surprise awaited at the hair salon at the top of the hill beside the hotel. So we trooped up there.

When we walked in, three female legal clerks in battle dress were lugging boxes and computers, and folding tables and chairs, and were converting the hair parlor into an impromptu legal office. In the corner stood a diminutive, squat Black female noncommissioned officer with short graying hair, gold wire-rimmed glasses, and a round, puffy face that somehow, improbably, looked harder than nails. She was barking commands at everybody, waving her arms this way and that, squawking to beat the band.

I almost ran across the floor to hug her. I didn't, though. She would've slapped me silly if I so much as winked. Katherine and Keith eyed what was going on and appeared instantly bewildered.

I said, "Sergeant Pepperfield, could you please step over here so I can introduce you?"

She looked up as though she hadn't noticed us until that very instant, which was balderdash because nothing ever happened within ten miles of Imelda that she didn't notice. She hiked up her Army camouflage trousers, lowered her spectacles, huffed and puffed once or twice like I was terribly inconveniencing her, then waddled in our direction.

Katherine was inspecting the cut of her jib.

"Katherine, Keith, this is Sergeant First Class Imelda Pepper-field, the best legal aide in the United States Army. She'll run our legal shop."

Imelda firmly planted her feet directly in front of Katherine, and the two of them stared into each other's eyes for what seemed an eternity but was probably only half a second. It was that kind of look.

"Nice to meet you," Katherine said, sticking out her hand.

Imelda grabbed it and snarled, "Don't you or none of your legal diplomas mess with me, y'hear. I run this show and you do what I say. This office is my turf. You remember that!"

"Okay," Katherine said.

"You got something you want, you tell me. Ol' Pepperfield will make it happen."

"All right," Katherine said.

At that very instant, Maria the grump and Allie the amazon came dashing out of an office in the back. Maria was actually smiling. It was a goofy-looking thing, but it was a smile, I guess.

"Would you look what this woman did! We've been here eleven days and couldn't even get a phone line. She's here two hours and she got a building, six phone lines, and five computers."

"Three cars, too," Allie chirped up. "With drivers."

"That's wonderful," Katherine said. "I don't mean to sound un-grateful, but is a hair parlor the best we could do?"

Imelda shuffled her feet. "They gave us this 'cause all of the Koreans that work here're on strike."

"And because it's a hair parlor and we're the gay defense team?" Katherine asked.

"Don't make a damn to me," Imelda snorted. "Got three offices in the back, air-conditioning, toilets, and lotsa electric outlets."

"You're right," Katherine said, giving Imelda a warm, proud smile. "It's perfect."

Imelda beamed like a happy child. Her mouth spread from one earlobe to the other. I was flabbergasted. This was a lovefest. They were all acting like big buddies, patting each other on the back and grinning like fools. It wasn't supposed to go down like this. Imelda Pepperfield was the grumpiest, gnarliest person God ever put on this green earth. One of the smartest, too. She did this great impression of a poorly educated, backwoods southern Black girl that somehow fooled nearly all the people, all the time. Not me, though. Imelda is as sly as any lawyer I've ever met and nearly as well educated. She has a master's in English lit and a master's in criminal law. She keeps all this well disguised because, like many professional noncoms, she knows the ship runs much smoother when the officers on the upper decks feel there's some tangible basis for their perch on the roost.

I stared hard at Imelda and she glared fiercely right back.

Katherine interrupted our silent showdown by announcing, "They still plan to turn Whitehall over to the Koreans at five o'-clock this evening."

The smile melted off Maria's tiny face, and Allie looked around the room as though she were searching for something to throw, or break, or kill. They really were an odd couple: complete opposites; one tall, one short; one loud and brassy, the other quiet, withdrawn, and well . . . grumpy. Not that I understood the first thing about gay relationships, but what the hell did they see in each other?

Anyway, I said, "I wouldn't worry about it."

"Why?" Katherine asked. "Do you think we scared them out of it?"

"I think they're on the phone to D.C. right now. They're both pissing in their trousers. Brandewaite's the ambitious type who'd like to be a real ambassador or an assistant muckety-muck some-day. And that big-lipped colonel has dreams of general's stars. The kind of public recognition you just offered isn't likely to further their careers any."

"Turn up the heat then," Katherine snapped. "Allie, call Carson from the *Times,* and Millgrew from the *Post.* Tell them I want to meet right away."

Allie took a step toward her office before I quickly said, "I wouldn't do that."

"And why not?"

"Because you don't want to set a precedent of running to the press every time you don't get your way."

"Bullshit," tiny Maria said. "You just don't get it, do you?"

"Get what?" I asked derisively.

"The press is our best weapon. The system's against us, and using the press is the only way we can level the playing field."

"Look," I said, as condescendingly as I could. "I know you all have this thing against the military, but I don't. It happens to be where I make my living. The Army's not perfect, but it's a damned sight better than you give it credit for."

Katherine and her coterie all did hairy eye-rolls for a brief second.

"Drummond," Katherine said, like she was talking to somebody who'd just said something a few leagues below stupid. "You're the one who doesn't get it. You come from the other side of the line. You have no idea how your side plays."

"Wrong. I'm from the other side. I know exactly how we play."

Katherine started to say something and I cut her off. "Besides, like my mother always says, a good threat's like a good steak: Let it marinate awhile. Give 'em three hours; then feel free to start babbling with your buddies in the fourth estate."

Katherine, Allie, Keith, and Maria all huddled together in a corner and began discussing it. I clearly was not welcome. I clearly was not part of the team. It took nearly two minutes before they reached some sort of consensus and Katherine walked back in my direction.

"All right, we'll wait," she said. "In the meanwhile, it's time for you to meet our client."

Like I couldn't guess what was behind this. She and the others thought I was finding it too effortless to barter our client's fate, since I'd never met him and therefore hadn't developed the sympathetic bond that often forms between an attorney and his customer. In their view, this whole thing was too impersonal for me.

They were making a big blunder, though. The truth is, I was probably more lenient on his behalf *because* I hadn't met him.

Given the crimes he was accused of, I dreaded how partial I'd be if I met him and became completely persuaded he'd actually done it.

But anyhow, there was no way I could turn them down, so I followed along behind Katherine and Maria as they walked out the door and climbed into one of the sedans Imelda, the traitor, had commandeered.

It took only ten minutes to reach the holding facility on base, an old, drab, one-floored building constructed of concrete blocks, very small, with your standard-issue black metal mesh on the windows. An Army captain with military police brass came into the front office and escorted us past a heavy iron door, then down a short hallway with about six cells on each side. Like most military facilities, the place was spotlessly clean. It reeked of disinfectant, but also cooked bacon. The captain informed us the prisoners had just finished lunch. It was BLT day.

We went down to the end and stopped in front of the last cell on the right. The door was made of steel, and the captain occupied himself for nearly a minute fumbling around for the right key. I paced nervously, because I didn't know what to expect, although I was anticipating the worst. Murder, rape, and necrophilia are as ghoulish as it gets. I was having flashbacks from that movie *The Silence of the Lambs*.

The door finally opened and I spotted a figure lying on a metal bunk on the backside of the cell. He got slowly to his feet and approached us with his right hand extended.

He looked youthful, maybe twenty-nine, maybe thirty, with short black hair, intense green eyes, thick eyebrows, a long, straight nose, a strong, narrow jaw, and thin lips that gave an impression of unhappiness. He was very fit-looking, with a lean, sculpted body that could come only from a steady regimen of weight lifting and heavy jogging.

"Katherine, Maria, I'm glad you're here," he said, shaking hands with the two of them.

"I'm sorry we didn't come earlier," Katherine said. "As soon as we heard, we rushed straight to the embassy to try to get it reversed."

"And did you?"

"We don't know yet. We put a good scare into them, but it's hard to tell which way it'll go."

Then there was an awkward moment as Whitehall studied me in apparent confusion.

Katherine finally said, "Thomas, this is Major Sean Drummond. You remember I told you I was firing the military co-counsel the command provided and requesting my own. This is him."

"Pleased to meet you," Whitehall said, thrusting out his right hand again.

I hesitated for only a brief moment before I shook it, but long enough for him to get the message. I then mumbled something incoherent that might've sounded like "Pleased to meet you, too," or "You make me sick." Whichever.

Whitehall sat on his bunk. Katherine and Maria followed and fell onto the bunk beside him. Me? I chose to prop myself against a wall in prickly isolation.

But I never took my eyes off my client. My first impression had been made the moment I heard the details of his crime, and I wanted to see how it squared with his physical presence. His uniform was sharply pressed and creased and his boots glistened as though he spent twenty hours a day rubbing polish on them. Maybe he did; what else are you going to do when you're sitting on your ass in a cell? The emblem on his collar identified him as an infantry officer, and the ring on the third finger of his left hand was an Academy ring with a big red ruby. He looked like a model young officer: handsome, fit, and meticulously tidy.

But he wasn't a model officer. He raped dead people.

"So," Whitehall asked, intensely studying me right back, "where do you come from, Major?"

"I'm assigned to a court just outside Washington. An appeals court."

That was a lie, but I had my reasons for misleading him.

"Have you ever defended an accused murderer before?"

"A few times."

"How about rape?"

"Plenty."

"Necrophilia?"

"No. None. Never."

"Then we have something in common."

"Really? And what could that possibly be, Captain?" I nastily replied, thinking we had nothing at all in common, except we were both in the Army. And we were both males. Well, he was sort of a male. Maybe.

"I've never been accused of necrophilia before," he assured me with a very bitter smile on his lips.

"You went to West Point?" I asked, avoiding that with a ten-foot pole.

"Class of '91."

"Are you gay?" I asked, deliberately diving right into it, a neat little lawyer's trick I'd learned, because I suspected he wouldn't be truthful and I wanted to see if the quick leap made him blush, or stammer, or emit some nonverbal clue that betrayed his true sexual druthers.

I needn't have bothered.

"In fact, I am," he said, sounding unaffected, like he wasn't embarrassed by it. Then he quickly added, "But you're not allowed to disclose that. Since you're my attorney, you're bound by attorney-client privilege, and I'll tell you what you can and can't divulge."

"And what if Miss Carlson and I decide an admission of sexual preference is in your best interest?"

Katherine was looking at me with a queasy expression, and it suddenly struck me what was going on here.

Whitehall said, "I'll reiterate again, Major. I'll tell you what you can and can't disclose. I was first in my class in military law at West Point, and like many gay soldiers, I've continued to study the law a great deal since. My life and career are on the line."

"Are you unhappy with us?" I asked. "Do you lack confidence in our abilities?"

"No, I guess you'll do fine. Just say I'm confident in my own judgment and abilities and leave it at that."

Katherine was now nervously running a hand through that

long, black, luxurious hair of hers. Her eyes were darting around at some invisible specks on the ceiling like the last thing she wanted to do was look at my face.

There's a term used in prisons: "jailhouse lawyer." The Army has its own version, "barracks lawyer." Both refer to a specific kind of foolish creature who stuffs his nose inside a few law books and suddenly thinks he's been reincarnated as Clarence Darrow or Perry Mason. They're a real lawyer's worst nightmare, because all of a sudden your client thinks he's smarter than you, which he very well might be, only he lacks a few essentials called experience and education, and in any regard is trying to transform a worm's-eye view of the world into an all-encompassing galactic perspective.

The great danger with barracks lawyers is that they very often don't comprehend their own gaping shortcomings until the words "guilty as charged" come tumbling out of the jury foreman's lips. Even then, some don't learn. Appeals court dockets are overloaded with motions launched by barracks lawyers, who graduate into jailhouse lawyers, who continue to believe the only reason they lost was because of the bungling attorney who took up space at the defense table with them.

I said, "Do I take it that you intend to direct the defense?"

"Mostly, yes," he said. "On all key decisions, I expect you to confer with me. And I have the final vote."

The law certainly gave him this authority, and by Katherine's pained expression I guessed this topic had already been broached at some length with our client. I decided not to press. Whitehall didn't know me, or trust me, so I wasn't likely to disabuse him at this early stage in our relationship. Depending on how full of himself he was, or how our relationship matured, maybe I'd never disabuse him.

I merely said, "You certainly have that right."

He said, "I know."

"May I ask a few questions pertaining to the case?"

"Uh . . . all right," he answered, as though he were doing me some big favor.

"What was your position on base?"

"The headquarters company commander."

"And how long were you in that position?"

"Eleven months. I'm on a one-year rotation. I was scheduled to change command in one more month."

"How were your ratings?"

"Outstanding. All of my ratings, my whole career, have always been outstanding."

"Uh-huh," I murmured, making a mental note to check that. Lots of officers lie and tell you they've got outstanding records, and because their personnel jackets are kept in sealed files in D.C., the layman has no way of checking. I'm not a layman, though. I'm a lawyer. I can check.

I asked, "So what were you and First Sergeant Moran, Private Jackson, and Lee No Tae doing at that apartment?"

He relaxed back against the wall. "They were my friends. I know officers aren't supposed to mingle with enlisted troops, but none of them were under my command. I figured it was harmless. I invited them over for a party."

"Could you elaborate on the nature of your friendship? Exactly what does that word mean to you?"

"You mean . . . was I romantically involved with them?"

"That's exactly what I mean."

He quickly bent forward. "You haven't tried any gay cases before, have you?"

"Nope," I admitted. "This is my first."

"In gay cases, Major, always direct your question more narrowly. Some gays are wildly promiscuous. Romantic entanglements can be irrelevant, even undesirable. You must always ask, was there a physical relationship, because often that's all there was."

Whitehall then studied me very carefully to see how I'd respond. I had the sense there was something here that was very weighty to him. He'd just lectured me on a point of law as though I were a first-year law student, so there was the matter of one-upsmanship to contend with. But he'd also made a somewhat provocative claim about gays—was this some kind of test?

At any rate, I coldly said, "Point taken. Did you have either a romantic or physical relationship with any of those men?"

He didn't answer. Instead, he bent farther forward, placed his elbows on his knees, and said, "Tell me something, Major. I've read that some defense attorneys would rather not know if their clients are guilty or innocent. In the dark, they give every client every benefit of the doubt. They throw their hearts and souls into the defense. Do you subscribe to that theory?"

"Nope. I sure don't."

"Why not?"

"For one thing, any decent defense attorney puts his feelings aside. For a second, it diffuses your strategy. If you believe your client's innocent, you spend all your time trying to prove that to everybody else. If you know or suspect he's guilty, you spend every second trying to invalidate or hinder the prosecutor's case. It's like what they taught you in military art about focusing the main effort on a battlefield, and economizing elsewhere. We've only got two weeks here. We can't afford to be diffused."

"But tell me truthfully. If you thought I was guilty of these crimes—murder, rape, necrophilia, engaging in homosexual acts, consorting with enlisted troops—would you put your heart and soul into my defense?"

"I've taken an oath as an officer of the court to provide you the most able defense I can offer."

That was a rhetorical sidestep and he knew it. And that seemed to tell him something important, because he leaned back against the wall and his expression got suddenly chilly.

"Okay," he said, "here's the way we'll work this. You go find out everything you can. Collect the facts, analyze what you've got, then come back to me with your questions."

"Will you answer them?" I asked.

"I didn't say that. Just bring your questions when you're ready."

We left Captain Thomas Whitehall in his cell and departed the holding facility. Neither Katherine nor Maria asked me what I thought. I figured they already knew what I thought. They knew, because they had to be thinking the exact same thing.

CHAPTER
6

★ ★ ★

Imelda had already accomplished an all-out miracle. Four desks with computers were up and running, giving the place the look of a long-established law office, barring the contradictory presence of hair supplies cluttered all over the counters. One of her clerks was typing, another was filing, and the third was taking dictation from Keith.

Imelda was seated in one of the four parlor chairs, feet kicked up, proofreading some legal document, slashing away with a thick red pen, looking like the Queen of Sheba. I swore I'd never forgive her.

A message awaited us, too. It was from the embassy and said that Katherine and I were invited to a powwow in the office of the Republic of Korea's minister of justice at 1:00 P.M. It being twenty till, the two of us frantically dashed outside and jumped into a sedan. We raced for the front gate, and it wasn't until we were almost there before I realized we were completely screwed. The gate was bound to be choked up with protesters.

But when we arrived, the Korean fellas in blue suits were already hammering folks aside to make room for us to pass. It had to be Imelda, of course. She'd obviously called ahead. The woman never missed a beat.

The ministry was located five miles away, and fortunately the traffic, which in Seoul almost always moves like constipated molasses, was suspiciously light. Probably everybody and his brother was out protesting against us Americans, which falls under the heading of what you might call a mixed blessing.

The overly elegant Mr. Brandewaite and his trusted henchman, Colonel Piranha Lips, awaited us at the grand entrance to the Ministry of Justice.

Hands were swiftly shaken while Brandewaite, with a very virtuous look, said, "Hey, I'm damned sorry for that testy meeting this morning. I'm on your side in this thing. Please believe that. I called the minister and persuaded him to at least hear your argument. Now it's in your hands. I wish I could do more, but my own hands are completely tied."

Bullshit. This guy was the acting ambassador in a country that thoroughly depended on us to keep the North Koreans from launching what businessmen call a hostile takeover. There were all kinds of things he could do. The only reason he'd even lifted a pinkie was because he was scared witless about being publicly barbecued by Katherine's gay buddies. But I kept that thought to myself.

We then trooped up some big stairs and walked across a wide hallway to a set of carved mahogany doors. Brandewaite and Janson seemed to know their way. We entered a cavernous anteroom with about six secretaries scattered at various desks. Brandewaite said something in Korean and one of the secretaries leaped from her chair in the obsequious way some Korean women have, bowed demurely, then led us to another set of carved doors. She knocked gently and we entered.

It was a big office with high ceilings, decorated, like most Korean official suites, with cheap-looking furniture, big scrolls on the walls, and a few watercolor paintings of peasants frolicking in fields, or big white cranes cruising through the air. I guess if you're Korean, they carry hidden meanings. I'm not Korean, though.

The gentleman behind the desk nodded politely and indicated with a stately wave for us to take the seats arrayed directly in front of his desk. It did not escape my notice that he chose not to shift our conversation to the corner where three couches were located. In Korea, symbolism counts for a lot. The symbol here wasn't hard to figure out. This wasn't going to be a chummy little chat, so let's not pretend otherwise.

The minister was elderly, white-haired, and had a broad, bony face, dark eyes, and a mouth so tight it looked as if it had been slashed on with a machete.

There was another Korean gentleman there also, even older than the minister, also white-haired, but more distinguished-looking, with a very handsome face and serene eyes. He sat quietly on a chair in the corner, the traditional place for notetakers and translators.

Brandewaite and the minister yammered back and forth in Korean. I couldn't understand a word, but this was one of those exceptions to my general rule about what you don't know don't hurt you. What Brandewaite was saying might be real hurtful. His posture and mannerisms were almost comically obsequious.

Finally they finished, and the minister, whose name was Chun Moon Song, turned to us and in passable English said, "Miss Carlson, Ambassador Brandewaite says you are protesting our request for jurisdiction over Captain Whitehall."

"That's correct," Katherine said.

"What bothers you so greatly? Do you not have confidence in the fairness of our Korean courts?"

In lawyer's terms this was what's called a verbal ambush, the legal equivalent of asking when you're going to stop beating your wife.

Katherine never blinked. "Aren't *you* the one who's demanding a change of jurisdiction? Don't *you* have confidence in the fairness of American courts?"

It was a nicely done turn of phrase, and if I didn't dislike her so thoroughly I would've been real proud of her.

The minister blinked a few times, then sat back in his chair. He was a very powerful man, and this was Korea, which is a very patriarchal, Confucian land. He wasn't accustomed to being challenged by anyone younger than him. He was painfully unaccustomed to being contradicted by a woman half his age.

"Miss Carlson, if a Korean soldier in America brutally murdered the child of your Secretary of Defense, how would your country respond?"

"In America, we honor our agreements. Our entire economic and legal system depends on it. If we had a contract, like our SOFA, we'd stand by it."

"But you agree, don't you, that the crime Captain Whitehall committed exceeds the bounds of ordinary criminality? Can't you see why our people demand that *we* determine the punishment?"

Katherine looked at him very curiously. "I don't agree. You're speaking as though you've already convicted Captain Whitehall."

"I'm sorry," he said, somewhat clumsily. "My command of your language is flawed."

"Is it really?" she asked, not missing a beat.

The minister ignored her, because the only other alternative was to simply throw us out of his office. In fact, I couldn't figure out why he didn't just do that.

Instead he drew his neck back a bit and said, "I assure you, Miss Carlson, that Captain Whitehall will get every benefit of the doubt. He will be treated as fairly as though he were in an American court."

I have to tell you, at this point, that I have an egregious flaw. Most lawyers live for long-drawn-out arguments. It's what attracts them to the profession. They love the interplay of opposing arguments, the commingling of subtle nuances and hair-splitting points, the thrill of intellectually besting a worthy, voluble, articulate opponent. I just don't happen to be one of them. I guess you'd say I'm impetuous, or impatient, or both.

Before anybody could utter another word, I blurted out, "Damn it, Mr. Minister, Whitehall's an American soldier. He's stationed here on the orders of our government to protect your country's security. He's here involuntarily. If he's convicted in your courts, using your legal standards, the consequences will be damned serious. Miss Carlson's movement will raise all kinds of embarrassing issues. They'll keep them alive for years. Whitehall will become a symbol, a martyr to a travesty of justice. His face will become as common on CNN as . . . well . . . as mustard on hot dogs. Is that what you want?"

Now I'd gone ahead and done exactly what Keith had accomplished in Brandewaite's office that morning. I'd brought their gay movement and all its political and media clout into this. But frankly, given the stakes of this case, philosophical debates weren't likely to have sway in this room.

"You really believe that?" the older gentleman in the corner suddenly asked.

"I absolutely do," I blurted out. "It's a damn shame what happened to that Korean kid, but he's dead and you can't bring him back to life. You need to seriously consider the damage this will do to the alliance."

The older man looked thoughtful. "And you believe we will harm our alliance?"

"Believe it? Buddy, I know it. I don't care what Mr. Brandewaite or Colonel Janson have told you. Their job is to kiss your asses, but it's not mine. I can tell you like it is. Americans might not be very sympathetic to the gay movement, but they're extraordinarily sympathetic to the rights of a serviceman serving on foreign soil. A West Point graduate, with eight years of distinguished service and an unblemished record. They'll make Whitehall sound like Joan of Arc. They'll make you all sound like Torquemada and his band of merry inquisitors. You'll have the same CNN legal correspondents who analyzed O.J. Simpson's trial spending months picking apart the very gaping differences between your legal system and ours. This is America we're talking about. There'll be a made-for-TV movie on the air before you can lock his cell door. And no matter how diplomatic we want to be in this room, face facts. Compared to America's, yours are kangaroo courts."

Brandewaite's face was crimson. He stood up and was just about to box my ears when the older man in the corner briskly motioned him to sit down. Then the minister and the older man in the corner exchanged some kind of hidden cue, a slight shifting of the eyes maybe.

The minister said, "Thank you very much for coming to see me. I will inform you of my decision later today."

That was the diplomatic equivalent of "get lost" and "don't let the door slam you in the ass" all rolled into one. We got up and hustled out of his office. Brandewaite stomped his feet the whole way, but he waited till we were outside before he attacked.

"Drummond, you stupid ass, do you know who that man was you were talking with?"

"No, I don't," I said. "And I frankly don't care. They're making a terrible blunder and they need to hear the truth."

Brandewaite stared at me incredulously. "That was Lee Jung Kim, the minister of defense. It was his son who was murdered and sodomized."

I'd like to tell you I handled this news with my usual debonair aloofness. But I didn't. I felt my face burn with shame. Somebody should've told us he was in the room. Actually, he never should've been there in the first place. No parent whose son was murdered should have to hear the lawyers wrangling behind the curtains of justice.

The fact he was there, though, was revealing. In America, the family of the victim would never be invited into the judge's chambers. How in the hell were we supposed to believe Whitehall was going to get a fair shake if he got turned over?

When we climbed into our sedan, Katherine put a hand on my arm. "Don't worry about it. You had no way of knowing."

"You're not the one who just stuffed his combat boot down that old man's throat."

We stayed silent for a few uncomfortable minutes. Then Katherine forgot all about my embarrassment. "Other than that, how do you think it went?"

"Hard to say," I told her. "If logic prevails, they'll leave well enough alone. The problem is, Koreans aren't known for being logical."

"What are they known for?"

"You know what the other Asians call them?"

"What?"

"The Irish of the Far East. See, they're not like the Japanese or the Chinese. For one thing, Koreans aren't inscrutable. They're mercurial. Don't expect them to be hyper-practical like the Japanese, or coolly calculating like the Chinese. Koreans run in deep drafts of hot and cold. They don't always decide in their own best interests, because their emotions sometimes overcloud their brains."

It wasn't funny but she chuckled anyway. "Anyway, Attila, you did real good in there."

"Yeah, well. You didn't do so bad yourself."

This exceptional instance of mutual bonhomie lasted till we got back to the hair parlor and I noticed that some asshole had hung a large sign over the entrance. In big, black, bold letters it said HOMOS. Then in pale, infinitely smaller letters underneath, "Home Office of Moonbeam's Office Staff."

Keith had to be behind this, since he was the only one who'd heard me use that nickname. He had a sense of humor, I guess. A perverse, sick one, but in his eyes I guess it seemed pretty funny. I looked every which way to make sure no one was peeking as I passed beneath that sign and entered our headquarters.

Katherine collected the lawyers and Imelda and dragged us into the office Imelda and her girls had set up for the lead counsel.

Imelda and Allie and Maria were cracking jokes with one another and acting real chummy. I needed to have a talk with Imelda. Maybe the poor woman didn't know they were all gay.

"Okay," Katherine said, once she had us all quieted down, "here's how it stands. Sometime in the next few hours, the decision will be made on jurisdiction. We've done everything we can. If it goes to the Koreans, you're all out of here, because none of us knows the first thing about Korean law. I'll help find a capable Korean attorney and stay behind to supervise his efforts. If it stays in U.S. jurisdiction, then we've just lost another day in preparing our defense."

We all traded glum looks, because this was a pretty disheartening summary. Accurate, but disheartening. The only thing we'd accomplished was to argue about where Whitehall would be tried, and frankly that wasn't going to help us get him off. Which was a pretty dim ambition anyway, if you asked me, but nobody was asking me.

Then giving us all a solemn look, Katherine said, "The strategy I've decided to employ is to prove he's innocent. We'll organize our efforts on that task."

I was sure I hadn't heard that right. "I, uh . . . could you repeat that, please?"

"I said we're going to prove he's innocent."

I immediately leaped out of my chair. "Damn it, Carlson, you can't do that. That's idiocy. We all know what the evidence says. Unless he was framed, he's as guilty as a fox in a henhouse with feathers crammed in his teeth."

"Good point," Katherine said, rubbing her chin. "That'll be our defense. He was framed. You're right. There's really no other option."

I couldn't believe this. No experienced lawyer would ever decide their strategy this way. Not in a murder trial. Not in any trial. No law school advocated the process of elimination.

"Damn it, don't do this!" I sputtered out. "Focus on the prosecutor's case. It's the only viable strategy."

Katherine shook her head back and forth. "Do I need to remind you I'm the lead counsel here?"

"Look, damn it, you got no idea what you're getting into. If you claim he was framed, you have to prove that. Nothing's more dangerous than a frame defense. You shift the burden of proof away from the prosecutor into your own lap. You'll give the prosecutor the opportunity to knock holes in our defense. Rule one of criminal law: When it looks like your client's guilty, make it impossible for the prosecutor to prove his case, not poke holes in yours."

Katherine stood up and placed her tiny hands on her thin waist. Her angelic face turned real unangelic. "Don't lecture me, Drummond. I went to law school, too. I've thought about it. Our client was framed for murder, rape, and necrophilia. That's our defense."

By this time, both of us were yelling and our faces were snarled with anger. Everybody else sat rigid and upright in their chairs, staring at us. I glanced at their stricken visages and felt this sudden burst of nauseating nostalgia, like we were back at Georgetown Law, making the other students restless and uncomfortable.

I just couldn't stop myself. I yelled, "You're wrong!"

She yelled back, "I don't care what you think! Or what the evidence shows! From now on, our client was framed. Someone else killed that kid and made it look like Thomas did it."

I kept shaking my head. I couldn't believe what I was hearing. "Have you discussed this with our client?"

"No. I don't intend to, either. Not yet, anyway. And don't any of you reveal this to him. I'll have your ass if you do."

"You don't think that presents a slight ethics problem?"

"Drummond, he's withholding from us. Why should we have any problem withholding from him?"

Unless we dove at each other and got our hands wrapped firmly around each other's throats, our conversation had reached a typically inelegant conclusion. But rather than commit murder in the presence of so many witnesses, I angrily stormed out and headed off to dinner. I went back to my room, picked up the phone, and barked at room service to send up a rare steak and an overcooked potato. I was in the mood for a red-blooded, manly meal. I consumed it alone, so I could stew in solitary self-pity. I chewed every bite like I had a grudge against it.

Carlson was wrong. Worse, though, I had a terrible premonition I knew why. The woman wasn't stupid, right? Nor was she professionally incompetent, right?

What I figured was this: Whitehall was now a symbol for all those antigay activists trying to overturn "don't ask, don't tell." If he got off on a technicality or because the prosecutor was too inept to prove his case "beyond a reasonable doubt," then Whitehall would go free, but that would only whip the antigay factions into an even more frothful fury. They'd portray it as a hideous injustice piled on top of an even more hideous crime.

Carlson's first loyalty wasn't to her client; it was to the movement that hired her, that made her famous, that signed her pay-check. Plus she was a fanatic. As Keith had quoted, sometimes you just have to break a few eggs to make an omelet. Carlson or the folks who hired her had obviously decided Whitehall was a break-able egg. The only way to get their money's worth was to go for broke. To undo the damage done by this case they had to prove Whitehall was innocent. It was all or nothing. Any other outcome and Whitehall would be turned into the eternal poster child for why gays have no place in the military.

There was one tiny insurmountable problem with that, though. It didn't look like he was the least bit innocent. And if we lost, Whitehall was facing the death sentence.

Apparently, from Carlson's point of view this was a reconcil-able technicality. Not from mine.

CHAPTER
7
★ ★ ★

The South Koreans made their call at ten o'clock that evening. They waived jurisdiction. Not pretrial confinement, only jurisdiction. Whitehall was to be transferred from the Yongsan Holding Facility to the Seoul High Security Prison at ten o'clock the next morning.

And when it came to the matter of punishment, if I guessed right, what the Koreans intended was to wait and see how the sentence came out. If Whitehall got death, they'd probably be shrewdly generous and allow us to yank the electric switch and fry him. If he got life, he'd spend the rest of his pitiful days and years in a South Korean prison.

Janson called to inform me of this. He didn't call Katherine, or Keith, or any of the rest of the covey. Just me. There was a subtle message there—I just didn't know what it was.

However, I immediately called Katherine to inform her of our extreme good fortune. A woman's voice answered. I had no idea who she was, and I asked to speak with Katherine. She said "okay," then I heard the two of them giggling. It sounded like that flirty kind of giggle you hear when two folks get interrupted in the midst of some heavy petting.

Katherine coldly acknowledged the news and hung up. No "Gee thanks, Sean, I can't begin to tell you what a great job you did in the minister's office." Not even the most grudging acknowledgment that I'd saved her bacon—just "okay," click. She was either as mad at me as I was at her, or she couldn't wait to get back to her girlfriend.

I was getting undressed when there was a knock at the door. I expected to see the maid coming to turn down my sheets and place a couple of those little chocolate tasties by my bedside. It wasn't a maid, though: not unless maids are late-middle-aged Caucasian males wearing trench coats who are in the habit of peeking searchingly down both sides of the hallway before they shoulder past you.

"Buzz Mercer," he announced, sticking out a hand.

I didn't feel any particular need to introduce myself, so I said, "Nice to meet you. You sure you've got the right room?"

"Oh yeah, Drummond," he said, with a man-eating grin. "You and I gotta have a short talk."

"Would you care for a seat?" I asked.

He went over and fell into the chair. He was a nondescript-looking type, with a squarish, unassuming face, a tight butch cut, clear-rimmed glasses, and what I guess you'd call a sardonic grin pasted on his lower face. Not his upper face, though. His eyes were too intense to be anything but somber.

He said, "I'm the station chief."

"Great," I remarked. What else do you say to a man who's just identified himself as the head of the CIA for all of Korea?

"Have a seat," he ordered, so I did.

"I thought about asking you to come to our facility, but finally decided this'd be better. You and I are probably going to have a few chats over the next few weeks. It would be best for all concerned if nobody knows about it."

You remember when I warned you I'm a bit impulsive?

I put a steely expression on my face and snarled, "Look, buddy, get this straight right away. You picked me 'cause I'm the only Army guy on the defense team. Not to mention the only hetero. Good thinking, except I'm not going to expose a single damned thing about this case. Not to you . . . not to anybody."

He seemed halfheartedly amused. "Settle down, Drummond.

That's not what this is about. I've discussed this with General Spears. He agrees that this is the right way to handle this."

"Handle what?" I asked, blinking wildly a few times, since in a matter of a few brief seconds I'd already managed to make a complete horse's ass out of myself. This wasn't a novel experience by any means, but humiliation is one of those things that doesn't go down more smoothly with practice.

"This is classified. Don't discuss it with anybody. Not even the rest of your defense team . . . no . . . make that *particularly* with the rest of your defense team. Got that?"

"Sure."

"Okay, here's how it is. This case is attracting attention in the wrong quarters."

"You mean in the South Korean government?"

"Right country, wrong prefix. There are folks in Pyongyang who get copies of the *Seoul Herald* within hours after it hits the newsstands. They watch our television news, listen to our radios, even read those half-assed tabloids about Martians in the White House. They know what movie star's screwin' what movie star this week, and the latest fad diet that'll help you lose forty pounds overnight. Kim Jong Il and his boys are well aware of what's going on down here."

I nodded right along. Given the rift our case was making in the alliance, of course North Korea was following it attentively. I hadn't thought about it until that moment, but of course they were.

He bent toward me. "Do you have any idea how many agents North Korea has down here?"

"No."

"I got news for you. We don't, either. Nor do the South Koreans. It's a lot, though. We know, for instance, that they left plenty of sleeper agents here in 1950, when MacArthur and his boys kicked their asses out of the south. And we know they've been recruiting more, and adding to them ever since. Some folks believe they might only have ten to twenty thousand agents. Others believe they have a few hundred thousand."

"That's a lot of agents," I said, because sometimes it helps to restate the obvious, if for no other reason than to show you're a conscientious listener.

"Yeah, it's a lot." He nodded, re-restating what I'd just restated, I guess to prove we were both conscientious listeners. "We've also noticed a step-up in North Korean infiltrations over the past two weeks. And we pick up the occasional radio intercept from North Korean cells here back to their controllers up north. That traffic's picked up these past two weeks. Normally that's a very grim sign that somebody's planning something."

"This is obviously not good," I said.

"We don't know yet. It's pretty damned obvious that how this thing goes down might well decide the fate of the alliance. Maybe the South Koreans are just blustering about throwing us Meegooks off the peninsula . . . or maybe they're not. But if I were a bigwig in North Korean intelligence, I'd sure as hell be sniffing around to see which way it goes. Quite possibly what they're doing is increasing their reconnaissance, just in the event we get thrown off the peninsula and they decide to attack."

"So what's this got to do with me?" I asked, which was the response I was sure he expected.

"Maybe nothing. Then again, maybe a lot."

"Have we been mentioned in some of this radio traffic?"

"There've been a few mentions, but we're not certain what they mean. See, the North Koreans know we listen in, and they're well aware of our sophistication at code-breaking, so they take precautions. They develop all kinds of ridiculous code names and circular puzzles to throw us off."

"But you must've developed some kind of opinion, or theory, or you wouldn't be here."

"Not really," he said. "But ever since that September 11 thing, we always play it safe better than sorry. Maybe your defense team's completely in the clear, maybe not. But if we come up with anything, we'd like to use you as our conduit. Of course, we'd like you to treat the information with the sensitivity it deserves. We sure as hell can't approach Carlson and her freak show directly."

He was right about that. The intelligence he was referring to was probably gathered through the most sensitive means available, and Katherine hadn't shown herself to be someone the U.S. government should entrust with such deep dark secrets.

He stood up and started walking for the door. "Anything more comes up, I'll keep you informed."

"Anything specific you expect me to do at this point?" I asked.

He had the door open and was just walking out. "Nope." Then the door shut behind him.

It was, all in all, a completely dopey conversation. He'd said something, and he'd said nothing. If I was the really suspicious sort, I might think he was probing to see if I was amenable to becoming his stooge, and I'd scared him off, so he'd resorted to that little cover story about North Koreans. That might sound fairly paranoid to most folks, but most folks haven't spent as much time around spooks as I have. They lie to their own mothers just for practice.

If nothing else, this little tête-à-tête had made me suddenly aware of the importance the U.S. government was placing on our efforts to defend Whitehall. Face it, they'd be stupid to be complacent. Carlson was a ruthless fanatic, and fate had just handed her the power to take a meat cleaver to the alliance. Those folks back in Washington probably wanted her watched like a hawk.

I got a lousy night's sleep. I kept trying to recall my Swedish stewardess with the Bronx twang and Italian name, but time and distance were rapidly diffusing her into a foggy ghost. Instead, a smallish woman with long, dark hair, an angelic face, and emerald-like eyes kept mulishly butting her way into my head. I knew I wasn't having desirous thoughts, because I've never been a sucker for unrequited lust. I like my fantasies reciprocated.

When I awoke in the morning I felt grizzly and raw. I opened the blinds to explore the day.

Back when I was in law school, there was this professor named Maladroit who taught legal ethics. I'm not making this up, either. His name was Harold Maladroit III; a great name for a barrister, if you think about it. Anyway, poor old Maladroit didn't put a whole lot of Sturm und Drang into his teachings, if you know what I mean. He normally arrived fifteen minutes late, shuffling into the classroom like it was the last place on earth he wanted to be. But he was actually a very brilliant and accomplished jurist.

He'd occasionally present us with case studies that were so waterlogged with ambivalence they made your head ache. I stared out the window at the skyline of downtown Seoul and got to thinking about one particular case.

The way Maladroit presented it, a private attorney had gotten a call from a man accused of murdering and then eating twelve people. He went and interviewed the accused, and to his vast surprise discovered a handsome young man, well-dressed, well-groomed, apparently well-educated, cultured, and almost impossibly likable. The attorney was astonished. He was also cautious. They spent five hours talking, because it took that long for the attorney to convince himself he was chatting with somebody far too sane and morally anchored to have committed such outlandishly heinous crimes. The attorney of course agreed to represent him.

The trial date was set for six months hence, and the attorney and his client used every minute of it to build their defense. They worked doggedly, becoming very close, achieving, if not a father-to-son relationship, then something not far from it. The most damning evidence against the accused man was a collection of tiny shards of bones that had been found in the old coal furnace in his cellar. The accused man swore the bones were those of Jackie, his beloved beagle, who'd died about two months before the police came. He'd considered taking the corpse to a pet cemetery, but in an effort to be thrifty decided he'd simply cremate the remains himself. This was before DNA testing, and successive medical tests ended up deadlocked: The bones could've been human, or they could've been a dog's.

The attorney believed his client. He put all his considerable legal brilliance into the case. He labored fifteen-hour days, ignored his other clients, borrowed money from the bank to keep his practice going, and worked solely, completely, singly on this case. It became his obsession. He gambled dangerously with his financial future. He traded his entire client base for this one man, this one trial.

The day before the trial opened, the attorney and his client went through their preparations one final time. The attorney was so utterly convinced of his client's innocence, and was so sure of the fine, wholesome impression he'd make with the jury, that he decided to take a great legal risk. He decided to put his client on the stand. They were rehearsing his testimony when they got to the part where the attorney asked his client about the tiny bone shards in the furnace.

"Oh, those," the client said with the kind of infectious chuckle the lawyer was sure would warm the hearts of even the most hardhearted jury. "See, I had a dog named Max. A cute little schnauzer, a real great dog. I loved him dearly. He died and so I cremated him."

The lawyer was gifted, or in this case cursed, with a fly-trap memory. Six months before, his client had told him the dog was named Jackie, only now the name was Max. And before the dog was a beagle; now it was a schnauzer. For the first time, he had grave doubts. If the story about the dog wasn't true, maybe nothing else was true, either.

He lost a great deal of sleep over the following week. The trial progressed. The prosecutor threw his best punches and the defense lawyer counterattacked with a vengeance. He was superbly prepared. He had a convincing rebuttal for everything. He poked holes of doubt every which way.

On the seventh day, the prosecutor was scheduled to call the witness the defense attorney most dreaded—the police officer who'd performed the initial search of his client's home. In the backyard, discarded behind some overgrown bushes, the officer had discovered some children's clothing. A mother who lived four blocks away had identified a red shirt as being the same type her son wore on the very day he disappeared. The boy had been missing for four months.

The clothing could have been hidden there by any Tom, Dick, or Harry who'd passed by, and the shirt might or might not have been her son's, since it was unmarked, and it was a popular generic brand. But the mere fact that it was there would be very damning with the jury. Everything about the prosecutor's case was circumstantial, but one thing every criminal lawyer knows is that the weight of two pieces of circumstantial evidence is far greater than the sum of the parts.

The problem for the prosecutor was that he couldn't introduce the shirt into evidence because in a pretrial ruling the defense attorney had convinced the libertarian judge that since the clothes had been discovered outside the premises of the dwelling, and the search warrant had specified the house itself, they were inadmissible.

The judge, however, wasn't a complete dolt, so he limited his ruling to say the clothing was inadmissible only so long as the issue of what was discovered outside the home was never raised. The prosecutor was then instructed that he was barred, under any circumstances, from *initiating* discussion about the evidence found outside the home. Sounds loopy, but you have to understand that legal rulings have a perverse logic all of their own.

The quandary was this: The defense attorney was suddenly shattered by self-doubt. He suspected his client had misled and manipulated him for six long months. He just wasn't sure. He'd built a strong defense. He'd covered every base. He was confident of his ability to neutralize the prosecutor's case. All the key evidence was either inadmissible or easily refuted.

That is, unless the defense attorney in his cross-examination of the investigating officer inadvertently triggered a discussion about the evidence found outside the house. That would allow the prosecutor to get the shirt introduced as evidence. It would compound the case against his client. It would place his client at great peril. It would also devastate his own legal career, which was hovering on the verge of bankruptcy.

The attorney couldn't sleep the whole night before. The nice, clean-cut young man he'd come to like so much might actually have murdered and then eaten twelve people, including six young boys. The thought sickened him. To rectify the situation, all he had to do was make one small verbal slip the next day, to allude in any way to the search of the grounds around his client's home. The prosecutor would hear the slip and pounce.

He was still wrestling with himself when it came his turn to cross-examine the police officer. The officer's name was Sergeant Curtis Lincoln, a big Black man with deepset, uncompromising eyes who looked positively tortured, no doubt because the prosecutor's case was falling apart. The defense attorney got up. He stood for nearly half a minute, so miserably conflicted that he became tongue-tied. The judge called his name three times. He looked at the police officer and Curtis Lincoln stared back searchingly. He looked at his client and the young man stared back even more searchingly.

In that instant, the attorney concluded that his lawyer's oath took precedence over his own deeply held personal convictions. He told the judge he had no questions and fell back into his chair.

His client was found not guilty. It was an incredible victory. The press lauded the attorney as the second coming. He was interviewed on talk shows and heralded as the most promising legal mind in the city, probably the state, maybe the whole damned country. Offers poured in from firms promising instant partnerships, from wealthy suspects who wanted to pay top dollar for his services, from publishing houses wanting to ghostwrite his story.

Within a year six more people disappeared. Sergeant Curtis Lincoln got another warrant, did another search, found six sets of bones in the client's basement, all neatly picked clean of meat. The client was arrested again, and the first thing he did was call the same lawyer.

Most everybody in the class chuckled when old Harold Maladroit III outlined this case. The irony was too excruciating, the story too perfect. It had to be fabricated. It simply couldn't be true.

I wasn't chuckling, though. I was watching old Maladroit's eyes.

As soon as the class was done, I rushed down to the law library and researched for four hours. I finally found the right case; it was named *State* vs. *Homison*. It concerned an accused cannibal named William Homison who was brilliantly defended by an attorney named Harold Maladroit III. The reason the case made the law books was because of the groundbreaking argument Maladroit constructed to get the clothing excluded as evidence. No wonder the old coot fled from the practice of law to teach legal ethics.

Like lots of ethical issues faced by lawyers, the lesson of this one took you into all kinds of dark, twisted back alleys. Maladroit had done what his oath required him to do. He'd steamrolled his own conscience and forged ahead. He'd also sentenced six more people to death.

My oath now dictated that I should follow Carlson's instructions to the letter and do everything in my power to prove my client innocent. Only, if I did, I might help sentence Whitehall to death. There were no guarantees either way, but a lawyer must appease his own sense of right and wrong. All attorneys gamble with the fates and lives of their clients: The trick is to gauge the odds, and make the bet you can live with regardless of the consequences.

The best bet for Whitehall was to pick apart the prosecutor's case. To do that, though, I needed to learn a great deal more about what had happened. So I got on the phone. I called Imelda and told her to have the case materials delivered to my room at noon. I would've told her to bring them up right away, but I intended to be present when Whitehall was transferred from American custody to the Koreans.

Carlson was going to be in for a rude shock, and I needed to be there to stabilize her. I called her next and made an appointment to accompany her to the military holding facility at nine-thirty.

That settled, I flipped on CNN and watched the coverage of the Antigay March on Washington. It was a sobering sight. Over a million marchers participated. There was a very dramatic shot taken at the Mall of a tightly crammed crowd that seemed to stretch off into infinity. There were quick glimpses of one frenzied preacher after another standing at a lectern, haranguing the crowd, and condemning the President, homosexuals, and about anybody who liked or supported either of them.

Thousands of placards were visible. Nearly all of them had a big photograph of a single face. I recognized the face, of course:

Thomas Whitehall. The common motto on the signs read ASK, TELL, GO TO HELL, a surprisingly un-Christian sentiment, if you ask me.

By nine-thirty, I was standing at the front entrance of the Dragon Hill Lodge when Katherine appeared beside me. Neither of us said a word. We exchanged cold, surly nods and climbed into the sedan.

A big black paddy wagon and ten sedans filled with Korean police were parked outside the holding facility. The Koreans must've been worried about being ambushed by a crowd of angry vigilantes and having Whitehall lynched in the streets of Seoul. It wasn't reassuring that they had to be concerned about that kind of thing.

Inside, a surprisingly tall, frightfully tough-looking Korean in a cheap-looking black silk suit was standing beside the Army captain in charge of the facility. The Korean had wide, knobby shoulders and a face that was more scuffed and scarred than the inside heels of my shoes. He was signing some papers I assumed were the transfer documents.

A sergeant led us to Whitehall's cell so we could exchange some brief words before he was taken away. Whitehall got up as we entered and coolly shook our hands. He didn't look the least bit anxious or concerned. He should've, though. He should've been quaking in his boots.

I opened with, "Good day, Captain Whitehall. You know anything about South Korean prisons?"

He offhandedly said, "I've heard stories."

"They're nasty places," I warned him. "But I guess they'll isolate you for your own safety. The accommodations, though, and the food, aren't nearly as swank as you get here."

"I went to West Point," he said, like that accounted for everything. "I can handle it."

I wanted to say, Oh boy, buddy, are you in for a surprise: Comparing West Point to a South Korean prison is like comparing the Waldorf-Astoria to a Bowery homeless shelter. But why throw fuel on a fire that was already lit? He'd feel the heat soon enough.

A moment later, the tall, oxlike Korean strutted into the cell, accompanied by two only slightly smaller thugs in blue uniforms. He gave an indifferent glance in our direction as he roughly shoved Whitehall against a wall, efficiently patted him down, then signaled the two policemen to come over. With the kind of lightning speed that comes only from ample practice, they cuffed Whitehall's hands and feet. The cuffs were connected by heavy black chains that were not nearly as elegant as the American variety.

They forcefully swung Whitehall back around and started pushing him toward the door.

"Stop this right now!" Carlson yelled.

They ignored her. Or actually, they didn't ignore her. They shoved him harder.

With a ferocious snarl, she stepped courageously into their path. She held up her business card and waved it across their faces. "I'm his attorney. I'm ordering you to stop shoving my client. Right now!"

One of the policemen looked over at the tall Korean in the black suit. A cold, peremptory nod was bestowed before the cop reached out and shoved Carlson so hard she flew against the wall and landed on her tush.

My manly ego told me to step in and clobber the officer who'd shoved her. And I started to, too. Then I heard the sound of a pistol being cocked. The tall guy in the dark suit, I now noticed, had a nasty-looking .38-caliber revolver pointed at my chest.

I smiled and humbly stepped back. Then Whitehall was whisked out of the cell by a series of more hard shoves.

Katherine was just lifting herself off the ground. I offered a hand, but she stared at it like it was the last thing on earth she'd ever touch.

I said, "I warned you they were rough."

She wasn't the type who liked I-told-you-so's. She just gave me a sullen glance before we rushed out to follow Whitehall's convoy. Our driver fell in at the end of the procession and we rode for the next forty minutes without exchanging a word.

The convoy turned off onto a street about midway between Seoul and Inchon, two cities that had grown so spasmodically they'd become all but connected. The huge, forbidding front gate of the prison swung open and the black paddy wagon, followed by eleven cars, proceeded inside. The Korean cars formed a ring and an army of police officers climbed out like ants and assembled into a cordon.

Two overeager Korean camera crews were already set up and ready to roll. They had their lenses focused on the black paddy wagon, so that all of Korea could witness the accused American getting his righteous comeuppance. Suddenly I noticed two of the blue-suited police officers step directly in front of the cameras to block their view.

Then the rear doors of the paddy wagon flew open and a body came sailing out. Whitehall landed on the ground with a loud *whoompf* and lay there a moment, perfectly still, like he was unconscious. Nice try. It didn't work.

Three of the Korean cops came over and roughly yanked him off the ground. I looked at him closely. I didn't see any visible damage, but maybe they'd limited themselves to body blows on the ride over.

His composure had evaporated. He looked scared as hell. I didn't blame him. This was the moment when the two police officers blocking the cameras' views stepped away and let the film roll. What the whole of Korea saw was a very frightened prisoner being dragged on both feet through some menacing-looking double doors. It was a picture sure to bring merriment to all those Koreans who wanted the homo rapist-murderer humbled and punished.

Katherine and I tried to follow him through the doors, but the tall cop with the linebacker's shoulders stepped into our path.

"We have the right to see our client," Katherine insisted in her most frigidly commanding tone. The cop grinned and stared down at her. For all we knew, he didn't speak a word of English.

"Please," I very humbly lied, "we are only trying to ensure our client is given adequate treatment. We have an appointment to report back to Minister of Justice Chun. Would you please be so kind as to allow us to proceed?"

"No problem," he finally replied, in almost perfect, oddly collo-quial English. Then he gave us a big, frosty smile. "You can visit his cell. But you may not speak with him. Not today. In Korean prisons we believe the first day is crucial. The prisoner must learn to re-spect our rules. He must learn his place in our order. Whitehall will not be damaged as long as he obeys our rules."

Odd that he chose the word "damaged," as though he was re-ferring to a piece of property rather than a human being.

Katherine had a horrified look, but frankly, even American pris-ons play by the same rule. Not as aggressively, perhaps, but it's the same principle. Make the right first impression and things go smoother for everybody.

The officer led us inside. We walked down some long, well-lit hallways and through several sets of steel doors, until we found ourselves inside a large chamber with three floors of cells. Unlike American prisons, which are rambunctious and kinetically noisy, this chamber was profoundly silent. I thought at first it must've been empty, but as we proceeded, almost every cell contained a prisoner. They were all sitting upright on the floors, legs tightly crossed, like they were propped up at attention. Not a one of them was so much as breathing heavily.

"This is reading time," our muscle-bound companion informed us.

"I don't see anyone with a book," I casually mentioned.

That brought a wolfish smile. "The book is inside their heads. We call it the Book of Regrets. They must spend three hours every morning contemplating their debt to society."

He stopped and dug a key out of his pocket. Opening a cell door, he ushered us through the entry.

The cell was maybe four by seven feet. It looked like a tall cof-fin. There was a thin sleeping mat on the floor, and a small metal bowl for the toilet. There were no windows, only a dim light inside a cage on the ceiling. The cell was cold. It smelled—of human waste, of vomit, of despair.

Katherine looked around and shuddered.

"Don't worry," the officer assured us, beaming even more broadly. "I am personally responsible for Captain Whitehall. I will take excellent care of him."

You can imagine how reassuring that was to hear.

CHAPTER
8
★ ★ ★

Four boxes were in my room when I got back. I called room service and told them to send up a fresh pot of coffee every hour, on the hour. Then I dug in.

It went down like this.

At five o'clock in the morning on May 3, First Sergeant Carl Moran called the desk sergeant at the Yongsan Military Garrison MP station and reported there was a dead body located in Apartment 13C, Building 1345, Namnoi Street, Itaewon. Then he abruptly hung up.

Ten or fifteen minutes of confusion erupted. The apartment building was on Korean territory, not American military property. The MP station shift officer was new to Korea and uncertain of the proper protocols. He finally reached the colonel in charge of the MP brigade and asked for guidance. The colonel ordered him to call Police Captain Nah Jung Bae, the commander of the Itaewon station, to notify him of the report and request a joint investigating team.

Itaewon is a fairly famous place. It is located right outside the back gate of the Yongsan Garrison, and one thing it's famous for is its thousands of tiny, cramped, goods-laden shops that cater to foreign shoppers. This is where tourists and soldiers go when they want a leather jacket, or a pair of Nikes, or a knockoff polo shirt.

What it's also famous for is a red-light district that also caters to foreign shoppers, only this is where foreigners go to pick up nasty cases of syphilis and gonorrhea. Because alcohol, whores, and soldiers are a notoriously flammable combination, the Itaewon Police Station and the MP brigade do lots of business together.

The shift commander did what his colonel ordered. He called the Korean police chief and then dispatched two military police officers to the apartment building. By the time the MPs got there, some twenty South Korean policemen, headed by a detective, were already on the scene.

Sergeant Wilson Blackstone was the ranking member of the MP team. He immediately got antsy and therefore radioed back to his shift commander and requested to be reinforced by somebody from the Criminal Investigation Division, or CID.

Sergeant Blackstone's written statement pointedly failed to explain what bothered him at the crime scene, but it didn't take a rocket scientist to make a few logical deductions. American police methods are the most advanced in the world. Fingerprint and fiber analysis, which have been used extensively by American police departments for over half a century, are only now working their way into the police arsenals of developing nations. More elaborate wizardry, such as chromosomal tracing or more sophisticated pathological techniques, is still vastly beyond the grasp of all but a handful of very wealthy, scientifically advanced nations.

When these tools aren't available to your police departments, you don't train your flatshoes to treat a crime scene like a hospital operating room, the way American cops get taught. What I guessed Sergeant Blackstone might've observed was twenty gloveless, low-tech cops scurrying around the apartment, disturbing crucial evidence, touching things they shouldn't have been touching, dropping their own hairs all over the place, and just generally contaminating the crime scene with all kinds of impurities. It was only a guess. However, it would be extremely helpful to our case if I was right.

It took thirty minutes for the MP station to roust a CID investigator from his bunk, for him to get dressed and drive to the apartment building.

His name was Chief Warrant Officer Michael Bales, and the instant he arrived he became the lead American investigator. I read his statement with great care. It was well written, highly descriptive, and very concise—all signs he was likely to be a highly observant, fairly bright flatshoe.

When Bales arrived, he observed Sergeant Blackstone in a heated argument with Chief Inspector Choi, the lead Korean investigator. Blackstone wanted the Korean inspector to make his folks back off. Choi wanted Blackstone to shut up. Choi was insisting this was his country, and his murder case, and a Korean victim, and he didn't like being told how to do things on his own turf.

We defense attorneys love this kind of thing. It's often said that more cases have been blown on cop territorial disputes, and the confusion that results, than on proof of innocence. I marked this as yet another possible vulnerability in the prosecutor's case.

Bales then approached Choi. Bales wrote that they knew each other and had a strong rapport. I guessed Bales sweet-talked him for a while, because things suddenly turned warm and friendly.

Choi led Bales to a bedroom where three American servicemen with nervous countenances were leaned up against a wall. Two Korean policemen stood guard to prevent them from confiding and building common alibis.

Choi then took Bales to another small bedroom where a naked body lay on a sleeping mat. The body rested on its back. There was a long purple welt around the neck, a sign that powerful force had been applied. The tongue protruded from the mouth, and the eyes bulged outward. The skin pallor was gray, an indication that a great deal of blood had already drained out of the head, presumably because someone had removed the tourniquet that caused the strangulation. Bruises and bloody abrasions covered the victim's arms, shins, and stomach. Bales hazarded the logical guess that the victim had put up a fierce struggle.

Choi informed Bales that when he and his investigators got there, the corpse was lying on its side. Something had been wrapped around the victim's neck, but one of the three Americans had removed it before the Korean police arrived at the scene. The victim's uniform was lying in a pile on the floor. Choi said the nametag on the uniform identified the victim as Lee No Tae. Choi said he had already called in that name to the Itaewon station for further identification.

A few minutes later came a call on the radio, and they all learned that Lee No Tae was the son of the minister of defense. That had a gut-tightening effect on the South Korean police officers, who until that point, according to both Blackstone and Bales, had been almost lackadaisical and haphazard in their activities. Murders were common enough in Itaewon, and South Korean police officers, like cops everywhere, adopt a kind of jaundiced, unhurried, seen-it-all approach, if for no other reason than to impress upon their peers that they're emotionally callused.

The calluses suddenly disappeared. They all looked like their asses were on fire. Three more South Korean detectives appeared within minutes, then the station commander, then the chief of police, then the mayor of Seoul himself. Bales described it as a long procession of busybody officials with worried expressions, all shouting out instructions and trying to appear more important and commanding than the last.

Crime scene photos were shot, evidence was bagged and tagged, the corpse was rushed off to a Korean hospital, and an immediate autopsy was requested.

The three Americans weren't interrogated until two hours after the first police officer arrived on the scene. They were first transported to the Itaewon Police Station, where they were booked, then to the American MP station at Yongsan Garrison. Bales handled the interrogation. Inspector Choi sat beside him and acted as the liaison.

Very interesting. There were some strong possibilities here—at least if you went with the strategy I'd advocated, of knocking holes in the prosecutor's case. Assuming, of course, that Whitehall didn't hang himself in his interrogations.

I was opening the folder that contained Whitehall's initial statement when the phone rang. It was Carlson. She coldly ordered me to get my butt up to the office. I told her I was busy. She said she didn't care if I was busy. I told her I was doing something vitally important. She said what she wanted to talk about was much more important. She hung up.

I just love it when somebody hasn't got a clue what you're doing, yet still insists that what they're doing is more important. Maybe I was tying a tourniquet around a severed artery in my leg. I obviously wasn't, but how in the hell did she know that?

Anyway, like a good soldier, I locked my room and headed up to the hair parlor with the HOMOS sign over the door. As before, I looked around and checked carefully to make sure nobody was watching.

Imelda was again ensconced on one of the big rotating chairs in the middle of the floor. A stack of legal documents rested on her stomach. Her nose was tucked inside a thick folder. I heard her snort with disapproval at something as I walked by.

I entered Carlson's office, where Keith, Allie, and Maria were seated and listening to their boss jabbering to somebody on the phone.

"Uh-huh," she was saying. "Good. The sooner the better."

She listened for a moment, then said, "CNN today, then NBC and ABC in the morning. That's the best order. CNN always presents flat news without editorial twist. Give ABC and NBC enough time and they'll make it look like a minidrama."

I listened as she continued coordinating details. I developed this real queasy feeling.

Finally Carlson finished. She triumphantly hung up the phone and then shared quick, satisfied nods with the other three.

"What's going on here?" I asked.

Before she could answer, the door swung open and in came a big, dykish-looking woman wearing way too much makeup, and hauling a microrecorder from a strap on her shoulder. She hugged Katherine, then they kissed. Uh-huh, I got that. Then a man with a big camera slung on his shoulder barged his way into the overcrowded office.

"Where do you want to do it?" the woman asked.

"Outside," Carlson answered, standing up.

"What is this?" I stupidly asked. I mean, it was damned obvious what it was. A catastrophically bad idea was what it was.

The other three happily followed the camera crew out the door while I threw my arm across the sill and blocked Carlson. I gave her a hard look. "I don't like being ignored. I'm going to ask one more time. What the hell is this?"

"Isn't it obvious? We've got a one-minute spot on CNN."

"Don't."

"It's already scheduled."

"Don't," I pleaded. "It's a really bad idea."

"Nonsense," she said with an apathetic shrug. "It's perfectly harmless. All they want is a quick puff piece on the defense team. Follow me. You'll see."

Some inner sense told me I shouldn't. But to my everlasting regret, I ignored it. I put my arm down and she squeezed past me. I shuffled a few steps behind her. She preceded me out the front entrance and then mysteriously paused till I was walking beside her. To my immense surprise, she put her tiny right hand on the crook of my elbow, started waving her left hand in the air, and began flapping her jaw.

I didn't pay any attention to what she was saying, though. I was too busy gawking at the cameraman, who had his lens pointed at the two of us. I felt like a spastic deer staring at the headlights of the thirty-wheeled semi roaring down on him. About five awkward seconds passed before I swiftly disengaged my arm and spun on her.

"What the hell—" I blurted.

"Major Drummond," the CNN reporter asked, jamming her microphone in my face. "Is it true your client was beaten by the South Korean police?"

I gave Carlson a blistering stare, and she tilted her head in a challenging cant.

I looked at the reporter, my face clouded with anger, my jaws tightly clenched. "No comment," I growled.

She paused, apparently confused, then asked, "Is that all you
have to say?"

"No damned comment to that, either," I roared, this time saying
it with enough emphasis in all the right places that she had to get
the message.

Carlson then took the reporter's arm and the two of them casually strolled to a shaded spot underneath a big tree. The cameraman followed them and Carlson gave a three-minute impromptu
interview. I watched and smoldered. You could tell Carlson was
very practiced in the art of interviews, because she even helped
arrange the cameraman to get the best angle—away from the
sun—and her movements in front of his lens had that theatrical,
picturesque quality of a born actress.

When she finally finished, she and the CNN crew warmly
shook hands and parted ways. My hands were shaking, too, only in
anticipation of getting themselves clenched firmly around her tiny
neck.

She ignored me as she walked by. I didn't ignore her, though. I
moved like a lion going after its prey. Her trio of co-counsels kept
their distance, because it was pretty damned obvious that Cher-
nobyl was about to bleed radioactive dust all over the countryside.

When we got to Carlson's office, I slammed the door shut behind me. There was a thunderous bang. The whole building rever-
berated.

"You've got a problem, lady!" I yelled.

She fell into her chair and looked up at me. Her expression was
anything but receptive. "I've got a problem?" she yelled right back.

"Yeah. A big one."

"No, Drummond, you're the one with the problem."

"Yeah?"

She nearly exploded. "You still don't get it, do you? My job is to
protect my client. That's supposed to be your priority, too."

"You don't protect your client by yammering in front of a camera every chance you get."

"When it comes to homosexuals, it's the only way you protect them. You have no idea how despised they are. No, that's not right. Maybe you do."

"What's that supposed to mean?"

"Come on, Drummond. I've seen how you look at Keith and Maria and Allie. What in the hell did they ever do to you to provoke that kind of disgust?"

There really was no way to answer that. She had me dead in the crosshairs. So instead I took the first resort of every able attorney: When caught with your hand in the cookie jar, point at the refrigerator.

"Look," I said, "you won't do our client any good by running your mouth on TV. You don't know the Koreans. Don't piss them off. Don't back these guys into a corner."

"You're acting like I started this. Don't tell me you didn't notice those cameras at the prison this morning? They were publicly humiliating our client. I'm fighting fire with fire."

Again, she was right. Only this time, she was also wrong. Horribly wrong.

"That was just for public consumption. They gave up jurisdiction so they had to save some face. This is Asia, lady. That's how the game's played over here."

"They beat him," she said, and her green eyes sizzled like tiny little hornet's nests with thousands of furious insects buzzing around.

"Did you see them beat him?" I demanded.

"I saw them shove him. And I saw him come flying out the back of that van."

"Maybe he tripped," I countered. "I'll ask you once again. Did you witness anyone beating him?"

"I didn't have to witness it. I saw the look on his face."

"You're supposed to be a lawyer. You're supposed to distinguish between assumptions and facts. You just told an international network that our client was beaten. Can you prove it? Can you back it up?"

She ran a hand through her hair. She knew I had her.

I said, "Call CNN and tell them not to run it."

She swallowed once, hard. "I won't."

"Do it. You were talking out your ass. We both know it."

"If I was, the Koreans can take it as a warning shot. They'll keep their hands off my client or I'll publicly pillory them every day of this trial."

We stared at each other for a long, fruitless moment. I finally spun around and left. I went back to my room. I paced around like a big, grouchy bear in his cave. Eventually I got tired of that, but I was too emotionally worked up to return to my reading, so I flipped on the TV.

Say this for those CNN clowns: They're damned quick.

The piece opened with a great shot of me and Carlson walking out a doorway under the word HOMOS in big, bold, black letters.

CNN's editors are real quick, too. And slanderously selective.

The next shot was borrowed from a Korean station. It showed Whitehall, looking like a miserable, saturated noodle, being dragged through some double doors. The next clip showed Carlson with her hand on my elbow and we looked frantically friendly, like we were discussing something and were in complete agreement. Then came the shot with Carlson under the tree saying, "My co-counsels and I are outraged at the beating of our client. He was worked over by several South Korean policemen. When I tried to stop them, I was assaulted."

Then came the cutout of me with the microphone stuffed in my angry, pouting face. I growled, "No damned comment," only the way it came across was like I was so damn furious that my client got beaten that I was too tongue-tied to spit out anything but "No damned comment."

The phone rang within two minutes.

"Hello, General," I said, before Clapper, the chief of the entire Army JAG Corps, could even begin to identify himself.

"Drummond, what in the hell's going on over there?" he belched.

"Hey, it wasn't like it looked. I swear, General. I got ambushed. Carlson set me up."

He paused for only a moment. "An ambush?"

"Right. She called me up to our office and I—"

"Office?" he interrupted, "Is that the goddamned building with that 'homo' word written on it?"

Feeling the blood rush into my face, I feebly answered, "That isn't like it looks, either. See, you have to read that sign real close. First, it's 'homos,' with an s at the end, and it actually stands for—"

The earpiece exploded. "Drummond! I don't give a shit what it stands for. The whole world just saw a picture of an American Army officer walking out a doorway with that damned sign. Have you got any idea what that looks like?"

"Now that you mention it, sir, I guess it—"

"You said she set you up?"

"Right. See, she called me to come up there, and then I—"

"Jesus, have I got the wrong man in there? Are you telling me she's too smart for you?"

That hurt. I mean, that *really* hurt. "I just wasn't expecting it. I will be next time, though. I swear."

"You better, Drummond. You really better."

He hung up hard. I didn't blame him. It was three o'clock in the morning back in Washington. He probably hadn't been lying around in bed idly watching the late-night news. Somebody must've called him and frosted his ear. Probably somebody big, like the Chief of Staff of the Army. Or somebody bigger, like the Chairman of the Joint Chiefs of Staff. Or maybe somebody even bigger than that.

My thoughts were interrupted when the phone rang again. This time it was General Spears. Personally. And he did this really excellent imitation of General Clapper. Next came Acting Ambassador Brandewaite, and I have to confide his imitation wasn't nearly as good, because he was so florid and incensed all he could do was spit and sputter and curse. He hit all the octaves right, though, I'll tell you that. Then Spears's legal adviser, Colonel Piranha Lips, called, and he did the shorthand version. No barrage of questions, no rude interruptions, just a simple, abbreviated "Now I really don't like you, Drummond. I'll fuck you for this."

It was really amazing. I'd been in Korea two days and already I'd managed to piss off every senior officer in the world, to get the acting ambassador so mad he couldn't work up enough saliva to spit, and to get my face plastered on the international news in a way that was thoroughly revolting.

I owed all this to a short, skinny girl with malice in her heart and no sense at all about what she was unleashing.

To give her credit, she thought she was protecting her client. And back in the good ol' U.S.A. what she'd just done might even have worked. Not here, though. Katherine Carlson was about to get a lesson in what the Asians call "face." The Mafia has a word for it, too: payback.

CHAPTER
9
★ ★ ★

As I later pieced it together, Keith had decided to slip out the back gate for a little shopping. That happened sometime around nine o'clock that night. He dodged across a heavily trafficked boulevard and entered the Itaewon shopping district. Maybe they started tracking him right then. If so, he apparently never noticed.

He began dashing in and out of shops, picking up a few things here and a few things there. He got himself a snazzy leather bomber jacket with a fuzzy fur collar, some Nike running shoes, and a spiffy new leather wallet. By eleven o'clock he was halfway through Itaewon. He'd made it to a major intersection with cars whizzing by, and had paused to wait for the pedestrians' traffic signal to show the little green man with his legs pumping, when a couple of strong hands lifted him off his feet and tossed him into the speeding traffic. He got bounced high up in the air by the first car and came down dead center into the bumper of the next. It took an ambulance twenty minutes to get there. Keith was loaded into the back and rushed to the nearest hospital.

The good news was he'd carried his passport with him, so the hospital got his identity and immediately notified the American embassy that some American had gotten hit by a couple of cars. The lady at the embassy night switch didn't recognize his name, so she made a note to give to the night duty officer the next time he wandered by. He came by around four in the morning. He didn't recognize Merritt's name, either. He followed his standard operating procedures and called and gave the name to the desk sergeant at the Yongsan Garrison MP station. The desk sergeant also didn't know who Merritt was, but he dutifully listed the news in his log. That's why we weren't notified until seven o'clock the next morning.

Now the bad news. Keith was in the ICU, unconscious, and the doctors were wringing their hands and mumbling fretful things. His skull was fractured, one kidney had been punctured by a broken rib, one leg and one arm were shattered into multiple pieces, and the doctors were still trying to trace the source, or sources, of a flood of internal bleeding.

I learned this via a very hysterical call from Katherine. I rushed straight to her room. The door was ajar so I walked in. Allie and Katherine were huddled in a corner, hugging each other and sobbing pitifully. Maria sat at the desk, her face looking like it had twenty-pound weights dragging at the corners of her eyes and lips. I idly wondered if Allie was switch-hitting on Maria. The room had the air of a funeral parlor.

"He might die," Katherine said, looking up at me.

"Uh-huh." I gravely nodded.

I sat on the edge of the bed and stayed quiet. I knew what was going through their heads. None of us had any real idea what had happened, but the timing and coincidence were too damned close. You couldn't escape the thought.

Finally, Katherine said, "Are these bastards that barbaric?"

I said, "Maybe."

I hadn't confirmed anything, but I'd equivocated enough to make them realize they'd been underestimating the risks.

I said, "Have your pictures been on Korean television?"

"We did a few interviews before you arrived," Katherine sulkily responded.

"All of you? Did you all get your faces in front of the camera? Maybe in the local papers, too?"

"That's right," said Allie, releasing Katherine and walking over to stand beside Maria. "We were on TV and in the newspapers. So what?"

"Then don't draw any hasty conclusions."

"What that's supposed to mean?" Allie asked in her typically defiant way.

"I mean it could have been somebody working for the South Korean government. They've got a couple of supersecret agencies responsible for internal security that have reputations for being pretty thuggish. Or it could've been someone else."

Katherine spun around; her face was bitterly scrunched up. "Who else could it possibly have been? Don't bullshit me, Drummond. It's obvious who did it."

"No, it's not," I said. "By parading yourselves in front of the media so much, you painted bull's-eyes on your chests."

"Bull's-eyes for who?" Allie asked.

"One of those anti-American student groups you always see rioting on TV. Or some group of South Korean soldiers who're pissed off at having one of their brothers in arms murdered and raped. The one thing we're not short of over here's enemies."

"Drummond, you are so full of shit," Katherine said, with a positively barbaric stare.

"No, I ain't. Now, I'm going to give you a little lecture. Maybe my timing sucks, but you better listen to me, for once."

Katherine slunk over from her corner and I finally had all their undivided attention.

"Korea," I explained, "is technically a nation at war. I'm not saying South Koreans are perfect, but they're pretty damned good people. There's an army of some three million men just twenty-five miles from where we're sitting. There's North Korean infiltrators and agents running all over this country. Only a few years ago, a North Korean sub got grounded on a sandbar off the eastern shore and out spilled ten commandos. Remember that incident? It was all over the news the entire week it took the South Koreans to chase them down and kill them. The only reason they were detected was because the sub commander screwed up and got his boat beached.

Any of you want to hazard a guess at how many other boats and subs have landed agents and commandos that *didn't* get caught?"

Maria had a disbelieving grimace, or maybe it was just her natural facial set, but when her lips came apart I cut her off with a quick slice of my arm through the air.

"Don't talk. Listen," I rudely ordered. "These people have been living like this since 1953. You got any idea what that's like? Every year, there's ambushes and shootouts on that border. This hotel room we're sitting in is within artillery range of North Korea's guns. In a split second this whole country could get pulverized. That has an effect on your psyche. This ain't like America. Stop thinking it is."

Katherine said, "Nothing justifies this!"

"I'm not justifying any damned thing," I told her with a stern glare. "Stop being so damned argumentative. Listen. And for God's sakes, don't go holding another of your idiotic press conferences and start blaming the South Korean government. Maybe they did it; maybe not. Hell, it might've just been some band of pickpockets, and he caught 'em, so they tossed him."

"You know better!" she said.

"I don't *know* any such damned thing. Neither do you. All I do *know* is that you embarrassed the South Korean people last night, and today one of our co-counsels ends up in the hospital. You can build a case on circumstantial evidence, but you can't build a case on coincidental evidence."

I got up and stood over Katherine. She was looking at me like she'd pay anything for a ticket to my funeral.

"This isn't the United States, Carlson. Remember what that big goon warned you yesterday? Learn to respect the rules around here. It goes better for everybody."

She started to open her lips and I held up my hand. "Look, I'll see what I can find out. Just don't hold another meeting with your press buddies while I'm gone. And skip those sessions with NBC and ABC I heard you planning yesterday. They won't do any good for our client, not to mention our health."

I left them in the room to stew. I can't say I was friends with Keith, since I barely knew him, but on general principles alone I was just as shocked and furious about what happened to him as they were, and I sure as hell hoped he wouldn't die. The problem was Katherine and her buddies had no idea what they were messing with here. I'd tried to warn them. They hadn't listened. Thomas Whitehall, guilty or innocent, was a symbol for all kinds of extremist groups with fiery views, and when you're standing next to a lightning rod, don't act surprised when a stray thunderbolt lands in your lap.

When I got back to my room, I called Spears's office and told that colonel with the world's snappiest salute that I needed to meet with Buzz Mercer. He said okay and hung up.

Twelve minutes later, the phone rang. It was a woman's voice. She told me to hurry downstairs and wait by the entrance of the hotel. So I did.

When I walked outside, a gray sedan was already idling under the entrance and a Korean woman stepped out. She peered around till she spotted me, then waved for me to come over.

"You're Drummond, right?" she asked when I got within earshot.

"That's me," I admitted.

"Please get in."

I climbed in, then briefly studied the cut of her jib. She was slender, conservatively dressed, probably in her late twenties or early thirties, and was somewhat attractive, but in a buttoned-down, stern, wintry sort of way. Her hair was cut short and was clearly unstyled. She wore gold wire-rimmed glasses that made her look like an academic who'd somehow gotten lost outside the ivory tower.

"So what's your name?" I asked, wondering who the hell she was.

"I'm Kim Song Moon. My friends call me Carol."

"Carol? How does Kim Song Moon get you to Carol?"

"It doesn't," she admitted. "I'm American. My real name is Carol Kim. Here in Korea, I use Kim Song Moon."

"No kidding? And you're with that same company that employs Buzz Mercer?"

"Buzz is my boss."

"Let me guess. You were raised in California, went to Stanford, or maybe Berkeley, got recruited there, and you've spent the last three years doing skullduggery here?"

"Oh my God, am I that obvious?" she asked with a shocked look.

"I'm throwing out stereotypes. Besides, telepathy is one of my strong suits."

"Actually," she said, "I grew up in Boston and went to Middlebury College, which was where I learned to speak Korean, then I spent a few years at Duke getting a law degree. And I wasn't recruited. After law school, I sought out the Agency and convinced them my language skills and Korean looks might come in handy. I've been here less than a month."

"Ah, so I got most of it right."

"Which part did you get right?"

"You went to college, right?"

She ignored that. "So you're a lawyer?" she asked. "You don't look like a lawyer."

"No? Well, what do lawyers look like?" I asked, fishing around for a compliment.

"They're usually very intelligent-looking."

"Oh."

"And they're usually very chubby, or very skinny and undeveloped."

"Ah," I said, perking up a bit.

"And the good ones, the really good ones, they usually have chewed-down fingernails and a perpetually nervous look about them."

"But you don't get that sense from me?"

She glanced at me again. "No. You seem far too confident, maybe even cocky." She let that sink in, then followed with: "I should tell you I'm the case officer for your trial. I was brought here to keep an eye on things for the Agency."

"And what nice eyes they are," I said, flirt that I am.

She gave me a weary look as she pulled the sedan into a parking place in front of the officers' club. We got out and she started walking in a way and at a pace that indicated she did a lot of speed-walking in her spare time. I followed her like a panting poodle up some steps and through a set of double doors into a small, comfortable lobby. She led me through a dining room that was completely barren of customers, then through another set of double doors and into a back room.

Buzz Mercer sat there, feet up on a table, tie loosened, sleeves rolled up, talking on a mobile phone that was far too big and clunky to be a commercial model. It had to be a secure phone. The moment I entered, he lowered his voice, murmured a few things, then uttered a swift good-bye and hung up.

He could've been ordering a pizza, for all I knew. CIA folks are like that—so secretive, it's beyond hilarious.

"Have seats," he said to Carol and me. So we did.

He examined my face a moment, then said, "I'm sorry to hear about Merritt." He didn't look real sorry, but then, why should he?

"Yeah, it's an awful thing. He's pretty beat-up, from what I hear."

"He slipped into a coma about twenty minutes ago."

"That sounds worse."

His eyebrows did this tiny shrugging thing. "Well, they've got the internal bleeding under control. The coma aside, at least he's not gonna bleed to death."

"Since you seem so well-informed, you got any idea who did it?"

He bent forward and put his elbows on the table. "Drummond, there's forty-six million people in the Republic of Korea. Rule out the ones in wheelchairs, the ones in hospital beds, and all the tots who're too small to have lifted him and thrown him into the road. That gets your number of suspects down to a nice workable number. Say thirty-five million or so. Oh, and don't forget the twenty-two million folks up in North Korea."

"Well, Carlson thinks the South Korean government's behind it."

He did that eyebrow-shrugging thing again. "Ten years ago, maybe. But frankly, we don't see much of that kind of shenanigans anymore. Not since they learned how to spell 'democracy' down here, anyway. I'm not saying they didn't; I'm only saying you better be damned careful with your assumptions."

"How about the guys up north?"

"Carol and I batted that back and forth, but frankly, we can't see a fit."

"But you don't rule it out?"

"Nope. But like I said, we don't see a good fit either."

"So that leaves some anti-American South Korean group. Or maybe some pissed-off vigilantes who can't get their hands on Whitehall, so they settled for one of his defenders."

"That's where I'd put my money. There're probably plenty of both groups around. The problem for you is, are they done?"

"So you think we're in physical danger?"

He stood up and walked over to the coffeepot. He poured himself a cup, but didn't ask if I wanted one. That meant one of two things: He was either a rude bastard, or this meeting was on the cusp of being over.

"I don't know what to tell ya."

"How about telling me you're going to protect us?"

He kept his back turned to me. He was done pouring his cup of coffee, so I wondered what was so damned interesting about the blank wall he was facing.

"That's not our job," he finally said. "But if it helps any, we're watching you."

"You're watching us?" I stupidly asked. I mean, he'd just told me we were being watched. But why, if they didn't intend to protect us?

"How else did you think Carol got to your hotel so fast? She was already in the parking lot."

"If you were watching us, how come you didn't see Merritt get tossed?"

He finally turned around and faced me. If I were to choose a metaphor to describe his facial cast, it was like a tiger studying some strange animal he'd never seen before and wondering if it was worth eating.

"Well, it's only a skeleton crew, so it's more haphazard than I'd like. He slipped away and we missed it. It would be much simpler if I could put someone in your office. Somehow, though, I don't think you'll let me do that."

He was right. I couldn't let him do that. Maybe he'd play it straight up and whoever he put inside our office would never whisper a word about how we were managing Whitehall's defense. Then again, maybe not.

Then Carol explained, "I've got three people keeping an eye on you. But that's all we can spare."

And I said, "But there's all us co-counsels, and there's the legal aides, and then there's twenty-four hours in a day, and your people have to sleep."

"I can count, Major. Look at the bright side. My job just got a little easier. Yesterday there were five co-counsels. Today there's only four."

I angrily said, "Merritt's not dead yet."

"Okay." She smiled. "Make it four and a half."

I found that smile really unnerving. She might have nice eyes, but I'd just come to the unwelcome realization she was as cold-hearted as a lizard. Maybe tomorrow somebody would toss me off the sixteenth floor of a high-rise, and she and Mercer would be trading high fives and talking about how much easier *I'd* just made their jobs.

I got all puffed up and said, "So that's it? All you're going to do is watch?"

"That's all we're gonna do," Mercer blandly admitted. "Our hands are damn full watching the bad guys up north, not to mention trying to keep an eye on our South Korean friends down here. I don't mean to sound cavalier, Drummond, but this Whitehall thing, it's way outside our bailiwick."

And here's what bothered me about that. If we were way outside his bailiwick, why'd he already have a team of four people watching us?

And that's the moment when I saw through all the odd glances and double-talk. No wonder Mercer had snuck up to my room in the dead of night. And no wonder Carol Kim and her goons were keeping an eye on us. As far as the CIA was concerned, Carlson and the rest of us were nothing more than expendable pawns in their big game.

It didn't make a damn whether we lived or died. No, actually, that's not right: It did make a damn. If somebody *did* bump off a couple of us, and North Korea did have a hand in it, and the CIA was there to watch it happen and be able to prove it—well, that would just be helpful as all get out. To them, anyway.

A few minutes later, Carol dropped me off under the overhang at the hotel entrance. She gave me that chilling smile and said, "Warn the others not to take any unnecessary risks. And stay together as much as you can."

I very bitterly said, "Do I take it this represents an official warning?"

"That's right," she said. "This is your official warning."

"You know what bothers me?"

"What bothers you?"

"I just can't figure what a lawyer like you's doing in the CIA."

She looked me straight in the eye. "After three years of law school, I decided I didn't want to practice law. I discovered I didn't like lawyers."

"Aha," I said.

"Aha," she frostily replied, then drove away.

I went back to my room, tugged another box out of the closet, then sat down to read what Captain Thomas Whitehall said to Chief Warrant Officer Michael Bales on the morning of May 3.

It began with the obligatory reading of rights, then the equally obligatory questions about name, assignment, etcetera. Whitehall waived his rights. He insisted that since he was innocent, he had nothing to hide. Dumb move there, I figured. An innocent man doesn't protest he's innocent until somebody accuses him. An innocent man naturally assumes everybody knows he's guiltless.

Like a skilled interrogator, Bales then spent a few minutes loosening up Whitehall with the standard warm-up questions: where did he live, what was his job, how long had he been in Korea, blah, blah, blah. The real purpose was to get the suspect comfortable giving answers.

Then Bales asked, "Did you know the victim?"

"Yes."

"How did you know him?"

"We met through a mutual friend. He was a Katusa, and we went shopping together a few times."

"Were you friends?" Bales asked, and I guessed it was a perfectly innocuous question. At that stage Bales had no way of knowing the circumstances of the death, or about Whitehall's sexual peccadillos.

"Not friends, no. Acquaintances, really. I didn't know him well. It was nice having someone who knew Seoul, who could speak the language. He showed me some good places to shop and eat, and helped me bargain on prices with shopkeepers, that kind of thing."

"What was he doing at your apartment?"

"I invited him."

"For what purpose?"

"I was having a small party. I thought he might enjoy meeting other Americans."

"What about Moran and Jackson? Were they your friends?"

"Moran's a friend. He brought Jackson along."

"Why?"

"I don't know. I didn't really ask. I guess he thought Lee and Jackson might hit it off."

"You'll excuse me, Captain, but that sounds a little odd. You're an officer and they're all enlisted."

"Not odd at all," Whitehall insisted. "It's hardly unusual for officers and senior NCOs to have relationships outside of work. And Lee's a Korean and had done me some favors. I saw nothing wrong with helping him make more American friends."

"I guess," Bales said, and I imagined that his tone was somewhat dubious. "There were a lot of empty bottles in your apartment. Was there drinking?"

"I served refreshments."

"Alcohol?"

"Yes, sure. Why not? They're all grown-ups."

"Drugs?"

"I don't like the nature of that question."

"Captain, a man was murdered in your apartment. You're going to get lots of difficult questions. Now please answer. Were there drugs?"

"No, no drugs," Whitehall finally replied.

"Why did the others spend the night in your apartment?"

"The party went late. Everybody was having fun. Before we knew it, it was nearly two in the morning."

"Were the others drunk?"

"In my opinion, they'd had a few too many, yes. I didn't think it was a good idea to let them walk the two miles back to base in their condition, so I invited them to stay."

"Uh-huh," Bales said. "When was the last time you saw Lee No Tae alive?"

"I don't remember exactly. Around two, I guess. He went into the bedroom and I made sure the apartment door was locked and went to sleep."

"The apartment door was locked?"

"That's right."

"There were only three bedrooms, weren't there?"

"Yes. I gave them the bedrooms and slept on the couch in the living room."

"Did you hear any sounds that night?"

"What kind of sounds?"

"Maybe someone entering your apartment? Maybe a struggle? Maybe an argument?"

"No. I'm usually a very light sleeper, but frankly, I'm afraid I had a few too many drinks also. I didn't hear anything."

"Are you the only one with keys to your apartment?"

"I suppose the management company that runs the place has other keys. Other than that, yes."

"So you have no idea what happened to Private Lee?"

"None. I was shocked when we discovered him dead. I have no idea how it happened."

Bales then said, "That's all I have at this stage of the investigation. Is there anything you want to add to this statement?"

"No, nothing. But, uh, well, uh . . . have his parents been notified yet?"

"His father was notified about two hours ago."

"Perhaps I can stop by and offer my condolences. He was a very fine young man. I'd like to tell his parents that. Would you happen to have their address? Do they live here in Seoul?"

"Are you serious?" Bales asked.

"I think it's the only proper thing to do. He was murdered in my apartment."

"You mean, you don't know who his father is?"

"No. Why should I?"

"Private Lee's father is South Korea's defense minister."

"Oh shit."

With that expletive, the initial interrogation ended. And things being what they were, it was a pretty fitting summary of what Whitehall had stepped into.

I tried to picture what was going through Whitehall's mind when he was being interrogated. I mean, that final discussion was a doozy. He had to know about Lee's father. That meant he was lying, and misleading, and blustering. He must've been scared as hell. Still, give me a break.

Had he really thought he'd get away with it? How could he? The body was found in his apartment, in his own bedroom, right beside him, for Chrissakes. There were two other witnesses in the apartment. Had they used the time before the Korean cops arrived to co-ordinate alibis? Wasn't Whitehall smart enough to know his semen would be found inside Lee's corpse?

And was he really so clueless that he thought they'd buy the assertion that he didn't know about Lee's father? He was obviously trying to get as much distance from the murdered man as he possibly could. A mere acquaintance, a shopping companion; someone he only barely knew and had invited over to his apartment so he could introduce him to some friendly enlisted troops. He had tipped his own hand.

As alibis went, it sucked.

I opened Moran's interrogation packet. Carl G. Moran was his full name. There was a photograph taken at the MP station clipped to the inside jacket.

It was a black-and-white that showed a large, powerful-looking man—actually, burly might be a better word. Maybe forty years old, with salt-and-pepper hair, a broad face, and a nose that looked like it had been introduced to a few fists in its day. But it was the eyes that really got your attention. Unnaturally large, they made an odd contrast to the rest of his face. They were like doe's eyes, with long, luxurious lashes, on a face that looked otherwise like a prize-fighter's mug. That Marlon Brando look, at least before Brando ate so much and his face got so bloated you could barely tell he had eyes.

Moran's expression was maybe confused, maybe irritated, maybe both.

Again, Bales went through the routine of reading him his rights. The strange thing here was that Moran interrupted him to ask if Whitehall had asked for an attorney. Bales said no, so Moran waived his rights as well.

I put down the packet. Why was that important to Moran? Was that some kind of litmus test? So what if Whitehall had declined an attorney? Something was odd about this; like maybe Moran was testing to see if he could trust Whitehall. Anyway, I made a mental note to think more about it later.

"What was your relationship to the victim?" Bales got around to asking after he'd exhausted his repertoire of warm-up questions.

Moran said, "He was a buddy of Captain Whitehall's. I didn't know him from shit, but the captain invited him over."

"Why?"

"Huh?"

"Why did Captain Whitehall invite him over?"

"Got me," Moran said. "Maybe they were buddies. Maybe he thought we'd like him."

"Had you ever met the victim before?"

"Nope. I might of seen him about base, but all these friggin' gooks look alike to me."

Gooks? I could just imagine the expression that must've popped onto Inspector Choi's face at that moment.

Bales said, "Was there any drinking at the party?"

"Yeah, of course. What do you think, we're a bunch of choirboys?"

"Any drugs?"

"Come on, Chief. You got a captain and you got a first sergeant there. Think anyone'd be stupid enough to use that shit in front of us?"

"Does that mean no?"

"Friggin' A, it means no."

"What time did the party end?"

"I don't know. Wasn't like I was checking my watch. Late, though."

"Had you or any of the others had too much to drink?"

"Hell, yeah. I could barely stand up, so the captain told us we could all crash there."

"And where did everybody sleep?"

"I . . . uh . . . shit, I was too drunk to notice."

"You discovered the corpse, though. How did that happen?"

"I got up at five. I was kind of fuzzy, you know. I mean, I'd put down easily a whole fifth of Jack Walker. I went and pissed. Then I went to the captain's room to check on 'em. Nobody answered when I knocked, so I opened the door. That gook kid was just laying there, real still. I went over and shook him. Nothing. So I rolled him over and seen this belt around his neck. He looked deader than shit, so I went and called the MPs."

"The belt was around his neck when you woke him?"

"That's what I said, wasn't it?"

"What kind of belt?"

"It . . . uh, it was a standard Army belt. Could've been anybody's, though. I mean, even the gook, 'cause he was a Katusa, he wore an American Army uniform, right? Might of been his own, you know. I mean, maybe the kid hung himself from the ceiling and he fell off."

"Did you remove the belt?"

"Never touched the damned thing."

"Do you know who did?"

"Nah. Never saw anyone else take it off, neither."

"So you don't know who did remove it?"

Bales was asking all the right questions. Absent autopsy results, he had to assume the belt was the murder weapon. And if he could find out whose belt it was, he might have his killer.

"Ain't got a clue," Moran announced.

"Did you wake the others up?"

"Yeah."

"And where were they sleeping?"

"I don't remember."

"You don't remember?" Bales asked, and I could only imagine the incredulous expression on his face. Of course, he still had no notion at that point exactly how critically important this question would later prove to be.

"That's what I told you. Like I said, I was still woozy, and the sight of that gook's corpse left me not thinking too straight."

I guess because Bales was not yet aware of the nature of the relationships among the four men, he took this response in stride and did not press further.

"So did you hear any sounds that night? Maybe a struggle? Maybe an argument?"

"Nope. A quart of Jack's better than a sleeping pill. Shit, somebody could've shot the kid, instead of strangled him. I wouldn't of heard it. I ain't gotta clue what happened to that gook kid. I swear."

"I, uh, I have only one other question," Bales said. "Did you invite Private Jackson to the party?"

"Yeah."

"Why? Isn't it unusual for a first sergeant to invite a private to a party at an officer's quarters? Especially when there's going to be drinking?"

"Hey, Jackson's my company clerk. A good kid, too. He don't have many friends, though, and I thought I'd give him a chance to get out of the barracks. I felt kind of sorry for him. It was probably bad judgment, but hey, ain't no crime in it, is there?"

"No, I suppose not," Bales replied, underscoring exactly how naive he was at that stage of the game.

I put the transcript back in the folder and thought about it. At this stage, Moran was obviously trying to cover Whitehall's ass. He

knew whose belt was around Lee's neck, he probably knew who removed it, and he damn well knew who was sleeping in whose beds.
He lied, though.

Like Whitehall, he had to know the semen inside Lee's body
would eventually be discovered. So why had he lied to Bales? And
what made him stop lying later and turn evidence against Whitehall?

This was all the more perplexing because Whitehall and Moran
had stupidly put themselves inside a tightly restricted box. There
were no signs of a break-in at the apartment. Whitehall had foolishly
admitted he'd made sure the door was locked before they went off
to sleep. He'd also admitted that only he and the management company that ran the complex had keys. Not very bright, if you think
about it. Why hadn't Whitehall claimed he'd left the door unlocked?
And Moran could've reinforced that by saying, yeah, sure he remembered hearing the sounds of a door opening and closing in the
middle of the night, but thought it was only Jackson or Whitehall or
Lee going to the bathroom. At least that would've opened up the
possibility that an uninvited guest had slipped in and strangled Lee.

Katherine was going to have a bitch of a time trying to prove
Whitehall was framed. The annoying fool had narrowed the spotlight to only himself and two other men, both of whom had already
turned state's evidence. That was yet another flaw in the frame defense. Court-martial boards turn skeptical when an accused man
claims he was framed by the very witnesses who are testifying
against him.

I reached into the box again and pulled out a slip of paper. This
was a photocopy of a transferal document for Lee No Tae's corpse
from the Itaewon Hospital to the Eighteenth Military Evacuation
Hospital in Yongsan Garrison. I checked the name of the American
officer who signed the receipt. I called the Evacuation Hospital.

"Captain Wilson Bridges please," I said to the cheery receptionist who answered.

"Just a moment, please."

An even cheerier voice finally said, "Doc Bridges here."

"Captain Bridges, this is Major Sean Drummond. I'm on the defense team for Captain Whitehall."

"What can I do for you?"

"You still got Lee No Tae's corpse in your facility?"

"We do indeed," he happily replied. "On ice in the basement."

"Would it be convenient for me to come over and view the corpse? Like right away?"

"For me, sure. I guess he won't have any problem with it, either."

He chuckled; I didn't. As morgue humor goes, that was one of the oldest and rottenest jokes there is.

"I'll be there in fifteen minutes. And could you please ask your experts on autopsies to be on hand?"

"You just did."

"You a pathologist?" I asked hopefully.

"A surgeon, actually. But we're only a small evac outfit, so everybody's got to carry a few extra loads."

"You must've done well in pathology at med school?"

"Nah. Nearly flunked it, but I never had a corpse complain."

That was the second badly overused morgue joke in only seconds. Originality did not seem to be the man's strong suit.

CHAPTER
10
★ ★ ★

The Evac Hospital was a sprawling, one-floored building that reeked of antiseptic and excessive cleanliness. I asked the receptionist where to find Captain Wilson Bridges and she spat out some quick-fire instructions that sounded like "Take six right turns, then three or four lefts, then two rights, then walk down a long hallway." It was a small place, so I figured no problem, and set off. Twenty minutes later I found it.

Bridges's office turned out to be a tiny hovel all the way at the back of the building, like maybe they were trying to hide him back there, out of sight of the observant public. I knocked on the door, it opened, and I immediately saw why.

Wilson Bridges was probably the sorriest excuse for an Army officer I ever saw. His white doctor's coat was wrinkled, stained, and splotched with things I didn't even want to imagine. His hair was way too long and wildly disarrayed, almost spiky. There were tiny hair sprouts on his face where his razor had missed, and the combat boots that protruded from the bottom of his medical robe were gray and cracked, so starved were they for polish.

Ever the optimist, however, I perceived these blemishes as fairly hopeful signs. A little-known rule of thumb about Army docs is to never, ever go near the ones with crew cuts, starched BDUs, mirrorlike shoes, and the upright bearing of a drill sergeant. Odds are they want to be Army officers more than they want to be doctors. It's the guys who look like they just got yanked out of the dryer you want operating on you. Chances are, their passion is for medicine, not marching and saluting. On the other hand, that theory sometimes turns out to be horribly wrong. Sometimes the doctor looks like a careless, disgusting slob because he really is. He's the guy who'll end up tying your aorta to your kneecaps.

He stuck out his hand. "Wilson Bridges. MD extraordinaire."

"I know," I said. "We just spoke on the phone, remember?"

"Yeah, sure," he said, grinning. "Sorry. It's just that you don't look like a lawyer."

"Really," I asked. "And what do lawyers look like?"

"Smart."

I could've retorted that he looked more like a field sanitation worker than a doctor, but why waste an insult?

"Listen, Doc, I hate to rush things, but I'm in a hurry. Where's the corpse?"

He waved a hand for me to follow, then led me to the absolute rear of the hospital and down some stairs that went into the dimly lit basement.

"We've only got a tiny storage facility," he explained. "And be sure you make your reservation well in advance, because there's only four drawers. Ordinarily, as soon as they expire, we stick 'em on the next plane going stateside."

"Why was Lee turned over to you?" I inquired.

"Damned if I know. I was told to pick him up and move him over here."

"Were you involved in the autopsy?"

"Nope. It was an all-Korean production. And don't draw the wrong impression from that. They're no slouches, believe me. This kid was done by a guy named Kim Me Song."

"He any good?"

"He's the guy they send to all the international conferences to make sure everybody believes Korean medicine is the best in the world."

I said, "Shit."

He looked over his shoulder and grinned. "Guess you'd expect them to use the best on this kid, what with him being the son of the big kahuna."

"I guess," I said. I said it in a dismayed way, too, because there was every chance Dr. Kim Me Song was going to end up on the witness stand, and it's never good to hear the prosecution's got the A-team on their side.

We took a left into a tiny room that was quite cold. A special air-conditioning unit was positioned in the corner, pumping out frigid air at full blast. Bridges buttoned up his spattered doc's coat and walked straight to a wall with four aluminum drawers. He reached down to the bottom row and slid one open.

"Voilà!" he announced as he unzipped the body bag and yanked it down all the way to Lee's feet, like he was a magician on a stage.

I glowered at him, then bent over and looked closely at Lee No Tae. The body was completely naked, stiff and pale. Somebody had obviously gone to the trouble to rearrange Lee's facial expression, because he looked content, even peaceful, which was a far cry from the description in Chief Bales's statement. What I guessed was that the father had come to have a last look at his dead son, and the Korean doctors had done the best they could to make it seem like he'd passed through the doorway to eternity without any pain and misery.

He was a very good-looking kid, with a narrow face, a long, aristocratic nose, a high, intelligent-looking forehead, and a muscular, well-proportioned figure. He looked much like what I suspect his father looked like as a younger man.

Bridges joined me in my inspection. He stood just to my left and I saw his eyes roving down the length of the body. You could still see the bruises and abrasions.

I asked, "Did anybody here get a copy of the autopsy results?"

"Yeah, I think I got a copy . . . maybe a few days after I collected the body. I haven't read it, though."

He walked over to a desk in the corner, opened a drawer, and rummaged around until he yanked out a manila folder. He stood and read it, while I continued observing Lee's body. I had no idea what I was looking for, in fact, had really only come over to get a firsthand look at the subject who'd caused me such immense misery. That really wasn't fair, since I sure didn't want to trade places with him, but it's so much easier to heap blame on an inanimate object than somebody who can argue back.

I found myself fixated on Lee's face. I have this theory that life gives most folks pretty much the face they deserve. We all start out as rotund little babies, with plump cheeks and tiny lips, a button for a nose, and lively, sparkling eyes. That cuddly cuteness wears off. By the time we're grown, some folks have grumpy faces, some thoughtful, some resentful and selfish, and some have no distinguishing look at all, just a bland emptiness, which I guess says something in itself.

Lee's face was nearly beatific. There was a clean, almost surreal wholesomeness, unblemished by sorrow, or anxiety, or greed, or any other petty emotional ailment. It was the face of someone who'd had a happy childhood, loving parents, no riveting insecurities or life-shattering failures. I found myself liking him. And it gave me an insight into his mother and his father, because nobody gets a face like that who wasn't embalmed in love nearly from the moment of conception.

I also found myself not liking Thomas Whitehall very much, for murdering and despoiling this cold cadaver on the table. He'd stolen this boy's life and robbed his parents of a cherished jewel.

"All done," Bridges announced from the corner.

"Huh?" I asked, surprised that I'd lost track of everything around me. I'm not ordinarily the sentimental type, so this wasn't good. If a brief look at Lee No Tae had that unsettling effect on me, just imagine how a court-martial board was going to feel after a voluble, able prosecutor spent a few hours leading them through Lee's life, his promise, and the thoroughly putrid things done to him.

Bridges, holding up the folder, walked over. "It's a really awful thing, isn't it?"

"It really is," I mumbled. It was a damned good thing he'd

stopped with the bad jokes. If he'd tossed another one my way at that moment, I might've popped him in the nose.

"Not good," he said, tapping the autopsy folder with a finger. "His blood-alcohol level was .051 at the time of death. He was legally sober. He's got some fairly hard contusions and abrasions on his stomach, his shins, his feet tops, his hands, and his forearms. Look at his stomach particularly," he said, pointing at each part of the anatomy.

I saw several large bruises and swellings on Lee's stomach.

Bridges continued. "It took some very hard blows to cause those contusions to his midsection. Really just short of sledgehammers. The tissue damage is extreme and there are several shattered ribs. The cause of death was asphyxiation. The purple welt around his neck was made by a thin, flexible object, and the bruising striations, which you can't see with the naked eye, indicate the object was roughly textured, like a cloth Army-issue belt. Judging by the contusions and broken blood vessels, it was pulled back with great force."

"How about the sex stuff?" I asked.

"There was fairly serious enlargement of his anus. That's highly unusual. We sometimes get cases here, men and women, who've engaged in anal sex and get something lodged inside. Typically, the muscle and tissue recover and return to normal size within ten minutes."

"But his didn't?"

"No. They measured it, and it was open nearly a full half-inch. There's only one way that could happen. He had to be dead the last time he was penetrated. His blood flow had stopped and the muscles lost their ability to retract."

We stared at each other a long moment, because this was a fairly disgusting topic, even for a doctor, much less a lawyer.

"You'd rule out any chance he was strangled while they were doing it? Like maybe one of those perverts who gets off being asphyxiated at the moment of climax?"

He stared again at the corpse. "First of all, the recipient in homosexual sex generally doesn't climax. Second, even if Whitehall was penetrating him at the moment of death, the muscles would still have enough elasticity to retract. Unless that is, Whitehall remained inside for at least ten minutes after death. That's possible, of course. And from a technical standpoint, that's still necrophilia."

"But you wouldn't rule out that maybe they were playing around and doing that asphyxiation thing, and maybe got a little carried away?"

"I might, except for those bruises," he said. "Those get in the way of that theory. He put up a fierce struggle."

"I guess," I morosely admitted. I'd ascertained that the autopsy results were apparently valid. They could be used to support every charge being leveled at Whitehall. I'd also ascertained that I didn't like Thomas Whitehall very much.

In the process, I'd put myself in the worst mood I could remember.

I thanked Bridges for his help. I went to the hotel and headed straight to the bar. It was five o'clock and I felt I'd earned a good stiff drink. And who should I discover in there but Katherine herself, seated in a dark corner, wedged in behind the jukebox, which was belting out some melancholy song about where all the cowboys went.

I told the bartender to send over two glasses of scotch and then walked in her direction.

"You look like hell," she said when she looked up and saw me.

She didn't look so great herself, but a real gentleman would never, ever reciprocate and acknowledge that observation.

"That right, Moonbeam? Look who's talking," I spitefully said.

She hiked up her long skirt and used a foot to shove out a chair for me. I couldn't help stealing a peek at that bare leg, since I couldn't ever remember seeing her when she wasn't wearing pants or a skirt that went all the way down to her ankles. For all I knew, she didn't really have any legs, only two stout poles she hobbled around on.

But she did have legs, I quickly discovered. At least one leg, anyway. And it was the real good kind of leg, too; slender, and quite nicely sculpted. What a shame to waste that artillery on a gay woman, I thought.

"You drinking?" I asked.

"Only a beer for me," she answered. "I can't handle the hard stuff."

"One beer," I yelled across the room to the bartender, who was putting the finishing touches on my scotch. To Katherine I sourly remarked, "I guess they didn't drink much in that commune you grew up in."

She shot me this irritated look, because it was pretty damned transparent what I was thinking about her parents' drug of choice.

"Have you ever been on a commune?" she asked.

"I saw some in Israel," I admitted. "Not the flower-power kind."

"You think the whole thing's pretty asinine, don't you?"

"Asinine . . . stupid—yeah, that sums it up."

The bartender appeared with our glasses, and I called a truce long enough to take the first long sip from my scotch. It burned the whole way down my windpipe.

"What's got a burr up your ass?" she asked, her eyes glued to my glass, which was now only half full.

"Try that you're the one who dragged me into this, and I just came back from the morgue, where I spent twenty minutes with someone who looked like he used to be a real nice kid. Only he's not breathing anymore. And our client seems to be the cause of it."

"Did you review the autopsy results?"

"Yeah."

She picked up her beer with both hands, took a long sip, then stared at me over the lip. "And what did you think?"

"What I think is our client's going to end up strapped to a chair in a dark room in Leavenworth with a few thousand volts coursing through his limbs to teach him a lesson. He'll deserve it, too."

She put her elbow on the table and took a smaller, more lady-like sip from her beer. "Unless he was framed," she finally said.

"Come on, Katherine, even you can't really believe that crap."

"Give me the benefit of the doubt for a moment," she said. "You keep ordering me to listen, now give me a turn."

"All right," I said, with an expression designed specifically to let her know she was being humored. Nothing pissed off Katherine Carlson more than the suspicion somebody was humoring her.

She somehow ignored it. "Say, for the sake of argument, Thomas was so drunk he became virtually comatose. Say he was sound asleep when Lee was murdered, and the body was placed there to make it look like he did it."

"Ah, come on," I said.

"Suspend your disbelief for a moment."

"Okay," I said, "then you got two suspects. Moran or Jackson."

"Which of the two would you home in on?"

"Moran. He's big and he's powerful. Lee No Tae wasn't any weakling himself, and his body was covered with welts and scrapes and bruises. The doc told me the stomach bruises looked like they were done by a piledriver. Whole ribs were shattered. Whoever subdued him was probably pretty big, and damned strong."

"Unless Lee was so drunk he couldn't fend anyone off."

"The problem with that," I countered, "was that his blood-alcohol level was only .051. Maybe he was technically drunk at midnight, but by the time he was killed he'd sobered up enough to fend for himself."

"Okay, good point," she said. "And the autopsy showed no contusions on his head, like he'd been knocked out?"

"Nope. There were contusions all over his stomach, his arms, his hands, his shins, and his feet tops, but none on his head or face."

"None anywhere on his face?" Katherine asked, sounding surprised, although I suspected this was a ruse, because she was too diligent not to have already reviewed the autopsy results.

"That's right," I admitted.

"Isn't that odd?"

"Not that I can see."

"Well, figure that he's in a fight with his attacker. They're struggling and Lee's doing everything he can to get away. Why no blows to the face?"

She had a good point, but I had a better one. "Think about it, Katherine. If a guy was trying to rape him, he'd be coming at him from behind. That's how the geometry works out between men."

"Then how did his stomach and shins get bruised?" she asked.

"I don't know. Maybe the assault started from his front, then the attacker wrestled himself behind him. Remember, too, that somebody got a web belt around his neck, and the autopsy shows that the belt was being held from behind him."

"Maybe," she said, but without the slightest trace of conviction, mainly, I figured, because she was grasping at straws to build her frame defense and didn't want to be particularly bothered by any distractions, like conflicting evidence, or good common sense.

I said, "Look, I know you don't want to get into this again, but the more I learn about this case, the more dubious your frame defense looks."

"Then you stay dubious," she said. "Maybe it'll do me some good to have an in-house skeptic."

"Maybe. But you think about what you'll do to our client if it turns out you're wrong."

"Speaking of which," she said, taking a deep gulp from her beer, "are you up for visiting Thomas again?"

"For what purpose?"

"A health-and-welfare visit. He could probably use some cheer."

"I'll go with you," I muttered, "but if I had my druthers, I'd rather bean him with a baseball bat than cheer him up."

The car was out front and it took us about two hours and more wrong turns than I can remember before we found the prison again. All the signs were written in Korean, and Katherine kept berating me, like it was my fault this country was filled with folks who put those goofy sticklike symbols on their signs. Some women are that way.

It was turning dark when we pulled into the courtyard. We left the driver with the car idling. It took a few more minutes to explain to a guard at a desk who didn't speak any English why we were there. He kept looking at us like we were door-to-door salespeople, while I kept trying to use sign language to explain what we wanted. I was pointing at the white wall, and repeating "Whitehall," over and over. I thought it was pretty clever, but Katherine kept glaring at me like I was a complete dolt. At least until the guard finally grinned and started shaking his head up and down, like an overeager puppy who finally got it.

Then he left us there a few moments till he came back accompanied by the big goon with shoulders like an ox.

"You wish to see Whitehall?" he asked, giving us that toothy grin.

"Please," I humbly said. "Only for a few minutes."

He crossed his thick arms across his huge chest. "You should've called ahead."

"So sorry about that," I said. "We are relying on your overabundant generosity to allow us to see him."

He scowled at me a few seconds, like he thought I was pulling his leg, or maybe he didn't like being called a generous person, but then he dropped his arms and indicated for us to follow him. We made the same trek. Again, it was so eerily quiet, I swear I heard a guy break wind up on the third floor.

"What's this, reading hour again?" I remarked.

"No, this is prayer hour."

"How's that one work?"

"They pray to God for forgiveness."

"They're all Christian?"

"Not when they get here. But they all leave Christian."

We were at Whitehall's cell by that time, and the big Korean was digging through his pockets for the key.

"I am the only one with one of these," he said, as he stuck it in and gave it a hard twist. "It is for Whitehall's safety. There are many men here who would gladly kill him. Even guards."

I let that one pass as Katherine and I stuck our heads inside

the cell. What I didn't say was that I wouldn't mind killing him myself.

It took a moment to adjust our eyes. The dim light in the over-
head cage barely emitted enough rays to make it to the floor.

"Thomas?" Katherine said.

There was a slight rustling in the corner of the tiny cell.
"Katherine, is that you?"

"Yes. How are you?"

"I've been better," he said. "Come in."

So we did. The room stank. Obviously Whitehall was using the
little metal bowl for his toilet, and just as obviously the bowl
wasn't being emptied.

"Excuse me," Katherine said, talking to the big Korean, "why
don't you have someone collect his waste? For God's sake, this is
disgusting. He'll catch some terrible disease."

"Not to worry," the man assured her. "We collect the bowl
every third day. He shouldn't have eaten so much before he entered. Soon his body will be purged, and his new diet will correct
the problem."

In other words, pretty soon Whitehall would be getting only
small portions of rice and water, so he wouldn't be producing
much human waste. Very economical, these Korean prison officials.

I said, "Could you relocate about fifty feet away? We have to
discuss a few things with our client, and American law affords us
the privilege of confidentiality."

"Certainly," he said, smiling like it was a particularly stupid request.

My eyes were now fully adjusted and I carefully examined our
client. He was wearing Korean prison garb that consisted of some
coarse gray cotton pajamas and a pair of cloth slippers. His lips
and face seemed oddly misshapen, and either he had two pretty
serious black eyes or he was turning into a raccoon.

"Pretty rough?" I asked him.

"Very rough," he said.

"Who did this to you?" Katherine demanded, sounding pissed to beat the band.

"Don't worry about it," Whitehall said.

"No, I won't ignore this. I—"

"I said, forget it!" Whitehall yelled, so insistently I wouldn't have been surprised if he had reached out and punched her.

"Damn it, Thomas, they can't do this to you."

"Katherine, they can do much worse than this to me. Don't make them angry."

Katherine said, "I'll go see the minister of justice. If I have to, I'll hold a press conference and tell the whole world what's happening here."

Whitehall collapsed onto his sleeping mat. "What in the hell do you think caused this in the first place? They dragged me out of my cell in the middle of the night, took me to a room to watch you on CNN, then beat the crap out of me. No more damn favors, huh?"

I could hear Katherine draw in a deep breath.

Before she could say any more, I said, "Other than that, how's things?"

"Unbearable."

"Think you could stand this the rest of your life?"

There was a moment of still silence. Then out of the shadows he said, "I'd kill myself."

It sounded fairly bizarre because he didn't say it angrily, or forcefully, or even threateningly, like most folks would say it, either to garner some sympathy or to make you offer to do something. His tone was perfectly flat, absolutely unaffected, like it was just a fact.

I said, "Captain Whitehall, the more I look into your case, the more likely it seems you're facing just that. Your only chance is me and Katherine here. You're going to have to tell us more."

A reflective look came to his face. The truth was, I'd been sadistically hoping a few days of Korean prison would make him sing like a castrated canary.

"All right," he finally said, "I'll answer two more questions. So pick wisely."

"Tell me about Lee No Tae," I said.

I heard him release a heavy sigh, and he didn't say anything for a long moment. That moment stretched on so long, I worried that I'd picked something so vexing or embarrassing that he was going to go back on his word.

He finally said, "I'm sure this will sound sick to you, but we were in love. It started about five months ago. His sergeant sent him into finance to collect some forms and I was there checking on something, and we took one look at each other, and both of us just knew."

"Five months?" I said.

"That's right. That's why I got the apartment off base. It was our . . . well, I'm sure you get the picture. I could see him, spend time with him, be alone in our private space."

"You . . . uh, you what? You *dated* him for five months?"

"Regularly."

"Then . . . what about witnesses? There must've been witnesses?"

"No, no witnesses. At least, none I know of. When you're a gay in the Army, Major, you're extraordinarily careful about these things. You get very expert at sneaking around in the dark. And if you're a Korean, it's even worse."

"Why?"

"Why what? Why do we sneak around?"

"No. I think I got that part. Why are Korean homosexuals so paranoid?"

"You don't know?"

"No, I don't know. Educate me."

"Because in Korea, homosexuals are lower than any other life form. Many Asians are viciously prejudiced. They're all very big on their racial bloodlines, and they despise anybody who makes that blood seem in any way tainted or perverted. Korean homosexuals are nonpeople, pariahs, beneath contempt. They don't even peek out of the closet. That's the world No lived in. He was scared to death about being discovered. Even more scared than me."

"But everybody, the Koreans, the American Army, even Moran and Jackson, they're all saying he was straight. How do you account for that?"

"Moran and Jackson know better. The rest of them probably believe he was. He was very persuasive. He even went so far as to date women, just to elude suspicion. They liked him, too. He was beautiful, you know. When he'd walk into a room, they'd all start eyeing him, as though he were a stud bull."

"Did his parents know?"

"Absolutely not. That's the single thing that scared No the most. He adored his parents. He knew it would kill them. I sometimes had this fantasy that he'd move back to the States with me, but he wouldn't hear of it. He would never do anything to shame or disappoint his parents."

This sounded like some weird twist on Romeo and Juliet, the old doomed love story, only in this case I somehow didn't feel any surge of sympathy for the afflicted lover.

"Okay," I said, moving along. "Your apartment was locked. There were no signs of a break-in, so if you didn't kill Lee, that leaves only Moran and Jackson. If you had to pick one of them, which would it be?"

He mulled that over for a moment. For a frame defense to succeed, we had to have a scapegoat we could pin this on. We didn't necessarily have to prove Moran or Jackson did it, but we had to create enough doubt in the minds of the court-martial board that they weren't sure who did do it. In other words, there had to be a reasonable doubt that Whitehall was the guy.

What he finally said was, "Neither of them would've done it."

"That's not what I asked. Give us something to go on. Which one of the two?"

"Look, Major, maybe I'm terribly naive, I just don't believe either of them could've done it."

"Damn it, Whitehall, grow up. They're both saying you did it."

He snapped right back. "That's not what they're saying. I've read their testimonies. They're saying they thought they heard a loud argument. They're saying that No was in my room, with me. They're saying I removed the belt from No's neck. Except for the argument, that's all true."

I couldn't argue with him on that point, since I hadn't yet read the statements they'd made to Bales on the second go-around.

"Did Moran rape him?" I asked.

"You've gone beyond your allotted questions."

"Who cares? Just answer the question."

"No. You do some more research and come back to me again."

I wanted to thrash him. The guy was living on rice and water, had twice been beaten, and was facing either a death sentence or life in a Korean prison—which he'd already said was tantamount to a death sentence. Despite all that, he was still playing ring around the rosy. The guy either had sawdust between his ears, or he had a death wish.

Maybe that was it, I suddenly realized. Maybe the damned fool wanted to become a martyr to the gay movement, a suffering Lothario who'd sacrificed himself for the cause. But that would only succeed if he was innocent. Which he wasn't.

I glanced over at Katherine and she just shrugged her shoulders, like, What can you do?

"Look, Whitehall," I said, "I have to be honest here. You're starting to piss me off. We've got eleven more days to prepare your defense, so you better stop playing games."

"I'm not playing games, Major. I've got my reasons."

He was hunched over in a stubborn posture and it was pretty damned obvious I wasn't going to get him to relent. I felt my temper rising. One of his co-counsels was in a hospital room on the edge of death, while the rest of us were working feverishly to defend him. The hell he wasn't playing games.

I gritted my teeth and asked, "Could you at least tell me what the hell you'd like us to plead? Guilty or innocent?"

"Innocent, of course."

"Innocent of what? Of homosexual acts? Of consorting with enlisted troops? Of rape? Of murder? Of necrophilia?"

"You tell me, Major. Isn't that your job? You do your research, then come back and advise me."

I couldn't believe this. The guy was acting impudent. I glared at him through the darkness. He stared right back, unruffled. As for Katherine, the only sound I could hear coming from her was slow, shallow, tightly controlled breathing.

Why in the hell wasn't she as mad as I was? Why wasn't she jumping up and down and screaming at this jerk? She was the lead counsel, the anointed one sent over to save this guy. She should've been the one coaxing and boxing her client into opening up. She should've been livid with rage because he was being stupid and making it impossible for us to adequately defend him.

She wasn't, though. She was as calm as ice.

CHAPTER
11
★ ★ ★

I had to wait until eleven o'clock that night to call the chief of the JAG Corps. He wasn't in, but I got his deputy, a brigadier general named Courtland, which is another fabulous name for a lawyer, if you ask me. I'd worked with Courtland a few times over the years. We didn't know each other well, but we were on first-name terms. Which, in the Army, meant he called me Sean, and I called him General.

I said, "Good morning, General. I hope it's a nice day back there."

"It's hot and steamy back here. I've got a meeting in five minutes. What do you need, Sean?"

"I was wondering if you could tell me who's been assigned as the prosecutor for the Whitehall case?"

"Uh, yeah sure. Eddie Golden. You know him?"

It was a perfectly duplicitous query because everybody in the JAG Corps knows Eddie Golden. Or at least they know of him.

The Navy and Marine Corps aviation wings have this nifty title they bestow on their most hot-shit fighter pilot, the Top Gun, which everybody in the world now knows about because of the corny movie of the same name. Although the Army JAG Corps doesn't fly lethal arabesques like fighter pilots, we do have our own silly little version of this badge of honor, and it is known as the Hangman. It goes to the prosecuting attorney who's put away the most bad guys. For the past six years, Eddie's been the undisputed Hangman.

Eddie and I had faced off against each other twice in court, and obviously, since Eddie was still the reigning Hangman, I hadn't made a dent in his record. To my credit, nobody held it against me—except my clients, of course—because both were fairly hopeless cases. But having seen Eddie in action at first hand, I was awed.

He looks more like Robert Redford than Robert Redford looks like Robert Redford, if that can be at all possible. Eddie is boyish, witty, brilliant, and has an assassin's sense of timing. Women board members are Silly Putty in his hands. But male board members aren't immune to his charms, either. See, Eddie has what we attorneys call the Pope's Gift. What this means is that the Pope can walk outside on a perfectly cloudless, sunny day and flap open his umbrella and every Catholic for miles around will crack open theirs, too. After all, the Pope's supposed to be infallible. Eddie's like that, too, although only in a courtroom when the show is on.

Now I'm not the vindictive type, but I don't like losing twice. I can live with an even split, because I'm the kind of guy who figures a draw is damned close to a win. Not everybody loves a winner, but nobody likes a loser, and I'm perfectly content hanging out right in the middle of the pack. The thought of losing three times to Eddie almost made me sick.

That's because the other thing about Eddie is that he's not a nice winner. He sends every attorney he beats a baseball bat with a notch carved in it. I know this for a fact since I've got two of them stored in my closet at home.

I said, "Shit," and the general chuckled. "Anything else I can help you with?"

"No, thank you very much."

We then hung up.

The thing about that phone call was that it inspired me. Maybe I haven't mentioned it yet, but the truth is, I really don't like Eddie. No, that's not true. I detest Eddie.

In Latin, there's this wonderful phrase: *Palmam qui meruit ferat,* which, translated, means, "None but himself could be his parallel." That fairly well describes Eddie. He's a smug, arrogant, pompous prick who happens to win all the time and never lets anybody forget it.

Vowing not to receive another of his baseball bats, I stayed awake till one o'clock wading through more of the materials in the boxes. I started with Jackson's initial testimony.

Private Everett Jackson was his full name, twenty years old, from Merryville, Mississippi, and trained by the Army to be an administrative clerk. He'd been in Korea nearly a full year and nothing in his personnel file jumped out at me. He seemed to be just another guy who'd made it through high school, skipped or put off college, and signed up. Maybe he wanted some adventure, maybe he wanted to get away from home, maybe he had nothing better to do. He was bright, though. His GT score, a test administered by the Armed Forces, was 126. That's roughly comparable to his IQ, so he had brains.

I examined the photo appended to the inside jacket. I tried to overlook that I already knew he was gay, but frankly, he looked it. That's not easy to accomplish in a black-and-white Army photo, when you're standing rigidly at attention, in Army greens. But he did. There was an unmistakable willowiness, an effeminate slouch.

Before "don't ask, don't tell" came to pass, Everett Jackson would've been singled out and discharged ten seconds after he walked through the gate for basic training. Some stiff-necked drill sergeant in a Smokey the Bear hat would've taken one look at him, sniffed derisively once or twice, then dragged him into the latrine, rammed his face within two inches of Jackson's, and fiercely demanded, "Don't you dare lie to me, boy. You tell me where you like to put that little pecker of yours."

Moran claimed in his initial statement that he'd invited Jackson to Whitehall's party because the poor kid was bereft of friends, that he was a barracks rat in need of a reprieve. There was probably some truth in that. The other troops probably despised Jackson. They probably treated him like a leper.

What intrigued me was why Moran plucked Jackson out of the

ranks, made him his company clerk, and chose to have an affair with him. Moran was a tough, manly-looking guy, the last man anybody would ever suspect of being gay. Unless, that is, he hung out with a neon gay like Jackson. I was making an assumption here that Moran and Jackson were lovers, but the facts being what they were, that didn't seem like a real wild leap.

And, since Jackson was so visibly gay, why would Moran take the risk of associating with him?

Anyway, Jackson's initial testimony tracked closely with Whitehall's and Moran's. It did so because he cloaked himself in ignorance. He claimed he drank way too much. He claimed he drank way too fast. He claimed he passed out at 11:45 on the dot. I had some trouble swallowing that one. Not many people check their watches before they lapse into a drunken coma.

The next thing he claimed he remembered was being shaken by someone and told to go to the second bedroom on the left. So he did. He claimed he then slept soundly until Moran awoke him at 5:30 A.M. and told him Lee was dead. He said he got up, walked down the hall, peeked in the room and saw the body, but only got a quick glimpse, because the apartment was instantly flooded with Korean policemen.

I put down his packet and went back to the statement by Sergeant Wilson Blackstone, the first MP to arrive at the scene. According to Blackstone, he and his partner did not arrive at the apartment until 6:08, by which time the Korean police were already there in force. I then checked the statement from the MP shift officer who'd dispatched Blackstone in the first place. The shift officer happened to be the same Captain Bittlesby I'd spoken with to get the humvee and escort to go to the embassy.

According to Bittlesby, he'd taken the call from Moran at 5:29, and, after speaking with his colonel, he'd talked with the Itaewon station commander. The time of that call was 5:45 A.M. Figure it took the Itaewon station commander two or three minutes to call his own shift officer and order him to dispatch an investigating team to the apartment. Itaewon is a fairly compact district. If the traffic was light at that hour of the morning, it might've taken another ten to fifteen minutes for the Korean cops to get to White-hall's apartment. That meant the Korean cops could not have gotten to the scene before 6:00 A.M. at the earliest, barely ahead of Blackstone.

In other words, Jackson was lying about how much he knew, if he wasn't lying about everything, which he probably was. Anyway, there was at least a thirty-minute gap between the time Moran woke him and the time when the Korean cops arrived.

It was just a guess, but it seemed a pretty good one that White-hall, Moran, and Jackson used that thirty minutes to ponder their situation and conspire. Jackson had enough brains to try to cover that up, but not enough sense to get his times correct.

But so what?

The "so what" was that it eliminated any doubt there'd been at least a hurried, halfhearted effort at patching together a common alibi, at devising a common defense to cover one another's asses.

Something had gone wrong, though. Somehow the scheme had unraveled and Whitehall was hung out to dry. To understand how their plan got deconstructed, I had to first reconstruct it.

I tried to picture how it might've gone down. They were all soldiers—a captain, a first sergeant, and a private—and in a pure world, that would've dictated a cast-iron pecking order. Whitehall or Moran would've devised the scheme, and Jackson, since he was only a private, would've dutifully gone along. He was probably scared out of his wits anyway—at being exposed as a homosexual, at being implicated in a murder, at being arrested by foreign police in a strange country. He would've been malleable and compliant.

At least that's how it would've gone down under ordinary conditions. These weren't ordinary conditions, though. These were three gay men who were sexually involved with one another in ways and combinations I couldn't possibly fathom. Everything was topsy-turvy.

There was too much here I couldn't begin to comprehend, things that were beyond my ken. Whitehall had smelled me out right away; I knew next to nothing about gays and their peculiar relationships. I knew who did, though.

I therefore left my room, took the elevator down two floors, and walked to room 430. I knocked hard three times, then tried to look perfectly guileless.

A light came on inside the room, the peephole darkened, the bolt slid open, and the door swung inward.

Katherine was wearing a skimpy T-shirt that came a quarter of the way down her thighs. She did have great legs, with long, taut muscles, slender calves, and thin ankles. Her hair was mussed and she looked groggy. She audibly groaned. Delighted to see me she clearly wasn't.

I tried to hide my rapture at interrupting her sleep. With flawless insouciance, I said, "I'm sorry to awaken you"—which I wasn't—"but I've got a few questions"—which I did.

"Drummond, it's one o'clock in the morning."

"Oh, so it is," I admitted, barging my way past her. "Well, you're already awake anyway."

She followed me, quietly cursing. She leaned against the wall and crossed her arms across her chest. "This better be good. Really good."

"Right," I said, falling into a chair and kicking up my feet onto her desk, just to be sure she knew I was settling in for the duration. "Start with this. Do you believe Whitehall's claim that he and Lee were in love?"

She climbed back onto her bed, got under the covers, and hiked them up across her chest. "Drummond, in case you hadn't noticed, I'm an attorney, not a lie detector."

"Right. But here's my problem. You've got four gay guys at a party. One gets murdered. His corpse contains semen from two different men. One of those men claims he and the deceased were madly in love, an eternal love, the type that comes along only once in a lifetime. See my problem here? Don't gays get jealous like heteros?"

"Of course they do."

"Then how does it square? If Whitehall and Lee were an item, something doesn't fit here. If Moran raped Whitehall's amour, why in the hell would Whitehall invite him to sleep over?"

"I never assumed Moran raped him," she said.

"No?"

She gave me an outsize stare. "Do you have any idea how rare homosexual rapes are?"

"Frankly, I don't," I admitted. "See, my mind's all cluttered up with all those useless heterosexual things."

If she got my taunt, she ignored it. "It's almost unheard of. At least when the act is between two adults. Homosexuals are not nearly as sexually aggressive as heteros. Even in homosexual pedophilia, forcible rapes are rare, although of course, pedophile cases are automatically classified as statutory rapes because the victims are underage. But actual, forcible rape is almost unheard of. Forget everything you know about hetero rapes."

"So you're saying hetero rape and homo rape aren't the same?"

"Rape's rape, regardless of the sexual mix. I'm saying that in over half of hetero rapes, the victim and the attacker are at least acquainted with each other. That's also nearly unheard of in homosexual rape cases. Except in prison, that is. There, all the rules are upended."

"So what? You never believed Moran raped Lee?"

"You actually want my opinion?" she asked, with only the barest hint of sarcasm or skepticism.

"Why else would I be here?" I asked, failing to mention, of course, the sweet joy of waking her up in the middle of the night.

"Okay. Here's what I suspect. Moran and Thomas willingly swapped partners."

"And you believe the partners were willing, too?"

"These are grown men. It would've been almost physically impossible without their consent."

"But why would Whitehall swap a partner he claims he loved?"

"I'm only guessing, okay? I think, though, that you might've elicited a motive from Thomas this evening. He and Lee, they both knew their love was doomed. Thomas had only four weeks remaining on his tour. Lee wasn't going to join him in the States, and maybe Thomas—or Lee—decided the time had come to orchestrate a separation."

"So you think maybe this partner-swapping thing was an effort to separate? Like some kinky kind of divorce?"

"Maybe, yes. Remember, you're talking about gays. They were seeking a clean way to emotionally disentangle. Maybe they decided to start by physically disentangling."

"And they did this by engaging in some kind of switch-hitting orgy?"

"No, Drummond. I'd guess they tried to handle it in a very gentle, discreet way. They probably drank a great deal to deaden their nerves and fortify themselves for something that was emotionally trying. And I'd guess that at some point in the evening, they paired off and went to separate bedrooms."

"So this was how they chose to separate?"

"It's possible."

"Is that common? Is that how gays handle it?"

"Is there a common way heteros handle breakups and divorces?"

"Of course not."

"Don't assume there's a universal way gays handle it, either. Every relationship's different; every ending's different."

"Okay," I said, "then see if you can figure this out. There was about a thirty-minute gap between the time Lee's corpse was discovered and the arrival of the police. What did they do during that gap?"

She said, "Who called the police?"

"Moran."

"Really? And why'd he do that?"

"Huh?"

"Why'd he call the police? Think about it. He awakens to find a corpse in the apartment. Now if he was the murderer, or was implicated in the murder, why would he call the police? Wouldn't he and Thomas try to work out some way to dispose of the body? Wouldn't they put their heads together and try to figure out how to sneak the corpse out of the building so they can dump it in the woods someplace where it would never be found? Wouldn't they?"

"I suppose, yeah."

"But instead, Moran called the police, right?"

"But was Whitehall aware he was calling the police?"

"Almost certainly, yes."

"Then let me try a different tack. Whitehall's upset at Lee. The love of his life has just refused to run off and join him back in the States. He feels jilted, rebuffed."

"Okay . . ."

"They agree to try this partner-swapping merry-go-round, only instead of helping Whitehall get over it, it makes him insanely jealous. He gets incensed. They retire to the bedroom together. They start having sex, only Whitehall's emotions fly out of control. He gets rough. First he punches him silly. Maybe he hits him in the solar plexus and knocks the wind out of him. Then he slings a belt around Lee's neck, and before he knows it, he's killed him. Maybe it was deliberate. But maybe it wasn't. Maybe it was subterranean rage boiling to the surface. He lies awake the rest of the night and tries to sort through what to do next. Act one is to seem like he's sound asleep when Moran opens his door at five-thirty."

"Then why would he let Moran call the police? Why wouldn't he try to talk him out of it?"

"Because that's act two. He's smart. If he resists, that would be tantamount to admitting he killed Lee. Instead he says, 'Geez, gosh, oh my God, look at this! Somebody killed my boyfriend. Quick! Someone call the police!'"

"Unless Thomas really was surprised."

"No. Don't you see it? By feigning innocence, he's able to get Moran and Jackson to trust him, to go along with him, to conspire in his alibi. Nobody witnessed him killing Lee. The other two are completely confused, but they've got things to hide, too. They give him the benefit of the doubt, and he's hoping he can at least get them to tell a few fibs to help him with his story. He knows they've got things to hide. He decides to exploit their trust and their fears and take his chances."

"That's not exactly what I'd call a perfect plan."

"Yeah, well, you got a guy who just flew into a rage and killed his lover. He's distraught. He was drunk. He acted impetuously.

There are no perfect plans available. He knows he can't get the body out of the apartment without maybe waking Moran or Jackson. Or without maybe being seen by some Korean as he's standing in the elevator with a corpse slung over his shoulder. He's forced to ad-lib."

She said, "You know what? I'll bet that's exactly the case the prosecutor is going to present."

"It's sure as hell the case I'd present," I admitted, without confiding that was exactly what I'd hoped to accomplish that night: to get a handle on what Eddie would argue, so I could figure out a strategy to block him.

Katherine gave me a fairly friendly smile. "You know, Drummond, I hate admitting this, but you're a pretty good attorney."

I said, "Me? You're the one who figured it out," which actually was true. In fact, she'd had it figured out long before I came to her room, which made me suddenly suspicious about how much else she'd already figured out that she wasn't sharing with me.

She peered at me over the covers. "Is that a compliment?"

I smiled. "That's a compliment."

She stared at the far wall a moment. "I never thought I'd say this, but we make a pretty fair team."

I reluctantly said, "In some ways, I guess we do."

Katherine then dropped her covers and climbed out of bed. She pitter-pattered to the bathroom. A moment passed, then I heard water running. She came back in sipping from a tumbler. Maybe I was imagining things, but I could swear she'd brushed her hair, too, because it was no longer disheveled and mussed. It hung down like a long, captivating robe past her waist. She grabbed another chair, dragged it over in front of me, and fell into it. Swinging those delicately shaped legs up, she propped her feet right next to mine.

It was what you might call a very stimulating gesture. I mean, lesbian or not, she really had great legs. And I'm a guy, and even though I knew she was untouchable fruit, there are parts of my body that don't know the difference between fruit and cannoli. This was also the moment when I noticed she wasn't wearing a bra under that thin, tiny T-shirt. These two cute little things jiggled about a bit, and the bottom of her T-shirt was hiked up all the way to the tippy-top of her thighs. I guess because she was gay, she was unconscious of the effect all this was having on me.

I began fighting a chivalrous battle to keep my eyeballs pasted on the floor, on the table, on the wall—anywhere but on her. I wasn't winning, but I swear I put up a hell of a fight.

"All right," she said, apparently unconscious that Ol' Humungo really couldn't care less if she was a raging bull dyke, so long as she had all the right plumbing and equipment. And she did. Believe me, she did.

She asked, "You're still convinced Whitehall did it?"

"Uh-huh. Very convinced," I said, rubbing my forehead, so I could shield my eyes, so she couldn't catch me staring at her cute little feet.

"Do you buy my premise they were trading partners?"

"Uh, yeah, sure. Why not? I mean, it's not exactly how I'd break off an affair, but I guess it's plausible."

She took a sip of water and I could sense, but not see, her studying my face, because my own eyes were busy sliding from her shapely little feet up her velvety smooth shins.

"Humor me some more," she said. "Go back to what you asked Thomas tonight, about who else might've killed Lee. Start with Moran. He's Whitehall's friend, right? He knows what Whitehall intends. He obliges him by bringing a consenting partner."

"A true friend," I caustically agreed.

Katherine had marvelous kneecaps, too, I'd just noticed. Not too big, not too small, not too bony, not too fleshy. My mother always used to say the only true way to judge a woman is by her kneecaps. Sounds odd, but in a funny way, she's got a point.

Suddenly Katherine said, "Drummond, you've got to stop that."

"Huh?" I said, thinking I'd just been caught peeping.

"Stop making your hetero judgments. Gays live in a different world with different standards. Particularly gays in the military."

"Okay, so Moran's a great guy," I said, forgetting about her knees and feasting on her thighs. "The kind of noble buddy every man wishes he had. So who's Jackson? Is he Moran's steady? Or is he just some willing toady?"

"My guess is he's nothing more than a compliant partner. Maybe Moran's slept with him a few times. There's physical involvement, but they're emotionally detached."

In a valiant display of strength, I jerked my eyes up from her legs and looked at her face. Her eyes, I suddenly noticed, were the greenest things I ever saw, utterly infinite pools of grass and forest and shimmering light. There was something odd about the way she was looking at me. But that was all wrong. She's a lesbian. And we obviously disliked each other intensely. Otherwise, I might've sworn she was giving me what we men call the come-hither look.

I mean, we're in this hotel room, it's late at night, there's this big, comfy bed right next to us, she's damned close to naked, and she's so close to me I can smell her hair. Smelled damned great, too.

But this was idiotic. Hell, we didn't even like each other.

Idiotic or not, I decided I'd better leave, and damn quick, too. I mean, there's something about having a gorgeous, half-naked woman perched within arm's reach that's very corrosive to your self-discipline.

I quickly stood up and gave her a lopsided grin. "Hey, I gotta go."

She seemed momentarily stunned. Then she shot me a look that, had I not known better, seemed ever so slightly peeved. "You're leaving? But you woke me."

"I know. Sorry, really. It's just that . . . uh, my brain's fried. I'm, uh, exhausted," I said, making a brisk retreat.

I got the door open and was halfway out when I heard Katherine grumble, "God, you can be such an ass, Drummond."

Now where in the hell did that come from? She should've been thanking me for letting her get back to sleep. I closed the door and muttered to myself the whole way back to my room.

It took me a while, but I finally got hold of it. Most folks would guess I'd just made a rollicking blunder, that she'd just offered me a ticket to ride, that I'd been a damn fool and walked away. Maybe she wasn't a purebred lesbian. Maybe she was AC/DC, and I just happened to blunder in on a night when she was in one of those enchanting DC moods.

But then, most folks don't know Katherine Carlson the way I do. What I guessed was that maybe she wanted to teach me a lesson for waking her in the middle of the night. Or maybe she just wanted to put me in my place on generic principle. Some women can act that way: Please believe me about this. It's all about power, and the quickest, most surefire way to get it is to flash a little leg, smile a crooked smile, and then act terrifically outraged when the randy bull starts snorting and scratching the ground.

She'd pulled down those covers, and climbed out of that bed, and I nearly fell for it, too. I'd almost made a damned fool out of myself. I didn't, though. I didn't give her the chance to mortify me, to coldly order me to stop pawing her and get the hell out of her room. In the battle of the sexes, I'd notched up a victory.

If it was anybody but Katherine Carlson, this would sound too contrived and Machiavellian by half. Only I knew her. I knew her well, too. She was the most vindictive, conniving lawyer I'd ever met. Nobody can build leakproof firewalls; some of that chilling guile has to seep over the edge into her personal life.

At any rate, the shower water was so frigid it was like being scalded by ice cubes. I nearly got frostbite, but I got over it.

CHAPTER
12

★ ★ ★

The alarm went off at four. I almost heaved it against the wall and yanked the covers back over my head. But I mumbled to myself that the early bird gets the worm, and all that shit, as I rolled out of bed and knocked off fifty quick push-ups to get my blood circulating.

The particular worm I wanted was to force Katherine off that bankrupt defense she was planning. To do that, I needed leverage. Unbeknownst to himself, Whitehall was going to give me that leverage. He was going to be my ace in the hole.

I groggily lifted up the phone and told room service to send up a freshly brewed pot of coffee. I stressed that freshly brewed thing quite adamantly. I wasn't in any mood for the dregs of midnight's pot.

Then I jumped into my second cold shower inside four hours. When I emerged, my eyes were so popped open that to the nice kid who brought my coffee I must've looked like I'd just stuck my finger into an electrical socket. I tipped him handsomely, then positioned the pot by the window. I opened the blinds and stared at the lights in the distance.

Koreans are hungry, industrious, hardworking folks, and the city was already popping to life. Little scooters piled high with textiles and other goods were careening around the streets, making their early-morning deliveries to shops and warehouses. The drivers had to have gotten up at three to be out this early. Some life.

I lifted up the phone and asked the operator to put me through to the office of the registrar at the United States Military Academy at West Point. A high, timid female voice answered. I said I wanted to speak with the registrar.

The receptionist politely inquired, "You mean Colonel Hal Menkle?" and I politely said yes, and she politely asked me to wait a moment.

This being West Point, some inspiring martial marching music came on the line. I marched gently in place, until a gruff voice said, "How can I help you?"

"Colonel Menkle?"

"That's who you asked for, wasn't it?"

Sometimes you just know, right away, you're not going to like somebody.

I said, "I'm Sean Drummond, defense counsel for one of the less stellar graduates of that great institution of yours. Thomas Whitehall? Class of '91? Ever hear of him?"

There was a brief pause before he said, "I wasn't here back in '91. I know who Whitehall is, though. Everybody does."

"I'll bet."

"We've been flooded with press inquiries on that bastard for weeks. You wanta talk to his physics professor? His priest? We've even got one of his former roommates on the faculty. We gotta whole list. Who you wanta start with?"

"How about the roommate? That sounds good."

"Captain Ernest Walters. He teaches mechanical engineering. Just a second, I'll transfer you."

After a moment, then three rings, a clipped, perfunctory voice said, "Department of Mechanical Engineering. Captain Walters."

"Hello, Ernie," I said, as though we were the best of friends, "my name's Major Sean Drummond. I'm a lawyer and I'm on the defense team for your old roomie Thomas Whitehall."

"How can I help you, sir?" he asked, so starchly that it sounded much more like, Hey, you and me, we ain't buddies, and why don't you go screw yourself.

"Heh-heh," I chuckled, like I hadn't even noticed. "Must've been a tough coupla weeks for you I guess, huh, Ernie?"

"I guess," he coldly replied, still not cozying up to my bonfire of friendliness. This couldn't last, though. I mean, I'm a pretty charming guy when I put a little elbow grease into it.

"I sure as hell don't envy you," I plugged away. "I'll bet you've taken a lot of grief, huh?"

"If that's what you'd call getting seven bogus appointment slips to report to the dispensary to take an AIDS test, I guess so."

"Aw, come on, that's not so bad," I said.

"Yeah? That's this afternoon. Yesterday, some asshole stuffed my desk drawers full of pink underpants. Last week, some cadets broke into my classroom at night, painted my desk flaming pink, and changed my name placard to 'Mrs. Whitehall.'"

"Hey, Ernie, tell me about it. Been there. You know, the other day, some bastard even painted the word 'homos' above my office entrance."

"Yeah?" he said, suddenly sounding much more receptive. "I guess I saw that on CNN. That was you, huh?"

"That was me," I said. "You can only guess how I got my butt reamed over that one."

"Pretty bad, huh?"

"Shit, generals were standing in line to call me. You'd think I knocked up the President's daughter. I'll tell ya, Ernie, I've been catching some royal hell."

"Yeah?" he asked, sounding suddenly much more chummy, proving once again that misery really does love company. "Try this one for size. I been married to my wife eight years, right? We date all through high school, all through my time as a cadet. I mean, hell, we got three kids, right? So, the other night, we're layin' in bed, and she turns to me and she gives me this real quirky look, and she says, 'Hey honey, is there anything at all you want to tell me about? I mean, *anything*?' You believe that crap? I almost jackslapped her."

"Wow. Your own wife. That's one for the books."

"'Course I didn't. Jackslap her, I mean. I just jumped on her ass and gave her a taste of the old power drill till three in the morning. Lady walked bowlegged for two days, no shit. She won't be questioning my damned manhood again."

"Heh-heh," I chuckled, now that Ernie and I had bonded through our common woes. The ice was out of his voice, and he was getting relaxed, sounding much like one of those basic good ol' boys from the South Bronx. The talkative type, at least once you get them going.

Still chuckling, I said, "So Ernie, what can you tell me about Whitehall?"

"Depends. What are you interested in?"

"What kind of guy was he?"

"Hell, everybody asks that. I don't know. He's just a guy, right?"

"Come on, Ernie, I'm not everybody. I'm the guy who has to convince ten hard-nosed sons of bitches they don't really want to run fifty thousand volts through him. To do that, I have to know what kind of guy he really is."

He seemed to weigh that a moment, because there was a fairly extended pause before he answered. I was taking a big risk. Maybe he really didn't like Whitehall and wouldn't mind one bit if fifty thousand volts cooked him like a Christmas turkey. But what choice did I have?

"This's between us?" he finally demanded.

"Absolutely."

"I mean, this isn't the crap I tell reporters to keep my butt outta trouble, right?"

"Ernie, I swear. I won't say a word."

"Okay. Truth was I really liked Whitehall. I liked him a lot. We were pretty good buddies, y'know?"

He was backing into this tentatively, like a guy sticking his toe into hot water.

"Why?"

"Hell, I don't know. He was just a great guy, y'know. A fantastic cadet, though. He played the game, right? Only don't take that in no unfavorable way. He was a straight shooter. A guy you could trust in a bad moment."

"No kidding?" I said.

"Yeah, no kiddin'. Tell ya a story. Freshman year, which they call plebe year here, right? There was this kid in my company who was a real screwup. Y'know the type, right? Couldn't spit-shine his shoes, uniform always looked like shit, couldn't pass a room inspection, couldn't remember all that crap plebes have to memorize so upperclassmen can quiz 'em every day. This guy's a miserable klutz, right? So the upperclassmen, they start coming after this kid. I mean, we're talking like a pack of piranhas, giving him hell, hazing him every day, hazing him till late at night, so he can't study, so he's gettin' so bothered and exhausted he's on the verge of flunking out. 'Course, that was their game, right? They were trying to run him out, y'know. Either make him so friggin' miserable he quits, or so friggin' fried he flunks out. And right there in the same squad is Tommy Whitehall. We're talking Mr. Perfect hisself. He's just one of them gabbonzos that arrive at West Point and they've got the whole game figured out. You know the type, right?"

"Right."

"Yeah, so the upperclassmen, they just adore Tommy Whitehall. Like he can turn Coke into Pepsi, right? Always they're saying to this screwup, 'Hey klutz, look over there at Mr. Whitehall. How come you ain't like him, huh? What's your friggin' problem, huh?' So one day, to everybody's surprise, Whitehall shows up at formation, and his shoes look like he polished 'em with mud, and his uniform's got smudges all over it, and suddenly he can barely remember his own name. So the upperclassmen, they jump on his ass a bit, not too hard, though, 'cause it's him, Mr. Perfect, right? I mean, it's only a freakin' anomaly, right? A one-day thing, right?"

"Right."

"Only it don't get no better for Tommy Whitehall. Mr. Perfect seems to disintegrate. So these guys, they're like sharks, they forget all about the klutz and go after Whitehall. I mean, it's like one of them biblical things, like the only thing they hate more'n a common sinner is a saint who falls from grace. 'Course, what nobody knows is that Tommy's staying up till midnight every night so he can sneak outta his room, go over to the klutz's room, where Tommy spit-shines the kid's shoes and gets his room ready for inspection, and even helps him catch up academically. I mean, he saved that guy's ass. Tommy hadn't helped him, that stupid klutz would of either flunked out or been thrown out, for friggin' sure."

Ernie had spit out the tale in that dizzying, rapid-fire way that only purebred New Yorkers can speak, only it was such a long-winded and convoluted tale that even he had to pause to catch his breath.

Then he said, "'Course, you're a smart guy, right? You bein' a lawyer and all. You probably already guessed who the klutz was, right? I mean, I wouldn't be sittin' right here wasn't for Tommy Whitehall. I'm telling ya, nobody worked it harder'n Tommy."

"Why'd he work so hard at it?"

"Shit, who knows? I just thought he was gonna be a really great officer. I mean, he was like that, y'know? More mature than most guys here."

"More mature, like how?"

"Like driven. Never bitched, never whined, never acted stupid like most cadets do."

"No kidding?"

"Hey, no kiddin'. Hands down. He was like pretty close to the top of our class academically. Guy's smart as shit. And box? He took the freakin' middleweight Golden Gloves down in New York City. You know anything about boxing, that's like being the amateur national champ, 'cause the best kids from all over the country pour in for that one."

"I had no idea," I admitted.

"Yeah, well, Tommy's not easy to know. He can come off like a real prick, least till he decides he likes you. There's like this moat of ice around him, y'know? I never knew why that was. Least till now, anyway. Who'd of figured it, huh?"

Regarding that moat-of-ice thing, I would've figured it. I had him pegged on that one. Of course I didn't say that. Instead I said, "So you never suspected it?"

"Hellll, no. Shit, we got communal showers up here. You'd think, if it was for real, you'd see a little pecker pop, wouldn't ya?"

"Did anybody ever suspect him?"

"Nobody. I mean, lotsa guys are running around now, swearing they knew all along he was a pansy. That's bullshit, though. He never let on. I'll tell ya, he sure had lots of female cadets pantin' after him. Could of got laid every night, if he'da wanted."

"You ever see him date?"

"Nah. But I always figured it was, ah, y'know, one of them loyal-to-the-girl-back-home things. The whole four years, he kept this picture on his desk. I'm talking gorgeous, y'know? Dark-haired, big green eyes, face to melt your heart. I asked about her a coupla times, but he'd never let on. In hindsight, that picture, it was probably camouflage. Y'know, like one of those frames you buy with a picture of a model in it. Only he left the picture in so we'd all think . . . well, you know."

I was sort of half listening by this point, because I was getting ready to end-run him.

As nonchalantly as I could, I said, "So, Ernie, do you think White-hall could've committed murder?"

The reason for my coyness was because, unbeknownst to him, Captain Ernie Walters was about to be fingered as a character witness. I didn't give a damn whether he wanted to testify or not. He'd said so many glowing things, he'd be perfect. I was ready to book him a flight to Korea.

He reluctantly said, "Actually, Major, I gotta be honest here. Yeah, I think Tommy could of done it. I definitely do."

I nearly choked with surprise. "You do?"

"Sure. Only 'cause I've seen him fight, though. It's what made him so damned good. They called him 'Raging Bull,' y'know. He'd go friggin' crazy in that ring. Scared the bejesus outta everybody he boxed."

"Is that right?" I asked. "So you figure . . . what? Maybe there was some hidden anger, some deep pathological impulse?"

"Hey, I'm a mechanical engineer, not a head shrink. I never saw it outside the ring, but I sure as hell saw him get that way inside. It was like some monster got out of a cage. The guy wasn't boxin', he was committing murder. His arms and his fists were like those old ack-ack guns, rat-a-tat-tat, slamming back and forth, blood flying everywheres, and he just kept charging. I hadda take a guess, knowing what I know now, then sure, yeah, maybe it was some kind of lurking anger related to this homo thing."

And in that flash of an instant, Ernie Walters lost his free ticket to Korea. But I wasn't about to let go.

"So, tell me, Ernie, are there any other classmates you think might speak up for Tom?"

"Shit, I don't know. There was some guys used to like him. Everybody respected him, tell you that. And after plebe year, nobody screwed with him neither. See, lots of guys didn't know he was the Golden Gloves champ, but everybody knew he was the brigade champ. Three years running, in fact."

"Tell me about that."

"Okay, sure. Once a year, the entire corps of cadets troops up to the gym for the brigade boxing finals. It's like the big event of the year, y'know? Like the king of the badass contest. Shit, the way this's turned out, maybe it was the queen of the badass contest." He chuckled. "Everybody saw Tommy fight. Two or three of those matches, he got real freakin' ugly. Once, he was fighting this upperclassman who'd won the previous two years. Shit, I'll never forget it. Tommy just let loose on him. Blood everywhere. Put the guy in the hospital. Broke his nose, shattered his jaw. Hell, the poor guy didn't see daylight for two days. It was all anybody talked about for weeks."

"So everybody knew he had a violent streak?"

"Hey, look Major, you want me to climb on a plane and come testify Tommy Whitehall's this friggin' great guy, you got it. I'll do that. The Army'll probably kill me for it, but I'll do that for Tommy. I could probably name five or six other guys who'd do it, too. Hell, before this thing broke, I probably could of named a dozen guys, y'know. But you gotta hear the risk here, right?"

"Yes, I do, Ernie. I'd hate to have heard someone disclose this on the stand."

"Hey, no problem. Uh, Major, maybe I can offer you a little inside tip here? Y'know, on the sly. Between us gonzos. No further, right?"

"Ernie, I'm fishing for whatever I can get."

"See if you can talk with this guy named Edwin Gilderstone. He's like the oldest major in the Army. He was Tom's English prof. They got pretty close."

I said, "Ernie, I appreciate this very much. You've been more helpful than you know."

"Hey look, sir, anything I can do to help Tommy, you pick up the phone and call. Right away, day or night, okay? Tommy Whitehall's my paisan. Unlike a lotta these pricks, I still tell everybody that. Probably why I'm catching so much crap 'round here, y'know. And next time you see Tommy, you tell him I still love him like a brother. Be real precise about that, though. Only like a brother, heh-heh."

I said, "Thanks, Ernie. I'll do that. Switch me back to the registrar, would you?"

A moment passed, there were two rings, and Colonel Hal Menkle's irascible voice came back on.

"You get what you needed, Drummond?" he asked.

"Walters wasn't the least bit helpful," I lied. "Who do you think might be helpful?"

"Try Chaplain Forbes. Or there's a Lieutenant Colonel Merryweather who taught him math. Or, there's—"

I jumped in. "How about his old English prof? Edwin Gilderstone?"

"Gilderstone?" he asked, sounding surprised. And damned unhappy, too—so unhappy, in fact, I could swear I heard his teeth grinding.

"Yes, that's right. Major Edwin Gilderstone."

"I . . . uh—"

"He's still on the faculty, isn't he?"

"Maybe. What possible reason would you have for speaking with *him*, though? Trust me here, Drummond, the other names I'm giving you, they're much better qualified to speak on this issue. You don't want to set foot in the wrong pastures here, if you get my drift. You could find yourself in a pretty ugly pile of shit."

I sure as hell did get his drift. When something like this happens, an institution, any institution, flies into a frenzy of self-mortification and damage control. This was the well-storied Long Gray Line: Robert E. Lee, Ulysses S. Grant, "Blackjack" Pershing, Eisenhower, Omar Bradley, "Stormin' Norman" Schwartzkopf .... oops, ouch, shit . . . Thomas Whitehall. What the hell happened here? How mortifying.

And as a wise old commander I once worked for used to caution, mortification quickly begets cover-ups. Obviously, the Academy had a list of former associates who would say the right things, proffer the right innuendos, who would create just the right impression.

That impression was that Thomas Whitehall was living proof that "don't ask, don't tell" didn't work, that it allowed murderous homosexuals to slip through the net.

I said, "I want to speak with Edwin Gilderstone and I sure as hell hope you're not trying to hinder me. Because if you are, then I'll have you cited for impeding my defense."

He very coldly said, "Back off, Drummond. You can talk to whomever you want."

I made it a point to sound even colder. "I know. Connect me, right away."

Three rings later, a soft, gentle voice said, "Ed Gilderstone."

I said, "Hi, Ed, Sean Drummond here. I'm the lawyer who has the unparalleled honor of defending Thomas Whitehall. I'm told you were his English professor. I'm also told you knew him pretty well."

"I was. But I was not merely his English professor. I was also his faculty adviser. I therefore saw Thomas regularly the whole four years he was here."

"Wow. You must be spending a lot of time talking to the press these days, huh?"

Sounding suddenly grumpy, he said, "I've spent no time talking with the press."

"No?"

"I've actually been blacklisted from speaking to any journalists. Can you imagine? I even received a formal letter from the superintendent personally ordering to me to say nothing to the press."

"Really? Like a gag order, huh? Why would they do that?"

Now, sounding childish, he replied, "I suppose I don't represent the image they want portrayed to the press."

"What image is that?" I asked, knowing damn well what image he meant.

"I'm not one of these young, lean, square-jawed, Airborne, Ranger types who take a brief sabbatical from the Army, pick up a quick master's, then come up here and pretend they're teachers for a few years before they go back to troops. Warrior-scholars, they call themselves."

"Then what are you, Ed?"

"I'm a short, bald, fifty-three-year-old major who would've been cashiered fifteen years ago, but for one asset: I happen to have a doctorate in English literature from Yale. The Academy hates it, but it must preserve a few like me on the permanent faculty or it'll lose its credentials as a real college. But God forbid the press ever learn there are overeducated dinosaurs like me in uniform."

"How long have you been there?"

"Twenty-two long, disgruntling years."

"Yes, well," I said, having heard enough of his problems, "we each must serve our country in our own way."

"Don't patronize me, Drummond. I was a major when you were in diapers."

"Very likely true," I admitted, now fully understanding exactly why the folks who ran West Point did not want Gilderstone to be on the same planet with a journalist. Aside from whatever he might say that contradicted the party line about Whitehall, he was a whiny, bitchy, disillusioned old man. If it were me, I too would order him to hide in the attic while I strutted some gung-ho hard-cock with a Ranger tab in front of the press.

I decided to cut to the chase. "So, Ed, what can you tell me about Tommy Whitehall?"

"Thomas? What can I say about Thomas? Simply that he's one of the most remarkable young men I ever met. Brilliant, poised, an extraordinary scholar, a great athlete. I tried to get him to go for a Rhodes Scholarship. Were you aware of that?"

"Really? A Rhodes? I had no idea. What happened?"

"Damned fool flatly refused," Gilderstone moaned. "A crying shame, too. The boy stood a good chance."

"No kidding? Why didn't he do it?"

"He said that even if he could get it, he didn't want to waste two more years at Oxford, feathering his résumé. That's how he put it. Can you imagine?"

"I don't get it," I said.

"He was in a hurry to get to the field with troops."

"So what's wrong with that?"

"The poor boy was brainwashed by all the gung-ho propaganda they pump into these impressionable young cadets up here. Troop officers are a dime a dozen. You're a lawyer; you know that. Thomas had so much more to offer. He was a vessel filled with so many remarkable talents. He could've come back here to teach."

One of the things you learn to do as a lawyer is listen real closely. It wasn't only *what* Gilderstone was saying, it was *how* he was saying it, like an ugly duckling describing a swan. There was a reason Ernie Walters had pointed me toward Gilderstone. That reason was beginning to grow legs, and hair, and warts.

Thinking I was being slick, I said, "So you were pretty fond of the kid, eh, Ed?"

For a very long time, Gilderstone did not answer. And I knew, after the first few seconds, that I'd underestimated him.

When he did speak, he erupted. "Drummond, there was nothing between us. Not a damn thing!"

"But Ed, who ever said there was?"

"I've already warned you, Drummond, don't patronize me. Is this why you called me? How'd you get my name? Did Thomas give it to you? Is this one of those witch hunts? What? They're promising leniency if he gives up some more gays in uniform? Is that what this is about?"

"Gilderstone, I couldn't give a rat's ass if you and Whitehall boffed each other in the commandant's bed. I'm just trying to figure him out. That's all. I'm trying to keep Whitehall out of the electric chair."

There was another long pause. Then, still sounding grouchy as hell, he insisted, "I never slept with him. Never!"

"I told you, Gilderstone, I don't give a damn."

"Then what is this about?"

"Information. Anything you say is confidential. That's on the record."

"Nothing will be attributed?"

"Not if you don't want it to, no."

"Well, I don't. Don't think me stingy, Drummond, but I'm not coming out of the closet for Whitehall. You need to agree to protect me."

It was damned hard to disguise my disgust. This contemptible old codger was sitting back in the nice comfortable little nest he'd built for himself at West Point, refusing to lift a finger for "the finest young man I ever met." I guess that's what happens to a guy who spends a lifetime hiding in shadows. Pretty soon he's got no more character than the shadow he's hiding behind.

Anyway, I simply said, "You got it."

"All right. Tell me what you want to know."

"To start with, did you know he was gay?"

"I suppose so, yes."

"You suppose so? You mean you never talked about it?"

"No, never. We . . . well, we gravitated toward each other, like two tourists in an alien land."

"Then how'd you know he was gay?"

"A sixth sense, I suppose. No, that's not completely true. You see, Drummond, when you're a gay soldier, you learn to act in a certain way, and you learn to detect the same act in others. I just looked at Thomas in class, around his peers. I knew."

"But you never talked about it? Never discussed it?"

"No, never. We both knew, though. Right off the bat, as they say."

"So you weren't his lover?"

"I already told you that. Why would I go near him? Do you have any idea what they'd do if they caught me?"

"Did he have a lover while he was there?"

"No. I'm nearly certain of it. West Point is . . . well, it's the holy temple of the Army. Whatever traditions or taboos you find in the Army, magnify them tenfold at this place. Thomas was remarkably self-disciplined. He was determined to make it through, too. He wasn't going to take unnecessary risks."

I decided to keep fishing. "What made him so damned determined?"

"What makes anybody determined? A deprived upbringing. Exacting parents. Virulent sibling rivalries. Overheated genes, maybe."

"Which of those was it with him?"

"How the hell should I know? I told you, he's very reserved. Mysterious even," he said, only now, instead of sounding bitter, he seemed wistful. "I never met his family, and he certainly never talked about them. They never even visited, to the best of my knowledge. Maybe that's a clue in itself."

"Okay. Now, do you think he could've slung a belt around the throat of his lover and strangled him?" I asked, deliberately putting a hard edge on it.

He didn't even hesitate. "Yes."

"Over what? Jealousy? Spite? Rage?"

"Nothing so tawdry, I assure you. As I said, he's exquisitely disciplined."

"Then what?"

Instead of answering, he asked, "Drummond, have you ever been in combat? Ever killed a man?"

Actually, before I became a lawyer, I'd spent five years as an infantry officer. In fact, I spent those five years in what the Army euphemistically calls a black unit, which means a unit so spectacularly clandestine its very existence is classified top-secret. The name of my particular unit was the "outfit," which was shorthand for the 116th Reconnaissance Squadron. But what we did had very little to do with reconnaissance, and a lot to do with counterterrorism during peacetime, and some fairly grisly, very hazardous things in wartime.

Gilderstone had no business knowing that, of course. I'd been in combat, though. Twice, in fact—in Panama and later in the Gulf. And I'd participated in a few interesting operations in between.

All I said was, "Yes," and left it at that.

"Me, too," he said. "A tour in Vietnam, a very long time ago. Until then, I'd never thought I could kill anyone. I thought I was above such primal savagery. I was too educated, too cultivated, too self-realized. Even when I got there, I thought I'd spend my tour with my M16 cradled in my arms, ordering others to kill. Of course it didn't turn out that way."

"No? How did it turn out?"

Instead of answering, he said, "Tell me about the first time you killed a man."

I didn't like this game, but since I was trying to coax him to trade confidences, I didn't see that I had any choice but to play along.

"Okay, Ed. An open-and-shut thing. I had to get my team into a facility, and there was this guard, and he was in the way, so I killed him."

"How?"

"That's a stupid question, Ed. I killed him. End of story."

"What weapon did you use?"

"A knife."

"Did you sneak up from behind him?"

"Yes, Ed, I snuck up behind him."

"Did you slap your hand over his mouth to keep him from yelling out?"

"That's right."

"Where'd you cut him?"

"What do you mean, where'd I cut him?" I asked, becoming exasperated by his ghoulish curiosity.

"Did you slice his throat open? Did you plunge the blade into his stomach? Into his heart? Into his back?"

"I put it in the lower part of his stomach. Okay?"

"And then you yanked it up?"

"Yes, of course."

"Why?"

"Why what?"

"Why'd you choose that particular killing thrust?"

"It's quick. It's foolproof."

"How so?"

"Because the stomach's soft tissue, Ed. Because there's no bones or ribs in the way. Because a strong upward thrust rips up a lot of vital organs, and tears open at least two major arteries."

"Was that a deliberate choice on your part?"

I said, "Ed, I'm getting tired of this."

"Was it?" he persisted.

"All right, yes. Why?"

"What were you thinking while he was dying?"

"I don't know," I lied, very irritated.

"Yes, you do know. What were you thinking?"

Now sounding grouchy myself, I said, "Look, Ed, I just want to know what would make Whitehall kill a guy. Drop the game."

He said, "You're standing just outside the facility. You've got one hand over his mouth, and with your other arm you're holding him erect. Your bodies are so close you can feel his heart racing. You can smell the gases escaping from his bowels. Your two heads are so near you can hear his last dying breaths, his muffled groans of pain. It's a very intimate moment. What were you thinking?"

"I was thinking the same thing I'm thinking about you. I just wished the stubborn bastard would get it over with. I needed to get my team into the facility, so he just needed to hurry up and die."

"Then you're a cold killer," Gilderstone said. "A paid assassin. I wasn't like that, Drummond. That's not the way it happened with me. I snapped. I exploded into a rage. I just ran into a bunch of underbrush and started killing indiscriminately, brazenly, wantonly. I still don't know what triggered it. I started killing everything in sight."

"That's nice," I said. "What's it got to do with Whitehall?"

"Know what I did afterward?" he asked, doggedly oblivious to my protests and proddings.

"Okay, Ed. What did you do afterward?"

"I looked around at all the people I killed. There were maybe a dozen corpses, I have to tell you. I threw up. Then I shot myself in the foot. Right then and there, I simply pointed my rifle at my shoe and fired three shots."

Being cute, I said, "That must've hurt like hell, Ed."

"Want to hear the funny part?"

"I didn't know there was a funny part," I said. I thoroughly disliked this man.

"I got a Distinguished Service Cross for my valorous actions. And I got a Purple Heart, and a trip home for the wounded foot."

I don't often go speechless, but I did. I was dumbfounded.

A Distinguished Service Cross is only a tiny sliver below the Medal of Honor. Edward Gilderstone was a war hero. A thoroughly flawed, conflicted, self-loathing one, but a genuine hero nonetheless. But hero or not, he was the kind of guy who was so puffed up on his own sanitized sense of self-worth that the realization he could be as ordinary, as feral, as murderous as the next guy drove him to self-mutilation. That's pretty nasty stuff, in my book.

More perplexing than that, though, here was a guy who'd earned his country's second highest decoration for valor, and he was too chickenshit to help an old student stay out of the electric chair. Some hero.

Thinking I was being sarcastic, I finally said, "Gee, Ed, that must've been some rage you flew into."

Still ignoring me, he replied in a very dry tone, "Thomas White-hall's not like you, Drummond. He's like me. He could snap and kill somebody, but afterward he'd show horrific effects from it. His conscience would eviscerate his whole being. So how does he appear to you? Like a man who's still coping with himself? Or a man who wants to shoot himself in the foot?"

This was the moment when I decided I'd had enough of Edwin Gilderstone and his bitter, sanctimonious words. I abruptly thanked him and hung up. I poured another cup of coffee and stood looking out the window, trying to piece all this together.

Neither Whitehall's college roommate nor his college mentor had hesitated or equivocated a bit—yes, Thomas Whitehall could easily kill somebody. That obviously wasn't what I'd hoped to hear. On the other hand, how good was their judgment?

Ernie Walters had the New Yorker's gift of gab, which always entails a degree of exaggeration. He wasn't lying, he was taking forty-five seconds and making it sound like a minute. But he'd lived with Whitehall two years, been his close personal friend for twelve, described him as virtually a brother, yet had never suspected his homosexuality. That's a fairly gaping miscalculation. A man's sexual character is an integral part of his larger character, of his earthly essence. Ernie Walters never had a clue.

Gilderstone had known about the homosexuality, but his misjudgments, if anything, went closer to the bone than Walters's. What I figured was that like lots of older men, Gilderstone saw Whitehall as a younger figure he wanted to transform into a burnished, tidier image of himself. That's what lay behind all that gibberish about untapped talents and Rhodes Scholarships. He wanted Whitehall to be his shadow, to follow in his footsteps. Maybe because he was gay and would have no children, he wished to sculpt one. He wanted Whitehall to be something more than a typical soldier, fighting and garrisoning his life away. Only Whitehall said no.

One thing I was learning about the world inhabited by military gays was that it could make for some fairly confused bedfellows. I mean, here was Ernie Walters, a thoroughly decent but straight guy who was getting his balls clipped every day because he'd once roomed with a gay. Still, he'd volunteered to step up and trade his career to help Whitehall. Then here was Ed Gilderstone, a gay man himself, who maybe loved Whitehall, who should've been sympathetic as hell, a fifty-three-year-old major whose military career was already a shambling wreck, who wasn't willing to make any effort to help his old student.

Maybe Gilderstone was the scarred product of the old days and

the old system. He'd been a teenager in the fifties and served in the
Army of the sixties; back in the days when "gay" still meant joyful,
and "homosexual" meant ridicule, disgrace, and ostracism. When a
man is forced to hide in a closet that long, I guess it can get pretty
dark and lonely.

It's what writers term an appalling irony. I call it frustrating as
hell.

But the most surprising thing I'd learned was that Whitehall
was actually a pretty good guy. Actually, unless Ernie Walters was a
complete fool, Whitehall was a great guy. And if Gilderstone was
right, then Whitehall should be showing terrific emotional effects
from the murder. I'd seen no signs of that.

Too bad I'd also learned my client was a boxer with concrete
fists driven by powerful pistons, and with a psychic trigger that
could drive him over the edge. He had the kind of power to shatter jaws and noses—certainly enough to cause the hideous bruising I'd seen on Lee's body.

CHAPTER
13

★ ★ ★

The sign over the door read HEADQUARTERS COMPANY, YONGSAN GARRI-SON. There was nothing distinctive about the building. It was just a musty old red-brick barracks built by the Japanese back when the Korean peninsula was a colony they'd collected from the Russo-Japanese War.

The Japanese had not been generous or merciful rulers. In fact, they'd been boneheadedly cruel, plundering Korea's resources and treating its people like slave laborers. They had even drafted a few thousand young Korean girls and shipped them off to troop broth-els all over Asia, where they forced them to perform as sex slaves for the emperor's warriors. As insults to other cultures go, that's pretty vile. The Koreans remembered it, too. Vividly, in fact.

I walked through the entrance and asked the first soldier I saw to direct me to the first sergeant's office. He gave this quick, fleet-ing look of disbelief and then pointed me to the third door down on the left, where a big green sign that read FIRST SERGEANT stuck out into the hallway.

And you wonder why enlisted troops think officers are such dopes.

When I entered the office, I found myself standing directly in front of a dark-haired specialist four. She was seated behind a gray metal desk and talking on the phone, shamelessly flirting with somebody on the other end. She got my attention right away. She was a bit too fleshy and her features were too big for her to be considered real attractive, but she'd make heads swivel; no doubt about that. One look and you got this instant vision of bedsheets and heavy breathing.

The Army's got fairly stiff rules against female soldiers making themselves too alluring and seductive. This woman didn't just violate them, she knocked them miles out of the ballpark with her puffed-up bouffant hairdo, a pair of big, flashy gold hoops that hung from her earlobes, and enough blush, lipstick, and rouge to paint the Berlin Wall. She was ferociously chewing what seemed to be a gigantic wad of gum.

"Hey, wait a moment," she mumbled, putting a hand over the mouthpiece, then skillfully using her tongue to wedge the gum to the side of her mouth.

I gave her a nice, warm, cheery smile. "I'd like to speak with your first sergeant, please."

She didn't reply. Or she *did* reply. Her shoulders arched back a bit, a gesture I recognized right away as a womanly attempt to get me to notice her uptoppers a bit better. They were big uptoppers, too; so big she really didn't need to waste any energy to draw attention to them. Even through her baggy battle dress, I could see that right nicely.

Having gotten my attention, she smiled a bit more encouragingly. "And could I know the nature of your business, Major?"

"I'm the attorney for Captain Whitehall."

"Captain Whitehall?"

"Yeah, Whitehall," I said, looking around like maybe I'd wandered into the wrong unit. "Isn't he the guy who used to command this company?"

"Yeah, that's right," she said, hanging up the phone without saying good-bye and then standing up. "Well, I'm sorry. The first sergeant's not in."

"Uh, okay. Thanks," I told her, getting ready to depart.

Then I changed my mind.

"Wait a moment, Specialist, uh . . ." To check her nametag, I had no choice but to gaze once again at that huge chest of hers, an act she made all too easy by very generously pushing it even closer to my face.

"Uh, Specialist Fiori," I finished.

She seemed to like that a lot. Her gum slipped back into the chewing position and her jaw started chomping again. She coyly asked, "There something I can do for you?"

"Well, maybe. Did you know Captain Whitehall?"

"Yes sir."

"Did you know him well?"

"I'd guess so. I was *his* clerk before . . . you know, everything happened."

"So, you what? You worked directly for him?"

She nodded and chewed her gum even more vigorously.

"How long?"

"Seven months. I sat right in his outer office. I was, uh, his girl Thursday. That's what he always called me."

"Thursday?" I said, scratching my head. "You mean Friday?"

"Uh, yeah. Whatever," she replied with a ditzy look.

Very foolishly, I said, "See, it's from this novel called *Robinson Crusoe*. Maybe you read that when you were young?"

"Nah," she said, chewing even harder. "Reading wasn't never my thing."

No, it probably wasn't.

I leaned up against her desk and got comfortable. So she leaned up against her desk and got even more comfortable—a little too much so, maybe. She ended up about six inches from me.

I said, "Did you like him?"

Her eyes started searching my face, like maybe she was wondering how to answer that. If she was looking for a clue, I didn't give her any.

She sucked on her tongue a moment, then said, "Okay, yeah, I liked him. A lot."

"Why'd you like him?"

"He was just a swell guy. Everybody liked him. At least, everybody respected him."

Amazing, I thought—almost word for word how Ernie Walters had phrased it.

"Okay," I said, "could you tell me why everybody liked, or at least respected him?"

"He was a good officer. Y'know, you work in a headquarters company like this, you see scads of officers. I mean, there's probably two hundred on our roll. No offense or nothin', but most of them are either jerks or wimps."

"That bad, huh? And I always thought officers were the crème de la crème."

"Huh?"

"You know, the pick of the litter," I said, and she still looked perplexed. "The best of the crop," I tried again, and her befuddled look only deepened.

Not only did she not read much, but her knowledge of French, hogs, and farming was sorely lacking.

"Yeah, whatever," she finally mumbled, like, Why was I torturing her with these complex issues? "Anyway, Captain Whitehall was different. He was real smart, y'know."

I couldn't escape the thought that this woman considered anybody who could tie their own shoes stratospherically intelligent.

Then after a thoughtful pause, she said, "And fair. He was always real fair."

"Now, you're sure you're not just saying that because you were his clerk?"

"No way. You wanta know the truth? Word's been put out *not* to say anything nice about the captain."

I pulled back and gave her a shocked look. "Really? No kidding? Who'd put out something like that?"

"Well, y'know, nobody ever announced it or anything. I mean, there's nothing official. It's what I hear, though. Y'know?"

Yes, I knew.

The Army, like most big organizations, has two channels of communications, and this clearly wasn't one of those instances where the first sergeant could simply draw all the troops into a formation and scream, "The first one of you jerk-offs who mutters a single nice thing about Whitehall will be cleaning the shitters for the rest of your Army career!" A more subtle method was used. They simply whispered the same message into the right sergeant's ear, and in seconds flat it was the talk of the latrine.

Anyway, I said, "But you thought he was a pretty good commander?"

"Hey, it isn't just me saying so," she insisted, pointing toward a tall trophy rack in the corner.

I looked over and there were some very old, badly corroded antiques neatly positioned on the two top shelves, and six gleaming, brand-spanking-new trophies near the bottom.

In peacetime, you can't win any battles—there aren't any—so the Army channels all that dormant martial energy into having units compete against one another for various distinctions. The competitions get pretty fierce and bloodthirsty, since they're the only way the overambitious can outshine their peers and get noticed doing it.

I was staring at six months' worth of trophies declaring Headquarters Company, Yongsan Garrison, to be the top unit in all of Korea.

Thomas Whitehall, it appeared, was a singularly energetic and competent officer. Of course, he'd *told* me he was the first time I'd met him. But you learn to discount that kind of stuff, because if there's one thing most officers get pretty good at, it's spit-shining their own asses.

I turned back to Specialist Fiori, who, while I wasn't looking, had somehow gotten herself fully up on top of her desk and into this strangely contorted position where her hips were twisted sideways, and her shoulders were slung back, and her breasts bulged tightly against her battle dress. If she were wearing a bikini, it would've been a glorious sight. Even in camouflage battle dress it had its righteous qualities.

And that's when I realized what a sly dog Tommy Whitehall really was. No wonder he'd planted her in his outer office. If she wasn't a full-blown nymphomaniac, she sure pulled off a lavish impersonation. That slick devil. She was the replacement for that girl's picture he'd kept on his desk back at West Point; his latest piece of camouflage.

I smiled at Specialist Fiori and thanked her for her honesty. She sucked in her lower lip, fluttered her eyelashes, and swiveled her shoulders in this sideways, provocative, swaying motion that made her uptoppers undulate like a couple of humongous sand dunes in a windstorm. She'd seen a few too many Marilyn Monroe movies, if you ask me.

"So, you're a lawyer?" she asked, licking her lips.

"Yep, that's right."

"Does that mean you get paid more than other officers?"

"Nope," I told her, making my way steadily toward the door. She only had time to give me one more sizzling glance before I made it to the safety of the hallway.

I rushed straight back to the hotel to see if there were any messages. But the moment I walked into the lobby, I ran smack into the middle of a large gaggle of men. They were mostly in line, getting checked in. There were probably fifty in all; some wore black-and-white collars and some didn't. By their noisy chatter, they sounded like a convention of southern rednecks. How very curious, I said to myself.

I artfully worked my way to the end of the line and stood behind a fleshy older gent, tall and rotund, who had nothing but some frizzy fuzz left on his big head. He looked like a big walking peach, nudging his bags forward with the tip of his foot as he inched up in line.

I bumped up against him and he spun around.

I winced and said, "Uh, gee, sorry. I hope that didn't hurt."

"Not at all, son," he responded in a syrupy, deep southern drawl that made it sound like "not'all, sun."

I grinned. "Well, welcome to Korea. This your first time here?"

"Actually, nope. I was here in '52, as a private, during the war."

"Place has sure changed, hasn't it?" I asked.

This was always a surefire opener to use with old Korean War vets. The last time they laid eyes on Korea it was nothing but shell-pocked farming fields that reeked literally of shit, and countless tiny, drab villages composed of thatched huts, and miserable, squalling people who couldn't rub two nickels together. Now it was cluttered with skyscrapers and shiny new cars and, believe me, more than a few billionaires.

"The Lord surely has wrought a miracle," he pronounced.

"Indeed he has. Is this some kind of returning vets' group?" I asked, nodding with my chin.

"Nope. We're all preachers and deacons."

"Aha!" I said to Preacher Peach. "I suppose, then, that you're all here for some religious convention?"

"Not actually, no. We're here 'bout this Whitehall thing. Y'know, that murderin' ho-mo-sex-u-al," Preacher Peach intoned, painfully stretching out every single vowel, like it was just so damned hard to force that particular noun through his lips.

"Uh-huh. I guess that makes sense."

"We've been invited by the Army," he said, obviously immensely proud of that.

"The Army? No kidding? What? They asked you to come over?"

"They sure did. See, we were in Washington, for the big march. You see that on TV over here?" he asked in such a tone that it sounded like, Hey, did you see me land on the moon?

"Uh, yeah, I did. Very impressive," I assured him.

"Yep. Well, we're the fellas who put all that together. Anyway, a group of us was asked to stop over at that Pentagon, and the Chief of the Staff of the Army, he asked us hisself if we wanted to come over. Even loaned us a plane. A real nice fella, you ask me."

"Well, ain't that really something," I remarked, slyly slipping into my own version of a bacon-and-grits brogue. "Mind if I ask, what's the Army expecting y'all to do over here?"

"Ah, well, there weren't no conditions nor nothin'. We're just here to represent the views of all good Christian 'Mericans," he said. "We're here to show the cross."

"You got any plans for how to show the cross?" I asked as offhandedly as I could manage, under the circumstances.

"You'll be seein' us around." He smiled and beamed, nudging his bag up another yard or so. Then he looked at the lawyer insignia on my collar, and his eyes moved down to my boots and back up again.

"Say, you're a lawyer, ain't you?"

"Yep," I admitted. "Worst thing in the Army to be. Dregs of the profession of arms."

"Uh-huh," he said, like from his experience that surely was true. "So, you got any opinion how this Whitehall devil's gonna fare in court?"

"Sure do," I announced.

"And what's that?" he asked. Immediately seven or eight more of his preacherly brethren turned around to hear what I might say.

This was what you might call a golden moment. I mean, no way it was going to be a good thing having a bunch of fired-up, overzealous preachers demonizing our client. The environment was already poisonous enough. Besides which, the only leverage we had over the Korean government was its fear that American public opinion might be on our side. We didn't want anybody creating the impression that fear was unfounded.

I put on my most lawyerly expression and recklessly announced, "I think he's gonna get off."

His chin flew back and his big beefy jowls shivered like poked Jell-O. "Get off? Now, how could that boy get off? He was sleeping right next to the corpse. His own belt was wrapped around that child's neck. And his devil's fluids were inside."

His explosion was so loud that nearly twenty of the preachers and deacons began gathering in a knot around us, collectively eavesdropping on every word. There were more than a few apprehensive faces. The last thing they wanted was to publicly vilify a man who might subsequently be found innocent. How could they ever return home and look their flocks in the eye?

"Look, there aren't many lawyers over here, and y'all know how us lawyers love to talk, right? Rumors fly around pretty thick."

"That right?" another preacher stepped forward to ask. This one was a few years younger than Preacher Peach, and leaner, and weathered in that tough, parched, dried-out way some southerners get. He had hard eyes, too. What my mother used to call brimstone eyes. He would be Preacher Prick, I decided.

I said, "Well, I hear things."

Preacher Prick's neck shot forward an inch or two. "So what you hearin', son?"

"That maybe the police didn't do such a thorough job. They might've jumped to conclusions a bit, if you get my meaning."

"Nope," he said. "Don't get your meaning at all."

"Well, I'm only going on rumors now, but the word is the Korean police rushed into that apartment and messed up the scene of the crime something terrible. Contaminated the evidence, shoved around the witnesses. Also, given who died and all—if you'll excuse my language—they were getting their nuts squeezed something awful to name a suspect. Any suspect, even if meant cramming a square peg into a round hole."

The lids on Preacher Prick's tight eyes screwed down even tighter, until all there were were two thin black slits, and the part of his face beneath his nose started moving around, like he was chewing something hard with his lips.

"Don't say?" he asked, craning his neck forward dubiously.

"Just what I hear," I replied, glancing at my watch, as though I suddenly remembered I had some drastically important appointment.

He drew his shoulders together a bit, and in a voice loud enough for everyone to hear, said, "Son, 'fore we all dedicated ourselves to this lofty task, we got briefed by some two-star general back in the Pentagon. He went over every last detail about this case. Accordin' to him, now, that Whitehall boy's guilty as hell. He says he ain't got a rat's chance of gettin' off. Them's his words."

I suddenly tasted a rush of bile slithering up my throat. I swallowed it, though, and struggled to appear normal.

"Ah, well," I said, "and would you happen to remember that general's name? I mean, even generals sometimes get these things wrong. And he'd be back in Washington, wouldn't he? And we're out here, on the forward frontier of justice, aren't we? Besides, he ain't a lawyer, is he? So what's he know?"

"I can't recall the man's name," Preacher Prick frankly admitted, scratching his head a bit. Then he quickly said, "I mean, there was a whole room full of generals when he was talking. He was a lawyer, though, just like you. 'Ceptin', he's like the head lawyer, so I expect he knows what he's talkin' about."

The smile disappeared from my face. Then, since I'd already made a horse's ass of myself, I glanced down at my watch again and said, "Holy cow, look at the time! I gotta get going."

Preacher Peach smiled benignly, while Preacher Prick stared at my nametag like it was a name he meant to remember, and maybe even check up on.

I rushed straight to the elevator and up to my room. I was so furious, I could barely see straight. I lifted up the phone and gave the operator the number in Washington. A few seconds passed before Clapper's administrative assistant, a captain with the silly name of William Jones, answered.

Trying to contain my rage, I choked out, "Drummond here. Let me talk to the general. Put the bastard on right now!"

Somehow or another, Captain Jones detected I was miffed.

"Major Drummond," he said, in the calmest, most reasonable voice imaginable, "perhaps I should offer you some advice. You really might want to cool down, and call back later."

To which I replied, "Jones, put me through right away or I swear I'm gonna climb on the next flight out of here and come kill you."

"Uh, yeah, sure," he answered, quite wisely deciding that his definition of duty did not require him to get trapped in the middle of whatever was happening here.

A moment later, Clapper, all warm and bubbly, said, "Hello, Sean. What can I do for you?"

"What can you do for me?" I screamed. "Jesus Christ! I just ran into a lynching party made up of cornpone preachers. They claimed the Chief of Staff of the Army invited them over here."

"Now, settle down, Sean. It's not like you make it sound."

"No?" I replied. "Okay, listen closely to this, because I mean it exactly like it sounds. I am formally advising you that I'm considering filing an immediate motion to have this case dismissed. You'd better have a damned good excuse for this."

He didn't skip a beat. "The Chairman of the Joint Chiefs thought it might be a good idea if the Army tried to reach out to the southern religious community. While our position with regard to Whitehall is completely neutral, we can't afford to antagonize the religious right."

"You're shittin' me!"

"Did you know some forty percent of Army recruits come from the South? That's almost half the Army's enlisted strength. Hell, forty-five percent of the officer corps are southerners. I'm from Tennessee myself. And we nearly all fit into one profile. We're nearly all dyed-in-the-wool, corn-fed, red-white-and-blue Baptists and Methodists. Do you have any idea what'll happen to our recruiting statistics if these preachers take to the lecterns and start speaking out against military service? They very easily could, too. They'll get up and start talking against the immoral and godless policy of gays serving in the ranks, and before you know it, you'll swear service in the Army is the same thing as leasing a condo in Sodom and Gomorrah. You know us southern boys, Sean. When our mamas and our preachers talk, we sit up and listen. Christ, there won't be any Army left to join. Believe me, they've got us by the short hairs."

"How about you briefing them on the particulars of this case? Is that true?"

"It was perfectly aboveboard. They insisted on being briefed before they all climbed on an airplane to spend the next two weeks away from their churches. All I did was assure them the trial would go off as scheduled. I hardly told them anything."

"Is that right?"

"I simply went over a few things they could as easily have read in the newspapers. I disclosed nothing confidential. I said nothing that isn't public knowledge."

"Gee, General, now I'm thoroughly baffled. See, those preachers swore you said Whitehall's guilty as hell, that he hasn't got a rat's chance of getting off. Your words exactly, according to them."

Now here's where you have to understand that there's this list of cosmically dumb things you can do in the Army, and right near the top is catching a two-star general in a full-blown, bald-faced lie. You can *suspect* a general is lying, you can even *know* a general is lying, but to actually *acknowledge* that fact, to his face, falls under the heading of more than stupid: It's like putting a gun to your own head.

Then again, there are exceptions to every rule—like when you can file a motion to get this case dismissed, and get the general a front-cover picture on *TIME* magazine that will ruin his career, his life, and his reputation. In instances like that you can say you balled his wife last night and odds are all he'll do is grin and ask how it was.

And Clapper was no dummy. He knew that, too.

Sounding very legalistic, he said, "As I recall, I was answering a question, off the record. And to the best of my recollection, I caveated that response by clarifying this was only a personal reflection, not my professional opinion."

When you hear those golden words, "as I recall," and "to the best of my recollection," and all the rest of that specious gobbledygook, especially from the lips of a trained lawyer, you know you've got a guilty scoundrel by the balls.

I said, "Know what really pisses me off about this?"

"No, Sean, what really pisses you off?" Clapper asked, struggling to sound affable.

"I know the guy probably did it, but I still can't stomach it being done this way. He deserves every chance of squirming out of it everybody else gets."

"And he'll get that, Sean. He'll have a fair trial in front of an impartial board. You can voir dire anybody off that board you don't like."

I hung up on him. I was suddenly sick of listening to him. He and the rest of the Army were stacking the deck against Whitehall, who might even deserve it, only it was wrong, and unethical. I was tired of hearing soldiers tell me they'd been told not to say anything nice about Whitehall; and the State Department trying to trade him like a piece of rotten meat; and learning the Army had handpicked its most viciously successful prosecutor and a military judge who thought he worked for the prosecuting attorney. And now I was tired of preachers telling me the Army had actually flown them over here to publicly pillory my client.

What really fried me was that comment from Katherine about how I had no idea how my side played, and I'd stubbornly insisted she was wrong. Well, she wasn't wrong. That, I really hated. That, I hated more than anything.

As it was, I now faced one of those head-splitting moral dilemmas Professor Maladroit used to pontificate about. Based on what Preacher Peach and Preacher Prick had told me downstairs, I probably had a shot at getting this case thrown out. I could file a motion and ask the judge to hold an inquest to determine what the chief of the JAG Corps really told those preachers. Then, poof! Thomas Whitehall might walk out a free man.

Not an innocent man—a free man.

The South Koreans would of course go so insanely crazy with rage they'd probably throw every last American trooper off the peninsula.

The Army would reassign me to be chief counsel on some Aleutian island nobody had ever heard of—and leave me there till the next ice age.

My client, who was possibly a murdering, raping necrophiliac, would adore me.

Katherine would send me Christmas cards the rest of my life.

I'd hate myself forever.

These were all the points I listed in my head as I tried to reason through this. Although I shouldn't have been the least bit ambivalent, because, technically, there was no debate. It was open and shut. I was supposed to immediately inform my co-counsels and my client of everything I'd just discovered. That was the right and proper thing to do. That was the legally ethical thing to do. It even happened to be the expedient thing to do.

Of course, I wasn't about to do any such thing.

Some lawyers believe in winning any way they can. It isn't

about guilt or innocence—it's about winning no matter what it takes. I don't happen to be one of them.

Clapper had foolishly created an *impression* of command influence in this case that would be impossible for any military judge to ignore. But were Clapper's remarks to some bunch of preachers really prejudicial to Whitehall's fate?

Of course not. On the other hand, it wouldn't hurt to let Clapper sweat. It might even be helpful.

CHAPTER
14

I went to the hair parlor to see Katherine. Bedlam reigned: Phones were ringing, the clerks were jumping around taking messages, referring calls, scribbling and passing notes. The amazon and the grump were hunched over the fax machine frenziedly shoving papers through the slot and looking like a pair of hens with their tails on fire.

I ignored them and even Imelda, who glowered at me as I walked by. I guess she was pissed that I'd cold-shouldered her these past few days. Hey, what the hell? She'd betrayed me, right? She'd chosen her lot. Didn't she know they were all gay?

Anyway, I went straight into Katherine's office. She was on the phone; she shot me a distracted look and kept right on talking. I planted myself in the chair in front of her desk. I wasn't going anywhere.

Finally she hung up. "Well?"

"I've got some very bad news."

"This isn't about the religious delegation, is it?" She waved a dismissive hand through the air.

"You mean you already know about them?" I asked, surprised.

"Drummond, I knew about them five days ago. I knew about them before they even walked into the Pentagon to get briefed."

I got instantly suspicious. "Bullshit. How?"

"OGMM. They keep me informed of things I need to know."

"Is that so?"

She leaned back in her chair and ran a hand through that long, luxurious hair of hers, as she apparently weighed whether or not I was worthy to be entrusted with this knowledge.

"This stays between us, right?"

This was Katherine Carlson. Before I agreed to anything so open-ended, I said, "It doesn't involve breaking any laws, does it?"

"Come on, Drummond. If I was breaking laws, think I'd admit it? To you, of all people?"

She had a good point. I simply shrugged.

She leaned toward me. "Do you have any idea what OGMM does? How it works? What it is?"

I didn't, actually, though I wasn't going to admit that. Not to Miss Always Number One in the Class, anyway. "Of course I know," I said with a facial expression and arm gesture intended to imply supreme confidence. "It's one of those nonprofits that gets oodles of money from guilty-feeling rich liberals and gays, right?"

"Partly right. From a funding angle, anyway. But OGMM's unique from other gay rights groups. It was formed by gay service-members themselves. It was set up as a secret organization—secret in existence and secret in membership. Put simply, its purpose is to protect gays who want to serve their country without having their rights violated."

"Only it's not secret any longer, right?"

"Its existence isn't, no. It came out of the closet in '91 when the big debate erupted. However, the identities of its members remain closely guarded. Since all the active members are on active or re-serve duty, they can hardly afford to be identified as card-carrying members without betraying their orientation. Then there's the in-active rolls made up of veterans."

"So how big is it?"

She smiled. "You wouldn't believe me."

"Try me."

"Four hundred thousand members. Give or take a few."

"Did I hear that right?"

"That's right, Drummond. Most are veterans, sort of like a gay VFW, if you will. Some go all the way back to the days before the Second World War. The oldest living member served in World War One."

"And how many are still on duty?"

"About twenty-five thousand at the latest count."

It suddenly struck me what I was hearing. "You're telling me . . . what? You've got twenty-five thousand gays on duty right now? And these people . . . they, uh, they keep OGMM informed of things?"

She looked like the Cheshire cat who'd just swallowed the Cheshire canary. "You'd be surprised what we know and how quickly we learn it. We even have generals and admirals on the rolls. A few in very important positions, too. Last time I checked, about seven thousand of the active members are officers."

I couldn't believe what I was hearing. This was fantastic—like having an army of twenty-five thousand spies in uniform. You'd never know if you were talking with one, or sitting next to one in a meeting, or standing beside one at a Pentagon urinal—even in the general officers' latrine, apparently. They were invisible.

"This is outrageous," I blurted. "It's a large-scale conspiracy. I mean, it's espionage on an almost unimaginable scale," because, really, that was what it sounded like.

"Don't be overdramatic, Drummond. These people aren't giving OGMM the details of the global war plan. Nothing they disclose is classified. They simply call OGMM whenever they see or over-hear something that infringes on their rights. They're not disloyal, either. They're completely loyal to their own sexuality, and they're convinced they're defending the Constitution they've sworn to defend. They are, too, believe me."

"But they're breaking the law," I stammered.

"Yeah? Name a law they're violating."

I needed a moment to consider that one. I mean, there was something horribly wrong about this. I just knew there was—there had to be. I searched my memory banks of laws and precedents. I spent probably twenty seconds doing that while she sat and watched me with a look of amusement. As far as I could tell, though, she was right—if they weren't exposing classified information, they weren't breaking any laws.

Then it hit me.

"Aha!" I said, convinced I'd just found the fatal wrinkle in her argument. "How about when they have to list what organizations they belong to? Every single recruit has to admit that on the recruiting questionnaire. And to get a security clearance you've got to do it again."

"Good point," she said. "Except that since it's public knowledge that OGMM is composed of gay people, that means the mere admission they belong to OGMM is synonymous to admitting they're gay, right?"

"So?"

"And under 'don't ask, don't tell,' it's illegal to ask, right?"

"But they *are* being asked, Carlson. That's the point. And if they don't list it, they're lying on an official questionnaire. That's breaking the law."

"Come on, Drummond—I thought you were a lawyer. What happens if you try to enforce an unconstitutional law? It's the same as no law at all, right?"

I weakly countered, "That's circuitous logic."

And she smiled. "Circuitous logic? So? Isn't that what law is all about? It's the perfect catch-22. We didn't invent it. We're simply taking advantage of it."

I was still hung up on my misgivings about this, but as much as I hated to admit it, she did seem to have a point. It was exactly the kind of clever loophole lawyers are hired to find.

"Okay," I grumbled, not willing to verbally acknowledge her victory, and therefore struggling to move on. "So OGMM called and warned you about these preachers?"

"There's a clerk in the outer office of the Chairman of the Joint Chiefs of Staff who happens to be one of his most trusted assistants. He considers her like a daughter. She's been with him since he was a brigadier general. His heart would break if he knew she was a lesbian."

"You're shitting me."

"It's the truth," she said, smiling. "She was the one who actually typed up the memo that asked the Chief of Staff of the Army to meet with these preachers and invite them over here in the first place."

My mind was reeling. This was a lot to take in. Finally I said, "So what do you think about these preachers?"

If I didn't mention it before, one of the scariest things about Carlson is how incredibly fast she shifts moods. Before I could blink an eye, her smile vanished and was replaced by a snarling war mask.

"They're the most dangerous threat we've faced yet."

"Huh?" I was completely taken aback. "You've got to be kidding. Some bunch of overweight old southern hicks. How much damage can they do?"

I had misgivings about them, too, but the most dangerous threat we'd faced yet? Give me a break.

She leaned back in her chair and assumed this slightly superior air. "Look, Drummond, I know you find this difficult to accept, but we're engaged in a war. It's like the civil rights struggle of the fifties and sixties. These preachers, they're the most potent weapon the bigots and homophobes possess. They're the atomic weapons of the antigay side."

I gave her a disbelieving look like I just knew she was over-stating things. Because she was. Plus I knew it would piss her off. And it did.

She wagged an angry finger in my face. "Don't you dare give me that look. I'm not exaggerating. They preach the worst kind of in-tolerance. They preach that homosexuals are sinful perverts, un-natural creatures, depraved seducers. They're no different than the Catholic priests of the medieval era ordering their followers to burn witches and unbelievers at the stake. How can people listen to them? Just look how often they've been proven wrong—Galileo, Columbus, Scopes. Why do people believe them? If any other institution had been proven wrong on so many fundamental questions, it would be a laughingstock. It's astonishing."

"Katherine," I said, in a deliberately condescending way, "you're way too rabid on this. Like it's some kind of no-holds-barred war. It ain't to me. I'm a lawyer. We'll probably lose, and if we do, I'll just drink a beer, and maybe feel bad for a day or so, then start getting ready for the next court case."

Okay, maybe I was exaggerating a bit, but her response was way out of proportion. It seemed I'd really whacked her unfunny bone, because she looked at me like I was the lowest thing she ever saw. Every bit of angelicism fled from her features. She actually turned this deep, dark shade of red, like there was a fire burning beneath her skin.

"Get out!" she said, coldly, controlled, but clearly on the verge of screaming.

I shrugged nervously. "Hey, don't take it personally."

"Get out, right now! I don't want to see your face."

I momentarily considered defying her, but one of the things I've learned in life is that when a woman's angry at you, neither logic nor reason have a chance of prevailing. Like a vacuum sucks air from a room, a woman's fury sucks every bit of rationality from a situation. I therefore did the only wise thing I could. I swiftly got lost.

It didn't help that Imelda grazed me with another sizzling look when I passed by. Grumpy and the amazon stared at me, too, and they didn't look real pleased to see me, either.

I suddenly realized something here. I was sexually stranded, isolated, alone. I was the only straight lawyer, for one thing. I was also the only male left on the defense team. Well, there was Keith, but he was in a coma (which I vaguely envied), so that left only me.

I went back to my room and turned on CNN again. I was sort of idly watching out of the corner of my eye while I relaxed on the bed and tried to think through my next step, when I caught a quick glimpse of Michael T. Barrone, one of those flashy, thirtysomething megabillionaires who'd made more money than God by being one of the early Internet pioneers. I don't know why, because megabillionaires normally bore me to tears, but I turned up the sound.

"That's right," Barrone was saying to some hidden interviewer.

"I did contribute the money. And I'll keep contributing money until they tell me it's enough."

The interviewer's voice said, "You're a businessman, Mr. Barrone. And right now, this is a very unpopular cause. The Southern Religious Leaders Conference is calling for a boycott against your company. Aren't you afraid it will harm your business?"

Barrone's face got very steely. "The hell with my business. OGMM asked me for the money, and I'm only too damned pleased to give it to them. What's happening here is wrong. I've got gay employees . . . Everybody does. I'm putting my money where my principles are."

Then Michael Barrone evaporated into thin air, replaced by a shot of several hundred Americans in the cavernous lobby of what looked to me to be the Shilla Hotel, one of the swankest inns in all of Korea.

A female voice, struggling to sound dramatic, was saying, "And so, three more planeloads of gay activists arrived in Seoul today, adding to the three that landed last night, and three more are expected tomorrow, adding a new twist to what has already proven to be the most dramatic military court case in many decades. This is Sandra Milken, reporting live in Seoul."

I fell back hard and cursed loudly. The effect was lost, because Carlson couldn't hear me, and the cursing was directed entirely at her.

She wanted a cultural war, and by God she was going to have one. This had to be her idea, her response to all these preachers. And believe me, it was a fantastically awful idea.

You don't import a few hundred angry, screaming American homosexuals to Korea, of all places, and expect things to work out. She was courting the worst kind of calamity and grief.

CHAPTER
15
★ ★ ★

Chief Warrant Officer Three Michael Bales could not have been more amiable or polite. He smiled so hard it was a miracle he didn't break his face. He shook hands with holy fury and said "pleased to meet you" like he really, really meant it. He invited me into his office, offered me a seat, brought me coffee, asked me how I was doing, how I liked Korea, how I liked the accommodations at the hotel, and so on, and so on.

As performances go, it was a doozy; about what you'd expect from a professional cop who knows the way things are. See, Bales, being an experienced CID investigator, knew that he and I were on a collision course. He was the investigator who broke the case. He was the chief witness for the prosecution. He was the linchpin to every iota of evidence that pointed at my client.

He was going to end up on a witness stand where Carlson or I were going to try our best to bend him over backward and slip him the willie. We had to prove he was an incompetent bungler, the damned fool who messed up the evidence, jumped to conclusions, mishandled the witnesses, overlooked things that would exonerate my client, and just generally dicked it up.

This was inevitable. He knew it and I knew it. Any attorney representing a seemingly guilty client has no other option but to attack the credibility of the key prosecution witness.

That's why he was turning on the charm. As we say in the Army, he was presetting the conditions of the battlefield.

The moment I laid eyes on him, I silently cursed. Young, maybe thirty-five or so, dark-haired, strong-featured, with pleasant, pale blue eyes and a benevolent, engaging smile. Unlike most CID guys, who dress horribly, he wore a finely cut gray pinstripe suit with a plain white, freshly starched cotton shirt and a simple striped tie. Lord Fauntleroy he wasn't, but he looked dapper enough. Worse, he seemed competent and damned handsome in a very earnest, midwestern, likable way.

Here's why this was bad. Court-martial boards are as susceptible to appearances as anybody else. In fact more so. They're trapped in their chairs ten hours a day with nothing to do but observe the main actors. They watch and they listen, and they watch and listen some more, and they form opinions. And military men and women, just because of the screwy way they are, are more swayed by appearances than just about anybody else.

I would've been much happier if Bales was a middle-aged, balding guy with grungy teeth, a hefty beer gut, scuffed-up shoes, and a plaid sport coat and striped trousers. At least then, when I tried to persuade the board that he'd been criminally negligent, they'd look at Bales, and say to themselves, "Yep, I could see that."

Anyway, Bales got done with his pleasant routine, and we sat and stared at each other like a bull and matador.

Then I broke the ice. "So, Chief, I've read your statements, and, as you might imagine, I've got a few questions."

"Yes sir," he said, perfectly straight-faced. "I thought you might."

"Right. Question one, then. When you first got to Whitehall's apartment building, exactly how many South Korean police were there?"

Suspecting I was up to something clever, he paused, appeared thoughtful, then said, "To the best of my recollection, perhaps twenty."

"Perhaps twenty, huh? Does that mean you don't exactly know how many?"

Again, he appeared thoughtful. He said, "That's correct, Major. I don't know exactly how many."

"Pardon me for asking again. I just want to be clear on this point. You don't know how many Korean police officers were at the apartment building?"

He looked at me very steadily. Crime scenes are supposed to be tightly controlled, almost hermetically sealed. From reading his and Sergeant Wilson Blackstone's earlier statements, I already had some fairly strong suspicions that things had gotten out of hand. Now I had the feeling I was getting that big break—the stuff we defense attorneys dream about.

He said, "No."

"Then you have no idea who passed in and out of that crime scene? Is that right?"

Without blinking, he said, "I didn't say that."

"No? Well, that's what I asked you."

"No, you asked me how many Korean police officers were at the apartment building—and that, I don't know. There were two guarding the front entrance of the building when I arrived, but they might've put more there after I went upstairs—I don't know. There may have been some guarding the rear entrance—I don't know. Then there were three or four in the hallway leading into Captain Whitehall's apartment. There might've been more—I don't know."

He paused and examined my face. "But if you want to know how many entered Captain Whitehall's apartment, that I know for a fact."

"You do?"

"Sure. Sergeant Blackstone and I followed standard procedures. He and his partner arrived at the scene right on the tails of the South Korean police. They took the name of every police officer who entered the apartment. A control log was maintained, IDs were checked, and every visitor who entered was escorted."

"Funny, I saw no mention of that in either of your statements."

"You wouldn't, though, would you? We never list all the procedural things we do at crime scenes."

If I didn't know better, I might almost have suspected at this point that Bales had been playing with me, leading me on, then maliciously slamming the door on my nose. Maybe he was sending me a warning not to get too cocky or abrasive in the courtroom or he'd find some sly way to make me pay for it. If that was his game, it worked.

Anyway, I tried to appear unruffled as I said, "In your statement, you mentioned that when you arrived at the scene, you encountered Sergeant Blackstone arguing with Inspector Choi. Could you explain what that argument was about?"

"Sure. Just some standard jurisdictional issues. No big thing."

"Like what?"

"Like who was responsible for gathering and tagging the evidence. Like who should interview the witnesses."

"And these issues were resolved?"

"Certainly. Inspector Choi's a very professional and reasonable man. He's also an old hand. This wasn't the first time he'd had GIs commit crimes inside his beat."

"So what was the resolution?" I asked.

"His guys would bag and tag, and handle the autopsy. Our guys would handle the interrogations. Choi didn't have any problem with it, either. I think Sergeant Blackstone got a little overbearing and it rubbed him a little wrong. We got it straightened out."

"Uh-huh," I said. "So it was more a personality thing than a substantive thing?"

"That's how I'd describe it, yes."

"Were you comfortable having the Koreans handle the evidence?"

"Sure. Why not?"

"Well, you and I both know there are very distinct differences between Korean and American rules of evidence. Nor are Korean police taught to handle evidence the same way ours are."

He rubbed his jaw like this was the first time he'd ever heard such a thing and he needed a moment to think about it. He was very convincing. If I didn't know better, I would almost have believed it.

Finally, he said, "Well, to be frank, there probably are a few tiny procedural differences, but I can't think of any that would have a germane impact on this case. Can you?"

This was another very crafty move on his part, because I was obviously on a fishing expedition and he wasn't about to help me put the worm on the hook.

But to show him that two could play this game, all I said was, "I might have a few ideas, but I'll save them for later."

He blinked once or twice, but that was all.

I said, "Did you get a look at the lock on the front door?"

"I did."

"The crime summary states that the lock had not been jimmied or tampered with. Who made that judgment? And how can you be so sure?"

Bales said, "Look, Major, the Koreans are sparing no resources on this case. They brought in an inspector named Roh, a burglary guy they flew up from Taegu, because he's considered their foremost national expert on locks. I was there when he checked it. And I learned more about picking locks in that thirty minutes than I learned in ten hours at CID school. He disassembled it and carried it back to the lab so he could inspect every little piece under a microscope, then ran it all through radioactive testing, checking for dents or abrasions, or a scarred tumbler, any telltale signs somebody had tampered with it. There weren't any. By the way, we also learned it was a brand-new lock, installed by the management company the day Captain Whitehall moved in. You can try to challenge Inspector Roh's judgment if you want, but he sure as hell convinced me."

I paused to perform a swift mental inventory. I knew from reading Bales's written statements that he'd performed all the proper rituals when he'd interrogated Whitehall, Moran, and Jackson. He'd read them their rights, never coerced or threatened them, and performed what appeared to be a model interrogation. I now knew there had been proper police controls at Whitehall's apartment. I now knew the Korean doctor who performed the autopsy was an exceptionally competent pathologist. And I'd just learned that a national expert had checked the lock.

These were not hopeful signs. Where before I thought I had detected a few cracks, I now saw a blank white wall. There was only one more venue left.

"Chief, how did you get Moran and Jackson to testify against Whitehall?"

A look of impatience crossed his face. "Don't you all talk with each other?"

"Don't who all talk with each other?"

"You and that lady, Miss Carlson."

"What do you mean?"

"She asked almost exactly the same questions. Her and some guy in a nice suit named Keith something. A week ago. So I'll give you the same answer I gave them. I don't know why Moran and Jackson confessed. They lied and misled me in the initial interrogation, then after they were charged they experienced a change of heart."

"Uh-huh," I mumbled, trying to recover from the discovery that Katherine and Keith had already interviewed Bales. This was news to me. She'd never mentioned a word.

Anyway, I continued. "So what did you initially charge Moran and Jackson with?"

"Moran we charged with murder, rape, sodomy, committing homosexual acts, conspiracy to commit murder, conspiracy to obstruct justice, lying under oath, failure to obey orders, fraternization, violation of his general orders—"

"Stop! That's enough," I barked. "And Jackson?"

"All of the above. Well, except rape or sodomy. In his case, there was no inkling of evidence to support those two charges."

I should've expected this. An old lawyer's dictum has it that most divorces are unruffled and amicable until the attorneys get on the scene. So it goes with conspiracies as well.

What CID and the command had done was an old and reliable favorite—the junkyard dog strategy where you pile every imaginable charge on the shoulders of the co-conspirators, knowing damn well that if enough mud is thrown against the wall, something is bound to stick. Then, when Whitehall, Moran, and Jackson went fearfully to seek the advice of counsel, their lawyers probably took one worried glance at the nearly infinite list of charges and recognized that inevitably their client was going to be found guilty of *something*. And since lawyers instinctively advise their clients to act in the most selfish manner possible, they would immediately advocate a deal with the prosecutor. The odd man out in these things is always the man who has the most to lose, which in this case means the man who has the most incriminating evidence against him on the most serious charge—which in this case pertains to the charge of committing murder.

In other words, Thomas Whitehall never stood a chance.

I said, "Who cut the deal with the lawyers?"

"I did. With the permission of the commanding general, of course."

"Of course," I dryly observed. "And who might have handled this affair for the commanding general?"

"His legal adviser, a gentleman named Colonel Janson."

For some odd reason that came as no surprise either.

"And can you tell me, Chief, what have the charges against Moran and Jackson been reduced to?"

"You could easily check it yourself, so I suppose there's no harm in telling you. Committing homosexual acts."

"That's it?"

"That's it," he sheepishly replied.

I politely thanked him for his time, then stood up and got ready to leave. He sat calmly, and I'll give him credit for this—he didn't appear the least bit smug or elated. He had every right to be, but he didn't show it. It's a damned good feeling to be sitting on top of an airtight case.

It's awfully damned depressing when you're on the other side.

CHAPTER
16

★ ★ ★

The red message light was blinking incessantly when I returned to my room. I punched in the code and Edwin Gilderstone's voice angrily shrieked to call him right away.

It was after midnight in New York, but Gilderstone sounded way too alert and poised to have been sleeping. I said, "Hi, Ed, it's Drummond."

He instantly screamed, "You lying bastard!"

"That's me," I admitted, though I was sure my parents would've sternly objected to my conceding that second point.

"You promised this was just between us."

"And so it is, Ed. I haven't said a word to anyone, not even my co-counsels. What's the problem?"

"The problem? What's the damned problem? I'm being followed."

"Followed by *who?*"

"I don't know. When people are trailing you, they don't walk up and say, 'Hi, I'm John Smith from CID and I'll be following you the next few days,' do they?"

"So you think it's CID?" I asked.

"I just told you I don't know who they are. Aren't you listening?"

"I'm listening, Ed. I'm just trying to sort through this. What makes you *think* you're being followed?"

There was a brief pause and I could hear him draw in a deep breath, like he was trying to compose himself. "This morning, I went to the Post Exchange to buy toiletries, and as I left the academic hall a gray sedan pulled in behind me. It followed me the whole way to the PX. Later, when I went out for lunch, the same gray sedan followed me again."

"Ed, I don't mean to be argumentative, but couldn't it just be a coincidence? West Point's not New York City. It's a small community, right? It really wouldn't be odd to have the same car going to the same place you're going to twice in the same day."

"Drummond," he said.

"Yes?"

"I warned you before, don't condescend to me. Of course I considered that. Except the same gray sedan is parked halfway down the block right now. It's one o'clock in the morning. I see two heads silhouetted every time another car passes."

I supposed he had a point. "So you're being followed. What makes you think I've got something to do with it?"

"Come on, Drummond. Yesterday you called to talk about Whitehall."

"Look, I told you I wouldn't say anything. I haven't. I have no idea why you're being followed. Maybe you brought it on yourself. Maybe it's some guy you had an affair with and he's still pining for you."

That brought on a nasty chuckle. "Fuck off, Drummond."

"Okay," I conceded. "But I haven't uttered a peep to anybody."

We chatted a moment longer, him still accusing, and me maintaining my innocence. We finally hung up on each other.

Of course I had something to do with his being followed. My mind turned to that snarling son of a bitch with the colonel's leaves named Menkle, from the registrar's office. He knew I'd spoken with Gilderstone. Maybe he sicced somebody on him.

But what was the point of trailing Gilderstone? And if the followers were pros, they would never have been sloppy enough to get spotted, especially by a rank amateur. Unless they were either bungling amateurs themselves, or they were pros who meant to be seen. Assuming they were pros, why would they do that? To harass him, of course. But why harass some old gay who was on the verge of retirement anyway? Spite? Or were they trying to muzzle him?

I rolled that one around the noggin for a while and had a sudden impulse. I pulled my pocketknife from my pocket and pried open the ear and mouthpiece on my telephone. It was the only other possibility I could think of.

I was in such a hurry, I trashed the hotel's phone so badly I was going to have to add it to my room bill.

I wasn't worried about that, though. What I was *really* worried about was the little tiny black thing, hardly bigger than a ladybug, that was stuck inside the earpiece.

During my time with the outfit, I'd had instruction on electronic listening and tracking devices. I wasn't an expert by any means, and the technology had changed radically the past seven or eight years, what with miniaturization and digitization and whatnot, but I still recognized a listening device when I saw one.

I sat and fingered it and felt angry and befuddled. That son of a bitch Mercer and his whiz-girl Carol Kim.

I went to the window and peeked out at the parking lot. It was filled with cars, but I knew which one to look for, and sure as hell, there was a gray Aries four-door sedan parked near the back of the lot.

I guess I looked pretty pissed off, because the guy wearing sunglasses in the passenger's seat next to Carol Kim spotted me coming, tapped her hurriedly on the shoulder, and she quickly started the engine. She backed out so hard she rammed into the bumper of the car behind her. There was a hard crunch and red and yellow glass cascaded onto the tarmac, but she didn't pause or hesitate. She spun the wheel hard to the right and peeled away. All I had a chance to do was kick the side of the car as it sped by.

It was a pretty dumb thing to do. Not only was it infantile, but it hurt like hell and sent me flying back on my ass. I scraped up my hands pretty good, not to mention my butt, and thank God I wore

Army jump boots or I probably would've broken at least a few toes. I limped and cursed the whole way back to the hotel, back up in the elevator, and into my room.

I went through everything. I took the pictures off the walls, unscrewed the lightbulbs, checked under the bed, searched my clothes in the closet. I found two more bugs, but there could've been dozens more.

When had they done it? Had they known from my reservation which room I'd get and planted them before I arrived? Or had they broken in afterward? Maybe one of the maids did the dirty work.

So how much damage was done? Had I said or listened to anything that would harm my client? Nothing overly alarming popped out, but if you put everything together, you could draw some fairly strong conclusions about where I was trying to go with the defense. But then that was different from where Katherine and her crew were trying to go, so maybe it wasn't all that damaging.

On the other hand, maybe I wasn't the only member of the defense team being bugged. And if I were the prosecutor and could get inside the head of the defense team, I'd have a field day. A guy with Eddie Golden's murderous dexterity would do even better.

I wanted to call Katherine and warn her, but the damn phone was trashed on the side table. I raced up to the HOMOS building, walked briskly through the main office, and stuck my head inside Katherine's office.

For once she wasn't chatting on the phone, because there were three civilians hunched over her desk. They were studying a big map. They all looked perfectly normal, but the mood in the room seemed conspirational, so I assumed they were from the big contingent of protesters pouring into Seoul.

I politely said, "Excuse me, Katherine, we need to have a word. In private, if you please."

She shot me an exasperated look that quickly changed to a resigned look, then said to her friends, "Could you all please excuse us a moment?"

To which I replied, "We need to have this talk outside."

No doubt she anticipated I wanted to either apologize for my

earlier transgressions or launch another blistering attack on her.
She followed me into the parking lot and over to the big oak tree
where she'd so recently given that splendid interview that had
done so much to advance my career.

"We've got a new problem," I told her.

She hrummphed once or twice, like she was clearing her
throat, although the fact that she was simultaneously rolling her
eyes gave it a wholly different implication. "What's our new problem, Drummond?"

"I found bugs in my telephone and around my room. They're
fairly sophisticated, because they're real tiny."

It took her a moment to fully swallow this news. She stared at
me. Then she began taking her characteristically small, measured
paces.

"Who put them there?"

This was where it was going to get tricky, because I wasn't supposed to tell her about my secret liaisons with Buzz Mercer and his
spooky gang. Were it anybody but her, with her penchant for flying
into indignant fits and chatting up every reporter in sight, I
might've ignored the rules. But this was Miss Blabbermouth.

"I haven't a clue," I somewhat lied. "But I'd guess it's either the
South Koreans or our own government."

"What if we have these electronic devices analyzed? Will that
tell us?"

"Probably not. Anyone sophisticated enough to use them
makes sure they're untraceable."

She stopped pacing and gave me a discerning look. "Have you
said anything on the phone that could be a problem?"

"I don't think so, but you never know."

"Uh-huh," she said, resuming her walk as she tried to discern
the full context of this new twist.

"Katherine," I said, interrupting her thinking, "if they've done
up my room, maybe they've done yours and the others as well.
They may even have wired the hair parlor."

This was the point when her composure took a radical turn for
the worse, because if the prosecution had access to every conver-

sation we'd ever had, well, then our client was screwed. Picture being in a poker game where you can see through every card on the table; then triple the implications.

She cursed a few times in a real unladylike way and stomped her tiny feet like a pouting child. "Shit, I can't believe this."

"Believe it."

"This means a mistrial!" she finally declared.

"I don't think so."

"I've never heard of such a gross violation of legal ethics. You read about this kind of thing in novels, but I've never heard of it in real life."

To which I very intelligently said, "Yes, well . . ."

"You can't honestly think we can avoid a mistrial, can you?"

"Well," I said, in my most conciliatory tone, since it was actually a surprisingly dumb question from someone with her legal acumen.

"Well what, Drummond?"

"How do you get a mistrial for a trial that hasn't even begun?"

She began ticking off her angry little fingers. "Okay, you get the venue changed. You get the prosecutorial team disqualified. You get their bar licenses revoked. You lodge a motion to have the charges dismissed."

"And if it turns out it was only my hotel room?"

"You're a member of the defense team."

"And if I can't testify I said anything that compromises our case?"

"I don't care. The fact they've been listening is all we need to file a motion."

"No, you need evidence that ties the listening devices straight to the prosecution. You got that evidence, Katherine? I didn't think so. Besides, our odds of getting a change of venue in this case are about zero. So what would we accomplish?"

Since everything I'd said was true, for once Katherine was out of arguments.

I said, "Look, I'll arrange to get our rooms swept every day. Imelda knows how to handle it."

"All right. But if she finds any more bugs—and I mean one single bug—I'm blowing the whistle. Have her report directly to me."

"Okay, fine. There's one other thing you and I have to talk over."

"What's that?"

I put on my most afflicted, woe-is-me expression. "Aren't I sharing things with you?"

"Yes," she admitted.

"Aren't I being helpful and open? Like this little thing?"

"Well, yes," she said, completely unaware, of course, about the separate investigation I was so diligently conducting.

"I interviewed Bales this morning. He said you interviewed him, too. A week ago. How come I didn't know about it?"

"Oh that," she said, with an innocent pout. "I just never mentioned it. There's just so damned much on my mind. I forgot. Sorry."

I wasn't buying it. Carlson has a memory like a computer hard drive. It loses nothing. It overlooks nothing. And it's immune to viruses, power failures, and assorted other natural and unnatural disasters. She didn't get to be little Miss Always First in the Class on low brain juice.

"So it was a simple oversight?" I suggested.

"Yes, a simple oversight. That's all it was."

"I mean, you'd already studied the autopsy results. You'd already interviewed Bales. Is there anything else you've already done I should know about?"

"Like what?"

If it was anybody but her I would've taken that question at face value. "Anything?" I said, with a menacing look.

Her expression became suddenly thoughtful, as though she were rummaging through her memory banks for anything worth noting.

"Katherine?" I said, going on a hunch.

"What?"

"Tell me about Keith."

"What do you want to know about Keith?"

"I'm just wondering why he got picked. Was he a target of opportunity? Or was he doing something that caused him to be targeted?"

Again she went into her contemplative mode. "Off the top of my head, I can't think of anything."

"No?"

"No. Nothing."

"Because if I were to find out you were holding out on me, I'd probably get real pissed off."

Those green eyes searched my face. "Do you have some reason to doubt me?"

I had a thousand reasons to doubt her. A million reasons. Hell, I couldn't think of a single reason to trust anything she said. But in the interest of our newfound partnership, I thought it best to confine this discussion to the subject at hand.

"Only that in the embassy Keith claimed his specialty was suing the government. But he accompanied you in your interview with Bales, didn't he?"

"He was along, yes," she conceded. "But don't give it any significance. He has a good legal mind so I wanted him along."

"But you must admit it's curious that an attorney whose specialty is civil suits is collecting evidence in a murder investigation."

She smiled. "My specialty is civil rights narrowed down to homosexual suits. Look what I'm doing."

And I had to admit she had a very good point. Anyway, I needed to go get some things done, like arrange for Imelda to have all our rooms and offices swept for bugs.

CHAPTER
17

★ ★ ★

I went through the same rigmarole to get in to see Whitehall, only I went alone. His obstinate silence had me stymied. It struck me that if we met alone, he might become more loquacious. His being gay, maybe women made him nervous or tight-lipped.

At least that's what I told myself. The truth was, I figured I could get an inside edge on Carlson by building a better relationship with her client. I can be very sly that way.

I even snuck in some treats in my briefcase—three Big Macs and a six-pack of Molson.

The big Korean with oxlike shoulders did the routine of leading me to the cell and getting the door open. I told him I expected to be with the prisoner about an hour and invited him to lock us in together and then go do whatever big thugs do when their services aren't in any great demand. He smiled, but it wasn't a real fraternal smile, and I wondered if he was going to reappear when my hour was over.

Whitehall was giving me a curious once-over as the cell door banged shut and was locked behind me. "You're alone?"

"That's right, Tommy. I think it's time we get better acquainted."

He stood up and walked over, to shake my hand I thought at first, but he stood stiffly in front of me. "Welcome to my world" was all he said, and although my eyes weren't yet adjusted to the dimness, I thought I saw a slight smile. His world was claustrophobic, especially when you cram two full-grown men into such a tiny, coffinlike space. It was intimate, though, which met with my designs.

"I brought gifts," I informed him, setting down my briefcase, flipping the locks, and reaching in to pull out two of the Big Macs. The smell immediately permeated the cramped space. The burgers were cold, but they were still the most American of meals, and after a week of rice and water, I knew they would have the desired effect. I handed him the first two and he simply stood for a moment squeezing and sniffing them, like he just couldn't believe they were the real article.

Then the wrappers were ripped off and he began gobbling them like an angry gargoyle, with gnashing teeth and grunts for swallows.

"Slow down," I warned. "You're going to make yourself sick."

"Screw it," he replied, not slowing down the least bit.

"Hey, I've got another little surprise," I proudly informed him, withdrawing two cans of beer and opening the tops.

They made that lovely *pshht,* and "Jesus" was all he murmured before he grabbed one and slammed it up to his lips. Half the contents disappeared in a single gulp.

I patiently watched him finish it, as well as the second Big Mac, before I fell into the corner. He licked his fingers for a few seconds to get that final bit of flavor, then collapsed onto his sleeping mat. I handed him another beer.

"How's it going?" I asked.

"It sucks," he admitted, belching from the effect of drinking a full beer in only two sips.

I couldn't resist. "Worse than West Point even?"

He gave me a self-conscious, embarrassed expression. "I guess that sounded pretty stupid?"

"Pretty much, yeah."

We quietly sipped from our beers and stared at the walls.

I finally looked over at him. "You gettin' any exercise?"

"One hour a day I go out into the courtyard and jog in a circle.

They take me out at ten o'clock at night when the other prisoners are asleep. It's for my own safety, they say. Other than that, I spend most of my days doing push-ups and sit-ups in here. It kills the time."

I chuckled. "Christ, you'll turn into a beast."

"Yeah?" he said. "Watch this."

He stood up, kicked off his sandals, put his feet against one wall, fell forward and placed his hands against the other wall, then began scaling the cell, using his hands and feet. He moved quickly, gracefully, like a cat. He made it all the way to the ceiling, gave it a small bump with his ass, then came back down the same way. He wasn't even winded when he was done, like he could've done it a hundred more times.

"That's very impressive, Tommy," I said, shaking my head. "They teach you that at West Point, that climbing-the-walls thing?"

I heard a sudden gurgling sound in the back of his throat, the sound of a convulsive vomit being swallowed, then, "Oh shit. I never tried that after burgers and beer."

I chuckled some more. "Hey, I talked to some old friends of yours."

"Yeah? Who?"

"I had a great chat with Ernie Walters. He sends his best. He asked me to tell you he still loves you. But like a brother, he says. He made me promise to be real clear on that point."

I heard a small "hmmph" come from somewhere deep inside Whitehall's chest. "I'll bet Ernie's catching hell, isn't he?"

"Well, yeah," I replied. "The day I talked with him his desk was painted pink, the cadets changed the nametag on his door to read 'Mrs. Whitehall,' and his wife made him demonstrate he could perform his heterosexual obligations."

Whitehall brought his right hand up and began rubbing it across his lips.

I said, "Hey, he's keeping his sense of humor. And he's telling everybody who asks that he still considers you his best friend."

"Ernie's always been a damned good guy," he said, still rubbing his hand across his lips.

"He had great things to say about you. He even offered to climb on a plane and come testify on your behalf. Of course—"

But before I could finish he said, "No."

"Huh?"

"I said no. Don't even think about dragging Ernie into this. The Army would destroy him. He's got a wife and kids to worry about."

"Hey, Tommy, I wouldn't worry about other people's problems. He's a big boy. He knows what he's doing."

Tommy very firmly said, "I told you no. And don't go looking for any other character witnesses, either. This is my problem and I won't drag my friends down with me."

While I was deeply impressed by his loyalty, he wasn't in any kind of position to be so noble. But there was no use wasting arguments on this one, at least not yet, since I still hadn't found any worthy character witnesses to wrangle over. Besides, I had other, more important issues to resolve.

I said, "I wouldn't bring him over anyway. He told me about your boxing career. Shit, you must've been a terror in the ring. Unfortunately, that's not real helpful right at this moment, because four straight years of West Pointers watched you fight and they all generally agree you're a homicidal maniac. Couldn't you have played tennis or something?"

Of course, I was using this opportunity to broadly hint that I knew about the bone-snapping power of his fists, not to mention his penchant for flailing opponents nearly to death, and I wanted to hear how he'd reply.

But he made no reply, he just stared at the far wall. So I continued. "I also talked to Ed Gilderstone. Can't say it was a real chummy conversation or anything, but he still holds you in high regard. Not that he's willing to lift a finger. He seems to like it inside the closet."

"Yeah, well, that's Gilderstone."

"You expected him to react that way?"

"A lot of old gays are like that. He's spent decades hiding. The longer you do it, the more obsessive you get. You hide it from your parents, your family, your closest friends, from everybody. You don't come out unless somebody drags you out, kicking and screaming."

He paused for a moment, then said, "Remember that gay magazine that got its kicks outing famous gays?"

"Yeah, I guess I remember something about that."

"They caused two or three suicides, and more lawsuits than you could count. If you're straight you can't begin to understand the terror it can cause a gay who's been trying to preserve a normal life."

"Is that why you want us to withhold an admission?"

"It's got nothing to do with it. I mean, it's a fairly hollow denial, right? That part of the damage is done."

"What is it, then?"

"I won't give them the satisfaction. Besides, Katherine says I shouldn't."

Well, this was news to me. I mean, among many other things Katherine never mentioned was that she'd already advised her client on this issue.

"She say why?"

"She just thinks it's a good legal strategy. And I see her point. The more burden of proof we put on their shoulders, the better our chances, right?"

"Yeah, maybe," I admitted, because technically that was true. Most smart defense attorneys never freely concede a single point. They force the prosecutor to painstakingly prove everything, because even if he *can* prove everything, it still increases the odds he'll make a mistake in the process. Except when it's completely hopeless, because then the jury is apt to see the stonewalling as an admission the defense team hasn't got a leg to stand on. In those instances, you only end up losing the goodwill of the jury members. An admission of Whitehall's homosexuality struck me as one of those instances.

And Carlson should know that, too. What in the hell was she thinking?

"So, Tommy," I continued. "Does your family know you're gay?"

"They know. They've known since I was old enough to walk. Some gays don't realize it till pretty late in life. I knew it from the day I could think rationally."

"Why was that?"

"I guess because I had a great family. My parents are remarkable people. They weren't into pretenses or shame. They always just figured you are what you are."

"Speaking of which," I said, "I've been trying to track them down. Your personnel file says you were raised in Denver, Colorado, but there's thirty-two Whitehalls in the Denver greater metropolitan area. Nowhere in your personnel file does it list your parents' first names. Could you help me out here?"

"Leave them out of this," he said. He said it very firmly, too.

I let out a deep sigh. "Tommy, they're your family. I'm sure they want to help, and they could be damned helpful. The way things stand right now, good character witnesses are essential."

"I don't care," he said. "They stay out of this."

I wasn't going to give up this easily. "Look, there's an impression out there that you're some kind of nutso homo freak who beat, murdered, then raped a guy. It wouldn't hurt to have your mother on the stand telling the board how cute you were as a baby, and what it was like to see you learning to crawl. Or your father talking about how proud he was the day you got accepted to West Point."

"It isn't going to happen."

"Are there strains between you? Gilderstone said he never saw them visit you at West Point."

"No, no strains. I love them and they love me. They're doing everything they can, but I want them left out of it. And don't cross me on this, Major."

"Okay, okay," I said, recognizing a lost battle.

But what the hell did I know? Maybe he was worried his mother would get up on the stand and say, "Tommy? My little Tommy? Why of course he killed that boy. From the day he was born, he used to love to play with webbed belts, wrapping them around his brothers' and sisters' necks. Why, it was a terrible strain on all of us."

And his father would say, "Damn was that boy happy to get into West Point. He was always homicidal anyway, and they promised to turn him into a professional killer."

I said, "Want another burger?"

"You got another one?"

I reached into my case, pulled out the last one and another beer. "Here." I handed them to him. "Go slow. You'll make yourself sick."

"That's the least of my problems," he replied, and I guessed he was right.

I leaned against the wall. "So what was it like growing up and knowing you were gay?"

He didn't answer for a while, just sat and munched his burger and sipped his beer. Finally he said, "Look, Major, I appreciate the hamburgers and the beer and the company. I really do. But don't push it. You're not my friend. You're the lawyer the Army assigned to my case. Now, why'd you really come out here?"

So much for my guileful attempt to bypass his defenses.

"You're right about the burgers and beers. I thought it might soften you up a bit. Can I be candid?"

"I'm not going anywhere. Be as candid as you want."

"Here's the thing. I've spent the past five days going over every detail of your case. I've read the full case file. I've viewed the corpse and studied the autopsy. I've talked to Bales and checked out your background. And, Tommy, I can't remember seeing a stronger case. From a strictly procedural standpoint, it's perfect. I can't find a single flaw, not one. You know what that means?"

"I'm screwed?" he guessed.

"That would be my professional judgment. Unless we find something we haven't thought of, or the prosecutor or the judge make a fatal blunder, your chances of conviction are at least ninety-nine percent. And don't bank on the prosecutor or judge screwing up. They've brought in the best prosecutor in the Army. And the judge is one of those guys they keep chained up in the basement unless they absolutely need him."

"So they've stacked the deck?"

"Let's just say they're bringing in the A-team. I wouldn't want to face these guys even if I had a foolproof defense."

He considered that in silence.

Then I said, "Tell me something. And it better be the truth."

"What?"

I drew a heavy breath and fixed his eyes with my best prose-cutorial glare. "Did you kill Private Lee?"

It was the same question he'd told me earlier he had no intention of answering—only, having laid out the bleak facts, I now hoped he was willing to relent. Stonewalling his own attorneys never was a good idea. It had become a catastrophically bad idea.

And besides, I really wanted to hear how he answered.

"I did not," he answered very simply.

"Do you know who did?"

"No. You can't believe how much I've thought about it. All I can tell you is that I'm positive it wasn't Moran or Jackson."

"That's an assumption, Tommy. It could be a very dangerous one. They're the only other possible culprits."

"We've already been through this, Major. I'm not changing my stance. I don't believe they did it. It had to be someone else."

"Someone else? Your apartment door was locked. You were on the twelfth floor of a twenty-story building. The windows were locked from the inside. A lock expert was flown up from Taegu. He took the door lock apart and inspected every single piece under a microscope. There were no signs of tampering, no visual scarring. The lock wasn't picked."

"So maybe somebody had a key?" Whitehall suggested, although you could tell from his tone even he recognized he was throwing pebbles at the moon.

"Won't fly. You admitted in your statement that only you and the apartment management company had copies."

He tensed a little bit. "That's not completely true."

"What?"

"I, uh, I lied about that. No had a key. I gave it to him months before, right after I got the apartment. I didn't tell Bales, because it would've confirmed No and I were lovers."

"You're not making this up?"

"It's true. If you can't find his key, isn't it possible the killer might've stolen it from him and used it?"

"How? How would the killer have gotten the key from him?"

"I don't know."

I pondered that a moment before I said, "What about the possibility the management company lost track of the keys?"

"That's a possibility, too."

I reached into my bag and pulled out the second-to-last beer. I opened it, took a long pull, and handed the rest to Whitehall, who took a short sip and immediately passed it back to me. He was watching me, so I immediately took another long draw, guessing, I think accurately, that he wanted to see if I was too squeamish to drink from the same can as a gay man.

"This is one strange damn case," I said.

"You're telling me," he remarked.

"No, Tommy, stranger than you think. You don't know the half of it."

"Really?" He chuckled. "And I thought I was the only one who does know all the halves of it."

"You know why Katherine asked for me?"

"Tell me."

"Well, she and I went to Georgetown Law together. You know that old saying about cats and dogs? That was me and her. We were a walking combat zone. It got so bad the law school issued flak vests and helmets to the other students, just in case of stray rounds."

"She can be pretty stubborn."

"Tell me about it. Don't get me wrong, I'm not questioning her legal skills. Between you and me, if I was accused of something, she's one of the few lawyers I'd want in my corner. It would have to be something damned serious, though. Otherwise, I couldn't put up with her."

"My position's pretty precarious," he said, smiling curiously.

"The point is, Tommy, I'm not sure why she asked for me. The passage of time hasn't improved our compatibility. You need to know that, because we're at the point where you're going to see some fairly gaping differences in how she and I think and operate. I have an obligation to inform you of that."

He needed a moment to take that one in. I had to tell him, though, because unlike Katherine, I didn't believe in withholding critical information from my client. His fate was on the line, and this was another of those instances where what you don't know could very well hurt you.

"Anyway," I continued, "here's another thing that's got me hot and bothered. This thing is much bigger than just you and this crime. There's all kinds of hidden currents and eddies."

"I know," he said. "It's this gays-in-the-military thing."

"No, Tommy. Bigger than that even."

He hunched forward. "What do you mean?"

"Keith got tossed in front of a moving car and he's in a coma. I'll be damned if I can figure it all out. But there's something else here . . . Something."

He peered at the far wall, and the shadows accentuated the strong features of his face. If he weren't an accused homosexual murderer who was locked up in a Korean prison cell, he'd be the perfect choice for that "noble soldier" model you see on Army recruiting posters. Strong-jawed, clear-eyed, a perfect complexion. You think of murderers and rapists as guys with shifty, soulless eyes, swarthy, pockmarked skin, crooked teeth, and thin, cruel lips. Whitehall just didn't look the type. On the other hand, what we were dealing with here was most likely a crime of passion, not the cold-blooded variety, so that bent all the stereotypes in half.

"Tommy, be honest with me. Is there something here I haven't been told? Are you holding anything back?"

He put the beer on the floor and faced me. "Look, all I know is I woke up one morning and the man I loved was lying dead beside me. I don't know why. I don't know who did it."

"Then it's narrowed to one option. You had to be framed. Deliberately set up. That's what Katherine believes. At least that's what she says she believes. Is that what you believe?"

"I don't know. Maybe some gay-bashing group learned about us and decided to set me up. That's possible, isn't it?"

"It's possible. The hardest damned thing in the world to prove, but it's possible. Did anybody know you were gay? Aside from Moran and Jackson."

"Nobody. Gilderstone guessed, but he's the only one. At least, the only one who knew for sure."

"Come on, Tommy. Don't be bashful. Didn't you have affairs or platonic relationships with anybody else? Think hard. Anybody? Back at West Point, maybe? In high school? Any other place you've been?"

There was this rather awkward moment, and at first I was confused. Then I caught on. "You mean, Lee was your first?"

"Umm . . . ahh . . . yeah," he finally stammered.

"Jesus, it's nothing to be ashamed of," I said, then we both chuckled, because if you think about it, that was something of an awkward observation.

Then I said, "How about Lee? You said he was cautious, but isn't it possible he had enemies? Maybe a former lover with a grudge?"

"Anything's possible. Maybe he was lying to me, but he swore he was celibate before we met."

"So you were both . . . uh, what? Both virgins? Is that the term?"

"Yes, it's the term we use. And yes, we were both virgins."

So much for the old stereotype of gay men being wildly promiscuous. On the other hand, I couldn't help thinking his sheer raw inexperience in romantic attachments might have made him less stable, less able to handle the swings and shifts of his first affair. First-timers of any sexual predilection tend to be fairly immature and prone to wild mood swings.

I said, "Tommy, you already know I'm something of a novice about how all this works. Excuse me if I say something insensitive here. Gilderstone claimed he knew you were gay because he was gay, so he caught on to your act. All he had to do was watch you with other people. Is it possible you or Lee might've inadvertently tipped your hands?"

"Look, some gays are easy to identify. There's always the earring in the left ear or the flashy clothes if you want to be identified, or there's the unconscious effeminate manner, or maybe you overaccentuate your manliness. I don't think No or I fall into any of those categories."

"I don't guess you do," I admitted. "But how'd you recognize he was gay?"

"I, uh, after one look, we knew we loved each other."

"That's it? Some invisible spark?"

"What were you expecting? A secret handshake or something?"

"I just wasn't expecting some intangible emotional clue."

"Haven't you ever felt that with a woman?"

I had to consider that. I'd certainly felt an avalanche of lust for certain women. That happened a lot—too often, if you want to get strictly technical. And there were a few women I'd felt strong emotional attachments to, although that developed over time, a gradual thing, like a slow-motion magnet tugging me inch by inch in its direction. But I'd never looked at a woman and felt some headlong rush.

"Actually, Tommy, I really haven't ever felt something like that," I admitted.

"Too bad."

"Yeah, too bad. So do you miss Lee?"

I asked the question sincerely, although I'd never in my life imagined I'd be asking a homosexual how much he missed his mate.

"God, yes. As miserable as this situation might seem, the hardest part is knowing I'll never see him again. That probably sounds perverted to you, doesn't it?"

For the first time I actually entertained the notion that maybe Whitehall didn't murder his lover, that some bastard stole into his apartment in the dead of night and left the corpse beside him. How must that feel?

"Why was he your first?" I finally asked. "You're a very attractive guy. You told me lots of gays are fairly promiscuous. What makes you different?"

"Ambition, I guess. It's not a homosexual's world, is it? You can come out of the closet and make a handsome living as an interior designer, or a hairstylist, or even a writer, but what other profession welcomes gays into its ranks? The military sure as hell doesn't."

"Then why choose the Army?"

"Why did *you* choose the Army?"

"I don't know. My father was a soldier and, uh, it just looked like an adventurous way to make a living."

"My father wasn't in the Army, but I came to pretty much the same conclusion. The way I was raised was pretty loose and undisciplined. I was allowed to do whatever I wanted. I could stay up as late as I wanted, skip school, you name it. When I was a kid I thought it was great. When I got older, I didn't. That make sense?"

"I guess," I said, although frankly it didn't make the least bit of sense. I'd barely had a loose or undisciplined minute in my whole life.

"Anyway, I wanted something more disciplined, more structured. And I didn't want to grow up and become a hairdresser or a decorator."

I nodded.

"And until now, I really loved it. I just figured that as long as I could hold my gayness under control, I'd do really good at it."

"So why the Army? There are lots of other ways to avoid being a stereotype, aren't there? Or did you always want to be a soldier?"

"Hell, I don't know. I grew up reading war books and biographies of famous generals. Being gay, you're still susceptible to little boys' dreams. It drove my parents crazy, because they're pacifists. But they're also broke, and it didn't hurt that West Point pays you to go. That was no small consideration. Do you want to hear the funny thing? They never blinked when I told them I was gay, but they nearly vomited when I told them I was going to West Point. Pretty ironic, huh?"

"So you suppressed it? Your gayness?"

"Yeah. Outside the house, anyway."

"That why you boxed?"

"Believe it or not, I actually love the sport. And I guess I figured that if I could beat everybody who stepped into the ring, you know, really beat them, then everybody would say, 'Gee, what a macho guy.' What's more hetero than boxing? Who's ever heard of a gay winning the Golden Gloves or being the brigade boxing champ at West Point, for God's sake?"

"Why'd you turn down the Rhodes Scholarship? Gilderstone said you had a good shot."

"Maybe so, maybe not. There were lots of good guys going for it. Besides, I wanted to get to the Army."

"You still would've gotten to the Army."

"I wanted to be an infantryman. I wanted to go to the field and live in the woods and tromp around rifle ranges and lead men. Why waste two years at Oxford when I wanted to be with troops?"

He sounded completely sincere, and I must confess to a certain prejudice on my part. I, too, joined the Army to become an infantryman—which, if you don't know, is the truest form of warrior in the military. And were it not for a wound that made it no longer possible, I would still be an infantryman. Law is intellectually challenging, and often even emotionally fulfilling, but in my mind it is still, as they say in the computer world, a default mechanism.

Tommy Whitehall and I shared something in common.

Then we both heard the sound of footsteps coming down the metal ramp that led to the cell. The steps were heavy and leaden, and we'd been left in isolation nearly an hour. It had to be the big brute.

"He treatin' you okay?" I asked.

"Don't let his looks fool you. He's all right. In fact, I kind of like him."

I chuckled and he quickly added, "Of course, I like him like a brother. And strictly like a brother."

We were both guffawing as the cell door swung open.

The big goon sniffed the air, saw the crumpled McDonald's wrapper and the empty beer cans, and gave me a dreadful glower. I shrugged my shoulders, since considering the circumstances, there didn't seem any point in denying my crime.

I then reached into my briefcase, withdrew the last can of Molson, and held it up to him. "We saved one for you," I timidly said, as I did the *pshht* thing.

He took it from my hand, raised it to his lips, and drained it in a single gulp.

I left Tommy Whitehall alone in his cell, no doubt to climb the walls some more. The big Korean led me out while I mentally recounted my accomplishments. I had exploited Whitehall's loneliness, physical hunger, and susceptibility to alcohol to woo him out of his stony silence. It had worked, too. At least, I think it had worked. Before Carlson would know it, I would own our client.

But Whitehall had accomplished something, too. I found myself liking him. Some of it was what Ernie had told me about him, and some of it was just the fact that I had to defend him, which makes you susceptible to being sympathetic. But some of it was just Whitehall himself. I wouldn't be the first defense attorney who'd been gulled by his client, but he seemed like a decent, genuine guy. And for the first time, I wondered if maybe, just maybe, all evidence to the contrary, he might actually be innocent.

I hadn't changed my mind. I was just entertaining the notion.

CHAPTER
18
★ ★ ★

Two brief phone calls did the trick.

The first was to the American Bar Association. You pay your two hundred dollars a year in annual dues, and you're part of the club. They send you biennial brochures about the legal issues the ABA is currently lobbying in Washington. They keep you apprised of bar practices. They also maintain a registry of every lawyer who's authorized to practice law in the United States.

Unless Keith Merritt owned a small private practice in Florida that specialized in medical torts, or was a 1932 graduate of Duke law school who coincidentally was supposed to be deceased, he was not now, nor had he ever been a practicing attorney. The only other possibility was that he'd never taken or passed the bar exam. But after I called Yale Law School, where Katherine had told me Keith got his law degree, I learned that only six Merritts ever graduated from that august institution.

Not a one was named Keith.

It's not that I didn't trust Katherine, but I didn't. When you know someone the way I know her, you run traplines.

So who in the hell was Keith Merritt? And why had he been tossed in front of that car? As much as I would've loved to dig into these pressing questions myself, I had my hands full already. I needed help. I needed someone resourceful and sly and trustworthy. That last quality ruled out Katherine or anybody from her clique. And that left Imelda. She was richly gifted with all three attributes, except that trustworthy thing, at least lately. So I went up to the HOMOS building and hooked a finger in her direction. She grumpily followed me outside and fell in beside me as I ambled in the general direction of nowhere in particular.

Before I could get out a word, she snapped, "What the hell's your problem? You've been walking around like you got a brick up your butt."

"Oh, you've noticed," I spitefully replied. "I'm the one you worked with these past eight years. The one who flew you over here. The one who's wearing the same uniform you're wearing."

"I ain't forgotten."

"Damn it, Imelda, those people, they make me uncomfortable."

"What people? You mean Allie and Maria?" she innocently replied.

"Yeah, them two," I said. "Haven't you noticed anything odd about them? I mean, real odd."

"You mean, they're lawyers? So what? Ask me, all lawyers are stone-cold weird."

"Let me give you a little hint. When you were a kid, didn't your mother ever have one of those awkward chats with you? That birds-and-bees thing? Haven't you noticed those two have their stingers on backwards?"

"Oh." She stopped, adjusted her glasses on her nose, and gave me a discerning look. "You mean, 'cause they're lesbians?"

"Damned right. That's exactly what I mean."

"Hmmph," she said, shaking her head like this was really ridiculous. "I got no problem with that."

"You don't?"

"Hell, the Army always had plenty of lesbians."

"And you got no problem with that?"

"Any reason I should? They do their jobs, let well enough be."

I was getting exasperated. "Don't try telling me Allie and Maria don't give you the heebie-jeebies. Christ, the big one makes paint flake off the walls. The other one glooms up a room faster than anybody I ever met."

She stopped in midstride. "You know your problem?"

"I didn't think I had a problem."

"Oh, you got a problem, all right. You're a White man."

I very calmly said, "Imelda, it's got nothing to do with it."

"Hell it don't. You ain't never been on the spiky end of prejudice."

"Let me quote the illustrious Colin Powell. 'Skin color is a physical quality; homosexuality is a behavioral quality.' He's a Black man, if I remember correctly. He's not comfortable with gays."

"Ain't no rule says only White people can be irrational. Maybe it's a man thing," Imelda retorted.

"You can't have it both ways," I shot right back. "First you claim it's only White males. Now it's a man thing."

Her eyes got narrow and squinty, and she cocked her head to the side. Philosophical debates aren't a real good idea with Imelda. Debates in general aren't a good idea with Imelda. Not if you like walking on two unbroken legs.

She said, "Let me ask you something."

"What?"

"You ever seen me with a man?"

"Huh?"

"A man. One of them things with a poker and two balls between its legs."

"I know what the hell men are. Of course I've seen you with men," I stiffly replied.

"No, you ever seen me *with* one?"

"I, uh . . . no. So what?"

"You ever get to thinking about that? Never wonder that ol' Imelda's forty-nine years old and don't have no man around?"

"What are you telling me?" I choked out. I mean, I thought I suspected, but it couldn't be. Not Imelda Pepperfield. Not my trusted right hand . . . my able assistant . . . my girl Thursday . . . or Friday, or whatever.

"You can't ask, and I don't have to tell. That's the rule, ain't it?" she smugly replied.

"Oh my God," I groaned, suddenly confronting the inevitable truth. Okay, I'd never seen her with a man, but I'd never attached any seamy misgivings to it. I always thought she was such a dedicated professional that she was like, well, married to the Army. Or she was such a headstrong, resolute woman that she couldn't find a man who wasn't intimidated by her.

Without another word on the subject, she abruptly started walking again. I hurried to catch up. "Hey, wait."

She looked coldly over her shoulder. "I got nothing more to say," she frigidly announced.

"No, I, uh, hold on, damn it."

She stopped and turned toward me. "What?"

"I need to ask you something," I haltingly said, unable to come to terms with what she'd just told me.

She fluttered her lips and rolled her eyes, and, knowing her like I did, I recognized the look. I'd better get over this fast or she'd pop me in the nose.

"Do you think Whitehall did it?"

"Maybe."

"Maybe's equivocal."

"Maybe," she mysteriously reiterated.

"Why maybe?"

"Maybe, because Whitehall, he seems like a smart boy. And boys that smart don't screw up so bad they seem completely guilty. A boy that smart would figure some way to inject some doubt."

I hadn't considered it that way before, but like most things Imelda says, it made stunningly good sense. Here's a guy who graduated at the top of his class at West Point. And he had ample opportunity the morning of the murder to contrive something. Maybe he couldn't have erased every doubt, but he could've muddied the waters and blurred the lines. He hadn't, though. He'd lain on his sleeping mat beside a corpse until Moran discovered him. Then he'd made a sloppy, halfhearted attempt to get Moran and Jackson to tell a few tiny falsehoods. But the truth was he'd left every arrow pointing directly at himself. You might conclude he was overcome by the pressure, but that didn't fit, either. He was a champion boxer. He had the composure to get out of tight corners when fists were flying.

"Think he was framed?"

"How should I know?" Imelda asked, clearly peeved about my little gay prejudice thing.

I gripped her arm. Looking into her eyes, I said, "Stop this. I need your help."

She stared down at my hand, and I politely disengaged it before Imelda kneed me in the groin, or bit me, or just bored a hole through my forehead with her sulfurous eyes. If I haven't mentioned it before, Imelda can be mean as hell when you get her dander up. Sometimes you don't even need to get her dander up. Sometimes she bites your ass off just for sport.

She drew her chest up and asked, "What's this, now? You don't got no problem askin' help from a lesbian?"

"Damn it, Imelda, even if you are gay, you're not really gay."

"Huh?"

"Like Rock Hudson," I said, grinning stupidly.

She shook her head as though that was the dumbest thing she'd ever heard. Then she got a resigned look on her face, like it didn't matter if I was a complete dolt, maybe she could manage to fit a small-mercy favor into her very busy schedule.

"What help you need?"

I rapidly explained everything, from Katherine's unexpected request for my services, all the way through the bugs in my room. She patiently clucked and gurgled in the appropriate places, but didn't seem the least bit fazed or disturbed. Imelda was like that, though—as unflappable as a lead pancake.

"So what do you need from me?" she asked once I'd finally concluded.

"I need you to get all our rooms and the office swept every day. And I need to know who Keith Merritt is. What was he doing here?"

"Some reason you can't just ask Miss Carlson?"

"I have. She lied."

"Uh-huh."

"Come on, Imelda. You see my problem, right? Katherine's up to something. That bit—Well, she's always up to something. And Merritt was probably in the middle of it. People don't get tossed in front of moving cars just for kicks."

"You got a problem with her, too? With Miss Carlson?"

"I've always had a problem with her. You don't know her like I do. Trust me on this. You never met anybody more manipulative, treacherous, and deceptive. Don't fall for her act."

"I like her," Imelda said, confirming that she was already dancing around inside the spider's web. "I won't do nothing to hurt her."

"Who said anything about hurting her? Trust me on this, she's up to something."

"Okay," she said, then scooted away, like there was nothing more to be discussed.

"Thank you," I called after her.

She left me standing alone on the hot sidewalk, feeling somehow like we'd just crossed a Rubicon, or whatever you call it when two formerly close people take a gigantic step back from each other.

Imelda Pepperfield, gay? I was going to have great trouble adjusting to this. After eight years together, too. I suddenly knew how Ernie Walters felt when he found out about Whitehall.

How the hell could I have missed it?

CHAPTER
19

✪ ✪ ✪

Koreans can be infuriatingly bureaucratic when it suits them, which just happens to be most of the time. They can also cut through the crap when they want to, and my request to meet with Minister of Defense Lee Jung Kim and his wife in their home got approved within hours.

It obviously required Minister Lee himself to make that happen. Although we'd met only briefly—and on unfortunate terms—he didn't know me from Adam . . . or Kim . . . or whomever. I assumed he granted my request out of curiosity, or because he wanted the opportunity to box my ears, both because I'd been so curt to him and because I was helping defend the man who'd so cruelly slain his son.

At six o'clock in the evening, I was standing gingerly in my starchiest battle dress and my most sparkling boots, dead center on the floor mat in front of his door. The home was made of musty red brick and was larger than most Korean houses, particularly ones inside the city limits, although it would've seemed tiny and ordinary in any middle-class American neighborhood. Koreans have this thing against flaunting wealth, so they tend to live unpretentiously, except when it comes to cars and TVs. They're nuts for Mercedeses and Sonys.

Having been inside a few Korean houses in my day, I took the cultural precaution of bending over and halfway unlacing my boots, so I could smoothly step out of them. It's one of those Asian things, and I'm a worldly guy, so I know the drill.

I rang the bell, and a sharp-looking Korean Army major with a holstered .38-caliber pistol on his hip opened the door. He wore the Korean Army version of battle dress, and I guessed by the muscular, sinewy look of him he'd probably been handpicked from the Special Warfare Command, which is one of the toughest, deadliest outfits in the world. The guy could probably crack ten bricks with the bridge of his nose. I also noticed he was wearing his combat boots inside the house. I observed this right after I saw him staring curiously at my untied, mostly unlaced boots.

I said, "Hi, I'm Major Sean Drummond. I have a six o'clock appointment to meet with Minister and Mrs. Lee."

In fluent English, he said, "I know who you are. I advise you to tie your boots, so you don't look stupid."

"Uh, yeah, sure," I mumbled, bending over and lacing my boots as fast as my nimble hands could manage. Nothing like making the right first impression, I always say.

"Follow me," he said when I was done.

Like many Korean homes, this one was dimly lit inside and sparsely littered with old Korean chests and bric-a-brac. The walls were spotted with scrolls, and paintings of mountains, and more of those flying cranes. The Lee family tastes ran toward Korean traditional.

The major led me down a hallway and through the living room to a covered porch tucked off the dining room. I could see two old people seated and sipping tea.

The major stepped aside to let me proceed. Following me in, he stayed close behind me like a good bodyguard. This is what comes from living in a country known for its frequent coups and attempted coups, not to mention the occasional terrorist attack by the bad guys up north.

Minister Lee stood up and crossed over to shake my hand. His face was grave and unsmiling, but curious. He courteously said, "Welcome to my home. May I introduce my wife."

"Pleased to meet you, Mrs. Lee," I said, bowing in her direction and calling her Mrs. Lee, even though Korean wives almost never share their husband's name. I knew she wouldn't mind, though. Koreans have long since learned that Westerners, and Americans in particular, are too inconsiderate to learn their customs, so they politely ignore our bad manners.

I said, "Minister Lee, I apologize for what I said in the minister of justice's office last week. I had no idea who you were."

He nodded.

"Also, please allow me to express my condolences for the death of your son. I've learned a great deal about him. He was a remarkable young man. I can only imagine how terrible this loss is for you both."

Again he nodded. Then, the diplomatic necessities obviously concluded, he waved for me to sit across from him and his wife. I stole a glance at her while I arranged my trousers. She was small and slender, delicate-looking, and although she was in her mid-sixties, you could see the traces of astonishing beauty. A noble beauty. Her features looked carved, and although there was an aging puffiness around her eyes, they still reminded me of a pair of big dusky black pearls.

She was demurely studying me right back, and I couldn't even begin to guess what she was thinking. I knew what my mother would be thinking had it been me that ended up with a web belt around my throat, and the defender of the son of a bitch who did that to me was seated on her back porch.

Mrs. Lee, however, graciously rose and leaned across the small coffee table that separated us. She placed a small green porcelain cup in front of me, then filled it with pale, watery tea from a small, discolored, badly dented teapot. Had it been my mother, the tea would've been laced with strychnine.

"What an interesting teapot," I mentioned in an attempt to break the ice. "A family heirloom?"

The minister answered for her. "My father gave me the pot when I entered the army in 1951. He was a poor man. He made it with his own hands before he was murdered by the North Koreans. I carried it with me my whole career, through two wars, even during my years in prison."

I leaned forward and studied the teapot more closely while he said, "So what did you wish to see us about, Major?"

I looked up at him. "Sir, did the hospital return your son's possessions after his death?"

"Yes."

"I'd like your permission to search them. I have no right to ask, and if you say no, I'll certainly understand. However, I'm sure you want the right man convicted for your son's murder. Your son's belongings might hold an important clue."

Most folks would've told me to hit the street and don't let the door hit me in the ass. I was banking on the same streak of fairness Minister Lee had shown in the justice minister's office. On the other hand, I braced myself for a typhoon of anger.

He studied me with an intrigued glance. "May I ask what you're searching for?"

Well, we got past the typhoon, but this was the tricky part. I, of course, came here to see if I could discover whether the key to Whitehall's apartment was still in No's possession when he died. The problem was, as far as the minister, his wife, and everybody else was concerned, Lee No Tae wasn't gay, and he certainly wasn't having an affair with Whitehall—he was an unsuspecting, gullible hetero who'd been lured to a party where he got brutally beaten, murdered, and raped.

I couldn't very well admit I was looking for the key to the romantic hideaway where Lee No Tae went to make love with the man he supposedly *wasn't* having an affair with.

"Well, sir," I said as convincingly as I could, "my client claims there might have been some evidence in No's possession that would vindicate him."

"And how can that be?"

"Because we believe my client was framed for your son's death."

I watched his reaction, because I figured that if the South Koreans were the ones tapping my phones and bugging my room, he'd already know damn well we were preparing to claim White-hall was framed.

If he wasn't surprised, he fooled me. His neck reared back, his forehead crinkled, and his lips twisted in a funny way. He was ei-ther an ace actor or was genuinely unaware. Of course, no man was likely to rise to the atmospheric heights of minister of defense un-less he was fairly skilled at deception. Especially in the capital of Korea, where intrigue's an everyday sport.

Then he spoke in rapid-fire Korean to his wife, who nodded and looked instantly distressed.

He turned back to me. "What might have been in No's posses-sion that could help Captain Whitehall?"

"A slip of paper. Our client claims your son showed him a note that night. A death threat."

I made this up on the fly, but the minister's face became in-stantly alarmed. He stared at the floor, and the alarm changed to dread. I could literally see the blood rush from his face. I felt even more miserable about lying to him, but necessity is the mother of moral corruption.

"Did, uh, did he say who the note was from?" he stammered.

"Uh, no," I improvised. "And it was written in Hangul. Whitehall can't read Korean."

The minister exchanged more words in Korean with his wife, and she nodded a few times, but except for a mild crinkling around her eyes and mouth, I couldn't tell how she was reacting.

They stood up. "Please follow me," the minister said.

We walked back inside with the bodyguard staying tightly be-hind me. He was as well-trained as a Doberman.

We crossed through the living room and ended up in a hall where there were three or four doorways. The minister and his wife walked slowly and laboriously. This was clearly a journey they didn't want to make. It smelled slightly musty, as if the corridor hadn't been used lately.

They opened the second door on the left and walked in ahead of me. The instant I crossed the threshold I felt as though I'd en-tered a sauna of depression. The room was much more like an

American boy's room than a Korean's. It was completely out of
character with the Asian atmosphere of the rest of the home. Instead of a traditional Korean sleeping mat, there was a double bed
made of pine. Instead of scrolls or soaring birds, there were posters
of rock stars and sports stars, mostly Western ones. The room was
orderly to the point of sparseness. The inhabitant had been a meticulously neat person. That detail, at least, *didn't* match any American
boy's room I'd ever seen.

Mrs. Lee was staring at the bed, her face melting, the sharpness
retreating. Her shoulders sagged. The minister reached over and
squeezed her arm, not a common sight in Korea, where men normally show no public affection toward their wives. Toward their
mistresses perhaps; never their wives.

A box was on the desk. It was taped and tagged, and had not
been opened. It contained the personal possessions that had been
returned, a fact I easily surmised since Minister Lee stared at it a
long, difficult moment before he pointed his finger. "Please, you go
through it."

I broke the seal and pried open the lid. Inside was some money,
all in Korean currency, a wallet, and some keys. There was also a
rosary, a silver cross on a chain, a stack of letters wrapped with a
rubber band, and two Army medals.

I flipped through the letters. They were written in Korean and
all had the same sticklike symbols for a return address—from No's
parents, I guessed. I didn't open the envelopes, just looked to see
if there were any free papers stuck between them. I riffled through
the wallet and found more cash. There were charge cards and photographs of Minister Lee and his wife and another of a strikingly
beautiful girl. Camouflage, I figured, just like the picture cadet
Whitehall kept on his desk.

Minister Lee was watching me closely, and I could swear he
was holding his breath. His wife's eyes were on the empty bed. I
could hear her sniffle occasionally.

I stared intently at the key ring. There were six keys. Three
looked like car keys. The others were made of brass and were
about the same size and make as the key to Whitehall's apartment

I'd already collected from the Taejom apartment management company. I pivoted my torso to block their view while I reached a hand into my pocket and withdrew the key I had obtained. The bodyguard watched my every move like a hawk. The minister looked past my shoulder into space.

I handed the packet of letters to the minister. "Could you please look through these? I assume they're from you, but I can't read Hangul. Are there any here from anybody else?"

He took the letters and stripped off the rubber band. He began looking through to make sure all the return addresses were his own. While he did so, I turned my back and carefully lifted the key ring out of the box. I began pressing the real key against the three brass ones on the ring. The last one seemed a perfect match. I stared down at it. Every edge, every cut, every indentation was the same.

I heard the minister say, "They are from my wife and me. Have you found anything else?"

"Uh, no sir," I said, dropping the keys and turning around to face him. "I don't see any notes here. Nothing like the paper my client said might be present."

"This is everything we received," he assured me, sounding half relieved, and half something else.

"Well, I'm sorry I bothered you."

We stood awkwardly in the middle of the room, neither of us knowing what to say next. I had the feeling the minister wanted to talk to me, to say something. His eyes were fixed on his son's desk. His arms hung loosely at his sides. His lips opened and closed a few times. Whatever he was struggling to get out was a gut-twister.

"Is there something you want to speak to me about?" I asked.

He didn't answer for a long time. His mind was very far away. His expression suddenly changed.

"I . . . uh, I . . . uh, do you believe Captain Whitehall is innocent?"

A good defense attorney would instantly say, "Yes, of course my client's innocent. This whole thing's a rotten sham and he should be released right away." Only I didn't want to lie to this man and his wife. Misery has a way of stripping off all vestiges of power and conceit. He didn't look like a mighty minister in my eyes; he was only one more sad man who'd suffered a bottomless loss. And besides, he'd demonstrated a streak of fairness I knew I wouldn't have had the character to show.

"Truthfully, I don't know. He says he is innocent, but the evidence is not in his favor. As a member of his defense team, I owe him every benefit of the doubt. It's my sworn obligation."

He accepted that with a polite nod that I took as a benediction of forgiveness for my role in this despicable affair. He grasped his wife's hand and gently led her from their dead son's room. The bodyguard let them pass, then stepped swiftly in front of the doorway. I avoided his eyes for nearly a minute, until he finally spun around and led me back to the front door. I let myself out and he coldly watched while I trooped down the street and climbed into my sedan.

Whitehall had told the truth; No did have a copy of the key. Unfortunately, No *still* had that key when he died. Nobody had used it to gain entry to the apartment. No was murdered by someone who was inside that apartment when the front door was locked. Of course, there was still evidentiary relevance to the key—if we wanted to use it for that purpose—to persuade the board that No and Whitehall had been lovers.

I can't say I felt real good about that. Actually, that's putting too fine an edge. I felt like an utter cad. I felt like the kind of rodent that eats human dung. I had gained entry to the Lees' home on a contrived pretext so I could find proof their son was a homosexual. The minister struck me as a remarkably honorable man, and even a dimwit could see his wife's heart ached horribly—and I now possessed the means to expose their son in the most shameful way to a nation that believes homosexuality is a huge depravity.

The worst part was, it wouldn't do a damn thing to get Whitehall off. No had still been murdered and sodomized. So Katherine and I could destroy the memory of Lee No Tae, and by extension the reputation of his family, and for what?

As we drove through the streets, I couldn't shake the feeling the minister wanted to tell me something important. I don't think he really cared whether I considered Whitehall guilty or innocent. Maybe he saw me checking that key, figured out what I was up to, and was on the verge of telling me what a piece of nasty garbage I am. Only he ultimately decided not to waste his breath because it would only lower him to my plane.

CHAPTER
20
✪ ✪ ✪

I knew we were back in Yongsan Garrison because every street corner held a grinning clergyman handing out literature to everybody who passed. The preachers' brigade was all decked out in clerical garb, and in a few places gaggles of clean-cut soldiers and their wives were huddled around listening earnestly to whatever drivel the holy men were putting out. The American culture war had arrived full force in Korea.

There was a long table in the middle of the lobby, and my new friend Preacher Prick stood sternly behind it, overseeing three other preachers who were seated like a royal triumvirate, with high stacks of holy literature piled around them. He gave me a mealy look and I shot him a surly salute.

I went to my room and called Katherine in her office and asked her to meet me in the bar. She said she needed thirty minutes, so I decided to occupy myself watching CNN.

Another of those odious talk shows was on. There were four obnoxious, noisy journalists crowded around a table, yelling and interrupting one another. The overheated topic du jour was Thomas Whitehall and the trial. We were six days out and the journalists were trying to predict who would win and what were the costs of victory for either side.

A bald-headed, fat tout kept screaming that anything less than the death sentence would be a monstrous injustice. That was the word he kept using, "monstrous," to re-cue the viewers to the revolting nature of the crime. Another guy, looking glamorous in a thousand dollar suit and horn-rimmed glasses, kept mumbling that "don't ask, don't tell" was bankrupt. The third guy was apparently the only one with a military background—having spent three or four years hiding out in the National Guard during the Vietnam War. He found five or six ways to say the military was a manly business and no place for queers and pansies. A woman with a horsey face, no makeup, and long, unkempt graying hair kept trying to say it didn't matter whether Whitehall was guilty, that all gays shouldn't be tarred with the same ugly brush, but she barely got a word in edgewise. The men shouted her down every time she parted her lips.

I was instantly reminded of Imelda's edict that homophobia was a guy thing. Maybe it was, I realized. You never hear women using epithets like "fags" or "fudge-packers" or "dykes." Maybe this was another of those "men are from Mars, women are from Venus" things.

My idle thoughts were suddenly interrupted by a hard knock at the door. I was expecting Katherine, so I swung it open wide and *Wham!* a fist crashed into my nose. I saw blackness and felt an electric shock that went straight to my brain. I flew backward and landed on my ass. A body launched through the air and crashed down hard on top of me.

I tried shoving and rolling away, but it was no use. Whoever was straddling and pummeling me had at least fifty pounds of advantage and complete surprise in his favor. I finally straightened my fingers and got a clean shot at his throat. He flipped backward and rolled off, writhing and gurgling.

I wiped at the blood gushing from my nose down my lips and chin and sat up to look at my attacker. Son of a bitch! Colonel Mack Janson, General Spears's legal adviser, was grasping his throat, eyes bulging, face crimson, struggling desperately to force air down his windpipe. The fight was out of him, so I got up and went into the bathroom. I grabbed a nice white face towel, soaked it in cold water, and held it against my nose. In an instant, the towel was no longer white.

When I walked back out, Janson was on his knees, and while he wasn't breathing real well, he was getting enough air that he wasn't going to die.

"You bastard," he croaked. "I'll fuck you for this."

I shook my head. "What are you, some kind of stupid recording? What the hell's your problem?"

"I don't like you, Drummond."

"I know," I said. "That why you hit me?"

His speech was coming back now. "You had no business bothering the minister. You had no business going to his house."

He reached over to the minibar and pulled himself up to his feet. He was glaring at me with as much hatred as I've ever seen in a man's eyes. "You're a disgrace to the JAG Corps. And the Army. That poor man and his wife have been through enough. You should've left them alone."

"I did what I needed to do."

"And what was that, Drummond? Why were you nosing around the minister's house?"

"None of your business."

"I'm making it my business. I live here and it's part of my job to help maintain this alliance."

"Too damn bad."

His glare got more choleric. "Do I need to remind you, Drummond, that I'm a colonel and you're a major?"

"Up yours," I said. "You trashed your authority when you punched me."

"What were you doing?" he persisted. "Looking for evidence the kid was gay? Did you actually enter their home for such a disgraceful purpose?"

"No, I went for a cup of tea."

"I'm warning you, Drummond, leave their son alone. Bad enough the poor kid got murdered . . . then the disgusting things they did to him afterward. Don't you add to their pain."

"It's none of your damned business," I told him again.

"No decent gentleman would even think of it."

"I'm not a gentleman, I'm a lawyer," I replied. "Now get the hell out of my room. And if you ever try to hit me again, I'll break both your legs."

Janson was much bigger than me, but he had a fairly big paunch, and what he didn't know was that when I was back in the outfit I'd been fairly well trained to break bones. I could see he thought I was making an empty threat, and for a fraction of an instant, I think he considered hitting me again. I actually hoped he'd try. I wanted to kick his ass. On the other hand, maybe he was tougher than I gave him credit for, and it was me who was going to end up a bloody mess. Christ, that would've sucked.

Anyway, he spun around and went out the door. Of course, he couldn't resist announcing again, "I swear I'll fuck you for this, Drummond. You'll see."

I was starting to think there were only twenty words in the man's vocabulary and "fuck" was half of them.

I inspected myself in the mirror. The bleeding had stopped, but my nose was red and starting to swell up. I looked like a drunk on a binge. I changed into a fresh shirt and headed downstairs to the bar.

Katherine was already seated at her same table beside the jukebox when I came in. That same song about where all the cowboys had gone was playing again. This couldn't be coincidence—it had to be her who kept putting it on. Odd thing that—a lesbian obsessed with where all the cowboys went. Whatever happened to the Village People and Melissa Etheridge?

She had a beer and it was half empty. She stared at my face as I sat down. "What happened to your nose?"

"It was what we call a soldier's fight."

"And what's a soldier's fight?"

"One of those ones where there's no rank, no rules, no apologies."

"Why are you men so childish?"

So much for sympathy from my co-counsel.

"Look, all I did was open the door to my room and boom! I got hit in the nose. Guess who the assailant was."

"Knowing your forte for making friends, I'm surprised there wasn't a line at your door."

"It was Janson," I said, for once ignoring her gibes. "He was pissed as hell."

"Over what?"

"I went over to Minister Lee's house."

"You what?"

"Remember how Whitehall told Bales he had the only key to his apartment?"

"Yeah?"

"He lied. I went to see him yesterday. He told me he gave a key to Lee several months ago. I went looking for it."

She gave me a dubious look. "And the minister let you in?"

"Yeah, actually. He's quite a gentleman. Besides, I lied about what I was looking for."

"Did you find it?"

"Among the sealed possessions the hospital returned."

She took a sip from her beer, then reached up and fingered my nose. It was a surprisingly intimate gesture. It hurt like hell, too.

"It might be broken," she said.

"Wouldn't be the first time," I muttered in a callous, manly-like way. For that I got the aren't-you-an-idiot eye-roll I richly deserved.

She said, "We'll have to get the key sequestered as evidence. It'll help us prove Lee and Thomas had a relationship. It's not definitive proof, but it's a fairly inescapable conclusion, don't you think?"

"And what will it accomplish?" I asked, since that was exactly the question I was wrestling with.

"It puts a crack in the prosecutor's case. At the moment, the only crack we've got."

"At the price of humiliating the Lees and destroying a dead man's reputation. What else do we accomplish? It won't get Whitehall off."

"What about our client's reputation? Look what's happened to his good name."

"This is a little different, don't you think?"

"No, I don't."

"For Chrissakes, Katherine, at least our client's alive."

"In a Korean prison cell where he's been beaten, publicly humiliated, and nearly starved. He's being accused of the most despicable crimes imaginable and he's facing a death sentence. Don't get your sympathies confused, Drummond."

I might ordinarily have continued arguing, except this wasn't really a debate, because I'd known before I even uttered my first word exactly how she'd come down. It's how I'd come down, too, but I guess it made me feel better to force her to be the one to make the hard, bitter decision. She was the lead counsel. I was selfishly exploiting that fact.

She knew that, of course.

I said, "At least they won't be beating him anymore. With only six days till trial, they won't want him parading in front of cameras with bruises all over his face."

"Some consolation," she mumbled.

"Speaking of which, with only six days left, what the hell are we going to say in court?" I asked, reaching across and taking a sip from her beer. Actually, it was a bit more than a sip. I drained the rest of the mug.

She stared down at her empty stein. "I got a call from the prosecutor just this morning."

"From Eddie Golden?"

"He wants to meet this afternoon."

"He say what for?"

"No. What do you think? Does he want a deal?"

"If he's a damn fool. He's got the best murder one case I ever saw. Not to mention there's enough ancillary charges, he's guaranteed a win."

"Are wins important to him?"

Wins were important to every attorney, but I knew what she meant.

"Like you wouldn't believe. Son of a bitch even sends a signed baseball bat to every attorney he beats."

"Sounds like a sweetheart."

"Put it this way. Imagine a young Robert Redford with a gift for bullshit you'd die for. He once had a court-martial board rise to their feet and applaud when he finished a summary."

"You're just trying to frighten me," Katherine said, with a properly skeptical look.

"I saw it with my own eyes. I was the defense attorney. It was easily the crappiest day of my career."

"Wow."

"Katherine, Eddie's tried maybe seven or eight murder cases. He doesn't lose. He's the current holder of the JAG Corps's Hangman Award. Has been the past five years. I'm not trying to rattle your confidence, but the Army's got the deck stacked pretty good. A killer prosecutor, a judge who hates defense lawyers, and a case so lopsided, we're drowning under the weight of it."

I can't ever remember seeing any hint of anxiety or self-doubt on Carlson's face. But I thought I did this time. Just a flicker, but I was pretty sure it was there.

I said, "Say Eddie does offer a deal? Would you take it?"

She brought her hand up to her forehead and began kneading it, as though her head was about to explode into a thousand shards unless she held it together. I never thought I'd feel sympathy for Katherine Carlson, but I did.

"Would *you?*" she asked, staring at me with doleful eyes.

"Depends on the deal, I guess. Wouldn't take much, though. Anything less than murder one or a sentence less than death, and I'd probably leap at it."

"Why? Because we're six days out and all the evidence points at Thomas? Or because you believe Thomas is guilty?"

"Because it'll keep him out of the electric chair. That's maybe the most we can hope for at this moment. We can appeal later. Maybe we'll find something down the road that exonerates him."

"We, Drummond? As soon as this trial's over, you'll be assigned to your next case, right? And OGMM will damn sure try to shift me to my next case."

"He'll get somebody to represent him."

"It's not an option. Thomas won't buy it. He told me, no deals," she said, sounding as distressed as I'd ever heard her.

I reached across and took hold of her tiny hand. I tried to sound soothing. "Take a deep breath and count to ten. You're taking it too personally again."

"Damn right I am!" she exploded, suddenly yanking her hand back and giving me a perfectly pernicious glare.

I thought she was going to slap me. I don't pretend to understand women, and I'm even more perplexed when the woman is gay, like Katherine. But this caught me completely by surprise. This woman changed moods faster than models change clothes.

"Damn it, Katherine, I'm just trying to get you to think rationally. You better know what you're doing when you meet with Golden. Trust me on this—the guy can take you to the cleaners and have you steamed, pressed, and folded before you blink. He ain't called Fast Eddie for nothing."

Although, actually, we called him Fast Eddie because he could get into and out of a girl's pants faster than any human being on earth. Not that I worried about that part with Katherine, because, after all, her electrodes were upside down.

Her face was still surly, but she said, "Maybe you'd better come along."

"Love to," I said, although actually I wouldn't love to at all. In fact, I'd be perfectly happy if I never saw Eddie Golden again for the rest of my life. A man's got to know his own limitations, and Eddie had amply demonstrated mine, twice, before a jury of our peers. The truth was, Eddie scared the hell out of me.

CHAPTER
21
★ ★ ★

I'll give Katherine credit; she collected herself with inhuman speed. She was as cool as an ice pick when we got to Eddie's office. She bounced with confidence as she walked through the door, entered like she owned the place; as though *she* was the one who had the judge and every piece of evidence in her hip pocket.

Unfortunately, Eddie wasn't easily flustered. He stood behind his desk and flashed his most Redfordesque, gorgeous-boy-next-door, I'm-gonna-cut-your-ass-into-tiny-pieces smile.

"Miss Carlson, I can't begin to say what a great pleasure it is to finally meet you," he announced, warmly shaking her hand and playing the perfect gentleman to the hilt. Then he tilted his head and looked at me curiously. "You're, uh, Drummond, right? Haven't we met before?"

Eddie Golden, if I hadn't mentioned it before, is a master at playing mind games.

I nodded shyly and said, "We've . . . uh, we've met twice, Eddie."

"Oh yeah," he said, like he wouldn't have recalled it if I hadn't jogged his memory. "The Dressor case, back in, uh . . . When the hell was that? The summer of '95, right? And . . . uh, Clyde Warren, back in '99? You were defending them, right?"

Depend on Eddie to remember everything about every case he ever won.

"That's right, Eddie. I've got two of your baseball bats stored in my closet at home."

"Heh-heh," he chuckled, like, What a silly habit, but, aw shucks, I just can't help myself. "Well," he said, returning to his most-charming-host-in-the-universe routine. "Won't you be seated? Can I get you anything? Coffee? Soda?"

"No, nothing," Katherine said. "This isn't a social visit."

"Of course," he replied, still smiling, but with just the right amount of sympathetic edge on it.

Katherine and I sat side by side. She pinched my leg to remind me to let her handle this, especially since Eddie had already used our past history to pound me into place.

She said, "So what is it you want, Major Golden?"

"I just thought we should get to know each other before the trial convenes," he replied with a dimpled grin I would've dearly loved to wipe off his face.

"I already know about you. What is you want to know about me?"

"Oh, you don't need to explain anything about yourself, Miss Carlson. Anybody who's read a newspaper or magazine these past eight years knows about your brilliant legal exploits. I can't say what a great pleasure it is to finally meet you. At the risk of sounding redundant, it will be the honor of my life to tilt with you in court."

Had that come out of anybody else's mouth, it would've been instantly recognizable as an obnoxiously oozy, completely insincere sentiment. Not from Eddie's lips, though. He was the master. He could get standing ovations from juries. You had to look at his face, his physical bearing; you could swear he was being presented to the Queen of England.

I was praying Katherine wouldn't succumb to this unctuous horseshit.

I stole a glance in her direction, and Jesus! She was beaming and blushing like a high school freshman being asked to the senior prom by the captain of the football team. She crossed and re-crossed her legs once or twice. She twiddled her fingers.

"Thank you, Major Golden. I'm looking forward to it also."

"Call me Eddie, please."

"Of course, Eddie. And I'm Katherine."

"Of course you are. Are you sure I can't get you something to drink?" her new buddy Eddie asked again. I was getting sick.

"No, really. With this heat, I've been drinking all day," Katherine said, giving him a blast of her most angelic smile.

If I didn't mention it before, Katherine's a beautiful woman, but in a way you're almost afraid to touch, like a delicate porcelain doll. She's not the type you dream of taking to a cheap motel for an afternoon of wild, raunchy sex; she's the type you pray Mom sees you with.

Of course, she's also a lesbian, so Eddie's sexual charms and sterling good looks should've fallen on blind eyes. That's not the way it was going down, though. She was melting in his hands.

"I'm terribly sorry about the case you've been handed," Eddie said. "It's really a raw deal."

"Why's that?" Katherine asked, smiling sweetly.

"Well, there isn't a reasonable defense, is there? It wasn't self-defense. He wasn't framed. And the sexual perversions, Jesus! That isn't going to sit well with a board of Army officers."

"Some cases are more difficult than others."

"I'll say," Eddie replied with an agreeable grin.

"Of course, there's a great deal you probably haven't discovered yet," Katherine said, smiling coyly.

"Like what?"

"Come on, Eddie, a girl has to have a few secrets."

He chuckled amiably. "Right, of course," he said, as though this were complete baloney, but if Katherine wanted to fence, it was all good fun for him.

"So, Eddie, is there something specific you want to talk about?"

He took his eyes off her for the first time since we'd entered and toyed with something on his desk. He looked reluctant, like he really didn't want to talk business, he just wanted to bask and reflect in Katherine's glory. I mean, the guy was really, really good.

He finally said, "Actually, yes. I want to discuss the possibility of a deal."

"A deal?" she asked, as though the very notion couldn't have come as a greater surprise.

"I need to start by telling you," Eddie swiftly said, lifting his arms helplessly, "my bosses are opposed to this. They want a full-blown trial. They want to use the trial to bolster Korean faith in the American legal system. They want Whitehall punished. Severely punished. They won't be happy with anything less than a death sentence."

Katherine swiftly bent forward and her eyes grew wide. "The death sentence? Oh my God."

"That's right. Only a trial's a complete waste of time and needless trouble. You know that, right? And I know that, right? The outcome's obvious, isn't it? Besides, frankly, I've never been a fan of the death sentence. What does it accomplish? It doesn't bring the victim back to life, does it? It doesn't undo the crime, does it? So what's the point?"

This was part of Eddie's style. He liked to coax you into agreement by asking a thousand rhetorical questions that allowed you to think you were coming up with the answers. I thought it was a tacky stunt. It worked for him, though. I'll say that.

And he was playing to Katherine's obviously liberal tendencies, knowing damn well she must be opposed to the death sentence. He was trying to show they had common ground.

It was just a damned good thing he was having this conversation with her instead of with me, because I would've felt duty-bound to point out that Eddie's Hangman Awards were owed substantially to the fact that he'd achieved something like four death sentences. He had more death sentences on his record than any other three Army lawyers combined.

But Katherine was nodding right along, completely mesmerized, under the thumb of the spellbinder.

"So what's the deal?" she timidly asked.

Eddie leaned back in his chair and hooked both his thumbs under his belt. He sighed and appeared completely distressed by this whole thing, like the weight of the world was on his shoulders. It was an unbelievable performance. Truly remarkable. I have to admit that.

"Plead guilty to all counts. He'll get life, no chance of parole."

"All counts?" Katherine asked, in shock.

Eddie's hands came out of his belt and he bent way forward, nearly all the way across his desk. His hands were palms up, beseeching the heavens, and his eyes were so sympathetic you could swear he was bleeding internally for her.

"Katherine, Katherine, I have to tell you, I'm going way out on a limb for this. I swear I am. He pleads to all counts or I can't get a deal."

Now he was wheedling and cajoling like a car salesman—like, Hey, I'd love to sell you this car; you only have to come up a little in price so I can persuade that tightfisted, asshole manager in the back room.

Katherine was seated pertly in her chair, her eyes riveted on his. "All counts?" she repeated, as though maybe she had a hearing problem.

"Hey, I'm sorry. I truly am. It's all or nothing. But think about it. What's the difference? He pleads to murder one, who gives a crap about the other stuff? You get a life sentence for murder, the rest is peachfuzz, right? Doesn't really add a single year to his sentence, does it? It's as generous as I can go. Think about it."

Katherine's expression turned pleading. "You're sure, Eddie? All counts? You couldn't drop something as insignificant as the engaging in homosexual acts? Not even for me?"

He somehow came even farther across the desk, literally out of his chair, until his absurdly handsome face was within inches of hers.

"I'm sorry, Katherine, this is the way it has to be," he whispered.

"Fuck you!" she roared so loud even I bounced in my chair.

Eddie reeled backward. "Huh?"

"Fuck you, Golden! You want me to spell it for you? I'm going to take this case and break it off in your ass so deep it'll scar your tonsils. You arrogant jerk-off. You've got no idea what nasty little surprises Drummond and I have in store for you. Just wait, you puffed-up asshole."

Poor Eddie was in complete shock. Like General Spears, he'd just gotten his first unexpected dose of what I'd had dished at me for years. I almost felt sorry for him. She'd been so girlish, so pliant in Eddie's skilled hands. She'd walked him down the primrose path. One moment the poor putz was sauntering joyfully in the middle of a flat, open, warm meadow, and all of sudden, out of the blue, *Whoosh!*—an avalanche of snow and ice crashed down on his head.

Katherine abruptly stood up and I followed her out. I barely had time to turn around and give Eddie Golden the bird. It was juvenile as hell, but hey; I got swept up in the mood of the moment.

Outside the JAG building, I lost control. I literally grabbed Katherine, picked her up, and spun her around in the air. She smiled and giggled and ordered me to put her down right away or she'd knee me in the nuts so hard they'd pop out my ears. So I did.

"God, that was great!" I yelled, exultant.

"No, that was fun," Katherine corrected. "Great would be if I could back it up."

"Good point," I admitted, starting to come down off my high.

"Boy, he is a slick bastard, isn't he?"

"Slick? You think that was slick? Wait'll you see him in court," I ruefully warned.

We walked to the gate, neither saying a word, just privately mulling.

Katherine finally said, "Why do they want a deal?"

"They want to reduce the risk, especially on this case. And they want to prevent us from humiliating Minister Lee by outing his son. They must suspect we have something."

"You think your visit to his house might be behind this?"

"Yeah, I think. That must've been why Janson was so pissed. Unless I miss my guess, somebody damned important, maybe Brandewaite or Spears, ordered Golden to get a deal. Janson probably argued against it, lost, and got so incensed he decided to take it out on me."

I kept to myself that Clapper, the chief of the JAG Corps, might've authored the idea of a deal because, if we lost, I could always launch an appeal based on command influence, citing him as the cause. In fact, the more I thought about it, the more likely it seemed Clapper was behind it. Boy, would I have liked to have been a fly on the wall for *that* conversation.

She said, "I think you're wrong. I think they're afraid of the six hundred protesters OGMM brought in."

"That could be a factor," I admitted.

"A *factor?* They're scared to death of what we might do next. In fact, I think it's time to turn up the heat."

"And what would be the purpose of that?" I asked, sounding edgy and concerned, because I was.

"If things don't improve in five days, we may have to consider a deal. Let's see if we can convince them to sweeten the pot."

"To what?"

"Make them drop the engaging in homosexual acts and fraternization charges."

"What's the sense in that?"

"They're just the two I want dropped," she said, refusing to elaborate. "Trust me on this," she continued. "To quote your friend Fast Eddie, if they convict on murder one, the other stuff's just peachfuzz anyway."

Knowing Katherine, I didn't believe for a second she was being anywhere near so arbitrary. I wasn't sure what she was up to, but she was hatching some plan.

CHAPTER
22

★ ★ ★

I hit McDonald's again and picked up four Big Macs to go with the medicinal necessities I'd already bought, which included another six-pack of Molson and a bottle of Johnnie Walker Blue, which, if you don't know, is the best brand of Johnnie Walker money can buy. And in case you don't know, it cost a fortune. I almost cried because I wasn't going to get a drop.

The guard at the desk instantly recognized me, so I didn't have to pantomime or otherwise act like an overanimated clown to make him understand I wanted to see Whitehall. He went and got the big brute, who walked in grouchy-faced, not the least bit happy to see me.

He ordered me over to a side room, and once we were there, said, "No more contraband may be smuggled in to Whitehall. Open your briefcase so I can search it."

I did and the odor of the Big Macs poured out. He grinned, then bent over and reached his big paws inside. What he pulled out was the Johnnie Walker Blue, which he stared at like it was the Holy Grail.

"That's yours," I announced. "And two of the Big Macs."

His eyes fixed on mine, he tilted his head sideways, and his shoulder muscles got all bunched up. I couldn't tell if this was moral indecision or preparation to punch me for so blatantly trying to bribe him.

I quickly said, "You got any idea what a bottle of Johnnie Walker Blue costs?"

"Two hundred and twenty-two dollars," he murmured. Somewhat passionately, too. When it comes to a man's taste in booze, my prescience can be uncanny. Of course, anybody who looked like him had be a scotch man. He was too damned ugly to sneak up on any other kind of hooch.

He eagerly stuffed the bottle down his shirt, crammed the two burgers in his side trouser pockets, and closed the lid on my briefcase. He handed it to me, then slyly hooked a finger.

When we got to Whitehall's cell, he opened it and waved for me to enter. "One hour," he said.

"Thanks," I replied, and he locked the door behind me and disappeared. I turned around. "Hi, Tommy."

Whitehall didn't get up. He lay on his back. "Hello, Major."

I kicked my briefcase in his direction. "Open it. I brought you more treats."

My eyes still weren't adjusted to the near-darkness, but I heard him rustle around. The clasp clicked open, and the disruptive odor of fast food again permeated the cell. It was a good thing, too, because once again Whitehall's cell smelled like human dung, the consequence, I guess, of my earlier visit.

Then I heard him wolfing down that first hamburger. Then a *pshht* as he popped open a Molson, and another as he opened one for me. I accepted it and leaned smugly against the wall listening to the bestial sounds of him devouring his treats. I needed him in a good mood. I needed him pliant. The time had come for our most important discussion yet.

Finally done with the burgers, Whitehall said, "You seem quiet. What's the matter? Things aren't looking up?"

"No, Tommy, they're not."

He said, "Ummmh," which was either a statement of hopeless acceptance, or bland acknowledgment. I couldn't tell which. Maybe there's no difference between the two.

"Did you look for the key?" he asked.

"I found it. I went to Minister Lee's house and discovered it among No's sealed possessions."

He fell quiet again. Then, "What's he like?"

"Minister Lee?"

"Yes, No's father."

"An impressive man. Tall for a Korean, maybe five-ten, slender, silver-haired, strong-featured, calm, and uh . . . I guess stately is the best word."

"Sounds like No," Tommy said.

"His mother's no slouch, either. I'll bet she was an incredible beauty. She's still damned attractive," I said, then added, "the old man's hanging together, but his wife's brittle. When we went in No's bedroom I thought she was going to crumble."

I wanted to see how he reacted to this, but in the dimness I couldn't tell. I thought I heard a sigh, but maybe I was just imagining things.

Finally he asked, "But No still had the key when he died?"

"He still had it. The apartment management company still had all their copies, too. Know what that means, Tommy?"

"I didn't do it," he said, although in a very resigned tone, like he was tired of saying it and he knew I wouldn't believe him.

"Katherine and I met with the prosecutor today. He offered a deal."

"And what was his deal?"

"Plead to all charges and there'll be no death sentence. You'll get life."

"That means no trial, right?"

"There'll be a quick hearing, followed by a sentencing hearing, but the verdict will be predetermined. We'll be allowed to present extenuating circumstances and beg for mercy, but the sentence won't change. The key issue's this: By pleading, you lose the right to appeal on the basis of flawed procedure, or an unfair trial, or an overly harsh sentence. An appeal will take the discovery of new evidence."

"And what are the chances of that?"

"It happens sometimes. Not often, but sometimes. Occasionally the real perp feels guilty and comes forward and confesses. Sometimes a detective investigating another case stumbles onto something tied to your case. We can look into hiring a private detective to keep digging around. That takes money, though. Lots of it."

"More money than I have, right?"

"You'll be dishonorably discharged, so your pay will stop. A really good PI, you're probably looking at a few hundred thousand a year."

"And once I'm sentenced, OGMM will forget all about me?"

"That depends."

"On what?"

"On Katherine. She's been with them eight years. She's their top gun. Maybe she has influence."

He sipped from the beer and considered all this. I'm sure he'd thought about it already, because it wasn't long before he asked, "And if we go to trial?"

"Our only hope is that the prosecutor or the judge makes a calamitous blunder."

"And what are the odds of that happening?"

I stepped over and sat down right beside him on his sleeping mat. I pulled two fresh beers out of my case, opened them, and handed him one. We were getting to the raw, nasty truth about the rest of his life. My bedside manner could be key here.

"Most judges have a bias. They're supposed to be impartial, but they're human. Maybe they spent their lawyer years as defenders or prosecutors, and that leaves them looking at the law from that angle, or maybe they just interpret the Constitution a certain way. This judge is very pro-prosecution. He's also antidefense. That might sound like one bias, but it's not. They're two very distinct bents."

"So I drew a bad straw?"

"The Army drew the bad straw for you."

"Can Katherine handle him?"

"Katherine's legal tactics are shaped by the fact that the majority of cases she's handled are military gay cases, where the laws are written against her. Her strong suit is theatrics. She's a show-man. She's very expressive and can be fatally caustic. She has a rep-utation for judge-baiting. You know what that is?"

"Please explain it."

"A judge is responsible for everything in the trial. He's got to maintain proper decorum and he's got to temper the behavior of the attorneys. Depending on the complexity of the case he might have to make dozens of tricky judgments—about evidence, about the limits of examinations and cross-examinations, about the tone and conduct of the lawyers. He can sometimes recess and go to his chambers and contemplate a particularly thorny issue. Usually, though, he has to make his judgments spontaneously, on the bench. Katherine's forte is trying to get the judge to dislike her, to get overheated. She taunts them. She provokes them. It might sound crazy, but she actually tries to prejudice the judge against her. She raises lots of empty objections to get the judge in the habit of overruling her, then she slips in a valid one and hopes he re-sponds on autopilot. Maybe he allows a piece of evidence he shouldn't. Maybe he sustains a lawyer's statement that's prejudicial. She throws lots of empty motions at him, and somewhere tucked in the middle of the stack and vaguely worded is something ap-plicable. Her whole aim is to bombard an angry judge with rulings, to force him into a biased procedural error. That error later be-comes the basis for an appeal. Katherine's forte isn't winning cases, it's getting them overturned."

Whitehall said, "Sounds like smart strategy to me."

And I said, "Most lawyers think it's sleazy because it's a way to try to circumvent the law. I mean, if a lawyer gets his client off be-cause he got the judge overtorqued at a critical moment, has jus-tice really been served?"

"So you think Katherine's sleazy?"

"That's not what I said. Her specialty's defending folks accused of breaking a law she believes is morally reprehensible. She's fight-ing a wrong with a wrong. To her, I'm sure it all balances out."

"But you don't think it'll work with this judge?"

"Not with this judge and not with this prosecutor. Colonel

Barry Carruthers has been known to throw defense attorneys in jail. He's a real badass, Tommy, and he'll be expecting Katherine's game, because she's known for it. As for the prosecutor, he's probably the best in the Army. You need to know this. Eddie Golden's never lost a murder case. He's tried maybe seven or eight and he's gotten four death sentences."

"You think he's that good?"

"I've faced him twice. I lost both times."

"That why the Army brought him out here?"

"That's exactly why Eddie's here. The Army's taking no chances."

"Are you afraid of this Golden?"

"Scared shitless. He's the perfect lawyer, with the perfect case, and perfect witnesses, and the perfect judge. The moons aren't lined up right here, Tommy."

He chewed on this a few moments without touching his beer. He was hunched over and his jaw muscles were working like a pair of furious pistons.

Finally he said, "Why are you here telling me this? Why isn't Katherine here?"

"You remember I warned you that she and I share different philosophies on some things?"

"I remember."

"This is one of those things. I believe in open disclosure with my client. She doesn't. Another thing—but this stays between you and me, right?"

"Okay," he said, sounding hesitant and unsure.

"Katherine and I have different agendas. She's employed by OGMM. She's pushing the gay agenda. This is her life's work. If something jeopardizes that cause, I don't know how she'll come down."

"And what are you pushing?"

"I'm career Army, Tommy. I'm pushing truth, justice, the American way. I'm opposed to bending the rules or trying to beat the system. I don't judge-bait. I don't play games. If you're innocent, we try to prove that. If the prosecution makes a procedural mistake, that's fair game. We've got the best and fairest legal system in the world. You pay your nickel, you take your ride. Don't try to cheat the turnstile."

"Let me see if I have this right. She'll sell me upriver if I harm the movement, and you'll sell me upriver if I threaten your principles?"

"No, Tommy. Nobody's selling you upriver. But just like all judges are predisposed, so are us lawyers. There's one other thing I have to warn you about, too. Katherine's emotionally entangled in your case. She's taking it personally. Don't take that as a good thing, either. Lawyers are supposed to operate from cold hard logic."

Tommy stood up and began pacing his cell. Given the size of the room, he could only go three steps this way, three steps that way. But even in such a compressed space, he still moved like a caged panther, sleek and muscular, with long, graceful strides.

"So I've got one lawyer who'd do anything to win and one who's afraid to step on cracks. I've got one who's emoting and one who could care less about me. I've got one who's a fanatic for the gay cause and one who hates gays."

I didn't want to admit this was a fair summary, but it was damned close. Except for that last crack, anyway.

"Tommy," I said, "I don't hate gays."

"Don't kid yourself. We gay people, we can smell homophobia. It's got a real nasty odor."

"I'm not a homophobe, Tommy. I'll admit it makes me uncomfortable, but that's as far as it goes."

"Okay," he said, not like it was really okay, not like I was telling the truth; more like he wasn't willing to argue about it. "So I make you uncomfortable."

"Look," I said, "it's no big thing. Christ, my own mother makes me uncomfortable. Combat boots on a hot day make me uncomfortable."

"But you don't think your mother or your combat boots murdered and then raped somebody."

"No, you're right," I told him. "But I don't think you did, either. And that's the thing that makes me most uncomfortable."

He stopped dead in his tracks. He turned and stared at me. "You believe I'm innocent?"

"I didn't say innocent, Tommy. You're an officer who was having an affair with an enlisted soldier. And it happened to be a gay affair. I said I don't think you killed and raped him."

"Okay, why?"

"Call it instinct. I mean, every piece of evidence screams it was you, except one."

"And what would that be?"

"You."

"Why is that?"

"Because you don't fit the crime. Because you're too smart to have let it go down the way it did. Because I think you're probably a pretty decent guy. Because the key in No's possession proves you were lovers, and maybe, if you're telling the truth about that, you're telling the truth about everything."

"Then what do you think happened?"

"I haven't got a clue. But Katherine was right about one thing."

He chuckled at that, which was the last thing I expected him to do. "And what could Katherine possibly be right about?"

"You were framed. You were set up. Not by a rookie, either."

CHAPTER
23
★ ★ ★

I heard the church bells pealing over the pounding on my door. I peeked angrily at the clock: 5:15 A.M., Sunday morning. If I had a pistol I would've shot the bastard at the door. I'd fallen asleep only two hours before, because there's nothing I hate more than an innocent client who hasn't got a chance in hell of winning.

I threw on my pants and, since one punch in the nose was already one over my weekly allotment, cautiously spied through the peephole till I saw the top of Imelda's head. In case I haven't mentioned it, Imelda's only five foot one and maybe 140 pounds, although a hell of a lot of cordite is packed inside that tiny shell.

When I opened the door, she stomped in without asking. Another damned thing about Imelda: She thinks she owns the world. Somebody, someday, ought to disabuse her of that notion. It certainly won't be me, though.

"Okay," she spat out by way of introduction, "Keith Merritt."

"Right. Keith Merritt."

"This guy ain't named Keith Merritt."

Having already ably established that verity myself, I said, "Right. Keith Merritt is not the name of the guy in the hospital bed."

"Passport's phony, too."

"His passport's phony, too," I repeated. Now, how the hell did she know that?

"I checked at the embassy. There's a Keith Merritt with that passport number, only he's a lawyer down somewheres in Florida," she quickly added, accurately reading my thoughts, as she usually did, which I found incredibly disarming.

"So who's this guy?"

"Nothin' too hard 'bout that."

"No?"

"Boy's got fingerprints, don't he? Fingerprints can be checked, can't they?"

"Of course," I said. "And have you done that?"

"'Course I've done that. The man's in a coma; what's so hard? Go into his room, roll his finger in ink a few times. Not like he noticed. Only hard thing was getting a friend in CID to run the check."

"So who's this guy calling himself Keith Merritt?" I asked again, playing along, but of course I knew what she was up to. It was the old sergeant's trick of making me go through a lengthy disposition to find out exactly how clever and resourceful she was, how many strings she had had to pull. That way I wouldn't get any dumb ideas, like maybe I didn't need her or something idiotic like that.

"Name's Frederick Melborne."

"Uh-huh."

"As in Melborne and Associates."

"This is not a brokerage house I take it?"

"You take that right," she frostily announced. "It's a private detective agency in Alexandria, Virginia."

"So he's a PI?"

She drew in her chin and stared down her nose at me. "Well he probably ain't the receptionist."

It struck me the reason she was busting my balls might be because she was still sore about this gay thing. I'm very perceptive that way.

"And does Melborne have a license?"

"'Course he's gotta license," she barked, withdrawing a slip of paper from her pocket and reading from it. "Number AL223-987 issued by the state of Virginia in the year 1995."

"So he's real."

"Ex-Army, too. Used to be a lieutenant in the MPs. Penn State, ROTC grad, three years at Fort Benning, got out and went into private business. Should know his way around."

"Imelda, you do very impressive work," I said, offering her my most suave grin. I was trying my utmost to mend whatever little problem we were having here. That suave-grin thing works wonders for Eddie Golden, right? Why can't it work for me?

"I'm not done," she grimly replied, stubbornly oblivious to my charms. "Melborne got here before Miss Carlson even. Two weeks before."

"Interesting. Do we know what was he snooping around for?"

"'Course we know," she announced like it was the stupidest question in the world. "Some friends say he was askin' around about where gays go to party, that kinda thing."

"So it looks like he was either out for a little fun or he was trying to infiltrate the local gay community?"

"Ain't that what I said?"

"Why would he be doing that?"

She blew some air through her lips. "Want me to go back there and ask him that? He's in a coma. Not like he'll answer."

I went over and sat on the edge of the bed as Imelda studied me from behind her tiny glasses.

What I wanted to say was, "See, Imelda, just like I told you. That bitch Katherine's been sandbagging me, uh, you . . . uh, us." That's what I wanted to say. But she was tapping her hand on the side of her leg in a pent-up way, so I controlled myself.

What I said instead was, "I'll tell you what I think. OGMM hired Melborne and gave him the names of some local gays so he could come over here and infiltrate the local rings. Katherine was using him to run discreet background checks on Lee, Moran, and Jackson."

"Might be that," Imelda noncommittally replied.

"And I think Melborne found something, or got close to finding something."

Imelda indifferently said, "Maybe."

"So who used him to buff the front of that car? Some gays who got bent out of shape that he was looking into their affairs? Some fanatical antigay group that decided to make an example of him? Or somebody else?"

Imelda was still tapping the side of her leg. I could tell by her expression I wasn't getting her full cooperation here.

It was starting to distract me, so I said, "You got something you want to say?"

She lowered her glasses down the bridge of her nose, an apocalyptic sign, like a battleship raising its colors to signal it's ready for combat.

"You sure you wanta hear it?"

I wasn't, but I'd brought it up, so I said, "Sure."

"What I think is you and Miss Carlson oughta have your sorry asses kicked. That's what I think."

"Huh?"

"You oughta be ashamed of yourselves. Playin' all these games with each other, while you got a man facing the executioner. How'd you like to be that boy? How'd you like to see the two lawyers who're supposed to be savin' your ass running about pissin' on each other's backsides?"

Now, I could've told Imelda she was exaggerating, only that'd be splitting hairs. Or I could've tried telling her this was all Katherine's fault—which, believe me, it was—except Imelda Pepperfield was a throwback to the old Army. And in the old Army, there were only two colors, black and white, and any attempt to find cover in the middle could prove lethal.

So all I said was, "Okay, okay. I'll work on it."

"You better," was all she said before she stormed out.

She was obviously in a gnarly mood, partly because she'd just spent the entire night on the phones tracking down Melborne's true identity, and partly because, well . . . I guess, just partly because. You gotta know Imelda.

I got cleaned up and went downstairs and had breakfast. When I got back to my room, an envelope had been slipped under my door. I tore it open. In a tight scrawl it said I had an eight o'clock appointment in the office of General Spears. This time, "8:00" was underlined about ten times in thick marker, like, Don't be late again, Drummond.

It was already seven, so I killed thirty minutes spit-shining my boots, combing my hair, and meticulously pressing every square inch of my uniform. Although actually that's not true; that's what I should've been doing if I was an earnest, ambitious officer. Instead I watched some inane Sunday morning sitcom before ambling over to the big cheese's office.

The same colonel was seated at his desk, only this time he was the one wearing civilian clothes and I was the one in uniform, because it was Sunday morning.

Remembering our last tepid encounter, I ripped off a salute. It was an awesome salute, too. It left a smoke trail in the air. The most incurably fussy drill sergeant would've swooned.

I said, "Major Drummond reporting as ordered, sir."

I said it loud and crisply, too, and just knew the man would be impressed as all get out. West Pointers are so damned easy to please.

He shook his head and gave me a scowl ugly enough to melt tulips. "Drummond, you're a lawyer, right?"

"Yes sir. JAG Corps all the way, sir. Hoo Rah!" I popped off. I was Johnny Gung-ho this early Sunday morning.

"Then you should know that when inside a building, you don't salute a higher officer who is not in uniform."

My hand was still stuck to my forehead, and I all of a sudden started scratching a non-itch over my right eye.

I was frostily instructed to go to the general's door and knock twice. The colonel even quizzed me to make sure I understood it was knock twice—not once, not three times, but twice. He was a real sweetheart. We were getting along famously.

Spears glanced up from some papers after I knocked twice, not once, not three times. I walked straight to his desk and noticed he also was wearing mufti on this grand Sunday morning.

Knowing military etiquette like I did, I merely nodded and politely said, "Good morning, General."

He pushed aside his reading materials, got up, and walked around his desk. "Please, sit down," he said, gesturing at a couch group near the door.

We quickly positioned ourselves so I was sitting across from him, while he eased into his chair, hoisted up his trouser leg, and studied me.

After a moment, he said, "How's it going?"

"Fine, General. Couldn't be better," I lied.

He awarded me a nice grin. "We've got a long week ahead. The judge arrives tomorrow. Press people have been flying in by the planeload. By Wednesday there'll be more reporters in Korea than soldiers."

"It's the big show," I said, which was a needless remark, obviously, but he didn't seem to mind.

"You ever handled a case this big, Drummond?"

"Like this? No sir."

"You feel like you're under a lot of pressure?"

"Like a bicycle tire that's been placed on a ten-wheeler."

He chuckled briefly. "And how's your client doing?"

"Could be worse, General. Not a lot, but could be worse."

He nodded. "Korean prisons aren't for the fainthearted. But they're good people, you know. The Koreans. This is my third tour over here. I was here as a new lieutenant, back in the early sixties. And I commanded my brigade here, back in the late eighties. It's miraculous what the Koreans have accomplished. Really miraculous. They're incredible people."

"Yes sir, they're admirable folks."

Then came a quiet lapse, because we'd obviously exhausted the let's-pretend-we're-comfortable-with-each-other chitchat and it was time to tend to the nuts and bolts. Whatever that was.

He went right for the jugular. "Drummond, I have to tell you, I've been very unhappy with the way your defense team has conducted itself. And I mean, *very unhappy.*"

"Anything specifically?" I asked. Like I didn't know.

"Start with Miss Carlson's infomercials. I told you I didn't want this case carried to the press. This is not the time to be fanning the flames."

In my most humble tone, I said, "Look, General, telling a civilian defense attorney not to prattle to the press is like telling an addict not to go near a needle. It's compulsive. They can't stop themselves. It's also perfectly ethical."

I had the sense this was a throwaway conversational point, because I wasn't telling him anything he didn't already know, plus his face suddenly got more grave, or suggestive, or something.

"Then let me tell you what I really don't appreciate. Your visit to Minister Lee's home."

"I have an obligation to my client to follow every avenue to prove his innocence. I wasn't there for a social call or to harass them."

I wasn't going to disclose any more than that, because the existence of the apartment key in No's possession was the only surprise we had for the prosecution. Besides, it was none of Spears's business.

But, like I mentioned before, the general has these grittily intense eyes, and he was giving me a full-up dose. I squirmed uncomfortably in my seat.

He said, "Did you know I served with Minister Lee in Vietnam?"

I shook my head. How the hell would I know that?

His expression altered a little, maybe even softened. "I spent six months as the American liaison to the ROK First Infantry Division where Lee was a battalion commander. Most Americans don't even realize Korean troops were in Vietnam. But the ROKs, you know, they earned a reputation as tough fighters. The Vietcong were scared to death of them, so the ROKs didn't see as much fighting as most American units. The Vietcong made an effort to avoid them."

"I've heard stories," I said, which was true. And they weren't pretty stories, either. Maybe they were exaggerations, but there were rumors of South Korean troops collecting ears for trophies and putting Vietcong heads on stakes to discourage sympathizers. On the other hand, maybe they weren't exaggerations.

Anyway, Spears stared out the window, caught up in his reverie. "One day an ROK battalion was on a sweep, and before they knew it, they were attacked by two full brigades of North Vietnamese regulars. They were outnumbered nearly ten to one. What we guessed later was the North Vietnamese wanted to show the Vietcong, who were all southerners, that the ROKs could be beaten. Or maybe they wanted to try to knock the ROKs out of the war by inflicting a bloody defeat on them. They sure as hell weren't happy that another Asian country was involved in their war. Anyway, the battle developed quickly. I flew in on a helicopter and landed at the battalion command bunker maybe twenty minutes after it began. Lee was the battalion commander. You probably guessed that?"

I nodded again.

"The ROKs didn't fight like Americans. They didn't have fleets of jets and helicopters and thousands of tubes of artillery. They didn't rely on all that firepower. They just slugged it out, soldier to soldier, and the North Vietnamese knew that, so they threw everything they had at them. God, I never saw such a fierce, desperate fight."

"So what happened, General?"

"Usually, in battle, there are pauses and lulls as the two sides regroup or stalemate, then go at it again. Not that time. It was one long, relentless attack. Lee's troops were formed in a hasty perimeter, and several times the North Vietnamese broke through. There were bands of North Vietnamese running around inside the perimeter, shooting and throwing grenades. Some had bombs strapped to their bodies, trying to get to the command bunker. The North Vietnamese were smart that way. They knew that if they killed the head the body would follow. Within ten minutes after I'd flown in, I wondered what the hell I'd gotten into."

He turned away from the window and stared back at me. But I didn't have the feeling he was actually looking at me. His mind was in another place, another time.

"It was an inferno. I saw Lee rush out and kill three men with an entrenching tool. Can you imagine? He'd emptied his pistol so he literally ran at three armed men with nothing but a short shovel. That's how desperate the fighting was. It took three hours for the ROK division to borrow some helicopters from a nearby American division and bring in reinforcements. A quarter of Lee's men were dead. The medevac helicopters spent four hours pulling out the wounded. There were maybe four or five hundred North Viet- namese corpses strewn around, from outside the perimeter to the assault teams that made it inside."

I said, "I heard he was a great soldier."

He shook his head. "Great? No, great's not an adequate word. I knew your father, too, Drummond. Did you know that? Now, your father, he was a great soldier. A real bastard to work for, I hear, but a great soldier. Lee was more than that. I saw two of his officers throw themselves in front of bullets to protect him. Think anybody would've thrown themselves in front of your father to save him?"

Knowing my father as I did, I could see people shoving him in the way of bullets to save themselves. I mean, I love and adore my father, but the man has some serious warts.

The general had made his point, so he continued. "If there was any chance in hell your client was innocent, I'd have no problem with what you did. Hell, I'd lead the assault on Lee's door. I'd help ransack his attic. But Whitehall's guilty. A thorough Article 32 in- vestigation was conducted before I recommended this court- martial. I've never seen a more airtight case."

An Article 32 investigation is the military's version of what would be called a grand jury in the civilian world, only instead of a closed jury, the Army appoints a major or a lieutenant colonel to determine if there's enough evidence and grounds to convene a court-martial.

Anyway, I opened my lips and started to say something, but he sliced his arm through the air for me to keep my mouth shut. He was one of those daunting men who, even in civilian clothes, had an air of authority that brooked no disagreement.

"I've checked on you, Drummond. Everybody says you're a damned good lawyer and an ethical officer. So ask yourself this. We offered you a deal where you'd save your client's life in exchange for avoiding the character assassination of one of the finest men I've ever met. What's the point of destroying Lee's reputation, and maybe this alliance, just to try to keep a murderer out of jail? You've got plenty of courtroom experience, right? How do you gauge your odds in this case? This wouldn't even be a Pyrrhic victory; it would be a Pyrrhic defeat. Your client's the one who created this situation, not us. How far are you willing to go? How much damage are you willing to inflict in his name?"

These were profoundly worthy questions, and it was obvious the general was well-grounded in the kind of ethical issues that bedevil us lawyers. The problem was there was a new fly in the ointment.

I tried to keep my voice and eyes steady. "General, my client *is* innocent."

"You can't be serious."

"I've never been more serious. He was framed."

He closed his eyes, a sign of weary resignation.

Finally his lids came apart and he frowned at me with an expression of bottomless disappointment. "So that's how you're going to play it?"

"General, that's how I have to play it."

He abruptly stood up, so I stood up, too. He just stared at me until I got tired of being stared at and headed for his door.

"Drummond?" he called before I made it out.

I turned around and faced him.

"Just be sure you can still look yourself in the mirror when this is done."

I nodded and left.

I have to tell you that among the many mischaracterizations perpetrated by the media and Hollywood is the one that depicts Army generals as plump, cigar-chomping, ego-inflated morons who are so busy spit-shining their own asses they can barely find their way to the eighteenth hole of the golf course. There're some of those, to be sure, and if Spears's legal adviser ever made general there'd be one more. But General Spears was more redolent of the larger breed—serious, thoughtful, sharply intelligent, the kind of person you just can't help respecting. The kind of person you want to respect you, too.

Spears had commanded a unit in the Gulf War that tore the hell out of two of Saddam's best divisions, and, although he was unaware of it, I was there, and I witnessed it, and he was a hell of a soldier. And he was now sitting on top of an explosive situation. With less than a few minutes' warning, he could be entangled in the biggest war to hit the planet since World War Two.

The worst of it was, I possessed not a single shred of evidence that Thomas Whitehall was innocent. I had a hunch. And as anyone in the legal profession will tell you, when you act on a hunch it's like playing Russian roulette with five bullets in the cylinder. And Spears was right; when this was over, I'd better be able to look in a mirror and not have it shatter.

CHAPTER

24

★ ★ ★

What Katherine figured was that she would kill two birds with one stone. Colonel Barry Carruthers, the military judge assigned to our case, was set to arrive on a military flight at 7:00 A.M. at Osan Air Base. This much Katherine knew because it was widely reported on the news.

Katherine would have preferred to meet him at the ramp as he walked off the plane, but because he was landing at a military air base, there was no way in hell she'd be able to get her associates through the strictly controlled gates. She therefore calculated the time it would take to get the judge by military convoy up to Yongsan Garrison.

She arranged her welcoming party to meet and greet Barry Carruthers right outside the main gate at exactly 8:10 A.M. And at 8:10 exactly seven buses, two or three dozen taxis, and a few people on bicycles suddenly appeared. Then, after about a minute of people rushing off their conveyances and getting organized, there they were, 620 practitioners of backwards love, most dressed normally, but a select few making a statement with flamboyant outfits.

Right beside them, in front of God and country and some dozen film crews, stood yours truly struggling not to look as uneasy and abashed as I felt. I was in uniform, too. I knew I was going to pay for it, but hey, in for a nickel, in for a dollar.

I was there because Imelda's sharp criticisms guilted me into it. I was there because I wanted my client to know I was unconditionally committed to his defense. I was there because I wanted Katherine to trust me and let me in on her secrets. I was there because I prayed Katherine was right, that maybe we could gull the Army into cutting a better deal for Tommy Whitehall.

At least she'd done the wise thing and gotten a legal permit. She'd applied through the Seoul mayor's office using a false name, and under the guise we wanted to publicly welcome the judge. This was technically true, at least depending on your definition of the word "welcome." Since even the Korean papers had been describing Colonel Barry Carruthers as a Judge Roy Bean kind of guy—the last of the great hanging judges—I think the Koreans were fairly delighted at the idea of an American welcoming party, so they put all the appropriate stamps on Katherine's request and even promised to provide security.

That's why there were about two dozen Korean riot police in blue suits, wearing those spiffy shielded helmets and holding black batons behind their body shields. The shields looked badly scratched and dented, because one thing a Korean riot policeman gets plenty of is on-the-job practice.

I could barely imagine what the police were thinking when they spotted us, because there'd sure as hell never been a demonstration like this in the history of the Republic of Korea. The officer in charge of the platoon was on the radio, red-faced and screaming frantically at somebody on the other end, no doubt trying to inform the city officials that this wasn't a welcoming party after all, but a demonstration, and, hey, you'll never guess what kind of people are here.

So we locked arms and waited. The camera crewmen were all taking a particular interest in me, since after all, I was the only person in uniform in this crowd. I looked anxiously at my watch. I hoped Carruthers's convoy didn't have a radio, or, if it did, that nobody had thought to call and recommend they divert to a different entry point onto post. If that happened, we'd look like a bunch of dopes.

What worried me the most, though, was what would happen when the South Koreans came to a decision about how to handle us. The Koreans, like most Asians, aren't known for speedy decisions, because they have to go through that mutual consultation crap that's a cultural imperative for them.

They can surprise you, though. And I wasn't all that optimistic about how that might turn out. The city of Seoul has something like one hundred thousand riot police, as well as fleets of gray, caged buses parked at strategic locations around the city. And they have radios, and when there's the first sign of trouble they send up smoke signals and converge with lightning speed on a single point. Katherine had 620 unarmed civilians, about half of whom were women, although some looked fit enough to fend for themselves.

Anyway, I was still calculating the odds of disaster when six of those big caged gray buses came careening down the road from the Itaewon district. And tucked right in the middle of them were two U.S. Army humvees and a black Kia sedan, no doubt containing the hanging judge himself, Barry Carruthers.

The first bus kept moving toward us, although it slowed down considerably, and I could see a Korean in the front hollering something into a radio, no doubt asking for instructions. Apparently he got some, because he turned and yelled at the driver, and the vehicle ground noisily to a halt. Another long minute passed as the guy with the radio kept yipping at somebody.

Katherine breathlessly asked me what was going on. Like I should know. Face it, she had a great deal more experience on this end of protests than I did. She'd probably been in dozens of them, whereas I was a stone-cold virgin.

Then the door of the first bus swung open and riot policemen poured out. A few seconds later the other five buses emptied, until there were what seemed to be two hundred or so blue-uniformed troops, pulling down their riot visors, forming into lines, stretching their muscles, and moving toward us.

As this was occurring a number of blue-and-white Korean police cars began arriving at the scene. Within two minutes, there were about fifteen or twenty cars skewed at various angles across the road. Several dozen policemen were milling around, scratching their heads and wondering what to do.

Katherine had to find the scene unnerving, but she coolly lifted up her megaphone and yelled, "This is a peaceful gathering. We have the authorization of your city mayor to be here. We want no trouble."

I turned and said, "Think they speak English?"

She chuckled and lifted up her megaphone again. "I repeat, this is a peaceful demonstration."

I examined the riot police, and it seemed they either didn't hear her, or comprehend her, or care. They were in a rough semblance of ranks. They began moving steadily toward us, taking two measured steps at a time, straightening their lines, and getting their riot shields positioned into a straight wall. I could hear their officers yelling instructions. I wished I could understand Korean and knew what they were saying.

I looked at Katherine, and she was staring straight at them, but she calmly said, "It's okay. It's a standard technique. They'll keep moving toward us until they get a few feet away. It's called the bluff and run. They bluff, we run."

I glanced behind me at the other protesters. Nobody seemed alarmed. Most of these folks were veterans, I guessed. They knew the game. But what if they were wrong? What if the name of this tactic was run and crunch? After all, this was a different country. Maybe American riot-control tactics hadn't traveled this far.

As for me, I was scared as hell. I'm a soldier and I've been in battle a few times, but in battle I was always at least as well armed as the guy I was fighting, so the odds were squared up. Besides, there's something grim and terrifying in watching all these highly disciplined, robotic-looking creatures moving relentlessly toward you. You can see their batons peeking over their shields, and you get this ugly mental picture of one of those things cracking the top of your skull a few times.

Soon the line was twenty yards ahead of us, then fifteen, then ten, and still they kept right on coming, inexorably—two steps, stop; two steps, stop. When they were only about five feet away, just as Katherine predicted, they halted.

A few newspeople dashed into the narrow space between us and began lying on the ground, taking their camera and film shots from horizontal positions, I guess thinking they could win an Oscar, or a Tony, or a Nobel, or a Pulitzer, or whatever asinine award you get for doing something spectacularly stupid and having visual evidence to prove it.

Katherine stood steady, but I could hear her drawing deep breaths to control her nerves. I could also hear my own heart beating furiously.

Suddenly, out of nowhere, there was a dull pop behind me. Almost immediately, I heard a bunch more shots, the sounds of a weapon shooting quickly, only this racket was coming from somewhere in front of me. And all hell broke loose. People were diving for the ground and screaming, and it wasn't just the protesters, either, but the riot policemen as well.

I suddenly got knocked forward, right into the ranks of the riot police. I stuck my head up and looked around to see who was shooting. I spotted one man on the hill pointing a weapon—it looked like an M16—but I heard shots coming from somewhere else, too; somewhere off to my left, I was pretty sure.

The man I'd seen was a South Korean policeman.

I started shoving aside everybody in my path and working my way to the edge of the crowd. Two protesters right in front of me went down with sprays of blood flying from their chests and heads. I saw a riot baton on the ground, bent over, picked it up, then used it to bash my way through the crowd.

Ten feet in front of me, I saw another South Korean policeman lying flat on the ground. I swung my baton and gently whacked him on the back of the head, enough to stun him, then I stooped over and pulled his pistol out of his holster. His hands had automatically reached up to protect his head, so he didn't put up a fight.

It took only seconds before I was at the edge of the throng and running toward the gunman on the hill. He was still up there, about forty yards from me, and a voice inside my head was saying, Don't be stupid, Drummond, don't be stupid, don't do this, but my legs weren't listening to my brain, and they kept pumping of their own volition.

Then I got lucky. He'd emptied his clip and was drawing another from a pocket in his vest. He looked down and saw me swinging that baton, sprinting toward him. He made a quick judgment, threw the weapon on the ground, spun around, and fled.

I could still hear someone firing shots from off to my left, but I kept running. The Korean policeman I was chasing was one of those guys with short, squatty legs that pump a hundred times a second. I was taller and my legs were longer, and in a distance race I could take him hands down, but he was a faster sprinter. He was heading straight up a gently sloped hill for the Itaewon shopping district with its thousands of back alleys and shops—a perfect place to get lost and hide.

I looked back up and my target was nearly to Itaewon, about sixty yards ahead of me. I knew this because he was shoving people aside—old ladies, a few young kids, anybody in his path.

I tried to put everything out of my mind. I pumped my legs. My lungs were burning but I struggled to ignore them. I got to a corner street that formed the edge of the shopping district, and I went left. Korean pedestrians were diving out of my path, and for the first time I realized what this must look like to them. First they see a South Korean policeman running fearfully from something; next they see a pursuing American soldier carrying a pistol.

I looked around and couldn't see the Korean policeman anywhere. He hadn't crossed the street or I would've spotted him. He must've disappeared into one of the shops or alleyways on my side of the street. I'd only been to Itaewon two or three times before, so I didn't know it well.

Then, suddenly, luck again fell into my lap. I saw two women who looked like American housewives toting huge shopping bags loaded with goodies.

I rushed toward them; they both stared at the pistol in my hand.

"Hi," I puffed out. "Did you"—puff, puff—"did you see a Korean cop?"

One had her eyes frozen on my pistol. She nodded.

"Where"—puff, puff—"where'd he go?"

Her head swiveled toward an alleyway about thirty feet away.

I left them standing there. I came around the corner and *Bang!* The bullet took about an inch of skin and muscle off my left shoulder. The thing that saved my life was those years of shooter training in the outfit. My response was instinctive. I dove through the air, pistol pointed forward, searching for a target. I heard two more shots as I landed hard on my stomach without acquiring my quarry. The blow knocked the air out of my lungs, but I somehow rolled up to my knees, still sweeping the pistol in a semicircle. Aside from a few mamasans and papasans who were frantically scooted up against the sides of the alley, I didn't see the shooter.

I tried to draw some air, but it took a few precious seconds to get my lungs inflated again. I stood and moved down the alley, this time more slowly. I kept my pistol up and ready, moving it back and forth in a steady sweeping motion.

I heard a shot down to the left, and I ran. The alley split into two tiny, cramped side streets, and I wouldn't have known which way to go if it hadn't been for the Korean civilian lying in the middle of the street. There was a big dark hole in the middle of his forehead and blood was puddling on the cement. His eyes were open and glassy. I knew the look. He was dead.

I sprinted past him, noticing that the street ended abruptly at a big concrete wall. It was a dead end. Now, this is where these things always get tricky, because we all know the warning about the cornered rat, and that's apparently what I had on my hands.

I slowed to a walk. Staying up against the left wall, I edged along, my pistol raised, ready to shoot the next thing that moved. Something suddenly lunged out of a doorway right in front of me, and I lowered my pistol and nearly pulled the trigger. Thank God I didn't. It was a small Korean kid who stared up at me with a blank expression. I guess he thought the pistol in my hand was a toy gun, or that I was a movie star and his street was being used as a set, because he then started looking around, like, Hey, where's the camera?

Keeping my gun up with my right hand, I reached down with my left and grabbed the kid by his collar and tugged him back behind me. He seemed to think this was great fun, because he giggled a lot, and hung right on my tail.

I continued inching forward, when, out of the corner of my eye, I saw a flash of movement. I grabbed the kid and fell backward just as three shots struck the window next to where I'd been standing. On the way down I let loose three quick, wild shots at the spot where I'd seen something move, knowing I had no chance of hitting him, but trying desperately to drive him back behind cover.

A few seconds passed. I heard another shot, then nothing. I slowly got up. The kid had realized my gun wasn't a toy and this wasn't a Hollywood extravaganza, because there was this stunned look on his face, and his lips were wide open, and he was getting ready to wail. He was staring at my leg, which hurt like hell. I glanced down and saw it was bleeding. Not from a bullet, though. When the shots struck the window, the glass had shattered and a big angular chunk had fallen down and was now protruding in an ugly way from my left thigh.

I have to confess that I'm not the kind of tough guy who can glibly wrench a big splinter of glass out of my leg and just grin and bear it. But I had to do something, so I reached down and tugged on that big splinter of glass and screamed a scattershot of words that thankfully the kid couldn't understand because his mother would've been seriously unhappy with me.

I sat for a stunned moment, trying to make the pain stop, before I realized that no matter how much it hurt I couldn't stay where I was. So I got up and limped in the direction of the shooter. I kept my pistol pointed ahead. Reaching the corner that led into the shop he'd fired from, I put my back against the wall and edged forward. A few seconds later I was at the doorway.

Most trained police officers will tell you, this is what's called a truth-or-consequences moment. So let's start with truth. The only way to get into that shop was through that doorway. Although you see guys do that in the movies all the time, it's suicide. Doorways are very narrow things, and the shooter's expecting you to come through, and he's stationary, and he's got his gun poised and ready, and he's going to get you. It doesn't matter if you go in flying, or rolling, or doing backward somersaults. He's going to shoot you and then it's over.

That's why policemen carry stun grenades and soldiers carry hand grenades, so they can fling them through doorways, wait till they go boom, then rush through.

Only I didn't have any grenades.

So I stood there for a long difficult moment and contemplated my options. Up against the wall a few feet down there was a big basket filled with clothes. I limped over and retrieved it. I stuffed my pistol in my belt, lifted that basket, and threw it through the doorway.

Nothing. Not a shot, not a sound. Either the shooter had sharp eyes and recognized it was a basket of clothes, or he was simply too smart for me and was holding his fire. Maybe he'd already fled through a back entrance to the shop. If that was the case, with all this warm blood spilling out of the wound in my leg, this game was over.

So here's where we get to that consequences part. I held my breath, dove through the doorway, and wildly fired my pistol until there were no rounds left. I lay perfectly still on the ground, my ears ringing, paralyzed as I waited for the shooter to peek up from behind a counter and pop me in the forehead.

It didn't happen. I waited a long time, helplessly sweeping my empty gun through the air. I won't say I was disappointed, although it looked like my shooter had gotten away. So I got up and looked around, until I eventually peeked over the far side of the counter. And voilà! There was my shooter. He was lying on his stomach, facedown, and there was a big chunk blown out of the back of his head.

Now it's time for a little secret. Among my many shortcomings is a complete inability to fire a pistol with any accuracy. It's true. I almost didn't get into the outfit because of it, and over the next five years they brought in all kinds of weapons experts to coach me. All of them gave up in frustration.

I looked at that hole in the back of the cop's head and said a silent prayer. I mumbled again and again, Thank you, God, for doing this thing for me. When did I get him, God? Was it when I went down back in the street? Did one of those wild shots catch him in the forehead and send him flying backward over the counter? Or was it when I came diving into the shop, guns blazing?

I bent down and turned him over. The first thing I noticed was the barrel of his own pistol stuck inside his mouth. The second thing I noticed was that he was wearing white cloth gloves that were soaked in blood.

CHAPTER
25
✪ ✪ ✪

The initial count was twelve dead and nineteen wounded, three of whom were in sufficiently perilous condition that the doctors said the authorities could just as well call it fifteen dead. Two of the dead and four of the wounded were journalists. None were South Koreans, unless you wanted to count one Korean-American reporter who carried an American passport. He was among the dead. Or unless you wanted to count one South Korean policeman who'd eaten his own bullet and another who'd been whacked on the head by an American officer.

That same hapless American Army officer was currently in a small, cramped, smelly jail cell in the Itaewon Police Station. He was a very unhappy guy, too. And I mean, royally unhappy. He was under arrest for assaulting one police officer, for the theft of a lethal weapon—to wit, a pistol—for shooting a Korean civilian in the head, and for cold-bloodedly murdering a Korean police officer.

Eventually I was led from the cell into an interrogation room in the rear of the station. Actually, "led" is an exaggeration. I was shoved, kicked, punched, and bounced off walls the whole way. By the time I got tossed like a rag doll through the doorway and into the interrogation room, my ears were ringing, my nose was bleeding, my brain was groggy, and my leg, the one I'd cut earlier, was bleeding profusely.

I looked up from the floor and saw two gentlemen in civilian clothes seated at a long wooden table. One was Korean and one was American. One was named Chief Warrant Officer Three Michael Bales, and the other could've been called Chop Suey for all I knew. I was so spitting mad, I almost couldn't see straight. All I wanted to do was punch somebody's lights out.

"God damn it, Bales," I mumbled through badly swollen lips. "Get off your ass and come help me. I've been beaten silly."

I was on my knees and wasn't sure I could get up, but I was still a major, and Bales was still a warrant officer, and Army rank isn't supposed to shed its obligations outside the gates.

He smiled. "Fuck you, asshole. Get yourself up."

I shook my head and tried to clear my ears. Did I hear that right? What the hell was happening here? Did those words come from the lips of Michael Bales, the ace investigator, the all-American midwestern boy?

I grabbed the corner of a chair and struggled to my feet. Having been in a few interrogation rooms in my day, I knew the drill. I fell into a seat and studied the room. What I saw I instantly disliked. Unlike American interrogation cells, this one didn't have a two-way mirror, and as best I could tell there were no video cameras in the corners of the ceiling. This was not a hopeful sign. Those cameras and two-way mirrors are to keep interrogators from acting out their most extreme fantasies, if you get my drift.

I studied Bales's face and didn't like what I saw there, either. He was smiling, only it wasn't anything close to a friendly smile. It was the merciless kind of smile.

Considering his expression, I opened with, "I want to see an attorney. I'm not saying a word until I have an attorney present."

Bales chuckled and started to study his fingernails. "The crimes you're accused of were committed on Korean territory, Drummond. They're running this show. And they don't believe in all that crap."

"Then I want a representative from the embassy. I'm an American citizen. I have that right under international protocols."

The Korean bent forward. "I'm Chief Inspector Choi and I'm in charge of this investigation. I decide what the rules are, not you. This is my country, Drummond."

Then, almost faster than I could see it coming, and certainly faster than I could do anything about it, his fist flew across the table and landed on my jaw. I careened backward and somersaulted off my chair, ending up somehow on my stomach. I had to shake my head a few times to be sure it was still connected to my body.

A man's got to be pretty damned strong to throw a punch that hard from a sitting position. I made a mental note of that.

"Get up, asshole," Bales ordered.

I scrabbled around for a few seconds trying to get some balance and finally made it to my feet. I was woozy and kept slipping on the blood that was pooling on the floor. My blood—from my shoulder, from my leg, from my nose, and God knows where else.

I bent over, lifted up the chair, and sat back down.

I very politely said, "May I ask what I'm charged with?"

"Murder," Choi said.

To which I replied, "I didn't murder him. I saw him shooting into the crowd at the gate. I chased him down and he killed himself."

Bales leaned back into his chair and stroked his chin. He looked terribly amused by this whole thing.

Choi said, "Actually, double murder. The civilian you murdered was named Kang Soon Moo. He was a retarded adult, forty-two years old, and you shot him right in the head. The police officer you murdered was Lee Kim Moon. He has been an officer in this precinct for twelve years. He has been decorated for courageous service four times. He was a reliable, dedicated, outstanding police officer. He has a wife and two young daughters."

And I said, "I'm telling you, I saw him up on the hillside with an M16 pouring rounds into the crowd."

Now Bales bent forward and sarcastically asked, "And what? You broke out of the crowd and charged him. Without a weapon? You made him drop his M16 and run?"

"That's exactly what happened," I angrily snarled, realizing how ludicrous it sounded.

Bales snickered. "I would've thought a lawyer should be able to come up with a better alibi than that."

For some reason that really pissed me off. "Up your ass."

This time it was Bales who swung his fist across the table and punched me. But I only fell backward and landed on my bottom. Bales wasn't nearly as strong as Choi. I added that to my mental notes.

When I finally looked up, Bales was standing over me. He kicked me twice in the stomach and I made big "ooof" sounds and folded up like a beach chair. His kick was harder than his punch. Much harder.

While I was struggling to get some air back in my lungs, Choi said, "There was only one shooter at the gate, Drummond. And he jumped into a car and was chased halfway around the city before he got away. And it wasn't Officer Lee."

I slowly got to my knees and Bales was still standing over me, so I begged him, "Please. Please don't kick me again."

He stood there a moment, and then took a step backward. I thought he was going to leave me alone, but he suddenly twisted around on his heel and let loose a roundhouse kick that caught me in the head.

I'm not sure how long I was out, but when I came to, Bales and Choi had hoisted me back up onto a chair, and I was wet all over. I guessed they'd thrown a bucket of water to try to revive me. I hurt about everywhere a man could hurt, except maybe my groin, which, all things considered, could be counted as a hidden blessing.

I couldn't work up enough strength to get my eyelids open. I heard Choi laughing and telling Bales, "Damn it, Michael, be careful with your feet. I warned you of that with Jackson. You almost killed him."

Bales halfheartedly chuckled. "The little fag sang, didn't he?"

"And I had to write a report that he was beaten senseless by his cellmate. Don't press your luck."

All things considered, the best thing I could do at this point was play possum. I was feeling spectacularly sorry for myself, and I'd had more ass-kickings than any one man should rightly get, so I kept my eyes shut and played dead. And let me tell you, that's damned hard to do when you hurt all over and you can feel blood trickling out of various cuts and wounds.

Choi finally got tired of waiting for me to revive, so he criticized Bales for his kick again and left to get some officers to drag me to a cell.

The two cops came in and each took a hold under my armpits. I hung limp, although my left shoulder, where the bullet had grazed me, burned like somebody had dropped acid on it.

They laid me on a sleeping mat, and, much as I would've loved to sleep, the pain was too great. I could peek through one of my eyelids, although the other one seemed to be fused shut. A guard was positioned right outside the bars, reading a skin magazine and apparently waiting for a sign I was conscious. Choi probably had told him to let him know as soon as I was awake so they could bring me back in the interrogation room and ass-kick a confession out of me.

I, of course, did some thinking about the Whitehall situation, although I will admit it was not at the top of my give-a-shit list at that moment.

I had badly misjudged Michael Bales; that was obvious. He wasn't Dudley Do-Right at all. He was Dirty Harry with a little extra malice thrown in. And he and his buddy Choi had knocked the crap out of Private Jackson, and probably Moran also, to extract their statements.

Anyway, so what, because I was facing another of their physical interrogations. The thought nearly made me sick. I was sure Choi was in there telling him, "Hey, Michael, stick with your fists so we can get this jerk-off to break." Two hours passed, and just as it was starting to become late afternoon, I heard footsteps and keys jingling, and I guessed they had run out of patience. I lay still and played dead and prayed desperately for myself. Korean voices chattered in the distance. I felt so hopeless I wanted to die. I'd been lying perfectly prone long enough for my body to stiffen and my bruises and wounds to begin to ache terribly.

I couldn't withstand another beating. If Bales or Choi wanted me to confess to killing everybody in that crowd, I'd do it and take the chance I could sort it out later.

I felt myself being lifted by a couple of pairs of strong hands. I moaned pitifully until I heard a voice.

"Oh God, Sean, what the hell did they do to you?"

I opened one eyelid, because the other was swollen completely shut from Bales's final kick. I tried to smile but my lips were pretty swollen so it probably looked awful.

I never thought I'd be happy to see Katherine Carlson. I was, though. If my legs weren't so wobbly, I would've rushed across the cell and hugged and kissed her.

But that was an empty, fleeting thought, anyway, because my body finally decided to give my nerve endings a break. I fainted.

CHAPTER
26
★ ★ ★

You'll never guess the first face I saw when I regained consciousness. Captain Wilson Bridges, M.D., was standing, head bent at the neck, studying what appeared to be my medical chart. The good news was he was operating in his capacity as a surgeon rather than pathologist. His medical coat had lots of dried blood all over it. The bad news was a fair amount of it was mine.

I said "Hello, Doc," but that's not how it came out. I sounded like a bullfrog with laryngitis.

His eyes shifted from the chart to my face, and he moved closer. Holding a finger in front of my eyes, he said, "Follow this."

I did so as he moved it back and forth.

Then he squeezed my left wrist and looked down at his watch, and I didn't say a word because I didn't want to disturb his concentration. It was my body he was scrutinizing. This was no time for him to make mistakes.

He jotted something on that ubiquitous clipboard and placed it back on a hook. I saw two IVs going into my arms.

Captain Bridges smiled. "You're going to live, Major."

To which I grumpily replied, "I hurt so damned much, I don't want to live."

He chuckled.

"Yeah. Yuck, yuck," I said.

He chuckled again, which was easy for him, because he hadn't been shot, knifed by a piece of glass, and had the shit kicked out of him by too many people to count.

"How long have I been here?"

"Since yesterday afternoon. We sent an ambulance to get you after your lawyer called. By the way, you're a big hero."

"Yeah? Tell me about that," I insisted. After all, how often do you go from being a kung-fu punching bag to a hero?

"One of the network news cameras filmed you running through the crowd and chasing off a shooter. It's been on all the news. Even CNN's carrying it."

This, I suppose, explained how Katherine got me released from the Itaewon station.

I said, "How bad was it?"

"You mean the massacre?"

The fact that he chose that particular word to describe what happened was my first indication. I nodded.

He shook his head. "We lost two more this morning. That makes fourteen dead. Ten of the wounded are here; the rest are being treated in Korean hospitals around the city. Our little basement morgue couldn't handle it. We had to rent a refrigeration van for all the bodies. If you hadn't chased away one of the shooters there'd probably be two or three more vans parked outside."

Remember that old saying about how "all politics is local"? Apparently the same applies to hospital departments. The guy was more concerned about morgue space than the pathetic fate of the folks who got in the way of a bullet. Down the hall was probably some little old lady complaining about how many forms she had to type. Three doors away was a supply clerk moaning about . . . Well, you get the point.

And on that thought, I asked, "And how am I doing?"

"Not bad. You're probably going to walk with a cane for a few weeks. You've got two broken ribs, but from the X rays it seems you've broken some ribs before, so you know the drill. I've taped them and you'll have to refrain from exercise or strenuous activity for a while."

This was no problem as far as I was concerned, because, oddly enough, I'd lost that urge I usually felt to get up and run a marathon.

He reached over and grabbed a hand mirror and placed it in front of my face. I took one look and immediately felt an elephantine wash of pity for the poor ugly bastard staring back at me. You could barely see a single square inch that wasn't bruised or swollen or scabby. One tooth was missing and another was broken in half. My nose was skewed at an odd angle.

"You were beaten up pretty badly," Bridges said, in what had to rank as the understatement of the year.

"Oh Jesus," I murmured, barely able to recognize myself. He quickly yanked the mirror away.

"Hey, you won't be getting any dates for a while, but it'll all heal," he assured. "And you'll get some shiny enamel teeth that won't get any cavities."

Captain Bridges, I was learning, had the bedside manner of a rottweiler puppy.

He grinned and said, "Anyway, there's a lady waiting outside to see you. She's been here since you were brought in. In fact, I was instructed to keep you in isolation until she spoke with you. I can throw a towel over your face or put a blindfold on her and lead her in."

Did I say a rottweiler puppy? I was wrong. A full-grown pit bull.

I was expecting Katherine, but in walked the heartless, bloodthirsty Miss Carol Kim. She stopped at my bedside and looked at my face, then picked up the doctor's clipboard and studied something. Like I needed this. She was checking the name on the board to make sure the battered wreck on the bed was indeed me.

"Wow, you look awful," she murmured, studying the clipboard.

I straightened a lock of my hair. "How's that? Better?"

"Much," she said with a cold smile, then lowered her tight little butt onto my bed.

She reached out and lowered the bedsheet to my waist. She clinically examined my body, and I looked down, too; there were more black-and-blue patches fairly regularly spaced. There was a bandage on my shoulder, and white tape running around my ribs.

"Wow, they really kicked the stuffing out of you."

Like I didn't know that already.

Then she said, "It was a really wonderful thing you did, by the way. We're very proud of you."

And I said the perfunctory, "Yeah, well."

That out of the way, she pulled out a tape recorder, pushed a button, and laid it on the bed.

In an officious tone, she said, "Major Sean Drummond, the United States Army officer who was present at the massacre. The date/time is 10:15 A.M., May 23. The location is the Eighteenth Military Evacuation Hospital."

She got a very businesslike frown on her face. "Major Drummond, could you please describe what you saw at the massacre site yesterday morning outside the main gate into Yongsan Compound?"

Now she and I, both trained lawyers, were speaking our own phlegmatic language, so I proceeded to detail everything that occurred as factually as I could recall it, from the moment the protesters arrived at the gate right through the multiple beatings I'd received at the hands of the South Korean police. And the kick from Michael Bales, don't let me forget that point. In fact, I dwelled on Bales and Choi for quite a while, although she didn't seem interested, even though I wanted it all on the record, real clear. In fact, what I really wanted was Michael Bales's scalp hanging off the end of my bed for the rest of my life, where I could wake up every morning, gaze fondly at it, and say, "Take that, you prick."

In case I haven't mentioned it before, vengeance is one of my strong suits. Or weak suits. Whatever.

When I finally finished, after nearly thirty minutes, Carol Kim picked up her recorder, withdrew the tape, and inserted a fresh cartridge. She went through the introductory motions again, then set the recorder down and studied my eyes. Or should I say, she studied my one eye, because the other one was still swollen shut.

She said, "You stated you heard a single shot behind you before the automatic fire began. Where did that shot come from?"

"I don't know. It was just a quick pop. But it was from somewhere in the rear of the protesters . . . or maybe behind the protesters. It didn't sound too close."

"Was it a pistol or a rifle?"

"I couldn't tell. Why, what's the point?"

"Please Major, answer my questions. I'll explain later."

"Okay, fine."

"Are you sure the Korean police officer you chased was shooting into the crowd?"

"He had an M16 aimed in our direction, the weapon was bucking, and people were getting hit and falling over. Yeah, I'm sure."

"But he stopped shooting when he saw you coming? Why?"

"At the moment he saw me, he had just emptied a magazine. I saw him reaching into his vest for a fresh mag, then I guess he made a quick assessment and decided he wouldn't get it inserted before I got to him."

"How long does it take to change magazines?"

"A highly trained soldier can accomplish it in maybe ten seconds. Someone less familiar with the weapon might take twenty, thirty seconds. You need to push a button to get the old mag out, then ram in the new mag, then pull back the charging handle to chamber a round."

"The film we've viewed shows you were still twenty to thirty yards from him when he dropped the weapon and ran. Why do you think he ran?"

I thought that was a stupid question and responded accordingly. "How about because he was killing people and didn't want to get caught."

"Major, please, this is important. The camera shots we got from the news organization are blurry. The cameraman was under fire and swinging the camera around, so the focus wasn't good. You had a good look at the shooter. Tell me what you think went through his head."

"What I think was that he wasn't going to take any risk of getting caught. I had a riot baton in my hand. I was running fast. He was thirty or so yards away and he was a very fast sprinter. He made a split-second choice and it was the wrong one. He should've jammed in that magazine and blown me away. Alternatively, maybe he just figured he'd murdered enough people already."

She cocked her head. "Jump forward to the point where you had him cornered in the shop in the dead-end alley. He fired some shots, and you went down with a shard of glass in your leg. That's what you said earlier, right?"

"Right."

"You went in and his corpse was behind the counter?"

"Correct."

"You rolled him over and the pistol was in his mouth?"

"Correct. At first I thought I'd hit him with a lucky shot, because he was lying on his stomach and there was a big hole in the back of his head. Then I rolled him over and saw his own pistol stuck inside his mouth."

"So you believe he committed suicide?"

"Unless someone helped him stuff his pistol inside his mouth, I think that's a fairly safe conclusion."

"But you saw no one else inside the shop?"

"No. Nobody. And I checked for a rear entrance, because I wondered why he hadn't simply fled. There wasn't one."

"Why would he have killed himself?"

"I don't know. However, I'd like to go on record as saying I'm damn glad he did. It's probably the only reason I'm alive."

She was starting to reach down and shut off the recorder when I reached over and grabbed her hand.

"There's another thing," I said. "He was wearing gloves. A pair of white cloth gloves, like you see taxi drivers over here wear. They were soaked with blood."

"Gloves?"

"Yeah, white ones. I mean, it's May, so it's damned hot, and I thought that was odd. What I think is, he was wearing the gloves so there wouldn't be any fingerprints on the M16. Maybe he and the other shooter planned all along to just drop their weapons and run."

"You're sure about the gloves?"

"Of course I'm sure. Check with the Korean police."

"We've talked with the Korean police. They haven't mentioned anything about it."

"Well, he was," I insisted. I mean, it wasn't a big point, and it certainly wasn't conclusive, except it implied a degree of premeditation on the shooter's part.

She shut off the recorder.

"Okay," I said. "What's this about?"

A big gush of air came out of her lungs, like someone who's under a great strain.

"While you've been in this hospital a very ugly dispute has erupted between our government and the Republic of Korea. The slaughter, it's all that's been on the news. The problem is nobody knows what happened, or why. There's a war of finger-pointing going back and forth."

I sat up. "Finger-pointing over what?"

"The protest, or demonstration, was approved by the city of Seoul and was under South Korean civil protection. That much is indisputable. The South Koreans, of course, don't want to be blamed for the massacre of fourteen American citizens and the wounding of seventeen others. They're claiming an American protester fired the first shot, then one or two ROK policemen returned fire in self-defense. You yourself admit you heard the first shot fired somewhere behind you. Other eyewitnesses corroborated the same thing."

I thought about this. It met with the facts. It made sense out of a chaotic event. But it didn't make complete sense.

"Then why did my shooter run? If he was simply returning fire, why'd he flee? And what about the other one, the second shooter?"

"Nobody's sure. It's believed the second shooter was an ROK police officer as well. He was wearing a police uniform and he dropped his weapon and ran. It was an M16 with all the serial numbers filed off. Nobody has any idea who he was."

"He was an ROK police officer? And they don't know who he was? How can that be?"

"That's the question of the hour, isn't it? There was a lot of confusion at the massacre site. A number of ROK police cars were dispatched to the scene, but nobody was taking a roll call as they arrived. He made his getaway in a police car. That proved to be a very clever move, because the ROK police dispatchers immediately put out a net call for every unit to look for a ROK police car and . . . well, you can imagine how chaotic that became."

"And you believe they honestly don't know who he was?"

"Who can tell? Maybe they're just covering up. Or maybe they really don't know. It's terribly convenient for their side of the story not to have him around for questioning . . . but it's also inconvenient, isn't it?"

"And the shooter I chased, he's dead, so there's nobody to say why they opened fire."

She stood up and straightened her dress. "That's the gist of it."

"And it's their country."

"Basically, yes," she replied, picking up the recorder and placing it in her purse. "I've got to hurry and get this transcribed and sent back to Washington. For obvious reasons, your testimony is considered crucial."

Before she could walk out on me, I said, "Hold on. What's my position in this thing? I mean, if the two police officers were merely responding in self-defense, where do I stand? And what about the fact that the guy I was chasing popped a South Korean in the head?"

"That's all under continuing investigation. The ROKs admit that you were very brave for chasing him off that hillside. It saved lives. They also think it's possible he committed suicide. They're doing an autopsy on his body now. But you're still being charged with assaulting a police officer, and for stealing his weapon. As for the other body that was found in the alley, there's still questions about who popped him in the head, as you put it. The bullet that killed him passed through his cranium and hasn't been found. The poor guy was a mentally handicapped adult."

Her eyes suddenly narrowed. "I don't mean to imply that you murdered him in cold blood, but you were involved in a gunfight. You were tense and under great strain, probably on a hair trigger. You didn't shoot him, did you, Drummond?"

Which I guess was a fairly good indication of what she thought of me.

My response was fairly short of being politically correct. But then, I'm a lawyer. If she tried to slap me with one of those gender crime suits, well, I was drugged and delirious with pain, and therefore wasn't responsible for my filthy tongue.

CHAPTER
27
★ ★ ★

Imelda and Katherine showed up two hours later. Make that two hours after I started frantically calling them. I wasn't happy about it, either.

But after one look at Katherine's face, I softened my mood. There were deep, dark circles under her eyes. They were puffy and swollen and bloodshot, the way eyes get when somebody's been crying a lot. She'd obviously gotten no sleep since the massacre.

Imelda, I noticed, was being very custodial toward Katherine. She was holding the door for her, getting her a chair, hovering over her shoulder like an anxious aide-de-camp.

Imelda looked down at me, studied my face, blew some air out of her lips, then returned her attention to Katherine. Imelda Pepperfield, after all, was a woman. In the female Hierarchy of Miseries, physical beatings are a few notches down from afflictions of the soul.

Katherine sniffled. "You look like hell."

"Yeah, well, I feel like hell. Thanks, though, for getting me out of that rathole. I couldn't have taken another beating. One more and I was ready to confess I'm your co-counsel."

She smiled and acted like she got the joke, but you could tell from her eyes she'd lost her sense of humor. Actually, she'd never had much of a sense of humor. At least none I'd ever been able to tap into.

"What you did, Sean . . . it was incredibly brave. The cameraman called me as soon as he was able to review his tape. He wanted to know who you were. He said he had this film of a complete wildman running through the crowd, people dropping over dead all around him, rushing the assassin."

"Yeah, well," I said, blushing beneath my bruises. "So how you doing?"

"It's been the worst day of my life."

"Yeah, mine wasn't so hot, either," I complained, because I just couldn't let her score higher on the misery index.

Then Katherine and Imelda exchanged some kind of private look, and Katherine looked even more tortured.

She made a very obvious effort to exert control over her emotions. "Uh . . . Maria got shot."

"Maria? Maria the grum—uh, our Maria?"

Katherine looked down at the floor and nodded.

I felt a small knot in my stomach. "How is she?"

Katherine never took her eyes off the floor. "Dead."

I had to take a moment to consider that. It's not like I knew Maria real well. We'd shared some room space, but we'd barely said ten words to each other. Except for a few odd smiles, the sum of our communication had been to either exchange frowns or vaguely ignore each other.

I said, "I'm sorry," which is an entirely inadequate thing to say, but because it's so commonly muttered in situations like this, it's a passable sentiment.

Katherine nodded.

"How's Allie?"

"Not well. They've lived together for ten years. They . . . uh, they were very much in love."

I nodded because again I was at an embarrassing loss for words. I sort of liked Allie, partly because she was so wildly eccentric you either liked her or hated her, and I had no reason to hate her, which I guess left me sort of liking her. And partly because she was so damned tough and I just naturally admire that quality, even in a six-foot-three lesbian with a face like a South American parrot.

Anyway, Katherine spared me the need to mutter more empty sentiments. She stood up and started pacing. "I knew these people. They were my friends. I'm angry and I'm frustrated. The South Koreans are trying to cover it up. They murdered my friends and now they're trumping up some horseshit about how the first shot came from us. Like we started it."

"The first shot did come from our side of the fracas. I heard it and so did you. Is it possible one of the protesters had a gun?"

She angrily shook her head. "Come on. They all took civilian flights over here. They passed through metal detectors and customs."

"So what? It's possible to smuggle plastic guns through metal detectors. It's possible to smuggle disassembled weapons in your luggage. Hell, it's possible to acquire a weapon here. American servicemen are even allowed their own private weapons, as long as they register them with the MPs. No offense, but some of your friends are angry social misfits. Maybe one of them decided to make a bold point."

"Don't be stupid. Why would our people fire on the South Koreans?"

"Reverse that question. Why would the South Koreans fire on us? With television cameras right there?"

I could see from her expression she wasn't in the mood to discuss this in a rational way, so I asked, "What's the status of the trial?"

"I've filed for a two-week postponement."

"And have you heard anything?"

"Only that Golden's fighting it. He claims the massacre is irrelevant to the case."

"I could've guessed that. He's got all his ducks lined up. He wants his moment in the sun. Eddie's in a mad rush to be famous."

"Well, the judge is here, the witnesses are here, everything's ready. How do you think they'll decide?"

"It's up to Spears and Brandewaite to make the decision. Brandewaite's a diplomat, so I'm sure he wants to get this over with yesterday. He'll see an early conviction as a way to start healing the rift."

"There's only one hang-up. It seems two of Thomas's co-counsels could be facing charges with the civilian authorities."

"Really? What are they looking to charge you with?"

"Filing a misleading statement to get authority for the protest. Inciting a riot. Also, it seems South Korea has this law called the National Security Act. They say I may be charged with something called 'endangering the security of the Republic of Korea.'"

I was vaguely familiar with the law she was talking about. It was a controversial statute that had been on the books for thirty years, ever since one of the earlier dictators imposed it. It's the kind of law every dictator dreams of, since it's amorphous enough to be twisted and contorted in any direction.

I should've been sympathetic, but I couldn't let her have the upper hand. "You think you got problems? I'm charged with assaulting a police officer and theft of a weapon. Oh, and I'm also under suspicion for murdering a mentally handicapped man."

Imelda, who'd been quietly listening to the two of us talk, suddenly moved around Katherine until she was close to my bed.

"You two done?" she asked in a sharp tone.

"What?" Katherine asked, looking up in surprise.

Imelda glared down her short, pudgy nose at both of us. "Are you two done with this woe-is-me shit? Have you got all that shitty self-pity outta your systems?"

I drew a deep breath, scratched my hair, and looked away. I could smell what was coming. Katherine had no idea. She'd never experienced an inspirational assault from Imelda, which I'll briefly describe as a conversation where Imelda does the talking, and you keep your mouth shut and nod your head at all the appropriate moments, and generally try to look inspired as hell. Oh, you can try to ignore her, or argue, but I really don't recommend it.

Katherine had a baffled look on her face.

"Okay," Imelda said, sliding her feet back and forth like a boxer, "you got a client in jail. His trial might or might not start Friday. You got one lawyer laying on his ass, actin' hurt. You got the other with

a case of the self-moanies. At least you two're alive. Least it ain't neither of *you* iced up in one of them meat wagons parked out back.
Right?"

I nodded enthusiastically and looked wildly inspired. Yes, yes,
that's right, Imelda. At least it's not me.

Katherine looked even more bewildered. Wrong answer.

"You got a problem with this, girl?" Imelda barked, bending
over and spitting her words into Katherine's face. "You not hearing
ol' Imelda right?"

Katherine's lips opened, but Imelda's finger popped up right in
front of her nose. Imelda's face was now directly in front of Katherine's, scrunched up in fury, and her eyes were sizzling.

"Don't you talk," she barked. "Don't you dare talk. If it was me
was your client, I'd shoot you two. I shit you not, girl. All this
moanin' an' groanin'. Hmmph! Hmmmph!" she stomped a boot on
the floor like she was crushing a bug.

Katherine's eyes peeked over in my direction. She quietly observed me nodding my head so hard I was about to break my neck.
My eyes, at least the one I could get open, communicated awed rev-
erence.

As I said earlier, Katherine's no dummy. She started nodding . . .
weakly at first, then like a piston.

"All right, now." Imelda spun on her heels and faced me. "I'm
gonna get me a wheelchair and roll your bony ass outta here. Don't
let me hear no bitchin' from you, boy. You ain't hurt. You only *think*
you're hurt."

Yes, yes, I only think so, I nodded. Forget these bruises and
stitches and bandages. Figments of a fevered imagination.

She turned back and faced Katherine. "Forget about what happened yesterday, hear me? Focus on that boy in that cell. Let me
and the major handle them South Koreans, got it?"

Katherine was nodding even more ferociously than I was. Her
neck was snapping like a birch tree in a hurricane. I swear I saw
saliva fly out of her mouth.

Of course, I then made an effort to look even more wildly inspired than her, and let me tell you, that's not easy when your face

is all swollen and bruised and you're missing a front tooth. I looked like an overanxious Halloween pumpkin who just couldn't wait for the big night.

I said, "Raring to go, Imelda. Hot damn! Can't wait. Go get that damned wheelchair. Get me the hell out of here."

She studied my face a moment, decided I was sufficiently galvanized, turned and examined Katherine, who was still jerking her head up and down. Instant and unquestioning obedience was all Imelda ever wanted, so she yanked up her trousers and stomped noisily out of the room, clicking her teeth and grunting curses, which was her way of expressing rabid satisfaction. She made the same sounds after polishing off a really good steak.

As soon as the door shut, there was the sound of two people letting a roomful of air out of their lungs.

"Jesus," Katherine said, gently massaging her neck. "I never imagined. She's so tiny."

As for me, I was trying to get my damaged face to recover its normal expression of rubbery nonchalance. "Well, you asked for it," I said. "Sitting there feeling sorry for yourself like that."

"Attila," she said, with a murderous look, "don't go there."

"Only kidding," I replied, and I'll be damned if she didn't giggle.

Then I said, "Hey, Moonbeam, we got what, three days?"

"Three days. Right."

"He was framed, right?"

"No question about it. Framed."

I stretched out my hand and we shook.

I grinned and appeared completely sincere, but if you think I was buying it, you haven't been paying attention. This was Katherine Carlson. I had to test the limits of our new partnership.

I grinned harder and said, "So, when were you gonna tell me about Frederick Melborne?"

Surprise popped onto her face. It quickly turned into a sly smile. "You found out about Fred, huh?"

"Yeah. Who is he? Really."

"A crackerjack PI. He was once an Army officer. He knows how to get around and he specializes in gay cases."

"Hah! Exactly what I figured from the start."

She smiled. "Of course you did, Drummond, of course you did."

"Well, I did," I lied.

"Drummond, Fred had your number the instant he laid eyes on you. Christ, he had you so fooled I thought you were going to faint. You should have seen your face when you shook his hand that first night. He did that Liberace act and you sprinted over to the corner like a frightened squirrel."

I felt a rush of blood to my face. "What? That was an act?"

"Of course it was an act."

"Well, he *is* gay, isn't he?"

"Of course he's gay. He's also quite macho. He was testing you."

I guessed I hadn't done real well on that test. Anyway, I wasn't going to let her dwell on it. "So what was he doing?" I quickly asked. "Running background on Lee, Moran, and Jackson?"

"Just Lee. Moran's an open book. Fred ran some checks with a number of OGMM members who've been assigned with him over the years, and they helped us compile a profile. A promiscuous male hunk, and an accomplished bar brawler, but he's never beaten or threatened a lover. Appearances aside, he's supposed to be a very tender lover. As for Jackson, he doesn't matter. We judged him to be largely irrelevant. He was there that night, but we think he was bewildered by everything that went down. Lee No Tae is the key."

"And what did Melborne find out?"

"Nothing."

I gave her a dubious look. "Nothing?"

"I swear. Lee was never seen in any of the bars local gays frequent. He'd never dated anybody but Thomas. He never flirted with anybody, never got propositioned, never gave any hint he was gay."

"But if he did, he probably ran with Korean gays, right? Maybe Fred was looking for love in all the wrong places."

Forgive me for that, but I'd always wanted to use that line.

Katherine leaned back into her chair and shook her head. She was back to not getting my bad jokes. "Of course we considered that. Fred even hired some local PIs. He had them ask around with

Lee's high school and college classmates. He threw a pretty wide net."

"Could Fred have been meeting with somebody that night in Itaewon? Maybe somebody found something?"

"Possibly. He liked to operate without my breathing down his back, so maybe."

The door slammed open and Imelda reentered pushing a wheelchair with a cane hanging from it. I had to ask her and Katherine to give me a hand getting out of bed. Thankfully, I was wearing underpants, although to be perfectly technical, being naked in front of two lesbians probably isn't a whole lot different than walking around a men's locker room without a towel. Anyway, Imelda threw a hospital gown over me, then started wheeling me out.

That's when Doc Bridges showed up. He blocked the doorway, crossed his arms, and said, "And where are we going?"

I said, "We're leaving. Right now."

He was shaking his head so I said, "By the way, have you met my attorney, Katherine Carlson? She's a patients' rights advocate. She's here to see I get my way."

In case you haven't heard, there's no love lost between doctors and lawyers. This is because doctors sometimes make mistakes and kill or maim people . . . and, well, you know how it goes.

Doc Bridges stared at Katherine like she was the bogeyman, and she bared her teeth at him once or twice for good measure. He politely nudged himself aside and yelled at the top of his voice, "Okay, I've given you my best medical advice. You're leaving here of your own volition. Die of an infection and I'm legally absolved."

As I passed him, he actually winked. A man after my own heart.

CHAPTER
28
✪ ✪ ✪

Here's what intrigued me the most. What made that Korean cop commit seppuku? For those who don't know, seppuku's the Japanese version of suicide.

One scenario was the South Koreans were telling the truth—the cop saw one of the protesters pop off a round and lost his cool. He opened up, and then, once he saw me running up at him, he dropped his weapon and fled. The act of changing magazines gave him a moment to cogitate and realize that shooting wildly into a crowd was a very bad thing. During the time it took me to catch up with him he did some further thinking and realized he'd done not only a bad thing, but a stupid thing—he'd killed a slew of innocent people, he'd overreacted, and he was going to be in very big trouble. There was going to be an investigation that would bring great shame on himself, his badge, and his family. Then he found himself cornered and had no idea what an awful shot I am, so he figured he couldn't get away and suicide was preferable to capture and everlasting shame.

Some Asians can be that way. The rite of suicide is an act of honor to purge some horribly disgraceful thing. Like killing a bunch of unarmed, innocent people—that would qualify.

Okay, that's one scenario. Here's another: The two shooters were a team. They weren't firing in self-defense. They weren't firing in the heat of the moment. They weren't firing randomly. They were cold-bloodedly murdering as many Americans as they could, as swiftly as they could. They wanted to manufacture an atrocity. They wanted to get people's attention.

But here's the rub. Who'd do such a thing? The same people who tossed Melborne in front of a car? Or were the incidents un-related?

Since I never much believed in random theories, I was assum-ing, just for the sake of argument, that both acts were done by the same people, which was why I was in my wheelchair on the road just outside the front gate of the Yongsan Garrison, with Imelda pushing me around as I pointed this way and that. I looked like a cranky old man with an even crankier nurse.

The road was closed and the massacre scene was fenced off with yellow tape. Korean and American military cops were climb-ing all over searching for clues. There were chalk-haloed silhou-ettes where yesterday real bodies had lain seeping their life's fluids onto the tarmac. Their bloodstains were still visible in the con-crete, and crushed and abandoned protest signs were strewn about, discarded in the moments of bald terror when two men with weapons were pumping round after round into the densely packed crowd.

I sat in my wheelchair and tried to recapture the stream of events that led up to the slaughter. In my head, there was a mass of protesters holding up signs, holding one another's arms, breath-lessly awaiting the confrontation. There was a platoon of riot po-licemen standing off to the left, the first group, the ones provided by the city to safeguard our "welcoming party." Six buses were idling in front of us and police cars with flashing lights were ar-riving every few seconds. The line of riot police was clumping to-ward us—two steps forward, pause; two steps forward, pause; two steps forward—then only five feet away, a complete halt.

We were eye-to-eye: protesters and riot policemen totally, inex-orably, fatefully fixated only on one another. Everybody—journal-ists, television cameramen, bystanders—had their eyes glued on the point of the confrontation. Everybody was staring anxiously at the narrow, tense fault line between the two sides. Nobody was paying attention to a shooter at the rear of the crowd or to two Korean cops who were choosing their killing roosts on opposite sides of the road. Hundreds of possible witnesses were blind to anything but the confrontation about to occur.

I closed my eyes and tried to remember the first shot, a dull crack behind me. Far behind me. Too far to have come from the mass of protesters, I was nearly certain. It was possible one of the protesters hadn't been in the crowd, but had hung back behind it. But whoever it was should've stood out like a sore thumb. Presumably the police were rushing in cars to block off the road at the rear of the protest, just like they were at the front, so surely there were plenty of Korean cops back there.

Wouldn't one of them have seen a protester as he or she lifted up a pistol or rifle and fired a round? Surely it would've been observed. A shooter can't be inconspicuous.

I opened my eyes and looked up, because two men were walking toward me. One Korean and one American.

Michael Bales had his all-American, what-a-great-guy, just-everybody's-pal look pasted on his face. It no longer looked friendly to me. It looked phony, contrived, the mask of a malevolent beast.

"Jesus, Major, I'm really glad you're okay," he announced, his voice dripping with sarcasm. "Look what that bastard did to you."

And Choi immediately chimed in, "That was very bad man we locked you up with. We make poor judgment. He no get away with this, though. We bring charges. He get punished. You see."

For this particular episode of South Korean Masterpiece Theater, he had reverted to pidgin English, and his face was a portrait of pretend sympathy.

Then Bales said, "Thank God your lawyer brought over that film when she did. If she'd waited till the next morning, we wouldn't have looked in on you till then. That brute in your cell would probably have killed you."

They were good. Give them credit for that. They were telling me in their own inimitable way that they had already fabricated an alibi. They'd probably lined up a platoon of cops to attest I was pulverized to hamburger by my nonexistent cellmate.

I glanced up at Imelda, who had her hands gripped on the handles of my wheelchair. She'd picked up on the sarcastic undertone and was snorting with anger.

I wanted to get out of this chair and kick them in the nuts, but before I could say anything, Bales said, "Now, I hate to be pushy here, sir, but I'm afraid I'm going to have to ask you to please leave the crime scene. This is a quarantined area. We're involved in an intensive police investigation. We can't have bystanders contaminating the site, can we? You're a lawyer. I'm sure you understand."

He'd reverted to his courteous, I'm-just-a-humble-cop-trying-to-do-his-humble-job masquerade, and I had an almost irresistible urge to tell him where he could put his head.

But before I could say anything, Imelda deftly wheeled me around and began heading for the yellow tape that surrounded the investigation site.

Bales called out, "Hey, have a nice day."

And Choi echoed, "Yes, have a nice day."

When we were on the other side of the tape and back through the gate, Imelda coolly asked, "Them the two that ripped you up?"

"Uh-huh," I furiously mumbled.

She said nothing more, as though it were just a passing question.

When we got back to the hair parlor, Allie the amazon was all over me. She literally tripped over herself to help Imelda wheel me in. She planted me beside a desk and fetched me some coffee, then stood there like a worried hen studying an egg with an ugly crack in it. I'd been transformed in her eyes. I'd become worthy. I'd shed blood for the cause.

I told her how sorry I was about Maria and she glumly nodded and sniffled once or twice. She was shrouded entirely in black, for mourning no doubt. The sight of Allie, all skinny, six feet three inches of her, draped in black leotards and a long black shift, combined with her spiky hair, nearly took my breath away.

I was touched, anyway. I truly was. Maybe some of it was pity, but I actually felt a wave of deep affection for her.

I also decided that having a couple of women busting a gut to take care of my every whim wasn't too bad, so I hunched over in my wheelchair, occasionally coughing, or moaning, or working up a pained look. For half an hour the two of them sprinted around getting me more coffee and cups of water, and pencils and paper, until Imelda got suspicious and whispered in my ear, "Cut that shit out or I'll give you a reason to moan."

So I did. I perked up in my wheelchair and told her and Allie they'd accomplished a medical miracle, that I felt like a whole new man, thank you. Imelda rolled her eyes and Allie grinned like a shy debutante staring at the local stud coming to ask her to dance.

Then we got down to a drill they teach in law schools called mindmapping. The point of the exercise is to disaggregate a bunch of chaotic events, to list them on a wall, and search for possible linkages or connections. Allie was writing the events on the chalkboard while we spat ideas and linkages back and forth. And the thing that struck me right away was that I'd badly underestimated her. She had extraordinary recall of events and circumstances and facts.

At the end of two hours, the chalkboard looked like a giant cobweb spun by a schizophrenic spider on amphetamines. Lines crisscrossed every which way.

Here's what we had. We had three prominent nexus, or nexi, or whatever. One: Lee No Tae's murder. Two: the near murder of Fred Melborne, aka Keith Merritt. Three: the slaughter at the protest site. Link the three together and we had a web of death.

Off to the right of this, we tried to reason through some possible motives. Our reasoning went like this:

People kill other people generally as an act of passion or chilling self-interest. Passions like rage, hatred, jealousy, or lust. Cold self-interest like greed, politics, or to cover other crimes. Of course, people kill one another by accident, too, or sometimes just out of sickening curiosity, or for fun, or because they've got a screw loose, but the kind of murderers we were looking for most likely weren't the crossed-synapses types, or the whoopsy-daisy types, or the gee-ain't-this-a-gas types.

Most times when a hetero murders a gay, it's a crime of disgust. It's labeled a crime of passion or hate, though more thoughtful psychiatrists would tell you the hetero murderers are trying to prove something to their peers, to be worshipped as something they don't truly feel they are—to wit, a macho man of action. Thus it's actually a crime of nauseating internal weakness, of self-disgust.

If you assumed Whitehall was innocent of Lee's murder, and you connected all three events together, one conclusion would be that all this mayhem was perpetrated by someone with a grinding hatred toward gays. More than one person, though. A ring of gay haters. And probably not an American ring, because the men who'd shot the protesters were Korean. We also knew one of the shooters was legitimately a police officer. The other wore a police uniform, and used an M16, and fled in a police car. For the sake of argument, assume he wasn't wearing a costume; assume he also was an honest-to-God flatfoot. Then toss in my hunch that there was a third police officer located behind the crowd, who'd fired the instigating shot as a pretext for slaughter.

"Guess where every finger points?" Allie suddenly suggested. She then answered her own question. "At the Itaewon Police Station."

You know how sometimes somebody says something and the second you hear it, you realize how very obvious it is, and how easily you should have thought of it yourself? This was one of those moments.

"Yeah," I said, amazed.

Allie stared at the chart. "The Itaewon police investigated Lee's murder. They could easily have planted evidence and otherwise made it look like Thomas did it. Fred was in the Itaewon precinct when he was thrown in front of the car. The Itaewon police did the investigation and claimed they couldn't find any witnesses. And the police cars at the massacre were most likely from the Itaewon station. The officer you killed, Sean, was assigned to that precinct."

All this was true. She'd connected the dots. Her law school professors would be proud of her. I was proud of her. And if she was right, Allie had broken this case wide open.

She'd just given us our first suspect. Only that suspect was an entire police station. Although that sounds fantastic, the truth is that rotten precincts are stunningly common. Remember that New York City precinct that was using electric cattle prods to torture suspects? Remember that huge New York cop ring that Officer Serpico of later movie fame broke up? Or how about that more recent Los Angeles anticrime squad that kept shooting innocent suspects and planting evidence and covering up for one another?

And to tell the truth, I wanted it to be Itaewon Police Station. I mean, I really did. Call me vindictive, but there it is.

But where did Bales fit in? What was he? A dupe? A sadistic stooge who got his rocks off knocking prisoners around, who was too stupid to notice what was happening around him?

That was a gap we couldn't fill in.

But what Allie suggested made sense. Terrifying sense.

After thinking about it a moment, I said, "What's the motive?"

She scratched her head. "Hatred. They hate gays."

"Possibly," I muttered, so she wrote that down on the big board.

However, I wasn't entirely persuaded it was sufficiently compelling. So we argued awhile. I said the hatred motive required a large dose of mass antigay hysteria, and I suggested that might be far-fetched. Allie assured me she knew more about these things, and she was convinced such a thing was within reason. Look at how Blacks were treated in the old South . . . even the not-so-old South. Look how hippies were treated by Mayor Daley's Chicago cops. Look how gays are treated by the American military.

I said those were different things, and she strongly insisted they weren't at all different, that all forms of mass psychosis had the same roots. We went back and forth like that for a few moments, until Imelda barked out, "Move on. What's next?"

She'd been silently watching us this whole time, and for once she appeared to be somewhat mollified that we lawyers were starting to earn our keep. Of course, the shiftless, unruly children still needed a hard-driving referee if they were to make any further progress.

I wheeled myself back and forth in my chair a few times, then said, "How about a political motive? Like anti-Americanism."

"How so?" Allie asked.

"Say some of the Korean police are linked to one of those nationalist, anti-American groups that are so rife over here. Say they found out Lee No Tae was gay and was having an affair with an American officer. Easy enough. The apartment's in their precinct. They have stooges and spies on the streets. They see this American officer and his Korean boyfriend visiting the apartment a few times every week. They run traplines and discover Lee is the minister's son. Maybe they find that really disgusting. I mean, Koreans find it racially insulting that our GIs sleep with Korean whores, but this, homosexual sex, really gets under their skin. Whitehall was exploiting a Korean body—that's bad enough. But Lee, he was the one who was wantonly disgracing their race. So they killed him and they framed it on Whitehall, an American officer, a West Point graduate. They get two birds with one stone. Then maybe Fred was getting close to them, so they tried to kill him, too. Then the protest came up and they saw an opportunity to really do some havoc."

Imelda and Allie stared at me, then glanced at each other, then started shaking their heads.

"Sean, look," Allie said. "In the first place, nobody knew about the timing or nature of our protest. Katherine filed it under false pretenses."

I said, "The police knew about the demonstration. The mayor's office informed them. Maybe they figured out its real purpose."

She said, "Second, the men who fired on the crowd were police officers. How could they be members of this anti-American group?"

I said, "Did you watch the '88 Olympics on TV?"

They both shook their heads.

"The '88 Olympics were held here, in Seoul. It was a grand moment for the Koreans, a coming-out party, an international tribute to everything they'd accomplished. So it's the opening-day cere-

mony. The stadium is packed with a hundred thousand local spec-
tators holding these tiny national flags in their hands. The American
teams come marching out, and, I kid you not, nearly the entire stadium stood and booed. A while later, the Russian team marched
out, and nearly the entire stadium got to their feet and cheered."

Allie said, "I can't believe that. We're allies."

"I know. Here's the Russians, the same guys who put Kim Il
Sung in place, who were completely responsible for the attack on
South Korea, who fed and armed North Korea for fifty years, and
they cheered them. And here's our guys, representing the country
that lost thirty-five thousand lives saving their asses, and then spent
countless billions of dollars to protect them over the next fifty
years, and they give us the Bronx cheer."

Allie said, "It doesn't make sense."

"It's a paradox. But I know this: They're tired of having American troops on their soil. They're tired of being dependent on another country. They're tired of being told what to do by Americans.
They don't trust our motives for being here, and frankly our motives *are* damned hard to explain, even to ourselves. I mean, what
does Korea offer the U.S.? Immigrants, and cheap electronics, and
cars that American workers would rather manufacture themselves,
right?"

Allie leaned up against the blackboard. "And you think they'd
kill Americans to drive us out?"

There was a television running in the corner and just at that
moment CNN switched to a live broadcast of the Secretary of State
climbing off a long, sleek U.S. Air Force 747. He looked like a former general as he came down the stairs, shoulders squared, back
erect. He looked grim, too, like he wasn't the least bit happy to be
here.

At the bottom of the aircraft steps the president of Korea
waited to meet him. Normal protocol would be for the foreign minister, his direct equal, to be there to handle the reception. This was
a sign of how serious things were. He and the South Korean president pointedly didn't shake hands. This was a sign of the mood.

The story cut back to a correspondent in Washington who was

interviewing a florid, angry-looking gay congressman from Massa-
chusetts.

"Representative Merrigold, do you really believe your troop
withdrawal bill has any chance of passing?"

"Damn right I do," he yapped. "I've already got enough support
to get it on the House floor. And I'm picking up more support by
the hour. Let me tell you something. Let me tell *all* of America
something. This is no longer about gays, ladies and gentlemen. Forget their sexual preference, those were Americans murdered on
that street. If the Republic of Korea won't protect our citizens, why
in the hell should we protect theirs? If they continue with this
cover-up, every last American soldier will be out of that country by
the end of the month. We'll send Federal Express to pick up our
equipment later."

There was another cutback to an attractive anchorwoman who
was struggling to look appropriately severe and apprehensive. "And
so the Secretary of State has been sent by the President to try to
salvage whatever he can out of a situation that all commentators
agree is virtually hopeless. The death toll in Korea has now reached
fifteen. Four of the wounded are still listed in critical condition. The
Republic of Korea continues to insist that its police officers were
provoked by sniper fire from the protesters, while sources on the
Hill say chances a troop withdrawal bill will pass are excellent."

Imelda went over and turned off the television. We got back to
work.

CHAPTER

29

★ ★ ★

What Katherine was attempting was actually very clever. And ballsy, too. Moran and Jackson were being held in the Yongsan Holding Facility and Katherine faxed a request for Colonel Barry Carruthers to issue a judge's order to allow us to interview them.

Why was this clever? Because we now had valid reason to suspect Bales and Choi had coerced the two men into testifying against our client. I had courageously sacrificed my own body to make that discovery. See what a noble guy I am?

The reason it was a ballsy move was because they were both listed as witnesses for the prosecution, and thus, technically, our first chance to speak with them should come in the courtroom, during cross.

But Katherine slyly justified her request on the basis that Moran and Jackson, aside from our own client, were the only living witnesses to what happened inside that apartment, and we therefore deserved an equal chance to determine whether their testimonies might be beneficial to our client. This might sound specious at this late stage in the game, but speciousness is what American law's all about.

Fast Eddie opposed the request in the strongest possible language. With the strength of his case, you'd think he'd cut us a little slack, but Eddie never took prisoners. Therefore Carruthers responded that he wanted to meet with Katherine to hear her logic. Protocol required me to accompany her.

Imelda actually wasn't happy about that. Her game plan was to keep Katherine and me separated. She knew Katherine and I were hormonally destined to eternal conflict.

Anyway, the two of us were standing outside the door that led into Colonel Barry Carruthers's office. We were both pacing nervously. Actually, Katherine was pacing, while she quietly rehearsed her logic. I was limping on a cane and quietly cursing, because my body was aching to be back in that wheelchair. I just didn't want the judge's first impression of me to be in that contraption, like I was crippled. I wanted him to see me with a cane, like I was only partly crippled. That's how macho logic works.

The judge's secretary, who'd flown over here with him, was strenuously buffing her nails and ignoring us. We were defense attorneys, after all—her boss's well-known disdain for our breed was infectious.

She glanced up occasionally to inspect a small blinking red light on her telephone. Finally it died. This was the signal that the judge was free and Katherine and I could enter. She gave us a glacial nod, and we trod fretfully into the lion's den.

The first thing I noticed was that the room was dark. Really, really dark. The shades were tightly drawn, as were the curtains, so that the only light came from a small desk bulb that illuminated only the figure it was directed at—the judge.

The second thing I noticed was that Barry Carruthers was what you might call a visually imposing man. He'd once been a left tackle for Notre Dame, and he'd gotten meaner-looking since then. He was Black, and by that I mean ebony black, with a big, broad face and thick, bushy eyebrows. Everything else was sharp angles—angled nose, angled eyes, angled lips. His face looked like it could slice you to ribbons. A human stiletto.

He was wearing an Army green short-sleeved shirt, and you knew the instant you laid eyes on him the man pumped some serious iron, because his sleeves were precariously tight around his brawny biceps. One flex and he'd have to make a hasty trip to the Post Exchange for a new shirt.

"Sit down," he said. Not nicely. Not angrily. Just coldly.

Katherine sat in the chair to my right. I bent forward on my cane, then ungracefully collapsed into my chair.

Carruthers was staring at his right fist and kneading one of those rubber squeeze-me balls. I was damned glad I wasn't the ball being pulverized inside that beefy mitt. You could see the sinews on his huge forearms tensing and untensing.

I stole a glance at Katherine; she was holding up okay. As far as I could tell, anyway. Between the eerie darkness and the man's sheer size and appearance, I wanted the hell out of there. But Katherine was somehow managing to mask whatever anxiety she felt.

"You got my request, Your Honor?" she asked, firm but polite.

"You're the young lady who arranged and led yesterday's demonstration?" Carruthers responded, deliberately ignoring her question. That "young lady" thing, that was a nice touch. Very condescending. Very overbearing.

"I am," Katherine admitted, trying to sound casual.

"It was designed to embarrass me, wasn't it?"

"Not in the least. It was an expression of public outrage at the captivity of an innocent man. Thomas Whitehall did not murder Lee No Tae, and if I'm given a chance, I will prove that."

Good so far, I figured. Katherine's voice was cool, unemotional, detached. She was holding her own. It was one of those David-wrestling-with-Goliath moments.

Carruthers stared at his fist. "Fifteen bloody bodies in a morgue. A rupture in a fifty-year-old alliance that may not be reparable. A public embarrassment for both our nations. Not bad for a day's work, Miss Carlson. Wouldn't you say?"

Katherine's face was static. "It was supposed to be a peaceful, legal demonstration."

The judge was still staring at his hand, and it was squeezing the ball even harder. His forearm looked like a bunch of snakes slithering up and down in a slow dance.

"You were warned by General Spears, weren't you? You were told things were brittle here, weren't you? What's the matter? Couldn't resist?"

Katherine couldn't answer that. There was no answer for that. His Honor was mad as hell and was putting her in her place. Frankly, he had every right to. Regardless of the awful consequences that neither Katherine nor anybody else could've foreseen, no judge likes to be taunted by press statements and public demonstrations. She'd been waving a match underneath a stick of dynamite, and the dynamite was now letting her know it didn't appreciate it.

Nor did it escape me that the judge was exploiting the situation to try to put his strong boot on Katherine's throat. Smart move on his part. It would save him from having to crush her like a bug in front of the whole court.

I peeked at her. Instead of looking like she wanted to crawl under her seat, she appeared ready to leap across the table and slap him.

She said, "Are you trying to blame me?"

The stick of dynamite was squeezing the ball harder and faster, and I realized that Katherine might enjoy this game of taunting judges, but it wasn't my idea of great fun. Before either of them could say another word, I quickly intervened. "What's your decision on our request, Your Honor? I'm asking on the record."

Carruthers placed the ball in the center of his desk. He stared at it awhile, and I got the point. That ball represented Katherine. If it weren't for that little piece of rubber, he'd probably rip her arms off and beat her over the head with them.

His eyes shifted to me for the first time. "That's why we're here, isn't it, Drummond? To discuss your request."

In case I haven't mentioned it yet, the judge has a deep, resonant voice. The type of voice that batters its way through the air and penetrates your skin and bounces right off your bones.

I coughed a bit, and bent forward. "Miss Carlson and I feel it's imperative to meet with those two men."

"Then you better have a more compelling legal justification than the one I read."

Katherine said, "We do. Neither of us were present for the Article 32 pre-court-martial investigation. We haven't been given the right to full discovery. If this request is denied, we'll consider it certain grounds for an appeal."

Her tone was respectful, but she might as well have stuck her middle finger in his face. When a lawyer brazenly threatens to take a judge's decision and use it for an appeal—no matter how politely it's couched—that's pretty much the same thing as . . . Well, actually, it's worse than that. The truth is I can't think of anything as bad.

A big angry snort erupted from Carruthers's nose and his body jerked forward. His slitty eyes were dead on her pretty face. "Was that a threat?"

She coolly said, "Yes, Your Honor, I threatened you. Respectfully, of course."

"Well, I—"

I saw a vision of two trains racing full speed at each other, so I said, nearly yelling, "Please let me explain. We've just learned that Moran and Jackson have knowledge that could be crucial to the proof of our client's innocence. Unless we're able to obtain that knowledge in a timely manner our case will be fatally weakened. Our client will be denied a reasonable defense. We'll have no choice but to appeal."

His head cocked to the side, and he scratched his ear. "Go on."

I looked at Katherine and she nodded for me to take over. In fact, she conceded the discussion so hastily I wondered if she was using me to play a little game here; her version of good cop/bad cop. Only in this case, a more accurate name would be brave cop/chicken cop.

Anyway, I swallowed and said, "We believe the statements provided by Moran and Jackson were physically coerced."

Carruthers contemplated that a moment. He picked up the rubber ball and began kneading it again. This time, I was the pitiful little thing trapped inside that meaty fist.

"You'd better have a reasonable basis for this suspicion."

"We do. Yesterday I was interrogated by the same officers who questioned Moran and Jackson. As you can see by my physical condition, they have . . . shall we say, a very persuasive way about them."

The room was so dark that he had to get up and walk to the light switch and turn it on. He circled around a few times, inspecting the damage.

He returned to his seat. "Look, Drummond, it's not news that Korean interrogation techniques aren't as humane as ours. But if you're considering a dismissal on that basis, go study your precedents. American law doesn't recognize the misbehavior of foreign police authorities operating on their own soil as grounds for dismissal."

"I'm aware of that, Your Honor. A CID officer was present for my beatings."

"That's lamentable, but CID can't be expected to control the behavior of the ROK police, either. Same precedents apply."

"Agreed, but he participated. And the same CID officer was present for the interrogations of Moran and Jackson. In fact, he's the lead witness for the prosecution."

"Then file a complaint against him. But the fact that he struck you doesn't lead to the conclusion he beat the other two."

"No sir, it doesn't. Except there was a point in my interrogation when he and his ROK counterpart thought I was unconscious. I overheard them refer to the beatings they administered to Private Jackson."

Carruthers was obviously familiar with the case file. "This is Bales you're referring to?"

"Yes, Your Honor."

He began bouncing the rubber ball on his desk. "Watch it, Drummond. Of course you want to discredit the star witness, but I don't allow attorneys to assassinate the reputations of good people. Not in my court. Bales is the youngest CW3 in the Criminal Investigation Division. He has a record any police officer would die for. Let me put this frankly. Don't be pulling any crap here."

"May I be equally frank?"

"You'd better be, Drummond."

"Okay. Here's the thing. For three hours before Bales and his ROK counterpart interrogated me, a long line of Korean officers kept appearing with keys to my cell. I got my ass thrashed more times than I could count. Can I prove that? No. Then I got dragged in to see Bales and his ROK buddy Inspector Choi. They knocked me around so hard they cold-cocked me. Will I ever be able to prove it? No. Enough guys in that precinct got a piece of my ass that there'll be a wall of silence harder than a woodpecker's lips."

"Then what do you hope to accomplish with Moran and Jackson?"

"We need to ask them if they got their asses crushed, too. We need to know if their testimony was coerced or not."

"Assume for the sake of argument they claim it was coerced. Will you be able to prove that in court?"

"It's doubtful, Your Honor. Choi has already filed a fabricated statement that claims Jackson was beaten up by his cellmate. I don't know what Moran's story is."

"Then what's your point? Why should I permit this if it'll still prove irrelevant?"

"Because it could lead us down other paths."

"And do you want to tell me what those other paths are?"

Carruthers, I suddenly realized, was considerably smarter than I'd given him credit for. I think he suspected from the beginning that we had some larger ulterior motive here.

I looked at Katherine and she looked at me, and we both realized that if we confided to Carruthers that we suspected the Itaewon Police Precinct of a mass conspiracy that included the massacre the day before, he'd wring both our necks.

Katherine, being the lead counsel, took over. "No, Your Honor, not at this time."

. He leaned back in his chair. He was still brooding and bouncing that little ball on his desk. "But you expect me to approve your request?"

"Yes sir," Katherine said, and it did not escape my notice that

she sounded and looked as meek as a housebroken kitten. Suspiciously so, in fact. She'd apparently switched to good cop/good cop
routine.

Smart girl. There's a time for in-your-face, and there's a time for
laying back.

The ball stopped bouncing and the judge bent forward again.

"All right, I'll let you know my judgment. But if I allow it, the
prosecutor has to be present. Moran and Jackson are his witnesses
and he has the right to share in the fruits of your discovery. Another
thing—call it point one: I want to know whatever you find out, as
soon as you find it out. I don't want to get into court and have any
big surprises. Not on this case. Capisch?"

"Capisch, Your Honor," we both respectfully replied.

"Point two: Don't forget point one. God help you, don't forget
point one. Miss Carlson, don't confuse me with those pansy-asses
you baited and sucker-punched in the past. I'll rip off your head
and poop down your throat."

Katherine sat and stared at him, and I have to tell you, there
wasn't any doubt in my mind that Barry Carruthers was not a man
to tangle with. Nor was there any doubt that he'd researched
Katherine's trial history and was well aware of her theatrical tactics.

He then said, "Now, you step outside, Miss Carlson. I need to
have a word with Drummond here."

It wasn't like she could say no. It was his office, after all. For
once, she didn't backtalk, or grumble, or anything. She got up and
left.

I sat nervously in my chair and anxiously wondered what this
was about. If he didn't want witnesses, it had to be bad.

He picked up the ball and started squeezing it again.

"Drummond, do I need to tell you that our friends in Washington aren't real pleased with your performance out here?"

So that's what this was. He'd asked the civilian to leave so we
could have a soldier's heart-to-heart. He was about to deliver the
mail, as they say. I slumped down in my chair.

"No, Your Honor. I think I've guessed that."

"You're a SPECAT special attorney, right?"

"Yes, Your Honor," I replied, although my mouth was agape.

What I was admitting was that I'm a Special Actions attorney assigned to a secret court that handles the ultra-sensitive cases of soldiers assigned to what the Army calls "black units." In other words, units whose purpose and missions are so absurdly secret and sensitive the military won't admit they exist. There are a lot more of these units than the public has any idea exists, which is actually paradoxical, because the public supposedly is unaware *any* of these units exist. With the marked exception of Delta Force, of course, which has to be the most widely publicized nonexistent unit in history.

Although the soldiers assigned to black units take strict vows to never mutter a word about what they do, when one of these "black" troopers gets accused of a serious crime, most of them instantly forget that vow and start threatening public disclosure unless they get a favorable plea bargain. There's also the danger that a public court-martial would expose information that could be hazardous to the nation's security.

Thus the SPECAT tribunal, where I work. The judges are handpicked. The lawyers are handpicked. We all have security clearances that run down the length of our arms. I got to be one of these attorneys because I was in the outfit, which happens to be the "blackest" unit of them all, and I got wounded so badly on a mission that my career as an infantry officer, such as it was, was over. The powers that be decided to send me to law school and then make me pay it back by working as a SPECAT lawyer.

I'm sure they were all regretting it now.

Judge Barry Carruthers wasn't supposed to know this, of course, because the existence of the SPECAT court was kept as secret from the rest of the JAG Corps as it was from the rest of humanity.

He was grinning. "Drummond, I spent four years as a SPECAT prosecutor."

"I had no idea," I admitted.

"Long time ago. But I'm not keeping you here to trade chummy stories about life as a SPECAT lawyer."

"No, I don't guess. You're here to tell me to straighten up and fly right."

"I've never heard of a court case that caused so much godawful carnage. You realize, don't you, that this alliance is on the brink of disintegrating?"

"That's what they say on the news."

"The news don't know the half of it, Drummond. The Secretary of State's here on a last-ditch effort to keep it together. Personally, I don't have any money on him. You should see the messages flying back and forth between here and Washington. It's ugly. And if you and Miss Carlson come into my court and start trying to prove this Lee kid was gay, then don't wait till the last American flight to get off this peninsula, because our boys will be loaded on troopships, and it won't be long before Uncle Kim up north decides it's time to come south for an extended visit."

"Your Honor, I—"

"Knock off the 'your honor' crap. We both know this isn't a proper judge-to-lawyer conversation. This is a mano-to-mano chat we're having here."

"Right."

He fixed his eyes on my face. He paused for a moment to let me know this was a decisive moment. Then he asked, "Do you really believe Whitehall's innocent? Don't screw with me now, Drummond. I'm not the jury. You don't have to persuade me. Give me a no-shit answer."

I did not pause or hesitate. "Of murder, rape, and necrophilia, I do. The other crimes, I suspect he did."

He leaned back in his chair and kept staring at me. I guess he was trying to look into my soul to see if I was capable of telling the truth or if I was just one more prevaricating, weasel-faced defense attorney.

Finally he nodded that big head of his and said, "All right. Do what you have to do. Talk to Moran and Jackson. On Friday, we're gonna have a trial, and you and Carlson come in and give it all you've got. No holds barred. I won't be easy on you, but if an American soldier, of all people, can't get a fair trial, then you and I chose the wrong profession."

I thanked him, left, and hooked back up with Katherine. As soon as we got outside, we stood right where we were, in the sunlight, blinded and awestruck for a second.

I said, "We've got permission to talk with Moran and Jackson. Also, trial starts on Friday. No holds barred."

She nodded. "Friday. No holds barred."

We fell quiet.

I finally laughed. "Ah hell, he's not so tough. He's a big pansy."

Katherine giggled, too. "Did you hear what he said? He threatened to rip off my head and *poop* down my throat. *Poop?* He'll *poop* down my throat? What kind of a man uses that word?"

"A man who means it."

She sighed. "God, I'm not looking forward to this trial."

CHAPTER 30

✪ ✪ ✪

Imelda waited impatiently by the front door to the hair parlor. She grabbed my arm and dragged me into a back room, then closed the door behind us.

She said, "Michael Bales."

"Right, Michael Bales."

"I checked his ass out."

"You checked him out."

"In country five years. Came over on a three-year tour, married a Korean, and extended."

"So he's a homesteader?" I asked, or concluded. Homesteaders are troops who get tired of being shifted from one end of the earth to the other and fight to remain in one place. It's a fairly common thing with troops in Korea especially, because so many of them marry Korean girls who aren't real eager to leave Mamasan and Papasan to go live in a strange culture on the other side of the globe.

"Guess who his wife is."

"A girl who's into S&M. On weekends they send the kids to stay with Grandma and Grandpa so they can tie each other up and beat the bejesus out of each other."

"Choi's sister."

"You're kidding, right?"

Actually it was a stupid question, because one of the things

BRIAN HAIG

about Imelda Pepperfield is that she never kids. I've heard her try to tell jokes, but frankly her timing sucks. Imelda's one of those folks who're only funny when they're not trying to be. A natural comedienne, I guess you'd say.

Unlike me—a forced laugh a minute.

"Bales is the number one boy around here. A tough case rolls in, he's the man. Boy's broken more cases than Jesus saved souls."

"And now we know how he does that, don't we?"

"He busts their nuts and don't get caught."

By the time we walked out of the office, Katherine had already called Fast Eddie and arranged for him to meet us at the holding facility. We had two days left. Katherine wasn't wasting time.

Since both witnesses were soldiers, it seemed obvious I should come along. We decided to bring Imelda as well, technically as our recorder, but really because she was a senior noncommissioned officer and might catch something we missed. The Army's like that. All kinds of hidden cues pass among the troops that officers and civilians can't begin to detect.

Twenty minutes later, we walked into the holding facility. A tall, gangly MP lieutenant met us at the door and lethargically escorted us to an interview room. Eddie was already there, seated beside a short, wispy, skinny kid who looked frightened as hell. The kid had wavy blond hair, a sallow, skinny face, reddened rudiments of popped, scabby pimples, and big, round, frightened blue eyes. I recognized his face from his photo. He looked even more effeminate in person.

"Good morning, Eddie," Katherine said, giving Golden a perfectly churlish smile.

"Have a seat," Eddie said, no longer using any of his famous charm on Katherine or me. Eddie's a smart boy. He doesn't waste ammunition.

Katherine instantly extended her hand across the table at Jackson. "Hello, Everett, I'm Katherine Carlson, the attorney for Thomas Whitehall."

She gave him a positively dazzling smile, and she was a beautiful woman, and although Jackson was gay, a smile on a beautiful

woman's face is still a glorious thing to behold. I mean, I was staring at her. Of course, I'm hetero. But then, she's not, which just
goes to show how chaotic everything was in this case. Anyway,
Jackson shook her hand.

"And this," she pointed at Imelda and me, "is Major Sean Drummond, my co-counsel, and Sergeant Imelda Pepperfield, our legal
assistant."

He gave a brief glance in our direction, then turned immediately back to Katherine. Imelda, I noticed, had backed herself into
a corner with a pained expression on her face.

Katherine continued. "Everett, I've been hired by OGMM,
whom I've worked for, I guess, for about eight years now. I'm a
civilian, of course. My specialty is military gay cases. I'm what you
might call an advocate. I believe gays should be allowed to serve,
and I make my living fighting for that right in the courts."

This was a very clever move on her behalf. She was informing
young Everett Jackson, a soldier imprisoned and about to be dishonorably discharged for committing homosexual acts, that her
life's work was fighting for guys like him. By implication, she was
saying, Hey, about that legal pretty boy on your right—that's right,
the good-looking stud in the green uniform. Don't be taken in by
him; sure he might act like a nice fella, but he's the guy who gets
paid for getting guys like you shoved out of the service. I'm the
good guy here, Everett. We're simpatico. Let's be chums.

Jackson was nodding like he understood. I was trying to look
invisible. I didn't want him looking at me and thinking, Hey, what
about him? Isn't he one of the gay haters, too?

But Eddie wasn't any chump, either. He quickly said, "Don't be
fooled by her, Everett. She's the attorney for Thomas Whitehall, the
man who murdered Lee No Tae and got you into this mess. She
doesn't care about you. She cares only about her client."

Jackson's eyes shifted back and forth a few times from Eddie to
Katherine, and I couldn't tell what he was thinking.

Katherine swiftly said, "Of course, he's right, Everett. My job is
to defend Thomas Whitehall. And I do it willingly, because I know

he's being railroaded, just like I suspect you were railroaded into giving the testimony you provided."

Jackson so far had not said a word. He had not been asked to say a word. The prosecutor and defender were too busy fussing and fencing over his loyalty.

"Now, Everett," Katherine continued, "let me tell you what this is about. In your testimony, you said you were invited to Captain Whitehall's apartment by First Sergeant Moran. Is that right?"

Jackson looked at Eddie, who nodded at him that it was okay to speak. The fact that he looked over at Eddie, this wasn't a good omen.

He said, "That's right, ma'am."

A big, warm, friendly smile. "Please, Everett, drop the 'ma'am' stuff. Call me Katherine. I'm not one of these stiff-lipped Army guys here."

"Okay, Katherine. Yes. First Sergeant Moran invited me."

"Didn't you find that strange? I mean, how often do you get invited to an officer's quarters for a party?"

"A little odd, yes. But I was, uh, well—"

"You were First Sergeant Moran's significant other?"

"Yes, that's right. I thought, well, you know, I thought I was invited like his date."

"Of course," Katherine said, as though this were the most innately aboveboard thing in the world. After all, she *was* a gay rights advocate. He didn't have to be embarrassed to disclose these intimate details to her. He didn't have to feel awkward. He could say it like it was. She, after all, was Jackson's only *real* soul mate in this room.

"Anyway," Jackson continued, "I felt odd at first, but Whitehall, uh, the captain, he was a real nice guy. I mean, he seemed real nice. He kept pouring me drinks, and he spent a lot of time talking with me. I, uh, I felt pretty comfortable."

"And what was Carl Moran doing? Was he talking with Lee No Tae?"

"Yeah. Part of the time, anyway."

At this point, Eddie lurched forward in his chair. "What in the hell's going on here? What does this line of questioning have to do with the interrogation?"

"I'm sorry?" Katherine stiffly replied, like, What the hell do *you* mean by what in the hell?

Eddie gave her a taste of his friendly-exterminator expression. "Lady, you're not here to practice your cross-examination on my witness. The judge's written order is clear. You can ask questions pertaining to Jackson's interrogation. That's it."

Katherine archly said, "Let me see your copy of the order."

In our haste to get back to our office, we hadn't actually stuck around to get a copy. Shame on us.

He triumphantly tossed it across the table at her. She picked it up, read it, then handed it to me, and I read it, then I handed it to Imelda and she gave it back to Eddie without looking at it herself.

It was a limited order. Carruthers was nobody's fool. We'd said we were investigating the possibility the witnesses were tortured. We could ask about the sequence that occurred after the arrest— period.

Katherine took a moment to regroup. She drew a couple of deep breaths, then smiled at Jackson again. This time it was a forced smile.

"Okay, Everett, let's review what occurred after you were arrested. Where were you taken?"

"To the Itaewon Police Station. We all were."

"And what happened there?"

"Well, first they separated us into different rooms. Then they took my fingerprints. Then they asked me a bunch of questions and—"

"Who asked you the questions?" I interrupted.

"A Korean police officer. I can't remember his name. It was like, uh, like—"

"Like Choi?"

"Yes . . . maybe."

"A uniformed cop, or a detective in civvies?"

"He was in civvies. I think he said he was like a chief inspector, or something like that."

"Where was this?"

"In a room in the back."

"Were any Americans present?"

"No."

"Okay, then what?" Katherine asked.

"Then I was put in a cell till some MPs came and got me. They brought me to base. They kept me in a room in the MP station. Then Chief Bales and the same Korean guy came in and asked me some questions."

"Did they touch you?" I asked.

He suddenly broke eye contact. He looked at Eddie, and Eddie nodded for him to go ahead and answer.

He said, "No . . . uh, they didn't touch me."

I bent toward him. "You're sure?"

"Yes sir, I'm sure."

"Then what happened?" Katherine asked.

"After an hour or so, I was released to go back to my unit."

Katherine turned and looked at me. I shrugged. She looked back at Jackson. "You went to see a lawyer, right?"

"Yeah, that's right."

"Why?"

"I dunno. I'd been at a murder scene. Who knows what the Korean cops thought, right? I thought I'd better be safe."

"And did the attorney advise you to go back and revise your initial statement?"

Jackson looked at Eddie again. Then he fidgeted for a moment. "Yeah. He said I should tell the truth. I mean, I didn't kill or rape anybody."

"Did you contact Carl Moran before you went back?"

"Yeah. I mean, I thought I owed him that. I couldn't leave him hanging."

I said, "Does that mean you knew Moran lied in his official statement to the MPs also?"

Eddie came forward. "Drummond, you're crossing the boundary."

"The hell I am. Your witnesses were interrogated twice and

their initial and final statements conflict. We have the right to know why."

Eddie scratched his chin for a second. Then he said, "I don't agree. Do we need to get on the phone and ask the judge?"

"We're only trying to get the truth. What the hell are you afraid of?"

He smiled. "Nothing. When you get him on the stand, ask anything you want. As long as it's relevant, of course. Otherwise, I'll break it off in your ass. You remember what that feels like, don't you, Drummond?"

If I hadn't mentioned it before, I don't really like Eddie Golden. In fact, I dislike him intensely. And not just because he'd bested me twice, but because he was such a puffed-up prick. I guess I was letting my feelings show, because Katherine put her hand on my arm to quiet me. I simmered but kept my mouth shut.

Then Katherine asked, "Everett, this is very important, now. Were you brought to the Itaewon station for a second visit?"

Jackson looked nervous. He turned to Eddie again, but Eddie stayed quiet.

He said, "I, uh, I'm sorry. What was your question again?"

"I asked, were you brought to the Itaewon station for a second visit?"

"No. Uh, I never went back there again."

He was lying. He wasn't even a good liar, because his eyes turned away from her, and his face turned red.

Katherine got forceful. "Were you ever beaten? Did Chief Bales or Inspector Choi touch you? Did they attempt to coerce you?"

Then, in a quick, taut, almost frantic rush of words, "No, never. They never touched me. I wasn't beaten."

To which I quickly said, "How odd, Everett. I have a copy of a statement from the Itaewon station that says you were beaten."

His face suddenly became alarmed. "What?"

"You heard me. I have an official police statement that says you were beaten at the Itaewon station."

Jackson's lips were just parting, but before he could say a word, Eddie grabbed his arm, and said, "Show me the statement."

"I didn't bring it with me," I replied, which was technically true. Since I didn't have any such statement, I obviously didn't have it with me. But such a statement did exist—the cover-up statement I'd overheard Choi confide to Bales that he'd filed, the one that claimed Jackson was beaten by his cellmate. I made a quick mental note to lodge a request with the Korean Ministry of Justice to see if they would produce it. I made a second note not to hold my breath.

Eddie, in the meantime, was smiling. "You're claiming you have evidence that contradicts my witness. I expect to see that evidence before he has to answer."

I wondered at this moment how much Eddie knew. Was he aware his witnesses were liars? Or was he just so eager to get another victory notch on his belt that he didn't want to know what he didn't want to know? Or did he really just think Katherine and I were a couple of sleazebag defense counsels trying to pull rabbits out of the hat?

Anyway, we'd reached what's called a deadlock, and Eddie was looking at his watch. "Now, if you two don't mind, I have a very busy schedule to keep. Unless you have a reasonable objection, I'm going to have Jackson returned to his cell and I'll have Moran brought in."

Without waiting for our reply, he got up and sauntered to the door and signaled a guard. Jackson was led out with his head hung low. I found it telling that he never turned and looked at us before he left. Not once. He got out of there as fast as Eddie could arrange it.

Then it was just us lawyers. And Imelda, of course, still standing quietly in the corner, observing us.

Eddie chuckled. "You guys are really grasping at straws. What's the matter, Carlson? I thought you said you and Drummond had some big surprises for me."

Like I mentioned earlier, Eddie was into playing mind games.

I was steaming, but Katherine was calm and unruffled, since mind games were her idea of sport also. "Oh, we do, Eddie, we do. We're just cleaning up a few loose ends."

"Sure you are, Carlson. You're hoping to assassinate Bales on the stand. Not unexpected, but a very bad idea."

"Really? Why's it a bad idea?"

"Because Bales is clean. He's rated one of the top three CID agents in the entire system. He's got the second highest arrest record, the highest conviction rate, and he's never had a single brutality charge leveled against him."

Katherine stared him right in the eye. "He's dirty."

And he stared right back. "Say that in court, and I'll make you regret it. This is a court-martial, Carlson, not a trial in some Black inner-city ghetto. Our jury's going be made up of ten Army officers. They respect CID officers. You open the issue, and I'll spend three days proving what a great guy he is. Don't waste your time."

"We'll see," Katherine said.

That was the moment when the door opened and First Sergeant Carl Moran was led in. His eyes roved around the room and locked on each of us for a brief second.

Eddie stood and held out a chair. Moran lumbered over and sat.

If I had any lingering misperceptions that you could pick gays out of a crowd, they went right up in smoke. He looked much like his photograph, except the picture didn't do justice to his size and apparent physical strength. The man was a mountain of muscle. An instant mental picture formed of him with his big paws gripped around an Army web belt as Lee No Tae coughed and choked and bucked out the last moments of his life.

Katherine went through her introductions again; same routine—I'm your real buddy here, not the well-groomed creep to your left. He believes gays should be drawn and quartered. Just tell me everything.

Carl Moran, though, wasn't Everett Jackson. He didn't look frightened, or vulnerable, or cowed. He was an old soldier, leathery and scarred, and despite what Katherine had confided to me about him being a big teddy bear in the bedroom, he looked like a king-size hardass to me.

Katherine then proceeded through the same drill of asking about his arrest, and he said essentially the same things as Jackson:

a trip to the Itaewon station, a standard booking, a brief stay in a Korean cell, a trip to the MP station, a by-the-book interrogation, a tortured battle with his conscience, a visit to a lawyer, a voluntary return to the MP station—a progression that ended in a voluntary, full-up confession.

I sat still and patiently waited for Katherine to get through her questions. I didn't intervene or interrupt once. She did a first-rate job, too, although it was completely hopeless. She made no headway. When she was finished, I bent forward, placed my elbows on the table, and stared skeptically at Moran a long time.

He tried to ignore me, till that grew awkward, then he said, "What? You got somethin' you wanna ask, Major?"

"Yeah, actually. You said you were never beaten?"

"That's right." He chuckled. "Do I look like a guy who'd take a beating from some gooks? Shit, one of them slant-eyes touches me, I'll bury his ass."

He was staring at my bruises and lumps, and I had the sense he knew how I got them. I had an even stronger sense he was taunting me.

I said, "Not if you're in manacles or tied to a chair, Moran. Not if they're ten of them and one of you. Not if you're scared stiff about being charged with murder. Come on, now, there's no shame in it. Tell us. Did anyone touch you?"

He leaned across the table and looked me right in the eye. "Nobody never touched me. I swear nobody touched me. No gooks touched me. Bales never touched me. That's the God's-honest truth. Nobody never touched me."

Then, on a quick instinct, I said, "One last question. You went to see your lawyer, then what'd you do? Did you at least warn Jackson you were about to confess?"

"Yeah, sure. Jackson's just a kid, y'know? I felt responsible for him."

And that's all it took. Voilá! The man's ego tripped him up.

Eddie, instantly aware of the disconcerting discrepancy, hastily announced, "All right, all right, we've exhausted this angle. First

Sergeant Moran, thanks for your help. Go ahead and return to your cell."

Moran's face revealed his puzzlement. He knew he'd said something wrong, he just wasn't sure what. Anyway, he got up and lumbered back to the door, where two MPs were waiting to return him to his cell.

The door closed, and Eddie sat back and smiled. It was his man-eating smile, one of those things where the corners of his lips stretched so far they touched his earlobes.

"Satisfied?" he asked.

This was the one risk we'd run by coming over here. Now Eddie knew where we were trying to go. And like us, he'd just heard his witnesses walk on each other over who'd gone to see the lawyer first, and who'd advised who to confess. There was a chink in his armor, but now he knew where. Knowing Eddie like I know Eddie, I had no doubt he'd walk them through a few rehearsals and make sure they got all the kinks ironed out by the trial.

"Very satisfied," Katherine said, and both of us did our best to smile confidently, like we had just learned something providential and compelling.

"Drop it," he sternly warned, standing up and looking at his watch again. "Trust me on this, Carlson, don't screw with Bales on the stand. I won't allow it. This judge won't, either."

He walked out with a satisfied strut. The instant he was gone, our phony smiles turned into gloomy pouts. We had nothing to smile about. Katherine and I did the usual lawyer's second-guessing when you come up short, wondering what questions we should've asked that we didn't, what we should've phrased differently, how we misplayed the witnesses, how we blew our big chance.

Then we walked out and dejectedly headed back to the parking lot and our sedan.

"You two did good back there," Imelda announced.

"What?" Katherine asked.

"I said you did good."

"We did?" I asked.

"Got it all figured out now, right?"

"Uh, yeah," I said. "Which part are you talking about?"

Imelda spun around and faced me. She reached up and adjusted her glasses around her ear. "Moran wasn't lyin'. They never touched him."

"Of course they didn't," I said—uncertainly, but I said it.

Imelda turned back around and chuckled. "That Bales, he's got good instincts. A man like Moran, he's all ego. A man like that, you could beat him silly and he won't talk. Nuh-uhh. Imagine pickin' the weak one to make the big one break." She chuckled some more.

And of course, Imelda was right. That's exactly what had happened. Bales and Choi had somehow gotten the two of them back in the Itaewon station for a second visit. They had somehow figured out the relationship between Moran and Jackson. They figured that Moran had an ego like a battleship, which wasn't too hard to guess, so they kicked the crap out of Jackson until Moran, the big teddy bear, broke to protect his boyfriend.

I looked at Katherine, but her eyes were still fixated on the back of Imelda's head.

I said, "Did you know the JAG office keeps a log of everybody who stops by to seek legal counsel?"

She smiled. "No, I didn't. How very convenient for us."

"Yes," I said. "All we need to do is check what day Jackson and Moran sought counsel, then we'll have proof of whether they were persuaded by their lawyers, or by a bunch of sadistic cops. If there's a discrepancy, maybe you can break it off in Eddie's ass."

"Already done that," Imelda mumbled from the front seat.

Katherine bent forward. "I'm sorry. What was that?"

"I said I've already done that. Jackson and Moran didn't visit no lawyer till a week after they made their final statement."

See, that's the thing with Imelda. She doesn't play fair. She knew before we even sat down with them that Moran and Jackson were lying about the lawyers. That's why she was able to unravel their fabrications.

If I were twenty years older, I'd marry that woman.

CHAPTER
31

✪ ✪ ✪

So here's where we were.

Two key witnesses were lying; one had been tortured, and both had been coerced into false statements. I figured the lie in their testimony was that part about hearing Whitehall and Lee fighting that night.

Another key witness, Michael Bales, was also lying. He'd beaten the crap out of Jackson to build his case.

Lee No Tae had a key to the lover's nest, although Eddie wasn't going to have great difficulty inventing a plausible alibi. He'd probably argue that Whitehall was smart enough to plant the key in Lee's pocket after he murdered him.

We didn't know how anybody could've broken into the apartment and killed Lee. Unless the police were lying. Unless the lock expert did a sham job. Unless there was a full-blown police conspiracy that extended even beyond the Itaewon station.

We knew our client was being expertly framed. We didn't know by who, for what, or how, which are not insignificant questions. We suspected an entire police precinct, and unless we could show insurmountable proof of that, we'd be laughed out of the courtroom.

I called Colonel Carruthers and told him what we'd discovered. I told him about the discrepancy. I told him about the JAG log and about the fact that Jackson and Moran were lying about who advised who to confess, and when they first sought counsel.

He listened politely. He thanked me for calling. He informed me we had nothing compelling. I already knew that. He told me to stay with it. He said the inconsistency was curious. I already knew that, too.

As soon as I hung up, Allie grabbed my arm and tugged me into a side room. Actually, that's an understatement. She nearly yanked my arm out of its socket, and I yelped as I catapulted through the doorway.

"Ouch!" I said, giving her a menacing glare.

"Don't be such a wimp."

"But that hurt," I complained. And it did. It hurt a lot, partly because I was already beat-up and shot, and partly because she was strong as an ox. It struck me that if Allie wanted to wipe the floor with me, she probably could. Even if I were in top form, she'd probably tear me to pieces.

She ignored my suffering. "How did it go?"

"Not good," I admitted. "Moran and Jackson walked on each other a bit, but it's nothing Golden can't repair with a little careful coaching. We're still nowhere."

Her face melted into a mask of deep unhappiness, which looked quite odd—one, because she had that kind of face; and two, because I'd only seen her expressions range between anger and disdain. No, that's not true, because I'd also seen her gaze affectionately at Maria, so this new expression reminded me how very agonizing this case had become for her. She'd lost her lover, maybe in a way not directly related to Whitehall's guilt or innocence, but clearly on behalf of the cause. Proving Whitehall's innocence was now the only way she could salvage her loss.

While she seemed like the last kind of woman you'd feel pity for, I did. I just couldn't think of anything helpful to say.

"I'm sorry," I told her. "I'm plain out of ideas."

She stewed on that a moment. She said, "What about the films of the massacre? Why don't we study those?"

"For what? The whole world's already looked at them a few hundred times and nobody's seen anything worth talking about."

"It can't hurt."

I didn't want to waste my time, but I also didn't want to disappoint her. "You know it's a long shot?"

"We're into any kind of shot, aren't we?"

I couldn't argue with that, so I dumbly nodded. Allie then called the local ABC affiliate and actually sounded quite charming and maybe even sexy as she sweet-talked some guy into letting us come over and view the film. It was quite odd hearing her sound so girlish and flirty, but it worked.

But just wait till the guy on the other end of the line actually got an eyeful of the woman behind the voice.

The studio was located on the twelfth floor of a huge, gleaming new high-rise on Namdung Plaza. We took the elevator up, and the Koreans who rode up with us stared curiously at Allie, who was about two feet taller than any of them, but would've been a sight even if she were two feet shorter.

Then they glared at me, I think because they suspected she was the one who'd beaten me to a pulp.

From their faces, you could picture what they were thinking. Americans! Such an odd people. How did they ever get so rich? So successful? So powerful?

Good questions, actually. I've often asked them myself.

Anyway, a skinny guy in jeans and a raggedy T-shirt met us in the lobby of the tiny studio. He stared at Allie in sheer shock, and it was immediately obvious he was the one she'd sweet-talked. Allie winked at me, and I had to work hard to suppress a laugh, because until this moment I hadn't thought of her as a woman, with feminine wiles and some of the necessary skills in the battle between the sexes. At least the two sexes.

The guy said his name was Harry Menker. He was the cameraman who'd captured the massacre on tape, and he was very proud of this. He spent a moment reliving how he'd dared shot and shell to get the film that was aired by just about every network in the world. He bitched for a moment about how he got no royalties for

that, because he worked for the network, and the network pock-
eted all the profits from his daring.

Allie and I listened patiently and cooed sympathetically. It was
his film. He led us to a room in the back he called the review room.
Two technicians awaited. The film was loaded and ready. They told
us to sit, then they dimmed the lights.

Harry helpfully explained, "What you saw on TV were clips. We
cut out the particularly gory scenes, you know, like bodies getting
blown away, the sounds of people cursing. What you're about to
see is the full, uncut version."

I glanced at Allie and she smiled back triumphantly. The trip
might be worth our time after all.

The first five minutes were switchbacks from the protesters to
the riot police. I was prominently on display a few times. Harry
said, "We were surprised to see an Army guy there. In uniform, no
less. You got balls."

Then we heard the recording of the first shot and the camera
went crazy. We stared at flashes of tarmac, of feet, of legs. The camera was being jerked and swung around so hard, it was enough to
give you vertigo. You could hear Harry's frantic voice on the tape:
"Shit . . . crap . . . oh Jesus."

Harry slid down in his seat a little. "I . . . uh, I got scared."

I said, "Me too."

As if on cue, I was on the big screen. I was shoving people
aside, and bodies were flying everywhere, not from my shoves, but
because most of the bodies around me were being shot and
knocked over. I hadn't realized how close I came to being hit.

"Oh my God," Allie murmured, and I felt her hand grip my arm
so hard I almost groaned.

She must've seen something, so I said, "Could you stop the film?
Run it back to when the shooting started. Run it in slow motion."

So they did. Then they did it again.

"You're friggin' lucky to be sittin' here, man," said Harry the
cameraman.

He was right. The shooter was aiming at me from his opening
shot. There was no question of it. He was trying to hit me. The peo-

ple being struck by bullets around me were simply the by-product of his lousy marksmanship.

But what I didn't notice until the third replay was what Allie had observed in a single glance. The protester directly to my rear deliberately shoved me forward, right into the ranks of the riot police. She'd had her head turned to the left so she saw the two people beside me get hit, and she sensed the next shot would hit me, so she just reached forward and shoved me. She was such a tiny thing, it's amazing she could muster enough force to drive me off my feet. But she did. And she saved my life, and deliberately exposed herself to the bullet meant for me.

I watched for the third time as her head exploded in a shower of blood. It was Maria, of course.

I turned and looked helplessly at Allie. Her chest was heaving and tears were streaming down her cheeks. She was moaning from pain and loss. I felt something deep inside my chest get thick and sour.

I put an arm over her shoulder. Her being so much bigger than me, and the way she looked, we must've seemed a very strange-looking couple. Harry and his two assistants watched us until they recognized that Allie and I were terrifically affected by something. They froze the projector and diplomatically slid out of the room.

I finally said, "Allie, I'm so sorry. I had no idea."

She didn't answer. She just sat and cried and moaned, and I felt as miserable as I could ever remember being in my whole life. Or maybe miserable is the wrong word. Maybe what I felt was shame and inadequacy. Maria had owed me nothing. No, actually she'd owed me less than nothing. From the moment I'd laid eyes on her, I'd judged her and ignored her, which, if you think about it, is maybe the worst form of disdain there is.

You always read stories about heroes who save people's lives, where they recount what they were thinking and how they felt in that fleeting instant when they did something unbelievably courageous. What you never read is what it feels like to be the one who gets saved, particularly when your savior dies. So I'll tell you what it feels like. It makes you feel so guilty you want to rip your own heart out of your chest.

Somehow, I guess Allie sensed that, because she slipped her long arm across my shoulder and pulled me toward her. And that's how we sat for the next few minutes, neither able to say a word, sitting in mutual misery, her because of her loss, and me because I wished more than anything I could trade places with Maria, even as I was guiltily content that I couldn't.

Allie finally withdrew her arm, stood up, and went to retrieve Harry and his boys. They flipped the projector back on and we grimly returned to our viewing.

There was one sequence where I quickly bent over to pick up the riot baton. On the film, the second I leaned over to get that baton, three more protesters right behind me got their heads blown open like splattering melons. If I hadn't bent over, the bullets would've hit me.

Harry said, "Wow! Man, look at that."

So the cameraman replayed the scene in slow motion twice more, until I was tired of watching people die from bullets meant for me.

"Move on," I barked.

The next sequence showed me sprinting toward the shooter. I looked damned good, too, if I do say. Allie even reached over and squeezed my arm, I guess to make me feel better.

Harry had focused his lens on me, so the figures around me were blurry and unfocused. I saw myself swing the baton and knock the cop on his noggin, then bend over and steal his pistol. I thought I saw something else, too, though it didn't register.

I was running up the hill at the shooter, and I relived that moment where he yanked that magazine out of his vest. Then I noticed something else. He glanced over to his right. Then he looked back at me and dropped his weapon.

I made them replay that moment of decision five or six more times. The more I studied it, the more apparent it got. There wasn't anything aimless in that sideways glance. The shooter was looking at somebody off to his right. He was searching for instructions. He was looking at his boss, or his lookout.

Then I remembered that I'd noticed something earlier in the film. I said, "Take it back to the point where I'd just emerged from the crowd. Slow motion again."

So they did. Probably they thought I was reveling in my moment of glory. Truth be known, I'm not above such things.

This time, though, I stopped looking at myself and saw it more clearly. The figure was foggy and blurry, but there was something about him, something odd.

"Take it back and freeze it when I say freeze."

It was impossible to be sure. The film was too out of focus. The figure was twenty, maybe thirty yards from me. What made him appear out of place was this: He was standing perfectly upright. He wasn't diving for the ground, or running, or anything. He was standing with his hands on his hips, a pose of command. He was located at almost exactly the spot the shooter had looked for his signal.

I turned to Harry. "Can I have a copy of the film?"

He said, "Sure, man."

So Allie and I collected the film, and then I took her hand and we left.

When we got outside Allie said, "What did you see?"

I felt bad about it, since reviewing the film was her idea, but I had no choice. "Nothing."

She looked at me in disbelief. "Nothing? Why'd you ask for the film?"

"Hell, who knows? I guess so I'll always remember how Maria saved my life."

Constructing that particular alibi made me a real louse, but I knew it would end any further curiosity on Allie's part, because really, how could she argue with that?

She smiled grimly and nodded, and we returned to base, me wondering about that figure in the film, her reliving the nightmarish sight of the woman she loved getting struck in the head by that bullet.

Back at the office, I furtively stepped outside and used a cell phone to call Spears's office. I told my favorite colonel I needed to see Mercer and I needed to see him right away. I gave him my number, and he said okay and hung up.

I stood under a shady tree for three minutes before my cell phone rang.

He said, "Drummond, Mercer here."

I said, "I need to see you. It's important."

"I'm busy. How important?"

"Damned important."

"All right. We're gonna have to be tricky about this. You're being watched."

"By who?" I asked.

"I'll tell you later. Go down to the Post Exchange. Loiter around by the jewelry counter and we'll take it from there."

I grabbed my cane and told Imelda I'd be back in an hour. Then I hobbled over to the Post Exchange. The PX just happened to be the one support facility located on the other half of Yongsan, and I worked up a good sweat, cursing at Mercer as I hobbled around on that cane. The blast of air-conditioning as I entered the building nearly made me kiss the floor. I went to the jewelry counter and looked at watches. When I finally glanced up, the ruthlessly cold-hearted Miss Kim was perusing some earrings on the other side of the glass counters.

She held up a pair, shook her head, and then moved off toward the stereo section. I slowly followed her. She stood studying a gargantuan-size pair of Infinity tower speakers until a guy walked by her, she glanced at him, and he nodded. Then she hooked a finger in my direction for me to follow her.

I have to tell you I thought all this cloak-and-dagger stuff was simply hilarious. These people probably run Geiger counters over toilet seats before they take a squat. She led me through some doors and into the warehouse in the back.

We walked around stacks of boxes and cabinets, until we turned a corner and ran right into Buzz Mercer.

I said, "You moonlighting as a warehouseman on government time?"

"Heh-heh," he said, although I had the impression he didn't really think it was funny. Maybe it wasn't. "You got two trailers on you, Drummond. They didn't come inside, although if you're in here too long, they might get suspicious. And make sure you buy something before you leave—you know, for authenticity."

"Who are they?" I asked.

"We're not sure. We took their photos this morning. We're checking them with our friends over at the Korean CIA at this moment. In fact, the reason we diverted you all the way over here was so we could make them pass through the post gate. We had a man there checking their IDs as they came through. Maybe we'll have a better idea soon."

As he spoke I could see his eyes inspecting my damage. Some of the bruises I was sporting had started to yellow around the edges, so I was sort of a walking kaleidoscope of colors. He didn't seem too distressed by my condition.

I reached inside my trouser pocket and withdrew the videocassette tape Harry had given me. I handed it to him. "This is an uncut ABC tape of the massacre. You got people who can enhance it? Maybe clear up some of the blurring where the camera's not focused properly?"

"Depends how many color pixels the camera caught."

"Okay, here's the thing. There's a point in the film where I'm running out of the crowd, going after one of the two shooters. Then there's a point where the shooter pauses to draw a new magazine."

He wearily said, "We all know about that, Drummond. It's been on all the TV news shows."

"Right. Here's the thing, though. Study the shooter just before he makes the decision to drop his weapon and hightail it. He looks over to his right."

His interest perked up. "Okay, so there's a spotter, or somebody else who was there."

"Right. I think I passed right by him. I think he's in the film. He's standing perfectly upright, as calm as can be. Everybody else is either hitting the concrete or moving in confusion. Not this guy. He's watching. He's composed. That's what I want you to check."

Mercer took the videocassette tape. "Who do you think he is?"

"I haven't got a clue."

"Okay, we'll give it a try."

"How long?"

"Hard to say. Won't take us long to compress and code this and send it back to Langley by satellite. It's two in the morning there, though. They'll have to roust some techies out of bed and get 'em to work."

"It's worth it," I told him. "Trust me."

"Yeah? Tell me more, Drummond."

"Not yet. Get a clear picture of this guy."

At that instant, Mercer's cell phone rang. He pulled it up to his ear and turned away from me, so he could murmur and whisper with whatever spook buddy was on the other end. It was a brief conversation.

He put the phone back in his pocket and looked at me. "The guys following you are Korean cops. I guess they're trying to keep an eye on you because of all the trouble you've been causing."

"Yeah, I guess," I said.

It was Wednesday afternoon. The trial opened Friday morning. We had thirty-six hours left. I hoped I wasn't imagining things. I hoped the CIA's techies could find enough color pixels to get a reasonable picture of this guy. I hoped he wasn't just some guy who turned out to be deaf and blind and was standing perfectly still only because he didn't have a clue what was going on. What I really hoped was that he didn't turn out to be a tree.

CHAPTER
32
★ ★ ★

The time had come for Katherine and me to pay another visit to our client. With thirty hours left till the trial started, we'd reached what lawyers call the moment of decision. We climbed into the sedan and I insisted on hitting McDonald's and the Class VI store, which, to the uninitiated, is the military version of a liquor store, only the prices are much cheaper because the booze is untaxed. If the drunks of America had any idea how much Uncle Sam gouges them, there'd be another American revolution.

I splurged on two six-packs of Molson and another bottle of Johnnie Walker Blue. I wasted a moment trying to persuade Katherine to get her OGMM buddies to recompense me for my costs, but she's a stickler on these things. She said bribes don't fall within OGMM's idea of allowable expenses.

We actually had an amiable chat on the way over, although our discussion was intermittent and halting, and I could tell she was distracted and nervous. She kept tinkering with a leather band around her left wrist, and every now and again stared wistfully out the window, like she didn't want to be in this car, like she really didn't want to visit our client.

I guessed she was apprehensive about admitting to Whitehall that his defense was damn close to hopeless. That's never a great feeling. On the other hand, Katherine had spent most of her legal career telling clients they didn't stand a chance. I don't know what her win-loss record looked like, but if it was 0 for 100, I wouldn't be surprised. She'd won plenty of appeals, because that was the point of her strategy, but she was probably accustomed to seeing jury foremen shuffle their feet, and avoid her eyes, and look up at the judge, and say, "Hang the bastard."

So what was making her so pent-up? It wasn't the public spotlight, I didn't think. She'd bathed in the public glare more than any other ten attorneys combined. She'd been cover-storied on magazines, profiled on those television news magazine series, had her glitzy moments with Larry King and Katie Couric.

Was it because this was a murder trial? After all, the worst that comes from your ordinary gay trial is maybe a few years in the slammer. More often than not, it's a dishonorable discharge from the service, which is really nothing but a fancy epithet for being fired. Maybe the stakes were getting to her. Maybe the thought her client could get the death sentence was eating at her insides.

Anyway, the big bully rushed right down when the desk guard retrieved him. He broke into a huge, hungry smile when he laid eyes on me, and I winked and pointed a finger at the search room. He nearly sprinted for it.

He dug his hand inside the bag, withdrew his scotch, his two burgers, grinned hungrily, and then led us to Whitehall's cell. I could teach that Pavlov guy a few tricks.

Again he said one hour, ushered us into the cell, then wandered off, actually caressing the bottle of scotch. I was smitten with envy. I wanted to caress that Johnnie Walker Blue with my tongue.

Thomas got up and studied both of our bleak faces for a stagnant moment. Then he reached out a hand and I shook it. He actually hugged Katherine, and I'll be damned if she didn't collapse into his body, then start sobbing on his shoulder. I heard these small, muffled moans. Her body was quaking.

He stroked her hair and said, "Hey, hey, come on. Take it easy, okay. Katherine, really. Don't get all worked up. I know you're doing your best."

She finally pulled herself away, and I scratched my head a few

times. I've seen some things in my day, but a defense attorney crying on a client's shoulder? Everything was backwards in this case.
But even more backwards was seeing Katherine Carlson with tears
on her cheeks.

I decided it was time to immediately rearrange the mood in this
tiny cell, so I put down my legal case, opened it, tossed two Big
Macs at Whitehall, and then withdrew three beers.

I said, "Hey, Tommy, this guy walks into a bar with a monkey. The
guy takes a stool at the bar, and the monkey perches next to him.
The guy orders a drink while the monkey starts eating everything
it can reach—peanuts, olives, lime slices, even napkins. The monkey wanders over to the pool table, where a couple of guys are
playing, and he jumps up on the middle of the table, then lifts up
the cue ball and swallows it whole. The monkey's owner immediately knocks down his drink and says to the bartender and the
other customers, 'Hey, I'm real sorry. The little bastard always eats
everything he can get his hands on. I'll pay for everything, I swear.'
So he does, and then he leaves. A month later, he and the monkey
come back again, they take stools at the bar, and the guy orders a
drink. Everybody in the bar watches as the monkey reaches across
the bar, grabs a Maraschino cherry, holds it up to his eye, reaches
down and stuffs it up his butt, then pulls it out and eats it. It's so
gross, people are getting sick. The guy says to the bartender, 'Hey,
I'm really sorry. I know it's disgusting, but ever since he ate that
cue ball, he measures everything he eats.'"

Tommy started laughing like hell. These huge guffaws were
erupting from his throat. The joke was funny, but it wasn't that
funny. I guessed the tension and pressure had him teetering on an
emotional cliff.

As for Katherine, she coldly said, "Is that a joke?"

Tommy said, "Actually, I think it's a parable for my situation. I'm
like that monkey. Now that I've been locked in this cell for ten
days, I've measured my future."

Katherine frowned, but I chuckled because he was right.

Then we all went over and sat down on Tommy's sleeping mat.
Katherine was in the middle, and we all propped our backs against

the wall. For a few minutes, we took sips from our beers while Tommy wolfed down his burgers. This was actually a chivalrous attempt by Tommy and me to give Katherine time to stop sniveling and get collected.

Then Katherine skillfully explained everything that had happened over the past two days, from the massacre, through our meeting with the judge, through our interrogations of Jackson and Moran. She told him what we suspected and how disgustingly little headway we'd made in proving any damned thing. She explained how we expected Fast Eddie to handle our pitifully small inventory of revelations and courtroom surprises.

Tommy heard her out. He occasionally took another sip from his beer. Otherwise he was inert, peaceful, unresponsive. It struck me that he expected everything he was hearing.

I had to admire his self-control. If it were me, knowing I'd been expertly framed for murder and other hideous deeds, and I was hearing my attorneys say they were making a complete hash of my defense, I would've been screaming my lungs out.

When she finished, he got up and went over to my legal case and withdrew three more Molsons. He opened them and then handed one to Katherine and one to me.

"No shit," he said, grinning proudly at me. "You actually went to the demonstration?"

"Couldn't resist it," I admitted.

"God, I wish I could've seen that."

"You might be the only guy in the world who didn't. The damn thing was broadcast by every network."

"Think you'll get in trouble?"

"Probably," I admitted.

The Army's not particularly vindictive, but like any organization, it has its limits. A picture broadcast worldwide of an officer in uniform amid a sea of homosexuals ain't exactly what the Army means by "be all you can be." I wasn't looking forward to the next promotion board. But Tommy Whitehall's problems were a little more grim than mine. Enough said.

Then Katherine said, "Thomas, sit down, please. We need to make some decisions."

He squatted on his haunches and faced us. It was a very Asian gesture, that squat. Only ten days in a Korean prison and already he was going native on us.

Katherine said, "I'm going to be blunt. Golden's a very shrewd and experienced attorney. Maybe we can get one of his witnesses to recant. Most likely Jackson, but not Moran, who's a tough nut. And Bales is even tougher. He's going to come across like a knight in shining armor."

Tommy said, "Okay."

Katherine let loose a heavy breath. "I recommend we take the deal."

Tommy bounced up to his feet. "What?"

"Look, I don't like it, but it'll keep you out of the electric chair. It'll buy us time."

"I'm not pleading. Get it out of your head, because I'm not taking their deal."

"Thomas, please listen. We've got one day left. The second we walk into that courtroom, the offer's moot. It'll be withdrawn. I'd like to approach the other side and try to bargain off the charges of committing homosexual acts and consorting with enlisted troops. If we plead on murder and rape, I think we can get them to go for it."

"I don't care."

She reached over and grabbed Whitehall's leg. "You'll still be alive. I'll dedicate my whole life to getting you an appeal. I won't stop, Thomas. I'll never stop. You know I won't."

"So what? We'll both waste our lives over this thing? I won't permit it."

Katherine looked over at me. Her face was beseeching. She was pleading with me to intervene, to do my best to convince her client to take the rap.

I said, "Good call, Tommy."

"What?" Katherine roared.

"He's making the right call. It's an obvious frame-up."

"Can you prove that?" Katherine asked, knowing damn well I couldn't.

"Nope," I admitted.

"Then what in the hell are you doing? A few days ago you thought a deal was the right way to go. You helped convince me."

I knew that and I felt bad about it, too. But I couldn't tell Katherine I was working an angle with my CIA buddies. Granted, there were no sure bets, but if something broke we could be off to the races. So all I said was, "I changed my mind."

I looked up at Tommy. Katherine was still holding his leg. He was staring down at me.

I said, "We're going to break this thing. Maybe not before the trial, but we'll get it eventually. I don't care if I have to resign my commission and come over and do it myself. We're going to break this thing."

"You'd do that?" Tommy asked.

"I'd do that," I assured him.

And I would. I'd just decided that. For one thing, a lot of people had been killed and something had to be done about that. And one of those people had died to save me, and it might sound corny, but didn't I owe her something? For another, I'd had plenty of clients convicted, but I'd never had one where I was so thoroughly convinced he was being railroaded. I didn't approve of Tommy's lifestyle choices, but he'd been a damned good soldier. And as the judge said, if a soldier can't get justice, then I was wearing the wrong uniform.

Also, Bales and his buddies had beaten me to a pulp. And like I mentioned earlier, I'm a vindictive guy.

Besides, I'm so stubborn I'm stupid. Anybody who knows me will tell you that.

Tommy said, "I, uh—"

But before he could finish the thought, Katherine suddenly erupted. "Don't listen to him, Thomas!" She was glaring at me through a pair of blazing green eyes. "This isn't about Thomas, is it? This is about Georgetown, right?" She spun and looked back at Whitehall. "He's never forgiven me for being number one in the class. He came in second and he's never gotten over it. Don't listen to him. This isn't about you. It's about him trying to outdo me. Don't listen to him."

Whitehall's eyes were roving from her face to mine. And mine was exploding with surprise.

"God, you gotta be kidding," I blurted.

I mean, it was true she'd beaten me out—by one-tenth of a decimal of a hundredth of a point. By such an infinitesimal fraction the law school actually had to recompute both our grade points something like ten times. They actually had to go back and retotal three years' worth of exams and papers and moot courts. Know what the spread was? Katherine got one more multiple-choice answer right than I did. That's right—one lousy question. No kidding. And you know the worst part? She probably guessed on that one question: one lousy throw of a dart in a pitch-dark room.

Did that give me the gripes? Well, yeah, actually it did. At the time, anyway. I mean, had it been Wilson Holbridge Struthers III, the guy who lived in the library, the guy everybody agreed was the biggest legal geek who ever haunted the halls of Georgetown Law, I could've lived with that. It wasn't, though. Struthers limped in at third place. It was Katherine Carlson. Of all people.

I took three deep breaths. I wasn't going to let her provoke me. I was going to keep my cool and reason through this. Georgetown law school was a long time ago. Whitehall had said at the start that he wanted to make the tough choices, and, well, he was getting his chance. Maybe not the way he'd envisioned, but I had at least warned him it could come down to this.

With as much calmness as I could muster, I said, "I still wouldn't take the deal."

And Katherine contemptuously snapped, "Look, Thomas, you won't have a death sentence hanging over your head. And let me tell you, getting a death sentence overturned is almost impossible these days. The courts have lost their patience with death sentence appeals. I'm no expert on it but I've done some research. Only one in twelve gets overturned. Plus, even the civil courts are accelerating death sentences, and this is a military court. These uniformed stooges could give you a chair appointment a year, maybe even six months from now."

Thomas said, "Both of you, stop this right now."

Katherine and I looked at each other in surprise.

His face was perfectly calm. "It has nothing to do with either of you. I won't plead."

Katherine said, "Why, Thomas?"

"Because I'm innocent. Because my love for No wasn't wrong or evil. Because I won't."

He and Katherine stared at each other a long time. It was one of those moments where electricity flowed through the air, where words would only have gotten in the way. Finally Katherine got up and started shaking the cage and yelling for the guard.

The big goon showed up, weaving back and forth, and it was pretty damned obvious he'd broken into the goodies. He was so drunk he kept diddling with the keys. Finally he got the door open and Katherine stormed out.

I looked at Tommy. "I guess I have to go."

"Yeah, sure. Keep me informed, will you?"

I assured him I would before I solemnly shook his hand. Then I walked out. I walked slowly. I was in no hurry to catch up with Katherine.

It was a long, tense car ride back to base.

CHAPTER
33

⭐ ⭐ ⭐

At two o'clock in the morning, there was another knock on my door. I rolled out of bed and hobbled over, again checked the peephole to make sure there wasn't somebody on the other side who wanted to hurt me. Like another bruise was going to make any discernible difference at this point. Silly me.

Carol Kim and a shadowy figure I couldn't make out were standing on the other side, so I opened it. The other person was Buzz Mercer, looking tired and perplexed.

I was wearing nothing but my Army-issue OD green battle shorts, so I demurely grabbed a fluffy white robe from the closet and escorted my visitors to the pair of chairs by the window. I fell onto the bed.

"Did you get it?" I asked, which was a fairly stupid question, because what else would they be doing in my room at this hour?

Carol opened a valise and withdrew a series of color photographs, maybe thirty in all.

"Look through these," she said, handing me the stack. "Are any of them the person you're talking about?"

The first few were the wrong figures. They were standing upright, but the reason was because they were frozen with fear or confusion or shock. You could see that on their faces, in their stances, in their auras. The fifth one was the man I wanted. The CIA techies probably figured that out from his pose, because the next six shots were all of him.

It wasn't until I got to the fifth photo that the techies had somehow amplified, or contorted, or tantalized enough pixels to make his face recognizable. I had to fight a sudden gleeful feeling. There he was, hands on hips, and although the expression on his face was still murky, from the cant of his head and the lift of his chin he appeared to be surveying the crowd, the way a proud farmer might look out over a field of newly ripened wheat. Except what Inspector Choi was admiring was a full-blown massacre.

I pulled out the photo and held it up for Kim and Mercer to see. "That's him."

"Who's he?" Mercer asked, correctly perceiving from my expression that I knew the bastard.

"Chief Inspector Choi of the Itaewon Police Precinct. He was in charge of the Lee murder investigation. He was the first one at the murder scene, and he teamed up with Chief Michael Bales, of CID, to break the case."

Mercer and Kim began studying the photograph more earnestly.

I couldn't resist adding, "He's also one of the bastards who kicked the shit out of me."

Carol said, "So what is this photo supposed to prove? Admittedly, he looks a little odd standing there, but so what?"

It was a good question. The mere fact that Choi was attentively watching the massacre unfold meant nothing by itself. Maybe he was just a cold-blooded bastard who found it entertaining. Nor was there anything compelling about the fact that the shooter I'd chased had glanced over in Choi's direction before he dropped his weapon. The shooter could've been looking at any of two dozen other people. Maybe he was just working a crick out of the back of his neck.

I said, "Well, here's the interesting part. When I was first arrested and, ah . . . interviewed, Choi claimed there was only one shooter, the one who got away. He claimed the police officer I chased down had not been involved in the shooting."

Mercer was studying Choi's photo. He said, "He had to know

about your shooter. Hell, he's only about a hundred feet from the guy. He probably heard the expended rounds hitting the cement, much less the bullets going off."

"That's right," I said. "So why was he trying to make a case against me for murdering a guy he knew was a shooter? Hell, the dead cop was from his precinct. He knew him on sight."

Mercer, who had a pretty quick mind, said, "Because he's trying to cover something up. Because he's connected to the shooters and he didn't want the connection revealed."

"Okay, good. Broaden the scenario. Choi's the chief inspector in the Itaewon precinct. Lee was murdered inside his precinct and Choi's one of the two head investigators. He and his brother-in-law, Bales, tie all the ribbons and bows to make it look like Whitehall did it. Remember Keith Merritt, the guy who's in a coma? Well, the attempt on his life was made inside the Itaewon precinct, and Choi and his boys are the ones who investigated and claimed they couldn't find any witnesses. I mean, Merritt was tossed from a very busy street corner. Surely somebody saw it. Finally, the one shooter we know about was a cop from that same precinct house. I'd be willing to bet the other one was, too."

From the look on her face, even Carol was getting it.

I said, "You know the other thing that's really screwy?"

"What's that?" Mercer asked.

"The cop I chased down, when he thought I had him cornered, he stuffed his pistol inside his mouth and blew off the back of his head. That's pretty extreme behavior, isn't it? What kind of a guy would do that?"

Mercer nodded. "A North Korean."

Remember when I mentioned that North Korean submarine that got grounded a couple of years back? What happened was, once the sub was grounded, the entire crew of fifteen sailors and some ten or so commandos all evacuated and made it to shore. The sailors submissively lined up in single file, then the commandos walked down the line and shot each of them in the head. Then the commandos split up and tried to escape back to North Korea, since they knew their mission, whatever it was, had been bungled and compromised. What ensued was a wild few weeks while the entire ROK Army tried to hunt them down and kill them. Several of the North Koreans put up a good fight and killed a number of South Korean soldiers. The funny thing was, not one North Korean commando was captured. One or two disappeared, but the others either died fighting or killed themselves.

In fact, there's a long and ghastly history of North Korean agents and saboteurs killing themselves to avoid capture and interrogation. That's the frightening thing about North Korea. It's not a nation. It's the world's biggest cult, bigger than that Jones group, or that one in Africa, or that one in Waco, where everybody's willing to do suicidal things for the cause.

Buzz Mercer was rocking back and forth in his chair as he considered the possibilities. For him, the CIA guy in charge of the whole peninsula, it was a disaster. I'd spent the past day pondering it in its full glory, but I was still bowled over.

Here's what I guessed: Choi and at least some of the coppers in the precinct were North Korean operatives. And what a fantastic place to spy from. Itaewon is the one place in South Korea where nearly every American soldier and foreign tourist comes to visit. It's the foreigner's shopping mecca, and it's also the exotic fleshpot that caters to the lustful yens of non-Koreans. It's right outside the main gate of the headquarters that commands the entire Korean-American alliance, the headquarters where war plans are drawn up, where every bit of intelligence collected against the North Koreans is brought for scrutiny, where the assessments of the alliance's military strengths and weaknesses are analyzed and reanalyzed in the never-ending way that soldiers do.

Say, for example, Major John Smith from the intelligence center decides to sneak away from his wife one night for a bit of secretive muff-diving. Choi and his boys have spotters outside the brothels: When Smith has sated his loins and paid his bill, they pick him up and take him to the station for a little grilling. They can ruin his career and bust up his family, or they can trade favors.

Or maybe it's Congressman Smith who has come to Korea for a little official fact-finding tour, and some harmless, wanton fun on the side. Or maybe it's Sergeant Smith, the clerk for Colonel Jones, the operations officer in charge of war planning. The possibilities are both endless and boggling.

And the blackmail didn't have to be limited to the sex trade. Maybe it's an arrest for shoplifting. Maybe it's blackmarketing. Maybe it's a drunken brawl. Every crime committed by an American inside Itaewon would be reported immediately to the Itaewon station. Hell, the target doesn't even have to commit a crime. Maybe it's just something Choi and his boys trump up to entrap some particularly juicy target, rather than the random targets of opportunity who walk willy-nilly through their precinct doors every day.

Obviously such an opportunity presented itself in the person of Thomas Whitehall, who was renting an apartment so he could have a private enclave to meet his male lover, who just happened to be the son of the South Korean defense minister.

Mercer's eyes suddenly lost their normally granular look and became wide and intense.

I said, "Think about it. Choi sees an opportunity that's much juicier than running blackmail schemes and collecting intelligence. He sees a chance to burn down the entire alliance. He ignites the fire by murdering Lee and framing an American officer. He tosses on a thousand-gallon can of high-octane gasoline by massacring a bunch of Americans right outside the gates of Yongsan Garrison, right in front of twenty news cameras. He even shoots some of the reporters, just to spur their outrage."

Carol finally got it. She dropped her valise and said, "Oh my God."

Then I admitted, "Of course, I'm just surmising. I mean, there's maybe two or three other possible explanations. And believe me, I've tried to think them all through. But see if you can conceive of another that fits every angle."

"You really believe this?" Mercer asked. "I mean, you're not just blowing up some big conspiracy balloon to get your client off?"

"Hey, I'm a lawyer. Of course I am."

CHAPTER
34

⊛ ⊛ ⊛

At 7:00 A.M., I sat in Mercer's office as Carol dialed the Itaewon precinct station. Her phone was connected to a speaker so Mercer and I and a few other agents could overhear the conversation. Carol identified herself as Moon Song Johnson and asked to speak directly with Chief Inspector Choi.

He came on and she chattered away, sounding like a scatter-brained Korean-American housewife, saying she was married to a very important American Army colonel on post, saying she'd met Michael Bales and his wife, Choi's sister, through local acquaintances, and that Bales had once told her that if she ever had any problems in Itaewon, well, then she should feel free to call his brother-in-law.

Well, she did have a problem, she complained. A big problem. She'd been in Itaewon shopping the day before when some louse cut the straps on her purse and ran off with it. For the next five minutes Choi asked her the standard whens, wheres, and hows; from the sound of it, checking the blocks from a standard police questionnaire.

Then Carol started crying. She moaned for a while about all the vitally important things inside her purse, from her military ID to her passport, and how ruined her life would be if she didn't get them back. Choi kept assuring her he'd do his best. He insisted he had a strong grip on his precinct. It was all a matter of intelligence, he told her, and he had very good intelligence. He'd put out word to the local merchants and he'd know if the thief tried to use her charge cards or identification. Carol asked him if maybe it was an American who might've stolen it, since, after all, her wonderful husband notwithstanding, Americans are such uncultivated, lawless bastards. Choi admitted that Americans are certainly a depraved and crooked race, but said he doubted they'd commit such a crime off base, because the punishment for getting caught would be so much worse than being caught on base. Should she call the Post Exchange and Commissary to warn them?, Carol asked. Yes, he assured her. Call and warn them. Take every precaution. Ask them to watch for your ID and credit cards. She asked if he thought the criminal would escape his net. No, he assured her, he didn't think the criminal would escape. It might take time, but if the thief used anything from her purse, then Choi's many sources would notify him.

Carol thanked him and asked if she should check with Bales on the progress. Yes, please, Choi politely replied, check with Michael.

My estimation of Carol Kim increased. In a seven-minute conversation, she'd pried all the right words out of Choi's lips. One of the men leaning against the walls immediately slipped the tape out of the recorder and dashed off with it.

Next, a Korean in civilian clothes was ushered in. He seemed to know everybody in the office except me, so Mercer introduced us. His name was Kim-something-something, like nearly every third Korean you meet. He was Mercer's counterpart in the KCIA, the Korean version of our Agency, only there're some fairly gaping differences, since the KCIA isn't hamstrung by restrictions concerning domestic operations, nor is it held back by millions of human rights regulations. For example, if the KCIA wants to kidnap you and bust your kneecaps to get answers, it can do that.

Kim had a stack of dossiers tucked under his arm. He looked wrinkled and disheveled as though he'd been pulled out of bed by a frantic phone call. Which he had. By Buzz Mercer.

The files under his arm were the personnel dossiers of the 110 cops assigned to the Itaewon precinct. He set them down on Mercer's desk, dividing them into two neat stacks—one big, containing about eighty or ninety folders; the second smaller, containing twenty to thirty files.

He looked at Mercer. "We ran these through COMESPRO. This is how it came out."

His English was flawless. There was not even a hint of an accent, which was not uncommon for those Koreans selected for important jobs where they were supposed to interface with Americans fairly frequently. The Koreans choose folks who sound just like Americans, gnarled idioms and all. They do this not just because they're hospitable folks, which they are, but because Americans tend to be much more loose-lipped when they're around folks who sound just like them. This is an advantage in intelligence work particularly.

Anyway, Mercer nodded that he understood what Kim was talking about, which he most likely did, because he'd probably been through this a hundred times before. I, on the other hand, had nary a clue what Mr. Kim was talking about. I coughed once or twice to get his attention.

"Excuse me," I finally said, "what in the hell is this COMESPRO? Could you tell me what you're talking about?"

Kim looked over at Mercer, who nodded, which I guess was the cue it was okay to let me in on this little secret. He gave me a smug smile and I was instantly reminded of my sixth-grade teacher, an arrogant schmuck who spent his life surrounded by twelve-year-olds and therefore thought he was the world's smartest guy. Spooks often remind me of him, regardless of their nationality. Since they know all kinds of dark, fluttery things us normal folks don't, they have this slightly stuck-up, superior attitude. It's one of those knowledge-is-power things, I guess.

Anyway, he said, "Okay, Major. As you're probably aware, we have a gigantic spy problem here in South Korea. In the U.S., you generally have two kinds of spies. You have foreign nationals. They enter with foreign passports and then set up business. Most often they operate out of embassies, or the UN headquarters in New

York, or some other international institution that gives them a cover. They're fairly easy for your FBI to target and watch. Then you have the occasional citizen who betrays your country—in the case of American traitors, most often for money. Those are the type who're considerably more difficult to target."

I couldn't resist. "You mean like that Korean-American analyst who worked for the Defense Intelligence Agency who was on your payroll?"

"Of course, he wasn't working for us," Kim said, maintaining his perfect smile. "But somebody like him would fit a spy's profile. He had ethnic sympathy toward South Korea. He had money difficulties. He had sums of money entering his bank accounts that he couldn't legally account for. I can certainly see where your counterintelligence services would suspect he was one of ours."

Then his smile got a little wider. "Of course, he wasn't. We'd never spy on our closest ally."

He and Mercer chuckled merrily at this, like this was all part of the game. Their game.

"Anyway," Kim turned back to me. "Our problems are much more severe. Northerners and southerners, we're all Koreans. We speak the same language, look alike, dress alike, share the same culture. Millions of southerners were either refugees or descendants of refugees who fled North Korea when the Korean War broke out. Many southerners have families in North Korea. They're vulnerable to all kinds of entrapments. Then there are the infiltrators. For fifty years they've been coming in, some by submarine, some simply sneaking across the DMZ. Lately, though, the North Koreans have gotten more sophisticated."

"Like how?" I asked.

"Well, let's take your friend Choi."

"Okay, let's take Choi."

"According to our records, Choi Lee Min was born in the city of Chicago in the United States, the son of two South Koreans who immigrated in the year 1953. His parents were killed in a car accident in 1970, leaving him an orphan. He returned to Korea when he was seventeen, which is not uncommon. Many Korean expatriates have difficulties assimilating in their new countries, and eventually return. He dropped his American citizenship, attended his final two years of high school here in Seoul, got excellent scores on the national exams, and went to Seoul National University. This is our Harvard. At SNU he finished near the top of his class and could have fulfilled any dream when he graduated. Oddly enough, he chose to take the police exam. Believe me, that had to be a first for an SNU graduate. He could've waltzed into the executive ranks of Hyundai, or Daewoo, or any prestigious chaebol."

"So he used to be an American citizen?" I asked.

Kim shrugged. "Maybe he was. As I mentioned, the North Koreans have gotten very cagey. They know we run rigorous background checks on any citizen being considered for a sensitive position, so they've become much more creative at fabricating foolproof legends. Maybe Choi's parents were North Korean sleepers they planted in Chicago forty years ago. Or maybe Choi never set foot in Chicago."

"He sure as hell seemed like he'd spent some time in America to me."

Kim glanced at Mercer again, and Mercer nodded that it was okay to let me in on another little secret, too.

"We suspect the North Koreans have a secret camp for molding agents to appear to be Korean-Americans. The candidates enter this camp as babies and never set foot out of it afterward, until they take up duties as agents. They eat American food, are taught in replicated American classrooms, even watch American TV on satellite cable. An American author named DeMille wrote a novel called *The Charm School*, a fictional account of such a camp in the Soviet Union. We believe the North Koreans actually have such a place."

"And you think Choi might be a graduate?"

Mercer said, "Look, Drummond, we're not even sure the place exists. Over the years, we've heard rumors from a couple of high-level defectors. Supposedly it's staffed by some of the American POWs who were never returned after the war ended. Of course, some of these damned defectors'll tell you any goddamned thing. Who knows?"

I said, "Okay, so Choi looks like a guy who reverse-immigrated back to Korea when he was seventeen. What about his sister, Bales's wife?"

Kim scratched his head. "What sister?"

I said, "Chief Warrant Officer Michael Bales is the CID officer who worked the Whitehall case with Choi. He's supposed to be married to Choi's sister."

Kim lifted up a folder and glanced through it, searching for something. He said, "We have no record of a sister."

"So who's Bales's wife?"

Mercer said, "We'll do some checking."

Then I said, "So what's with this screening you mentioned?"

Kim said, "Our biggest problem is that before 1945 we were under Japanese rule and were administered by Japanese civil servants. In the last days of the Second World War, they destroyed their files, effectively eradicating our historical record of citizenry. Then between 1950 and 1953, thousands of our villages and cities were destroyed, and with them, even many of our municipal and regional records were lost. Millions of people lost their homes. There were massive internal migrations and millions of northerners fleeing south. The entire Korean race was on the move. It was like our country was stirred in a huge mixing bowl."

Mercer said, "That's why it's so damned hard to figure out who's workin' for who down here."

Kim nodded that this was so. "About three years ago, we developed a computer program to help us sift through large populations. We call it the Communist Screening Program, or COMESPRO. Admittedly not a very elegant name, but it works. The program employs special profiles to tell us who we might want to examine more closely, much like the one your immigration service employs to screen for likely drug mules at your customs points. For example, if we can't trace a citizen's family back three generations, it sends up a flag. If the citizen immigrated from a third country, that's another flag."

I said, "Then wouldn't Choi have popped up on your program?"

"Yes, except we've only used it to screen our armed forces and

BRIAN HAIG

intelligence services, some of our more sensitive ministries, and our foreign service. We frankly hadn't considered using it on our police forces. They're not involved in national security, so why should we?"

I pointed at the stacks of folders. "Is that what happened when you screened everybody who works at the Itaewon station?"

He pointed at the larger stack. "These were the ones COME-SPRO screened out." Then he pointed at the smaller stack. "These are the ones we would call suspect profiles. There are twenty-two in all."

So I said, "Then you could have a big nest of spies in the precinct house?"

Kim smiled condescendingly. "I don't want to sound dubious, Major, but a fifth of all populations we screen come up as suspects. There's nothing unusual about these numbers. A lot of these aren't going to pan out . . . probably none. Besides, we've never had anything like that before. Spies and agents operate in singles. They may be part of a larger cell, perhaps under a single controller, but they're quarantined from one another. It's good spycraft. If one gets caught, he can't compromise the others, because he doesn't know who they are. The controller usually has an alert system in place in the event one of his people is picked up, and a well-planned escape route he uses at the first sign of trouble."

"So you think I'm barking up the wrong tree?"

"Frankly, it's wildly implausible. You have a client you want to vindicate. Your imagination is in overdrive."

I looked over at Mercer. "What about you?"

Buzz looked up at his counterpart. "There's something here, Kim. Might not be as big and dramatic as Drummond thinks, but it's something."

Kim gave us both a skeptical shrug. I wondered what he really thought. The thing is, the South Koreans would find it awfully shameful if it turned out one of their police stations was riddled with North Korean termites. Of course, maybe this was my "overdrive" imagination at work again.

Anyway, Mercer looked at his KCIA ally and said, "Look, we're gonna try a little bait-and-flush here. What I need your guys to do is lock down the escape hatches." He handed Kim a photograph of Michael Bales that had been retrieved from Bales's personnel file earlier that morning.

"This is Michael Bales," Mercer continued. "If he tries to take a plane or ship out of Korea, I want him stopped. He's a smart boy. He's also a trained cop. He might be wearing a disguise and he might have a false passport, so have your guys alter this photo to show what he'd look like with a beard or mustache, or dressed as a woman, or with glasses and his hair dyed blond. I know all us White folks look alike to you Koreans, so make sure you distribute composites of what he'd look like if he took precautions. This is a no-fuck-it-up, Kim. Don't let me down."

Kim nodded. "No problem." He picked up his stacks of folders and prepared to leave.

Mercer said, "One other thing. Can your people put a watch on Choi?"

Kim smiled graciously. "Consider it done, Buzz."

"Good. If we break this thing, I'll make sure my boss back in Langley tells your boss here you were the man who broke it. I was mystified by some funny things going on, so I went to you for help, and you figured it all out."

Kim smiled even more broadly. "That would be very kind of you, Buzz."

Then the two of them shook hands and Kim left. I had to give Mercer credit. As embarrassing as it would be for the Koreans to discover this spy ring working right under their noses, it would be doubly humiliating if the credit went to the Americans. This way, the Koreans could save some face. And this way, Kim had a strong personal incentive to help us in every way he could.

CHAPTER
35
✪ ✪ ✪

I stopped by the judge's front office to pick up the list of potential court-martial board members. Then I went to the hair parlor for a brief visit so Katherine wouldn't think I'd been kidnapped, or maybe murdered and buried in some grove of woods. That's probably what she was hoping happened, so why not show my face and disappoint her?

The place was a hive of wild activity. The trial was set to start in less than twenty hours, and Katherine, Allie, Imelda, and all her worthy assistants were going through the last-minute frantic sweats any well-oiled law office goes through before the big show.

A stack of neatly typed motions lay on a table, and I shook my head as I stopped and riffled through them. Katherine obviously planned on filing them with the judge at 1559 hours, one minute before closing time. It didn't matter that Carruthers had warned her—Katherine was intent on pissing him off with a juggernaut of last-second requests for judgments. She couldn't resist. Eight years of legal habit wasn't going to be washed away just because some judge threatened to rip off her head and "poop" down the cavity.

When I stuck my head in her office she was chattering with somebody on the phone. She looked anxious but lovely. She glanced up and shot me the bird. It wasn't a casual gesture. She meant it.

I then went over to Allie's side office. I said, "How's things?"

She gave me a surprisingly cold look. "Where have you been? We're up to our ass and could use help."

I grinned. "I've been running around checking some last-minute details."

"Like what?"

"I spent the better part of the morning waiting at the judge's office for the list of potential board members."

"Did you get it?"

I nodded. "Longest damn list I ever saw. There are nearly eighty officers on it. They're obviously planning on losing a lot of members to voir dire challenges. They're probably right. Considering the nature of the crimes, a lot of these guys are going to admit they're so emotionally repulsed they can't make detached judgments."

Allie said, "But out of eighty officers, we should at least be able to find ten fair men and women."

"The problem is I never saw a list packed with so many infantry officers."

She said, "So?" in a tone that betrayed her naiveté about the Army. See, all Army officers aren't exactly interchangeable parts.

I said, "Look, the Army has some twenty-six different branches. There's lawyers like me, doctors, supply guys, maintenance guys, finance guys, and on and on. The more the job sounds like a normal civilian job, the higher your chance the guy holding it thinks like a civilian. The only difference between them and some guy you'll find on the street is they have to wear funny clothes to work every day."

"But infantry guys are different?"

"Very different. They're the Jesuits of the Army. They love discipline and they love to impose it. We JAG officers usually try to purge as many of them off a board as we can."

Allie said, "So we'll challenge them all off."

And I said, "Of the first thirty names on the list, two thirds are infantry. They've stacked it. We'd be lucky to whittle them down to half the board."

I felt a presence behind me. I turned around and Katherine was standing there.

She'd been eavesdropping. Her face was frigid. She said, "Well, you're the asshole who talked our client out of the deal. Still think it's such a great idea, Drummond? Still think you gave our client the best legal advice?"

"My two cents had no effect. He never had any intention of taking the deal."

She stared at me. "That's not what I asked. Do you still think you gave him the best legal advice?"

"I don't know if it was the best legal advice, but it was my best advice."

Her face was cold and hard. She was trying to stare me down, but I wasn't about to let her humble me. This was what psychologists call transference. She was teed off at her client, and because I'd agreed with him, and I happened to be a handy target, she was spewing her anger at me.

She pointed a finger in my face. "Be in my office at three this afternoon with your strategy for the voir dire. That's supposed to be your area of expertise. I want a survey of the potential board members and detailed lists of challenges and questions."

"Okay."

Her finger was still pointed at my face. "And keep your nose out of everything else. From here on, your duties are confined to advising me on matters of military law. You will no longer converse with our client. You will not meet with the judge. You will no longer participate in our strategy reviews. Take one step outside those boundaries and I'll have you removed from our team. Is that clear?"

"That's clear."

She stomped into her office. I looked at Allie; she refused to meet my eyes. From the look of things, Katherine and her staff had made some decisions about me in my absence. I was no longer a trusted member of the team. Maybe I never had been a trusted member of the team.

I took my board list and limped away. I mean, I could have

stayed and argued with Katherine, but what would be the point? Besides, this made things easier. I could dedicate my time to catching Bales without worrying about the trial.

I went straight back to my hotel room and went through the motions of developing a game plan for the voir dire. Having spent eight years screening potential boards, this was a fairly straightforward task. First, circle the names of officers who look like they might be favorable to the defense—in this case, women, minorities, and officers who work in the softer branches, in that exact order. Then put arrows next to the people you want to get thrown off. Target the infantry guys first; go after the higher ranks particularly, because the longer an officer serves, the more likely he or she is to buy into the culture and its hoary little peccadillos.

Then start developing the normal sequence of questions, like, "Have you read any newspaper articles or seen any TV news shows about this case that have left you predisposed or prejudiced in any way?" You've got to ask that question even though it can be a two-edged sword. It can eliminate as many sympathetic jurists as hard-nosed ones. Then you get to the questions only an experienced Army attorney would know to ask. "Have you ever punished a soldier for homosexuality?" Because Whitehall was a captain, all the potential board members were at least captains, and in the case of all those infantry officers, that meant they'd all held command positions. A fair number would've had troops who committed homosexual infractions they would've had to pass judgments on. I doubted many would publicly admit they'd gone soft on them. We'd get rid of a few infantry officers on that one.

I thought up a nice kicker: "Have you ever kissed or fondled another male?" Ask any average guy that question and you'll get a fairly negative response. Ask a high-testosterone guy—like an Airborne, Ranger, or infantry stud—and you'll get a nasty snarl, a derisive snort, and a very repugnant denial. In short, an inadvertent display of homophobic prejudice of the type that will wipe some more infantry officers off the board.

I added a few more of these sly stilettos, then considered my job done. I called Mercer and told him I was on my way. The early warning was because of the Korean cops who'd been following me. When I passed through the gate into the other half of Yongsan, where Mercer's office was located, he had guys in the guardshack to block the cops from following me.

I then hobbled back to the CIA complex. The place was as busy as an ant's nest. There were more spooks than I could count. Mercer must've brought in reinforcements, maybe from other offices around the peninsula, maybe from Japan. The agents seemed to be organized into seven or eight teams. Several of them stood directing pointers at stand-up easels and talking quietly to various groups. The air crackled with seriousness and tension.

I drew a few curious stares. I knocked on Mercer's door and he yelled for me to enter. He was talking on that souped-up cell phone again, and he automatically dropped his voice to a whisper. Pretty damned silly, if you ask me. I fell into a seat and waited till he finished.

That didn't take long. "You ready for the big time?" he asked.

"As ready as I'm going to be."

"Carol's with Bales's wife right now."

We'd still been trying to figure out how to lure Bales's wife out of their Army quarters when I'd left Mercer to go see Katherine. The whole operation depended on Mrs. Bales being gone from their house.

I was curious. "How'd you arrange it?"

"We had the wife of the colonel in charge of the MP brigade invite her to an impromptu luncheon. Carol's there as a waitress. The luncheon ends at two, so we've only got an hour."

I said I was ready to get to it, so Mercer led me out. The second we got outside the door, he yelled at everybody to go get into their positions, and, as we say in the Army, asses and elbows flew all over the place.

It took me ten minutes to limp over to the MP station. I went right up to the desk sergeant and said I needed to see Chief Bales. He got on the intercom, informed Bales he had a visitor, then pointed at a hallway and told me to go straight to the sixth office on the left. I told him I knew my way, and he went back to doing whatever he was doing.

Bales barely looked up when I entered. He didn't stand or offer to shake. He merely gave me a distracted, unwelcoming look.

I said, "I need to have a few words with you."

He pointed at the wooden chair in front of his desk. He leaned back in his seat and stroked his chin and rotated his head, partly annoyed and partly curious. Probably he figured I was making some last-ditch effort to finagle some piece of information about the Whitehall case. Or maybe I was here to bitch about my beating and make a few threats.

I said, "Whitehall's trial starts tomorrow."

"So I hear."

I glanced down at my watch. The big hand was between 12:04 and 12:05. The telephones in Itaewon were scheduled to be shut down at 12:05 on the dot. Buzz's friend Kim had arranged it. For thirty minutes, the entire Itaewon telephone grid was going to be disconnected. Like I said earlier, the KCIA could do things the CIA only dreams about.

I looked up and said, "You know the odd thing?"

He smiled. "What's the odd thing?"

"Well, it's having all these crimes occur in Itaewon. I mean, there's Lee's murder, then the attempted murder of Keith Merritt, then the slaughter outside the gate. And who's in charge of all those investigations? Choi from the Korean side, and you from the American side."

"Yeah, well, when you're the best, you get the tough ones."

"I guess you do."

"Comes with the territory," he said, brushing back his hair, like he really meant it.

"Must keep you pretty busy."

"I stay up with it."

"So it seems, Chief. You know, I even went back and reviewed the record of those cases you and Choi handled together. That's the beauty of computerized records. Just enter a couple of names and the computer does all your work for you. Hell, before this, it would've taken three paralegals a month to collect all that data. Isn't the modern age just wonderful?"

He placed his elbows on his desk, suddenly much more interested in what I had to say.

I continued. "How's it work? Does Choi call you every time something intriguing happens over there? Christ, for five years, you've led the station in case closure rates."

"I get my assignments from the brass, just like every other CID agent here. I can't help it if my closure rate's higher than the other guys. Maybe it's luck of the draw. Maybe I just work it harder."

I shook my head. "Come on, Chief, there has to be more to it. Your closure rate's over eighty percent. Four out of five. I doubt there's another CID agent in the world who comes anywhere near that. Hell, a CID agent's considered a golden cow if he gets fifty percent. You're a regular Sherlock Holmes."

He smiled impatiently. "What's the matter, Major? Do you actually have a problem with a detective who solves his cases?"

"Well, that's the other thing. Nearly eighty percent of your investigations were in Itaewon."

"What's so mysterious? I've been here five years. I've developed good sources, an army of snitches, and I know my way around. I've got a great rapport with the Itaewon precinct. The command knows it, so they throw a lot of that stuff my way."

"What gives you such great rapport with the Itaewon precinct? Is it because you're married to Choi's sister?"

"It helps," he said, still smiling.

"Well, that's the other odd thing I wanted to ask you about. I ran a background check on Chief Inspector Choi Lee Min also. Born in Chicago in 1954, emigrated back to Korea in 1971, attended Seoul National University, where he graduated at the top of his class. A very impressive guy."

"Yes, he is."

"A guy like him had the world at his feet. He could be sitting in one of those gleaming towers downtown making millions. He could be trading on the bourse. But he chose police work, of all things."

"Choi's not motivated by money. Like you said, he's quite a guy."

"Yeah, I guess," I said offhandedly. "Only problem is, he didn't have a sister."

Bales's elbows flew off the desk and he fell back in his chair, like this was the most comical thing he'd ever heard.

He actually chuckled. "I don't know who ran the check, but you better go back and start over. My wife was born in Chicago in 1962. She and her brother lived together until 1970, when their parents were killed."

I scratched my head and looked baffled. "Your wife's maiden name is Lee Jin May, right?"

"That's right."

"Born in Chicago?"

"That's right."

"There's no record of any Lee Jin May born in any hospital in Chicago between the years 1957 and 1970. For that matter, there's no record of a Choi Lee Min born in any Chicago hospital, either."

This was true. Mercer had asked the FBI to run a quick background check, and they had so far been unable to find any trace of Choi or his sister.

Bales came back forward and looked angry. "Maybe they were born at home. Maybe they used a midwife. Did you think of that? Their parents were poor immigrants struggling to survive. I've never asked Jin May, but I wouldn't be surprised."

"Ah, I hadn't thought of that," I said, like, Oops, gee, stupid me.

"Well, you had no fucking business going through my background anyway. Or my wife's. What the hell's going on? Do I need to file a complaint against you?"

"No, no need to do that," I assured.

He instantly became conciliatory. "Look, I know we've got this little problem between us. I don't blame you for being sore. Don't take it personally, though."

I gave him a full grin, so he had a bird's-eye view of the gap where I used to have a tooth. "Me? Take it personally?"

"Look, I'm sorry if things got a little rough back at the station. We thought you'd murdered an innocent cop. You know how us cops are when one of our own gets it. I'm not making an excuse, but I'm sorry, all right?"

"Yeah, sure," I said with a full dose of insincerity, although frankly the intonation was wasted because we both knew there wasn't any chance in hell I'd forgive him.

Then I abruptly got up to leave. I got to the door, then turned around like I'd just been struck with an afterthought.

I slapped my forehead. "Hey, one more thing."

The overconfident prick actually gave me his Dudley Do-Right grin. "Sure, how can I help you, Major?"

"That thing about your wife. I'm sorry if I overreacted, but when I got curious about not finding her birth records, or her brother's, I called the CIA station here and asked them to look into it. They've got smart guys, though. I'm sure they'll figure out she and her brother were born at home."

I wished I'd thought to bring a camera. You had to see his face.

I left the MP station, then walked two blocks to a gray government sedan that was waiting next to the curb. Mercer was seated in the front. I climbed in the back, next to one of his guys.

A radio was on the dashboard and a speaker was connected to it so we could hear what was happening inside Bales's office. Early that morning, one of Mercer's guys had gained entry and wired the office for sound, so Mercer had overheard every word of our conversation. He absently held up a thumb. His attention, though, was focused on the sounds coming from the speaker. My role in this affair was to give Bales an intimation of trouble to come, just enough of a whiff to put him in motion.

We listened for a while as Bales talked to somebody, probably an MP, about some details of a case they were working. He sounded impatient and curt, and was transparently struggling to hurry the MP along. Then we heard the sound of a door closing, then Bales dialing a number. One of the bugs was planted in the earpiece of Bales's phone. We could hear every sound coming through his receiver. What we heard at that moment was that scratchy, hissy noise phones make when the lines are out of service. He tried the number again, then slammed down the receiver, hard.

Half a minute of silence passed. We could hear him breathing. Full, huffy breaths. We heard him pick up the phone and dial again. We heard the hissy sound again. We heard him dial another number.

It rang about three times, then the voice of an answering machine said, "Hello, this is the Bales residence. We are out right now, but please—"

We heard Bales punch in two numbers to code his home answering machine, then we heard Choi's voice say, "Michael, take every precaution. Escape right away. American intelligence has us in their net. Change your identification and escape."

The voice came from a tape on Bales's answering machine in his quarters. And it actually *was* Choi's voice. The message had been cut and stitched together from the conversation Carol had had with Choi earlier that morning. As soon as Bales's wife had been lured out of their quarters, Mercer's techs had called and played their tape.

Bales hung up the phone, more softly this time, and we could hear his chair creak, probably from him leaning back into it and trying to catch his breath. We heard him open a drawer, and then the sounds of things being moved around. He was searching for something.

Then he picked up the phone and dialed another number. Only this time, the real Choi answered. It had to be a cell phone number. We should have considered that, but we hadn't.

"Choi, it's me," Bales said.

"Yes, Michael, what is it?"

"I got your message. What the hell's going on?"

"What message?"

"The one you left on my answering machine."

"I didn't leave you any message."

There was a moment of stunned, bewildered silence. Mercer turned around and we both smiled. The whole thing might be going south on us, but there's still something perversely satisfying when you hear the bad guys getting tangled up in your web.

Sounding frantic, Bales said, "God damn it, Choi, I had that asshole lawyer in here a few minutes ago telling me he stumbled onto the fact you and Jin May weren't from Chicago. He said he couldn't find your hospital birth records, so he turned it over to the CIA. Then I heard your voice on my machine telling me to run. I know your fucking voice, Choi. It was you."

Choi calmly said, "Michael, stay cool. I didn't call you. Somebody's playing games with us."

"Right."

Then Choi said, "Remember plan B?"

"Yeah, sure."

"Use it."

"What about Jin May?"

"Where is she?"

"I don't know. She was in the house when I left this morning. But she didn't answer when I called. That bitch could be shopping at the PX for all I know. Or they could already have her."

"That bitch," he'd called her. It didn't sound like Mr. and Mrs. Bales were what you might term a blissfully married couple.

Finally, sounding strained, Choi said, "Don't worry about her. I'll see if I can find her, but if she gets caught she knows what she's doing. Just get moving."

Then Bales said, "What about phase 3? Is it still—"

"Michael, get moving."

"Okay, okay," Bales said, then they both hung up. Three seconds later, we heard the sounds of Bales getting up from his desk, then pacing across his office, then his door opening and closing.

Michael Bales was now on the run, but not before he'd called his buddy Choi, which was something we'd hoped to avoid. We wanted Bales on his own, isolated, without resources, confused about what had happened to Choi. Frantic men make stupid mistakes and that's how we wanted him. Now we had to worry about plan B, whatever the hell that was.

The only good thing about the call was that it almost certainly confirmed I was right. What we had sounded like a full-blown espionage ring.

Mercer's driver put the car in gear and we raced straight back to the CIA office complex. We rushed inside to the communications console that had been hastily set up in the large room outside Mercer's office.

Five communicators were huddled around the console, each with headsets on, each taking reports or coordinating actions among Mercer's field teams. The CIA might not have been able to figure out when the Soviet Union was falling, but it looked like they ran a first-class surveillance operation.

I stood and watched. I was impressed. A tracking device connected to a GPS satellite had been planted on Bales's car, and there was a large electronic map display on the wall. You could see this little red light moving steadily away from Yongsan, toward the international airport located about forty minutes' drive from Seoul's city center. There must've been three or four chase cars following along with him, because progress reports kept coming in to the radio operators at the console.

One of Mercer's guys handed him a cup of coffee and he stood sipping from it as he proudly surveyed the operation. I went and found myself a cup, too, then found a chair, because my damaged and dented body was tired of standing up.

The basic idea was to let Bales get to the airport, buy a ticket and make his way to the departure gate, then arrest him. The original plan hadn't envisioned Bales calling Choi and thus had been built on the premise that there would be no evidence of his involvement in the plot. But Bales was a soldier; if he bought a ticket and attempted to flee, he was trying to desert, and that would put a nail in his coffin. Even now, he could make up some excuse about why he called Choi, but he couldn't do the same about trying to flee from Korea.

I thought it was a bit extravagant, and frankly didn't see why they didn't just arrest him, but Mercer insisted it was critical to have something tangible to hang on Bales. The first step in breaking a traitor is forcing him to implicate himself. Mercer was the spymaster; what the hell did I know? Besides, it wasn't my business.

About thirty minutes passed. After a while, surveillance operations get tedious, because all you're doing is following a car, and you can get lulled into complacency. I don't know if that's what caused it, but suddenly the radio operators started screaming into their mikes and Mercer looked like somebody had stuck a burning match into his shoe.

What we quickly pieced together was that Bales had driven into a long tunnel. The chase cars didn't want to stay too close to him, because they didn't want to make him suspicious. When his car emerged from the tunnel, they followed him as usual, which meant that every three minutes a chase car passed his auto to get a visual on the driver. The first pass after the car came out of the tunnel, it was no longer Bales driving. It was a Korean.

Mercer yanked a microphone away from a communicator and screamed at his chase teams to force the car to pull over. They did. The Korean driver immediately jumped out. He leaped directly in front of a passing car and was splattered all over the roadside.

CHAPTER
36
✪ ✪ ✪

You know that old saw about how when things get bad, they almost always get worse? Without hesitating, Mercer picked up the phone and called Kim, his KCIA partner. He hastily explained what happened and told him to pick up Choi immediately. Kim calmly explained that everything was under control, that Choi and three of his fellow cops were at that moment having lunch inside a kimchi restaurant in the heart of Itaewon. A KCIA agent had followed them inside, and four more agents were planted outside, observing the front of the restaurant. Good, Mercer told him. Don't waste another minute. Send them in to get him.

Kim called back ten minutes later. The team had gone into the restaurant to get Choi, only Choi and his boys were nowhere to be found. They did find the agent who followed them inside. His corpse was propped up on a toilet inside a stall in the men's room. His throat had acquired a nasty new gash that ran from earlobe to earlobe. While the surveillance team had kept watch on the front of the restaurant, Choi and his goons had fled out the back.

Kim was terrifically embarrassed by this, but Mercer was equally abashed about losing Bales, so it came out a wash. This was somewhat of a blessing. It spared me from having to witness the normal nasty catcalling and finger-pointing that would certainly have occurred if only one side had committed a gaffe. When it comes to government agencies, there's always a lofty comfort found in a joint failure. The fact was, Choi and his colleagues were obviously trained agents and both Mercer and Kim had underestimated them.

But Mercer and Kim were pros, too, and rather than rehash their mistakes, they immediately instigated a nationwide search to catch the bastards. They started arguing about whose job it was to ransack Bales's and Choi's offices and apartments but soon, after a few terse exchanges, they decided to form joint teams so both sides would have firsthand looks at every clue and piece of evidence. I sat and listened, but it didn't concern me, so I thought of other things.

Things like how Eddie Golden's case had just gotten the floor pulled out from under it. The walls were still standing, but they were teetering and maybe ready to collapse. Two of his prize witnesses had just gone on the lam, and that was going to pose fairly intriguing challenges for Eddie. As soon as he learned of this, he'd be calling Carruthers to ask for a postponement while he tried to rebuild the state's case.

Which reminded me: It was already after two-thirty, so I went to Mercer and told him I had other work to do, since I was still part of Whitehall's defense team, and we still had a trial that started at eight the next morning. He scratched his head and tried to think of a reason to keep me around, but couldn't, so he excused me, after making me swear not to tell a soul what had happened.

I said I wouldn't, as long as he'd call Judge Barry Carruthers and inform him that two of the prosecution's key witnesses had just disappeared and were wanted in connection with whatever plausible cover crime Mercer wanted to invent. He said okay, so I left.

By the time I got to the HOMOS office, Mercer had obviously already called the judge, and Carruthers had just as obviously called Katherine to break the news. Everybody was doing a war dance. Bad news travels fast, but catastrophic news moves like lightning bolts. Of course, what was catastrophic news to Eddie's pearly ears was manna from heaven here.

Imelda gave me a funny look when I came in, like she just

knew I had something to do with this, although she wasn't sure exactly what. Nobody else seemed curious or suspicious. The general mood was that God must really love gay folk because he'd just done a mighty big service for the cause.

I went back to Katherine's office and poked my head in. She was seated at her desk, swiveling back and forth in her chair, looking quietly elated.

"Hey, what's going on?" I asked, the picture of ignorant innocence.

"Haven't you heard?"

"Heard what?"

"Bales and Choi disappeared. A nationwide search has been initiated."

"No kidding? Disappeared, huh? Just like that, poof?"

"Weird, isn't it? Carruthers called to tell me."

"Yeah?"

"He wants to meet with me and Golden in his office in thirty minutes."

I stepped in and dropped some papers on her desk. It was the voir dire strategy. I said, "Great news. Here's what you asked for." Then I turned around to leave.

"Hey, where are you going?"

"Me?"

"Yeah, you."

"To the bar in the hotel."

"What?"

"Lady, my day's done. I busted my ass on these. I'm tired as hell, and I'm thirsty. I'm going to get roaring drunk and then climb into bed."

A quizzical, perplexed look popped onto her face. "You don't want to accompany me to see Carruthers?"

I shook my head. "Nope."

"Aren't you at least curious?"

"Not the least bit."

She stood up and came around to face me. She leaned against

the front edge, butt backed against the desk, legs and arms crossed. "You think I can handle him myself?"

"You? You were first in the class. I'm just some second-place dunce who never got over it."

"I didn't mean that," she said, taking a step toward me. "You know I didn't mean that."

"And you probably didn't mean that part about no more meetings with the judge? No more strategy sessions? No more talking to the client?"

"Drummond, I was angry. Don't you ever say things you regret when you're angry?"

I ignored that. "Look, it's no big thing. Really. I figure we've got, what—two, maybe three weeks of trial? I'm gonna treat it like the vacation you ruined. There's plenty of good bars in this town, and some of those Korean women are gorgeous."

"Damn it, Drummond, I'm sorry."

"What is it about me that always makes you so mad?"

"You don't always make me so mad."

"The hell you say. Every time you look at me, your face turns red and you look like you want to break something."

She walked right up to me. And she did the strangest damn thing. She reached up, pulled my head down, and kissed me. Not one of those puffy, wimpy, dry pecks either, but a glandular, wet, lingering one. On the lips, too.

I froze. She pressed her slim body against mine, and I froze more.

She finally pulled back, then looked up into my eyes, like she was searching for something. What, I didn't know, but my eyes were blinking madly, because I was utterly, unconditionally confused. Just a few hours before she'd been ready to strangle me, and now she was pressed up against my body in a most tantalizing way. The woman was like a typhoon spinning out of control. What in the hell was going on?

"What was that?"

"What do you think it was?"

I gave her an awkward, silly smile. "I guess it was a, uh, a kiss, but I—"

But before I could get that thought out, she did it again. Only this time, I pulled her tightly against me and all our curves and angles and hollows and lumps fitted together. I can be gulled and suckered as easily as the next guy, but I swear I felt some real heat and electricity here. Her arms were wrapped tightly around my neck, and her hips were grinding against my lower body in a way that was pleasantly beguiling, which is a courtly way of describing a biological response one doesn't bring up in mixed company.

I ran my fingers lightly down the middle of her back and felt her body tingle and shiver like a cat's. I heard heavy breathing, only maybe it was me, because my own lungs were starting to make that happy heaving motion that lets your head know the rest of your body's in the mood to do something naughty.

Now here's something you'd probably never in a million years ever guess about me. When it comes to fragile emotional situations, I'm like . . . well, hopeless. I'm afflicted with the romantic equivalent of the bull-in-the-china-shop disease. I can't help myself. I always say the wrong thing at the right moment. I'm brusque when I should be ticklish, blunt when I should be discreet, wisecracky when I should be mushy. In matters of the heart, I'm Dr. Kevorkian.

I felt this irrepressible need to say, "Hey, what the hell is this? Lesbians don't kiss like that. Lesbians don't rub their hips against guys that way. Lesbians don't flush and tingle and get body purrs when guys caress them."

I didn't, though. I was about to, except suddenly someone was rapping knuckles on the door. I was saved by the bell, or the knock. Whatever.

Katherine hastily stepped back, rearranged her dress, unmussed her hair, and took a few deep breaths. I just leaned against the wall and watched her. I was too stunned to move. I was utterly bewildered.

She opened the door and Imelda barged in. She took one look at Katherine, then at me, still pressed against the wall, and her eyes suddenly got real narrow and her lips twisted at an odd angle.

But all she said was, "Time to leave for the judge's office. You got everything you need?"

Katherine smiled demurely. "I think so. Major Drummond and I were just debating whether he should come along."

"'Course he should," Imelda huffed. "Allie, too. She's been workin' hard. Let her taste the moment."

Katherine nodded at Imelda like this was what she'd intended all along. Her eyes were glued on me, though. "Drummond here seems to think he shouldn't be there. I was just trying to persuade him that I might need his military expertise."

Imelda whirled at me with a fierce glower. "You got some problem with that?"

I said, "No, uh, absolutely not. I'd be only too pleased."

"Good," Imelda announced, then departed, whistling through her teeth; an unconscious gesture of hers whenever she encounters something she can't quite put a finger on.

Katherine walked past me, provocatively brushing her body against mine. "Come along, Attila."

CHAPTER
37
★ ★ ★

The look on Eddie's face when he saw Allie enter Carruthers's office made it worth the trip. He got to his feet like a good boy when the introductions were made, but for once the smooth bastard was running a little short of charismatic polish.

Eddie's shorter than I am, and Allie's taller than me, so she positively loomed over him. He stared up at her in shock. Also, Eddie's one of those guys who spends a lot of time in the gym buffing up for the opposite sex, but Allie nearly forced him to his knees when they shook hands. She made it seem effortless, but you could literally hear the knuckles and bones in Eddie's hand cracking. He had tears in his eyes when she let go.

I actually caught Eddie wiping his hands after he shook with her, and that really pissed me off. Allie saw it, too, and the look on her face reminded me of the way she'd glanced at me the first time I'd met her, that first night in Katherine's hotel room. I can't say I was real proud of that.

As for Carruthers, he never blinked an eye. He treated Allie respectfully, like the smart, upright, hardworking attorney she was. My estimation of him bounced up a few more notches.

He gruffly told us to have seats. He spent a moment overviewing the situation, noting that the trial was set to convene in sixteen hours and that some four hundred international journalists were now in country. They were lounging around every bar in Seoul, eagerly waiting to broadcast this intriguing and momentous trial to every breakfast table and living room in the world. He noted that all the appropriate preparations had been made. A special detachment of MPs had been flown over from the States to provide security. Army officers from peacekeeping and military assistance outposts had been plucked from the remotest corners of the globe in hopes of collecting a large enough assemblage of potential board members who weren't tainted by the blizzard of publicity that attended this case. He noted the case was being heralded as the trial of the century, bigger than O.J.'s even, because so much seemed to weigh on the outcome; because some ghastly crimes had been committed; because the fate of an entire alliance stood on the brink; because important laws stood to be changed.

Eddie squirmed in his seat, because what Carruthers was not too faintly intimating was that a postponement at this stage was unthinkable.

Then Carruthers searched each of our faces and concluded, "All that notwithstanding, Major Golden has asked for a postponement."

Katherine immediately barked, "On what grounds?"

Eddie said, "On the grounds that two key prosecution witnesses have mysteriously disappeared."

Katherine shook her head like he had to be kidding. "I don't get it. Two police officers have disappeared? I mean, please."

Eddie shot forward in his seat. "I'm sure it's just some silly mixup. And I'm sure they'll turn up within the next few days. All I'm asking for is an extension till Tuesday to get this straightened out."

Katherine said, "And if they haven't turned up by Tuesday?"

"Then I'll go with what I've got."

"I don't see why you can't go with you've got now."

"Because the state's case has been adversely affected by unforeseen circumstances. They were the two lead investigators, for God's sake."

"That's your problem," Katherine shot back. "You're responsible for the accountability of your witnesses. I can't help it if you mis-placed them."

I was enjoying this immensely. It wasn't often that Eddie had to operate from a disadvantage. Come to think of it, I'd never even seen him at the fringe of anything remotely discomforting. Till now. He was actually sweating.

But Carruthers barked, "Stop the fencing. This isn't the time to play lawyer games. Miss Carlson, can you live with the extension?"

Katherine coldly said, "Two days ago, after fifteen protesters were brutally slaughtered, I requested a postponement. Golden ar-gued that a full-blown massacre was too insignificant."

"I'm aware of that," Carruthers said, which he surely was, since he ultimately was the one who made the decision not to resched-ule. "But he didn't argue that it was insignificant. He argued it was irrelevant. Remember the distinction."

"All right," Katherine said, inching forward in her own seat. "I'll talk relevance. I've got an innocent client who's already spent nearly two weeks in a hellhole the Koreans call a prison. He's been beaten, mentally abused, isolated, fed only water and rice. The de-cision to put him there was made by our government. I don't see why he should be subjected to another day of torture because the prosecutor can't produce his witnesses."

Eddie defiantly mumbled, "He won't be hurt by another few days."

Carruthers was starting to grind his teeth impatiently. His voice got real prickly. "Miss Carlson, I asked whether a postponement would create significant problems for your defense. Not your client, your defense."

This was the moment when I decided to intervene. "Your Honor, could I have a private moment with my co-counsels?" I asked.

Katherine gave me a mystified look.

Eddie gave me a hopeful, pleading look.

Carruthers nodded. "The conference room is down the hallway to the left. Five minutes?"

Ordinarily, if you put three lawyers together in a room, five days wouldn't be enough. But I said, "Five minutes would be fine."

Then Katherine, Allie, and I filed out the door and down the hall. The moment the door closed, Katherine spun and faced me.

"What the hell's this about?"

"We might want to think this through."

"I have," Katherine said, quite firmly. "That little bastard hasn't given us a single break. Screw him."

"That's one way of looking at it."

"And there's some other way?"

I backed away and leaned against the wall. My eyes roamed across both their faces. "Say we start tomorrow morning. How sure are we we'll win?"

They were both attorneys and the answer to that was obvious.

Allie ran a hand through her spiky hair. "No trial's ever a sure thing."

And I calmly responded, "The first rule of law."

Allie said, "He'll have to reconstruct. He'll have to use substitutes. There's about ten other Korean police officers on his witness list and he has the two military policemen who first went to the scene. He has the pathologist and the lock specialist. They can fill in a lot of the gaps."

And Katherine said, "And if we give him till Tuesday, he'll use every minute to rebuild his case around those other witnesses. If we force him into court tomorrow, he'll be disorganized and behind the curve."

I rubbed my chin. "Yeah, that's true."

Katherine was now looking at me curiously. "But . . . ?"

"Look, nobody wants to cream Eddie worse than me. I've got two of his damn baseball bats in my closet."

"But . . . ?" Katherine asked again.

"But I know Eddie. He might look like a mess today, but he won't by tomorrow. Believe me. We don't call him Fast Eddie for nothing. An ego like his won't stay down long. In fact, when he comes to his senses and realizes he's got two dirty cops on his hands, he'll recognize his case is now less vulnerable."

Allie said, "He'd have to be pretty good to pull that off."

"Allie, he's not just pretty good, he's the best the Army's got."
She nodded.

Then I said, "But what if we could get the murder, rape, and necrophilia charges thrown out before the trial?"

"That's a silly question," Katherine said. Then she tilted her head sideways. "How?"

"Two days will buy us time to look into Choi's and Bales's activities. We know they're rotten. What if we can prove that?"

Katherine was chewing on her lip. She was the lead counsel, so ultimately this was her decision. She stared at me hard. You could almost see her wheels spinning with the possibilities.

"Drummond, no bluster. Can you come up with something? And I mean before trial."

"I hope I can. No guarantees."

There was a long, tense, awkward moment. All this was easy for me to say, but I didn't want to be in Katherine's shoes. Despite what I'd argued, if we went to trial in the morning, Eddie might be so tipsy he'd never recover. On the other hand, the opening day would mostly be spent on voir dire, and maybe opening statements. Then Eddie would have Saturday and Sunday to replan his case. Really, we weren't giving him much.

On the other hand, this was Fast Eddie we were talking about, and what would be one day for anybody else would be like two weeks for him. And what if I couldn't dig up anything more on Bales and Choi? What if all they'd left behind was a cloud of dust?

Katherine looked at Allie and she was nodding her head—reluctantly, but she was nodding.

Then Katherine nodded, too. She didn't look pleased, or confident, or satisfied, but her head was bobbing.

We trooped back into the judge's office two minutes ahead of schedule. Eddie was slumped down in his chair, prepared for the worst. We all knew that Carruthers didn't need it, but he badly *wanted* Katherine's assent to the postponement. Otherwise she'd run to the press and kick up holy hell—and an army of her journalist friends had flown over here, and Korea is not exactly a tourist haven, and they were all ready for the show to begin. Grumpy journalists are everybody's worst nightmare.

It just would be much neater for all concerned if she went along and agreed.

Katherine sat in her chair and gave Eddie a withering look.

"Well?" Carruthers asked.

"Okay, Your Honor."

"Okay?" Eddie asked, flabbergasted. I doubted if he ever once in his entire legal career had cut anybody an inch of slack. He's the kind of guy who probably went to the executions of the men he helped convict. Eddie's that way. Believe me.

Katherine said, "That's what I said, Golden. You're getting your two days."

I could see that Eddie wanted almost more than anything to say something sharp and nasty back, just to balance the ledger, except Katherine had a grip on his short hairs, so discretion stilled his tongue.

Carruthers said, "All right then, Major, you've got until 0800 hours Tuesday to locate your witnesses. Miss Carlson, the court thanks you for your equanimity."

Then we all got up and left. When we got outside, Katherine loitered by the door and asked Allie to go ahead. We gave her a minute to get beyond earshot.

Then Katherine said, "What the hell have you got up your sleeve?"

I held up my hands. "What do you mean?"

"Don't try to run a scam on me, Drummond. I know you."

"Me? A scam?"

Her stare hardened. "You do have something going, don't you? The only reason I agreed to this was because I assume you've got something. Some lead, something."

I shook my head. "Actually, no. I don't have a thing."

Katherine's big green eyes suddenly got bigger. "Look, Drummond, I just made the biggest decision of my legal career because of you. The biggest decision of my life. You have no idea how important this is to me."

"Why'd you ask for me to be your co-counsel?" I asked.

"Honestly?"

"No, lie and say it's because I'm so damned good-looking and sexy."

She sort of half smiled. "It wasn't that, believe me."

"See," I said. "You've got your secrets and I've got mine."

Her half smile disappeared. She gave me a very steady look. "Let me make this clear. I just gave that son of a bitch two more days. I let you talk me into that."

I nodded.

She continued. "That means you've got two days to come up with something. You've got two days to give me something that proves Thomas Whitehall didn't murder and rape Lee. If you fail to do that, I'll find some way to ruin the rest of your life. You won't be able to hide from me. I'll track you down and make your life miserable. Is that clear?"

I looked carefully into her eyes, and there was not the slightest doubt in my mind she meant every word of it. Without another word she walked away and left me standing on the hot cement, wondering what in the hell I should do next. Not that I was afraid of her or anything, but I suddenly felt desperate to come up with something. Something quick, too, because when I claimed I wasn't afraid of her, I might've been exaggerating a little bit . . . or a lot.

I went back to Mercer's office. He was seated behind his desk with the usual cup of coffee attached to his lips. As much coffee as that man drank, he probably had brown liquid flowing through his veins. If you took his java away, he'd probably deflate like a big balloon with a hole in it.

He looked astoundingly unhappy.

I said, "Hey, boss, what's happening?"

That "boss" thing was my sly way of intimating I wanted to do some more work for him.

He didn't seem to catch it. He grumbled something about how Choi and Bales seemed to have disappeared into thin air. Actually, they had disappeared in Seoul, which ain't exactly thin air, if you ask me. It's a sprawling metropolis with some fifteen million people and at least that many rabbit warrens and pigeonholes they could've run into. They might not even be in Seoul anymore. Hell, they might not be within a thousand miles of Korea.

I said, "Choi's probably got a million places to hide."

Mercer took another sip of coffee. He looked wrung out, and it wasn't hard to guess he'd gotten reamed pretty good for letting Bales slip away. He could at least pin the Choi screwup on Kim and the KCIA, but that's like saying you're only responsible for sinking the lower decks of the *Titanic*; some other guy let the upper decks slip under the waves.

The way spooks like to handle these things is to *catch* the spies. Then they like to vigorously interrogate them and gauge how much damage was done, and where, and how. Otherwise you have to assume the worst, and respond accordingly. The worst in this case was hugely ugly. The entire defense plan for South Korea might've been compromised and therefore needed to be rewritten. Thousands of units might have to be moved, minefields relocated, port security plans rebuilt, etcetera, etcetera. Millions of men and women would have to be retrained to execute a new plan. It could take years and many billions of dollars.

Still, that left the larger question of who Bales and Choi might've blackmailed and turned. Hundreds of people worked in sensitive jobs in the huge alliance headquarters. Choi had been in business nearly twenty years, and even if he'd only cherry-picked one sucker every year, that left a big army of informants. And just because Choi had hightailed it didn't mean his moles were out of business. The plumbers couldn't do their work if they didn't know where the leaks were.

Mercer looked like he'd had all this explained to him in painful detail by somebody with a real loud, brassy voice. I felt sorry for him.

No, actually that's not true. I'd brought him the breakthrough and he'd let the rats slip from his grasp. He should've arrested Bales and Choi right away. Maybe he should've had thirty cars tail Bales to the airport, or put a man in Bales's trunk. He took a gamble and he lost.

Anyway, I said, "Has anybody figured out what happened?"

He shrugged. "What we guess was there was another car and some accomplices waiting for Bales in the tunnel. We haven't got a clue who the guy was who drove his car out of the tunnel. He didn't have any ID, but he obviously worked for Choi. I guess that was plan B. As for Choi, he somehow figured he was being followed. After Bales called him, he must've taken precautions. Maybe he had some of his own people tail him and they detected the KCIA guys."

"He didn't waste a minute. He's really good," I remarked, which was as revoltingly obvious as anything I'd ever muttered in my life.

"Yeah," Mercer said, looking even more glum.

I hooked my cane on the front of his desk and fell into a chair. "You've got people going through their offices and homes?"

"Yeah."

"What about Bales's wife?"

"Carol arrested her at the luncheon. That's the only fuckin' thing that went right."

"Where's she now?"

"The KCIA's got her."

"What? You turned her over?"

"Yeah."

"How come?" I asked. "You arrested her on a military base. She's a military wife. You have jurisdiction."

His eyes shifted a little, like this wasn't something he was particularly proud to admit. "'Cause the KCIA has a bit more latitude than we do."

That was a nice way of saying that the KCIA could rip her fingernails out and flood her veins with truth serums.

I wasn't passing any judgments, though. I might've done the same thing if I were in his shoes. Hell, I might've done the same thing if I was in my shoes. Lots of innocent folks had been murdered, and Bales's wife was probably somehow connected to it.

"Besides," he continued, "they know how to handle North Korean stooges better than we do."

"Is there some trick to that?" I asked, genuinely curious.

"Ah, yeah. They're a breed apart. Know how Carol took her down?"

"How?"

"Drugged her tea. The second she saw her getting drowsy, she slipped up behind her and jammed a steel plate in her mouth so she couldn't bite down, while two other agents rushed over, threw ropes around her body, and pinned her in place."

"Sounds pretty extreme."

"There's a reason for it. Lots of these North Koreans have those poison pellets inside a tooth. No shit. Remember that KAL plane that got a bomb planted on it by a North Korean couple? The KCIA caught them, but the guy reached up, twisted a molar, and plunk! The bastard was dead before he hit the floor."

"Think the KCIA'll get her to talk?"

"Depends how tough she is. Usually they start getting results within seventy-two hours."

"That's too long, though, isn't it?"

"Yeah. Choi and Bales will assume she's been taken. They'll hide someplace she can't compromise. They'll alter their plans."

I rubbed my chin and gave him a full dose of the look people say makes me look just like a Lebanese rug merchant. "So, you got any ideas?"

He shrugged. "Maybe Bales's wife will tell us something helpful. Maybe we'll find something searching through their belongings."

"You don't sound hopeful."

"I'm not. These guys were trained agents."

"Choi maybe was. Bales wasn't."

He looked over his coffee mug. "You got something you wanna share?"

I kept rubbing my chin. "I thought maybe if I joined in the search, I might catch something you'll miss."

Mercer was no dummy. "You mean you'd like to go through their shit and see if you can find something to get Whitehall off."

I smiled. "I suppose if I came upon something that helped my client, that wouldn't be a bad thing."

He shook his head and rolled his eyes. He'd obviously had a hell of a day. "Look, Drummond, you wanna go through their crap, just say so. I owe you, and I always pay my debts. Feel free."

"Could you loan me Carol Kim?"

"Think I'd let you go through their shit without somebody looking over your shoulder? Take her."

He had a good point. I started to get up.

"One other thing," he said.

"Yeah?"

"Remember when Bales called Choi?"

"Of course."

"Think back. Remember what he said just before they talked about that plan B thing?"

"He wanted to know about his wife?"

"Nah, after that."

"I don't remember anything after that," I admitted.

"Bales asked him about phase 3."

"What in the hell's phase 3?"

Mercer looked sadder than any man I ever saw. "That's what we'd like to know."

CHAPTER
38

★ ★ ★

I asked Mercer to have Carol meet me at the snack bar on base. I hadn't eaten since the day before, and it looked like another long night ahead. I was halfway through my second overcooked burger and was noisily slurping a watery chocolate milkshake when Carol walked in.

How could I tell? Because when she entered, the snack bar was jammed with soldiers loudly bitching about what a lousy week they'd had, or making empty boasts about how they were going to get laid this Friday night, when suddenly everything came to a stop. The room just froze—the opposite effect of throwing a pebble into a still pond. See, Carol wasn't bad in ye olde looks department, but she wasn't any great shakes either—only these troops had been penned up on base ever since Whitehall's arrest, and anything with boobs that walked upright looked damned good to them at that moment.

There was an almost universal gasp of surprise when she wafted across the room and landed at my table. I still looked pretty ravaged from the beatings. And when a hundred or so young minds think exactly the same thought, at exactly the same moment, the psychic echo can be almost deafening: Jesus, what's she doing with that busted-up hulk? Friggin' officers get all the luck.

I looked around the room and proudly acknowledged their universal envy, because I'm a guy, and guys don't really care if jealousy is built on a false foundation. At least I don't. I take it anywhere I can get it.

"Congratulations on capturing Mrs. Bales," I said, after she'd sat down.

"Thanks," she offhandedly responded, like, You know, no big thing; just another day in a secret agent's life. Not even worth an entry in my diary.

"Hungry?" I asked, munching away on my burger.

She looked at the burger with disgust. "No, I, uh, I'll get something else to eat. Later."

"You sure? It might be a long night."

She was still staring at the greasy thing in my fist. "Quite sure."

"Okay, have it your way. Here's what I'd like to do. Can you get me in to see Bales's wife?"

"If you'd like. Why?"

"Curiosity. I just want to see what she looks like."

"All right."

"Then I'd like to spend some time going through Bales's and Choi's investigation files."

"They've already been taken from their offices. Bales's files are at our facility. Choi's are with the KCIA."

"But you can get 'em?"

"I suppose. There are a lot of them, though. Box after box filled with them. We could spend all night."

"I got nothing better to do."

"I guess I don't, either," she sighed, not the least bit happy about that.

"Good," I said, noisily licking some ketchup off my fingers. "Let's get moving."

Then, just as I was standing up, my legs suddenly buckled. If I hadn't grabbed the corner of the table I would've done a free fall onto the floor. Carol rushed around the table and took hold of my shoulders, helping me straighten up.

"Are you all right?"

I shook my head a few times. "I don't know. Must be the beatings. My body . . . uh, it's not working right."

"We don't have to do this tonight. We can reschedule."

"No, it has to be tonight. Please."

I bravely tried taking another step and my legs buckled again.

So she slipped her arm around my waist, and I put an arm around her shoulder and let her lead me out. After one or two steps, I straightened. Every eye in the room was on us. A hundred disgruntled young faces looked like they'd kill their own mothers to be me.

I'm so slick, sometimes I'm ashamed of myself. But like I said, I'll take it any way I can get it.

It took thirty minutes to get to the KCIA. It was a nondescript, blocklike gray building located on a busy street. You'd probably pass right by it, except it was the only building I ever saw that had no windows on the first three floors. They started on the fourth floor, and even those were small, pinched, scrawny-looking things.

Carol showed a guard her Agency ID, and she was allowed to enter a gated area and park. Then we left the car and went to the front entrance, where two fairly competent-looking guards took her CIA identification card, called a number, chattered in Korean for a few seconds, then gave us both plastic laminated passes with clips on the back.

Carol seemed to know where she was going, because she led me down a series of halls and up two flights of stairs and into a side office. There were about six men in dark silk suits lounging around drinking tea, smoking cigarettes, quietly bullshitting. They seemed to recognize Carol.

She jabbered in Korean for a few minutes, occasionally putting a finger to her lips in a fretful motion, like a sign of concern. Her manner seemed more reserved, almost subservient, in the presence of Korean men.

One of the men finally stood up and led us through two sets of doors and into another room filled with cigarette smoke. A Korean gentleman was hunched over a table, suit jacket on the back of his chair, tie loosened, sleeves rolled up. It was Mr. Kim, Mercer's KCIA counterpart.

He got up. Carol bowed and made no effort to shake hands. She was reverting to Korean protocols. Then Kim looked at me and stuck out his hand. "Major Drummond, it's good to see you again."

"My pleasure," I said. "How's it going?"

He grimaced painfully. "It's not been the best of days."

I couldn't resist. "Yeah, that was some screwup this afternoon, wasn't it?"

"That bastard murdered one of my men. He cut his throat like a pig's."

I gathered Mr. Kim was no longer dubious about my overheated imagination.

"So how's your prisoner?" I asked.

"She's going to be tough."

"Yeah?"

"She's had good training. She hasn't said a word."

I wasn't going to tell him, but when I was in the outfit, I'd had some training in interrogation myself. Only mine was always on the receiving end, because the outfit did most of its work inside the bad guys' territory and was therefore justifiably concerned about our ability to withstand torture and interrogation. Some sadist figured that practice makes perfect, and they gave us lots of it. I therefore consider myself something of an expert in interrogation methods—strictly from the victim's end of things, of course.

I said, "What are you doing to her?"

"Actually, we don't use physical techniques. Everybody believes we do, and frankly we encourage the perception." He lifted his shoulders a little. "It heightens the anxiety of our subjects. The truth is, we prefer sleep deprivation."

I grinned. Sleep deprivation doesn't get quick results like yanking out a few fingernails might, but it's much more effective, because once a prisoner breaks, they break all the way. I know. In training, I'd had it tried on me once. I ended up babbling like a baby.

"Can I see her?"

He shrugged. "If you'd like. Just don't talk to her."

We entered a room off to the side. The walls and floors were thickly padded in some solid white material. The padding wasn't for bouncing bodies off of, but was super-thick sound insulation. The lights in the ceiling were huge and very high-powered. The light was pure white and spectacularly bright, so bright it hurt your eyes and forced you to blink a lot, although even then it penetrated through your lids.

A woman was seated in a chair with her back turned to us. There were white straps completely immobilizing her, so she couldn't move a limb or even her head. There was some kind of eye halter strapped around her head that forced her eyelids to stay open, which after a while gets pretty painful because the eyeballs get dry and sore. Even the chair was painted white. In fact, the only color in the room was the flesh tone of her skin. She was entirely naked. She'd been stripped and left nude to add to her humiliation and sense of vulnerability. The monochromatic whiteness was done to amplify the effects of her sleep deprivation. To multiply her humiliation, they would keep feeding her liquids and foods, so she peed and shat all over herself.

By the second or third day, she would be thoroughly exhausted, degraded, bored out of her wits, physically miserable, and, hopefully, ready to tell all. Even a Zen Buddhist who was nuts for meditation couldn't withstand more than two or three days of this.

I walked to her front and studied her. She didn't say a word. She just gave me a sharp, haughty look, but her expression did nothing to hide one simple, irreducible fact. The woman was utterly, breathtakingly beautiful. She had classically high cheekbones, large, alluring eyes, full, sensuous lips, and an exquisitely shaped face. Her hair was so thick and shimmery it almost looked artificial. Her body was an athlete's fantasy, broad-shouldered, hard, sinewy muscles, and a washboard stomach. If there was an ounce of body fat on her, I couldn't see where she hid it.

I felt uncomfortably like a voyeur, but my interest in studying Bales's mate was purely professional. I had a theory bouncing around inside my head, and she was a vital piece in that puzzle.

I stared at her face, and she glared back defiantly. Faces can betray a lot about people. You can hide a lot of things about yourself, but a lifetime of expressions and attitudes eventually work themselves into a mask. Her mask spoke of supreme self-confidence, even arrogance. She had the face of someone who was used to commanding people. Well, sure, you might say, because beautiful women are often spoiled women, but this woman's haughtiness wasn't from being mollycoddled or indulged. She was an unusually disciplined, tough specimen, and her body didn't get that way from lying around the house munching on bonbons and ordering the servants around.

I finally nodded at Mr. Kim that I'd seen enough, and we quietly slipped out.

Once we were back in the waiting room, Kim lit up another cigarette and asked, "What do you think?"

"I think you're right. She's going to be a bitch to break. She's superbly conditioned, so the sleep deprivation will take much longer than normal. Plus she's got an ego like a rock, so the humiliation's going to roll off her back."

He looked painfully unhappy to hear that, although I suppose I was only voicing what he and his technicians had already surmised.

I said, "Have you checked her teeth?"

"Of course. We found a cyanide pellet in the number three molar in the back."

"No, I mean the quality of the dental work."

"Yes, that too. Steel fillings, shoddy, coarse work."

He seemed impressed that I would know to ask that. The one thing Communist spymasters nearly always overlook when they're building camouflage for their spies is how truly lousy the dental work is in their own societies. If this woman had been born and bred in Chicago, she'd have silver or porcelain fillings and the work would reflect the level of craftsmanship demanded by a vain society that likes even repaired teeth to look like jewelry.

I leaned against the wall. "Why do you think North Korea would send a female agent that looks like her down here to work with Bales and Choi? And why would they position her in Bales's house?"

"That's what we're hoping she'll tell us."

I glanced over at Carol, who was seated at the table playing the demure Korean girl who knew her place in this macho society.

"Did you hear her speak?" I asked her.

"I stood over her shoulder and listened to her most of the luncheon."

"What's her English like?"

"Excellent. Native quality, in fact. So were her manners. She used the fork and knife, even though the other American wives were using chopsticks. I thought that was interesting."

I looked at Mr. Kim. "Maybe she's one of those kids who were raised in that American village you mentioned?"

"Maybe."

I turned back to Carol. "Any other thoughts?"

"I think it's strange that she didn't arrive here until five years ago."

"Yeah, a little after Bales got assigned here."

Kim quickly suggested, "A honeypot?"

"The timing would fit, I guess," I admitted.

She certainly had the exquisite looks and body to be a honeypot, which to those uninitiated in the wormy arts of espionage is a woman who is used to lure a target into an affair, like bait, to entangle the target in an embarrassing predicament that can be exploited for blackmail.

Then I said, "But Bales wasn't married back then, was he? And he wasn't in a sensitive position with a high security clearance and access to valuable information?"

That seemed to obviate the way most honeypot ploys work. If the target is married and engaging in an affair, that makes him vulnerable. If the target has an important job and knows lots of important secrets, at some point the bad guys deliberately let him know the girl he's sleeping with is a foreign agent, and that can also make him vulnerable to blackmail. Bales fell into neither category. If the bad guys told his bosses he was sleeping with a North

Korean spy, his bosses would simply shrug and say, "Yeah, what's she look like? Is she a great lay?"

I said, "You know, the other intriguing thing was the way Bales referred to her when he called Choi this afternoon. He called her a bitch. And when Choi told him to forget about her and run, he didn't argue or sound the least bit upset. Doesn't sound like much of a marriage."

The other two were nodding, because the prisoner tied to that white chair was gaining significance. And an added layer of mystery.

But I had an advantage over them. I'd been thinking about Michael Bales for many days. And I had met him under several different sets of circumstances, so I had a greater window into his dark nature than they did.

I said, "How do you think Choi got Bales on his side in the first place?" I looked over at Carol. "Did your people have the FBI run a check on him?"

"Of course."

"And?"

She looked at a wall and began reciting the facts. She had the lawyer's gift of great recall, and it came pouring out crisp and factual.

"Bales was born in Warrenton, Nebraska, where his father owns a dairy farm. He joined the Army in 1987 when he was eighteen, right after graduating from high school. He enlisted in the MPs, did well, and made warrant. Never previously married, no money problems surfaced, no bad habits. He's been background-checked for his secret clearance and there were no signs of trouble. The checkers talked to some of his old teachers and schoolmates, and one former girlfriend. Everybody said he was a great guy, honest, reliable, an all-American boy. No previous arrests, no scandals."

I said, "So here's a guy who gets to Korea five years ago with an impeccable record and a great future ahead, then suddenly he decides to start working for North Korea. Doesn't make sense, does it?"

Kim said, "Money. It's easy to hide it. When it comes to Americans, always follow the money."

You might think he'd watched too many American movies and was starting to sound like a grade-B actor. Or you might say to yourself that he was a foreigner, so what the hell did he know. But you have to remember that Kim's agency had recruited its share of American traitors—both discovered and undiscovered—so he did have a certain claim to expertise.

I looked at my watch; it was after 11:00 P.M. I nodded at Carol and she got the message, so she stood up and began getting ready to leave.

I turned to Kim. "Thanks. If we come up with anything we'll call."

He said, "I hope you do," then sat back down.

I had the impression his punishment for letting Choi murder one of his men and slip away was to sit here and wait until the gorgeous, tough-looking lady in the other room finally started babbling. In other words, he was also sentenced to sleep deprivation.

Now that I'd looked at her, and at him, my money was on her.

CHAPTER
39
✪ ✪ ✪

There were probably many ways to approach this, but I persuaded Carol to have some minions deliver the boxes filled with Bales's and Choi's case files to my hotel room in the Dragon Hill Lodge. Somehow I didn't think it was my charm that persuaded her. It would be midnight by the time we got back to base, and she still hadn't eaten, and Korean restaurants close early. The hotel at least offered room service.

Besides, I had the impression she wasn't the least bit afraid my manly charisma would make her swoon and end up in my bed. So why not do our work in a comfortable hotel room instead of some musty office?

Three-fifths of the boxes were stuffed with Choi's files. They were written in Hangul, which posed an intractable problem for me, because the only Korean character I recognized was the one that meant "homosexual," since I'd seen it written on so many signs lately. Thus Carol. Her job was to rummage through Choi's files.

I waited till she got off the phone to room service before I explained what I hoped to accomplish. I wanted her to rifle through Choi's files and pull aside every crime sheet that dealt with an American committing a felony, witnessing a crime, or in any way being involved in aiding or abetting a crime in Itaewon. Don't bother to read them, I told her. Sift them out and place them in a pile. And nothing older than three years ago. And be sure to write the subjects' names and ranks in English on the cover sheets.

I dug through Bales's files. The good thing about being a highly experienced criminal attorney was that I'd spent eight years looking at crime sheets. You do develop a certain expertise. You know which data sections are substantively important and which are filled with meaningless procedural details. You know which pages to flip to immediately and which to ignore.

The other thing was that Bales was highly organized, precise, and not the least bit wordy. I recalled that from his statements in the Whitehall packet, and the same characteristics were evident on his crime sheets. Too bad he was rotten right down to his skivvies. Other than that, he was a dream cop.

I ruled out any crimes committed by anybody lower than a major. Not that lieutenants and sergeants and privates aren't possibly traitorous, or in vitally sensitive positions, because the clerk to the general in charge of operations sees almost everything his boss sees. I just couldn't be bothered at this stage. Somebody else could sift through later and see if any of those crime sheets were worth investigating more thoroughly.

I pulled out every crime sheet involving a major or higher, including those that involved their wives and kids. Army regulations require active files to be kept two years back, and a third year back for inactive files. So what I had was Bales's records going back three years.

It was surprising how many officers or family members were connected in some way or another with a crime. It took me three hours, and Carol and I ate as we worked, but I ended up with a stack of nearly one hundred files. Most of the crimes looked fairly petty—DUIs, shoplifting, blackmarketing PX goods on the Korean economy, Peeping Toms, that kind of thing. But you never know what pushes somebody's hot button. One guy's innocuous trifle is another's unbearable embarrassment. And some of the crimes looked fairly salacious. Several involved prostitution, including the wife of a full colonel who got caught three different times. An Army captain was arrested for armed robbery. A major was caught peeking in a window at a general's wife. A lieutenant colonel flashed some schoolkids.

Carol's stack looked twice as large as mine, and she still had another box to go. Both of us were rubbing our eyes a lot. We'd been awake since two o'clock in the morning the day before, when she and Mercer had knocked on my hotel door.

I got up and stretched and then went to the bathroom and threw some cold water over my face. When I came back, Carol was pacing and sipping from her third bottle of Evian. She'd decided to get more comfortable. She'd removed her shoes and stockings and her suit coat, so she was wearing only a short skirt and a thin, sleeveless blouse.

I said, "Tired?"

"Exhausted. This reminds me of first-year finals at law school."

I chuckled. "Now you see what us lawyers do for a living. See what you're missing?"

She collapsed onto the bed and her body bounced. "God, this bed feels great."

Before she could give up on me, I said, "Hey, why don't you go through that box? I'm gonna start cross-indexing the files."

She groaned but sat back up. "Is there a method to this?"

"Actually, yeah. Here's the way I figure their scam works. Choi does the initial investigation anytime an American is involved in a crime in Itaewon, right? He's the first one on the scene, the first one to gather the facts, interview the witnesses, and collect the evidence. Then he calls Bales. Say the culprit looks malleable and entrappable. What would they do next?"

She ran both her hands through her hair, massaging her scalp. "I don't know. He'd bring Bales in to meet the suspect, to have an American police officer on the scene."

"Right. When the suspect sees an American CID investigator, he knows the shit is hitting the fan. Suddenly it's no longer some infraction committed off base, limited to the Korean courts. Suddenly it's serious. It's going to seep into American channels, be reported to his commanding officer, put his career in jeopardy."

"Putting the fear of God into him."

"Right. Then maybe Bales's job is to decide if the victim's worth the trouble—maybe run a quick background check, see if the culprit's got any value, if he seems susceptible, if he looks like someone they want and maybe could get."

"In the meantime, the suspect's left twisting in the wind, wondering if his life's over."

"They let the fear and tension build."

"I can see it."

"Okay, say Bales comes back to Choi and says they don't want him, or he doesn't seem the right type. They decide to throw the fish back into the sea. How do they do that?"

"I guess Bales goes ahead and fills out an American investigation report on the suspect. He gets the crime entered into the garrison blotter."

"Exactly. They put the wheels of justice in motion. The suspect has no idea he's just been vetted and found unworthy."

"So we're looking for officers who were arrested by Choi but there's no corresponding American report filled out by Bales?"

I smiled. "In some cases, it may turn out somebody other than Bales handled it from the American side. In others, maybe the investigation didn't pan out. But I'm willing to bet we're going to see some that smell like they could get convictions, except they mysteriously stopped at the American fenceline, if you get my drift."

"And you really think Choi would keep those files around?"

"Any other course would be stupid. Dangerous even. My bet would be he stamps them 'closed for insufficient evidence,' or titles it a dead end, then stuffs it in with everything else. He's the chief of detectives at the precinct. Who's gonna backcheck his cases? Plus, what happens if anybody ever asks, 'Hey Choi, whatever happened to that old case with that American officer who got caught lifting that expensive Rolex from Old Man Lee's jewelry shop?' This way he can pull out the file and everything's hunky-dory."

Carol started going through another box, while I began cross-referencing the Korean and American files. I had organized Bales's files alphabetically. That made it go faster. When I was done, I had about twenty unmatched Korean files.

I put them in a neat stack. Carol had culled six more out of the last two boxes. I quickly crossed-referenced the first four, but the fifth caught my attention real fast. It was Colonel Mack Janson, aka Piranha Lips, Spears's legal adviser.

I put that one in a pile all by itself. The dessert pile.

Carol got on her knees on the floor beside me. We started going through our stacks. I asked her to read the crime, then what the witnesses said, and what evidence was collected. We eliminated six files right way, because the crime was too insignificant, or because the evidence was so flimsy the case probably fell apart under its own weight. Somebody else could double-check later to see if we underestimated or overlooked anything.

Then we hit the first one that looked suspicious; then after two more eliminations, another. When we were done we had nine that in some way smelled.

I had saved the best for last, of course. I handed Carol Mack Janson's folder and asked her to read me the pertinent details.

She put a finger to her lips. "Let's see. Arrested and detained on April 19, 1999, for . . . Oh my God, you're not going to believe this."

"Tell me," I nearly yelled.

"Pedophilia."

She flipped through several more pages, reading the details. Then she said, "Apparently there's an American housing area that's off base on the outskirts of Itaewon?"

"That's right. Two big apartment buildings. One for junior officers and one for senior enlisted."

"There were several reports of American children being fondled by a large Caucasian male. The reports went to the Itaewon station because the children were lured outside the grounds of the housing area before they were molested. In fact, it was Michael Bales who reported this to Choi and handled the American side of the investigation."

"Then there should've been a report in Bales's file."

Carol still had her perky little nose tucked inside Choi's file. "The Itaewon station put up a stakeout around the housing area at the request of American authorities. On April 19, a police officer

named Pang saw a large American male wearing jeans and a sweat-
shirt leading a small boy out of the housing area. He led the child
behind an office building and into a vacant courtyard. When Pang
moved in, the man had his trousers down and was in the process
of taking down the little boy's underpants."

I said, "Yuck, I hate child molesters."

"Don't we all. Anyway, the American was arrested and brought
to the Itaewon precinct house. Choi took a statement from the arresting officer and handled the booking. He called in Bales, and
they conducted a joint interrogation."

"Turn to the interrogation sheet and tell me what it says."

She flipped through the pages for a moment, then looked up.
"There's no interrogation sheet."

"Figures. The last page, the disposition, what's it say?"

She turned to the last page. "Closed due to lack of evidence."

"Lack of evidence my ass. The son of a bitch had his pants
down."

"You know him?"

"Yeah, I know him. Janson is Spears's legal adviser. He's a
lawyer. He's also the guy overseeing the disposition of the Whitehall case. He made sure it was put on a fast track and expeditiously
handled. He worked the deal to get Whitehall transferred to the
Korean prison. He picked the judge. He picked the prosecuting attorney. He's probably the guy who selected the potential members
of the court-martial board."

Carol dropped the file. "Wow."

"Yeah, wow. The son of a bitch has been putting loads in the
dice."

CHAPTER
40
★ ★ ★

It made no sense to sleep, so we kept working. Carol wrote down English summaries of every relevant point contained in the nine reports we'd culled out. I read through her notes and tacked on recommendations on how to further winnow down the pack.

All nine remaining files appeared in some way suspicious, but three others stuck out like outrageously rotten thumbs. For one thing, like Janson's, they contained no witness statements.

One concerned an Army major in the intelligence section whose Korean wife was caught running a blackmarket ring. When she was arrested, she was driving a van loaded with over a hundred thousand dollars' worth of American cosmetics. Korean women are nuts about foreign cosmetics, which have ridiculously heavy duties tacked on by customs in Korea's staunchly protected economy. As blackmarket goods go, they're hot sellers. Given that she was caught red-handed driving a truck filled with contraband, it seemed impossible the charges were dropped.

A second case involved an Air Force lieutenant colonel in the strategic plans shop who was arrested on charges of raping a fourteen-year-old Korean girl. You get an instinct for these things, and something smelled wrong. The girl's photo was in the packet; she didn't look fourteen. Not to me. But maybe she was just physically precocious. Another thing, though, there was a raw hardness to her face. It was like that hackneyed look an experienced street-walker acquires after her third or fourth hundredth john. The American officer swore she was a whore, that he'd paid her, while she claimed he'd yanked her into an alleyway and forced himself on her. No medical exam was performed. The girl claimed she had five witnesses, but none of them were ever interviewed. There was no way to tell on such thin evidence, but it smelled like a setup.

The third case involved the Navy captain who was in charge of protocol at the headquarters. Protocol is the office that plans for and oversees all important visitors, making sure they have hotel rooms, cars and drivers, experienced guides, and security if necessary. It even puts together their schedules. In this case, the captain was arrested for a hit-and-run that resulted in a death. He was investigated for DUI and manslaughter, specifically for running over a twenty-year-old pregnant Korean girl, who survived but lost her baby. He'd attempted to flee but was forced to stop by a crowd of irate Koreans who witnessed the accident. Case closed; no grounds for prosecution.

By four-thirty, Carol was napping on the bed, and I decided to slip into the bathroom and take a shower. My body stank and I needed to clean and re-dress some of my stitched-up cuts.

When I came out, Carol was hanging up the phone.

"Who was that?" I asked.

"Your co-counsel, Miss Carlson."

"What did she want?"

"She didn't say. She hung up."

This didn't sound good. "How come?"

"I don't think she was expecting a woman. I told her you were in the shower."

I had bigger fish to fry at the moment, so I merely grunted my acknowledgment, then asked Carol to call whomever to pick up these files.

We ordered a room service breakfast—in my case a greasy, cheesy omelet and another pot of coffee; in hers, a fruit bowl and two more Evians. Our eating habits, among many other things, implied we were not a compatible couple.

Then we straightened up the room and put all the files back in the boxes, excepting of course the nine we'd earmarked as suspicious. The food came. We dug in.

While we ate, I asked, "How come you get so coy and withdrawn around Korean men?"

She pondered that a moment, like it was some unconscious thing. "My father's a very traditional Korean man. He loves America, but he stays with his Korean customs. I suppose I picked it up from him."

"What? So every Korean male reminds you of your father?"

She chuckled. "I hope not. It makes Korean men more comfortable. Most American women get under their skin. They consider them bossy and pushy, rude even. They're especially peeved when the woman is racially Korean."

"Hah! And I thought you were liberated."

"Misjudgments abound. I once thought you were a brash, sloppy, obnoxious bore."

"Yeah?"

She looked around. "Your room's actually fairly tidy. How could I have thought you were a slob?"

I stabbed and shoveled another slice of omelet between my lips. "New subject. Something I've been wondering. Why'd you bug my phone and hotel room?"

She looked up in surprise. "We didn't bug your room."

"Bullshit. Come on, I'm on your team now. Tell me."

Her eyes narrowed. "We didn't bug your room."

"Well, I found a little black thing in my phone. And I found two more tucked here and about."

"When was this?"

"Remember that day I ran out to the parking lot and you pulled away?"

"Of course. I couldn't believe you did that. You might've been watched. You might've compromised me."

"Hey, I lost my head. I'd just found three bugs."

"And you thought we'd done it? What? You thought we were listening in on your plans for defending Whitehall?"

"Oddly enough, that's just what I thought."

"Drummond, believe it or not, the Agency's got a few more pressing issues on its plate than listening to some lawyer talk about a court case." Then a dumbfounded expression emerged. "How do you know your room isn't still bugged?"

"Because Imelda, my legal assistant, has it swept every day."

"So you removed the bugs?"

"Yeah. All gone," I confidently replied.

"Did you think about long-range listening devices?"

"Those inverted megaphone things?"

"That's exactly what I mean," Carol said, working her way over to the window. She pulled the curtain apart and looked outside. First light was just breaking. "Listen, Drummond, when you removed the bugs, you notified whoever was listening that you'd detected them. If you're a target of serious interest, they'll simply switch devices."

She was putting on a very good act, but I wasn't buying it. I'd fully expected her to deny it. I just wanted her to know I knew.

Her eyes were sweeping the parking lot, like she was looking for some vehicle, maybe a truck or a van, anything big enough to hide a long-range listening device.

I asked, "Can those things target a single room in a big hotel like this? Wouldn't they pick up all kinds of babble and noise?"

"If the rooms around you were talking, there'd be bleedover and distortion. But not late at night, like now, when everybody's asleep."

She was really putting on the act. Give the woman credit.

I walked over and stood beside her at the window. She turned and looked at me.

I pointed my finger out the window. I yelled, "Quick! Get on the phone and tell your folks to move in on that vehicle right there."

She started to say something, and I grinned. She looked out in the parking lot. Suddenly a gray van turned on its lights, backed out of its space, and literally tore out of the parking lot. You could almost hear the rubber burning.

"Jesus!" I yelled.

Carol ran to the phone. She punched in some numbers and waited impatiently for somebody to answer. She yelled, "This is Carol Kim. There's a North Korean spy van headed from the Dragon Hill to the main gate. It's gray and enclosed. Get somebody to stop it."

When she hung up, she shot me a furious look. I couldn't blame her; after all, I'd just ruined a perfectly good chance to catch some North Koreans. In my defense, I really didn't believe her until I saw this with my own eyes.

I was getting ready to make my excuse when I came to my senses. There was something else we'd better do. And we'd better do it damned fast, too, or else.

CHAPTER
41
⭐ ⭐ ⭐

Here's how the rest of the morning went. A number of Agency and military police cars raced around the base for hours trying to locate and collect the suspects Carol and I had immediately identified to Mercer.

Three suspects, it quickly turned out, had been reassigned out of Korea, so they weren't in imminent danger, although Mercer still took the precaution of sending messages to their new commands to have them taken into protective custody until everything got sorted out. He'd made enough mistakes. He wasn't taking chances.

A fourth suspect was on leave somewhere in Korea. Since we couldn't find him, there was no particular reason to expect the North Koreans could, either. An all-points bulletin was sent through American and Korean channels to apprehend him on sight.

Suspects five through eight were picked up without incident, including Piranha Lips, who was literally dragged out of his office with two members of his legal staff watching. What I would've given to observe that glorious moment.

The ninth suspect, the protocol officer, was the unlucky one. He was found alone at his kitchen table with a big wound in his head dribbling cranial fluid all over his breakfast.

Nobody had a clue how it happened. Nobody saw anybody enter his quarters. Nobody heard the sound of a shot. Probably the gun was silenced. Probably the assassin was a pro. The captain's skin was still warm and the blood was still moist, so the MPs who broke into his quarters guessed he'd been executed no more than an hour to thirty minutes before they arrived.

It was ten o'clock in the morning and I was having all this pointedly explained to me by Buzz Mercer himself. I would describe his demeanor as partly pleased, since he was arresting a bunch of suspected traitors, and thus was recouping some of the prior day's humiliations. The other, much larger part of him, was annoyed, since I'd cued the North Koreans that we were on to them, making an already chaotic situation even more snarled.

The two other guys who were having this explained to them were General Spears and Brandewaite, who were seated just to my left. And if Buzz Mercer looked agitated, Spears seemed deathly worried, while Brandewaite looked ready to leap off a cliff. I wished he would.

"Jesus Christ, what a disaster," he kept mumbling over and over.

Mercer was saying, "Of course, at this stage we don't know how bad it is. Let me remind you, the eight men we have in custody, or are still trying to apprehend, are only suspects. We're bringing them in for their own protection. And for questioning, of course."

Brandewaite sniffed once or twice. "And when will we know more?"

"Can't really say," Mercer told him.

He said it in a breezy, deflective manner that gave me the impression there was no love lost between the two men. No surprise there, I thought. Brandewaite was the quintessential immaculately coifed, oily, narcissistic man of the nineties. Mercer was more of a crew-cutted, austere, meat-and-potatoes throwback to the fifties. Spies and diplomats; if you threw them both in a blender, you'd get something poisonous.

For my part, I was trying to blend into the woodwork, because the room was filled with powerful men who had no particular reason to think highly of me right at that moment.

Spears's eyes kept glancing over from beneath those eaglelike, fierce brows. I wondered what he was thinking. On the other hand, maybe I didn't want to know.

Mercer went on. "Anyway, right now we're busy collecting legal counsels for all of them."

"Did they all ask for lawyers?" Spears asked.

"Nope. We automatically provide it. We don't want any procedural shit to come back and bite us in the ass down the road."

Brandewaite said, "How stupid. You'll slow the whole thing down." He looked spitefully at me. "Once the lawyers get there they'll all clam up."

Mercer impatiently said, "Look, you stick to what you know, and I'll stick to what I know."

Brandewaite pointed a manicured finger in his face. "Right now, Mercer, you've got a bunch of American military officers in custody and one dead body. Don't lecture me. Get results and get them fast."

They went back and forth like that for a while and I found myself wondering about the Navy captain who got shot in the head. Why him? I mean, whoever was eavesdropping out in that parking lot overheard Carol and me mention the name of every one of the suspects. Probably some weren't going to pan out. There'd be perfectly good explanations why their names weren't in Bales's file, or why Choi dropped the charges. But I was pretty sure there'd be no good explanations for at least three or four others. They were simply caught in Choi's web.

So why only the Navy captain? Carol had notified Mercer of our concerns at 5:20, and the MPs had burst into the captain's quarters at 6:36, which meant he could have been murdered as early as 6:00. In other words, as soon as the North Koreans learned what we'd figured out, they dispatched an assassin to bump him off. Mack Janson wasn't arrested till 8:30. Another suspect wasn't picked up till 9:00.

Did that mean I was wrong? That the others weren't guilty? That the captain was the only fish who ended up in Choi's net? Or were the others just too hard for the North Koreans to get to? Or was there something more here?

As much as I didn't want to emerge from the woodwork, I said, "Hey, Mr. Mercer, why do you think they knocked off this Navy captain?"

Mercer and Brandewaite were into each other's faces, so it took him a second to tear his attention away. "What?"

"That Navy captain?"

"Elmore. Harold Elmore."

"Yeah, right . . . Harold Elmore. Why do you think they popped him? I mean, if I've got this figured right, they had two or three hours to kill some more, right? Why'd they rush right over and clip Elmore? Why just him?"

Mercer's lips curled inward. "Damned if I know. Of all the suspects on the list, Elmore is in unquestionably the least sensitive position."

I said, "You knew him, right, General?"

Spears said, "Damned right I knew him. Harry was my protocol officer. I saw him every day. He briefed me every morning. We get lots of important visitors and Harry handled all of them. Before this morning I would've found this impossible to believe."

"Why's that?"

"Because Harry was a damned good man. A Naval Academy grad, twenty-five years of good service, hardworking, honest, reliable."

I gave him a respectful shrug. "Right, sir. And one night he went to a bar and had one drink too many. The next thing he knew he was driving home and there was a hard bump on his fender and a young mother was cartwheeling over the top of his car. Then he found himself in a foreign police station, being told he was gonna be charged with manslaughter and DUI, and he might be facing twenty years in a prison."

Mercer said, "What was his access to plans and sensitive information?"

Spears looked puzzled. "He was cleared for Top Secret, but limited to whatever he needed to know. In Harry's case it wasn't much."

I asked, "Did he sit in on briefings on war plans, or sensitive intelligence, that kind of thing?"

"Not routinely, no. Uh, actually, he might have sat in on some. Particularly if he assigned himself as the escort officer for some particularly important visitor."

Brandewaite asked, "You mean, like a senator?"

"We don't brief senators on war plans. Say the Secretary of Defense, or the Chairman of the Joint Chiefs. They get over here a few times a year. Even the President was here last year."

We fell quiet a moment.

Spears broke the silence. "Harry always handled the big ones himself. I never associated anything with that. I always thought Harry was just . . . well, taking responsibility for the tougher ones."

That's exactly what it was, I thought. Elmore's guests were privy to the most sensitive knowledge. He could sit in the back of the room at the heftiest briefings and report back to Choi. He'd be the last person anyone would suspect because his position was so drab and perfunctory. He was the only person in the room who came as a coatholder, a petty, unimportant escort, the guy who was there to make sure the VIP got from this briefing to the next on time.

Was that why the North Koreans hooked him? Why they took him out?

I said, "Was there something he knew that made him special?"

Brandewaite said, "Maybe he was the only traitor. Maybe the others are innocent. Maybe that's why they killed only him."

As much as Spears, Mercer, and even I would've liked that to be true, Brandewaite was blowing smoke. I had this picture in my head of a policeman walking into a courtyard and coming upon Janson with his pants down, trying to remove the drawers from some poor little tyke. It was a sickening thought. Add that to Janson's manipulations in the Whitehall case and Elmore definitely wasn't the only one.

Mercer said, "Probably he was also useful for telling Choi when big VIPs were in town. Like some powerful senator or general. Elmore maybe even knew what their personal peccadillos were."

Spears said, "Damn it, Buzz, we don't run an escort service for the command's guests."

"I know that, General. What I mean is, some of these guys get here, and it's a week away from Mama and the screaming kids, and they're on the other side of the world, and ah hell, who's gonna know if they run out and get a little Oriental nookie? I mean, who'd know, right? Well, Elmore and his guys would probably know. They talk to the VIP's security guys. Maybe they provide him with the car and driver."

I said, "I'll bet that's right. Maybe he was pimping targets for Choi to blackmail. Maybe the North Koreans eliminated him so he wouldn't compromise somebody. Maybe they're trying to protect some priceless asset. Maybe several."

It was a fairly ugly thought, and you could see it register on everybody's faces. But it did make chilling sense. If Elmore was trolling for Choi, he'd be able to identify others on Choi's roll. That could justify an immediate execution. That could mark him for special consideration.

"Jesus," Brandewaite muttered. "I hope to God this doesn't get any bigger. This is sickening."

Mercer, enjoying his discomfort, twisted it in. "Oh yeah, it's gonna get bigger. I won't be surprised if it reaches inside your embassy."

The look Brandewaite gave him would've boiled cucumbers.

We talked for a few more desultory minutes, until it was obvious we weren't making headway, and Spears and Brandewaite both had important phone calls to make to their respective bosses in Washington about the disaster unfolding around them. They got up and left.

Mercer went to get a fresh cup of coffee and this time he even brought me one. Either he was feeling sorry for me, or we were getting to be buddies.

Ah, how silly of me. He was CIA. He felt sorry for me, obviously.

"So what do *you* think, Drummond?" he asked. "They torched Elmore 'cause he knew too much?"

"No question of that," I admitted.

"Hard to feel sympathy for the son of a bitch. He was betraying his own country, for God's sakes. They spared him the anguish of getting caught."

"Yeah, I guess," I admitted, taking a sip.

He studied me over the lip of his cup. "You got enough to get Whitehall off now?"

I put my hand up in the air, palm down, and wiggled it back and forth. "How much will you allow me to enter into evidence?"

"Not a word. There's reporters climbing all over the place. I'm putting a lid on this so tight folks'll be suffocating."

"Then I wouldn't bet my mortgage on Whitehall."

I yawned. Having not slept in about forty hours, I was exhausted. All the adrenaline rush of the past few hours had dribbled away and left me an empty hulk.

"Jesus," Mercer finally muttered, "you look like crap. Go to bed."

I gave him a grim smile. "You mean I've done enough damage today?"

"Damage? Drummond, you're a walking earthquake. I can't wait till this goddamn trial's over and you get your overdestructive ass off my peninsula."

I smiled and got up. "You think Bales and Choi are long gone?"

"Hell yeah. Maybe they climbed on some North Korean fishing trawler or submarine. Maybe they had a private plane stashed somewhere that flew them out under radar."

"Too bad," I said, thinking of what that would mean to Whitehall's defense. Not to mention what it would mean to Katherine, who was expecting me to come up with the goods. If those goods were just getting settled into a hotel in Pyongyang, they were out of my reach.

"Yeah," the spymaster said. "Very fuckin' too bad."

CHAPTER
42
★ ★ ★

The way the law works, the defense and the prosecution start each case with a tug-of-war on pretrial discoveries. The first real skirmishes of any criminal trial are battles of discovery, which is simply everything you can learn about the crime, the evidence, and the witnesses. You like to learn about these things before the trial begins because it tells you how to mold your strategy. It also keeps you from getting embarrassed and having your case completely trashed by surprises during the trial. Like maybe the prosecutor walks into court with a videotape you didn't know existed that shows your client shooting a kneeling victim in the head, and all of a sudden your claim of self-defense has a gaping hole in it.

The prosecution, because it works for the state, has ready access to everything the police have, and that's a fairly telling advantage. The law recognizes that advantage and offsets it by allowing the defense great latitude in learning what the prosecution knows. The prosecution actually has to provide advance notification to the defense of every witness and piece of evidence it intends to produce in court.

There was a time when the courts were so libertarian that defense attorneys had nearly a one-way street. In other words, the prosecutor had to empty the contents of his briefcase, whereas defense counsels only had to share limited knowledge with the prosecutor. Those were the good old days to be a defense attorney. That was before Ronald Reagan and George Bush reigned for twelve straight years and the Supreme Court got a strong injection of conservative steroids.

These days, the exchange of notification and shared evidence is nearly equal. The whole idea is to keep either side from monopolizing critical knowledge and unfairly bushwhacking the other in the courtroom.

All this is by way of explaining why Eddie submitted a motion to Carruthers about me. Like I've said several times, when it comes to matters of the law, Eddie has few equals.

The gist of the matter was that Eddie demanded to know my role in the disappearance of his two key witnesses. He somehow found out I'd been beaten while under their custody, and he wanted to know if I'd pursued a vendetta against them. What he was suggesting was that I might've crossed over the line of serving as a defense counsel and become personally implicated in the case.

The law has some fairly quirky rules about the relationship of attorneys to anybody else in a courtroom. Say, for example, either counsel is married to, or sleeping with, the judge, or the jury chairman, then somebody's expected to recuse themselves. Those are ludicrously self-evident examples, but there are many others that are more slithery. For example, if a defense attorney becomes privy to knowledge about key opposition witnesses by working with a government investigatory agency, that also might imply a need for recusal or disqualification.

Eddie had no direct knowledge about my activities except his gut instinct, but in this case his washboard tummy was reliable. So he fired a well-placed shot in the dark.

How did I learn this? Because there was a big red sticker pasted on the door to my hotel room when I got back. The handwriting was Katherine's. It said, "My room! Immediately!!"

Her chilling reception spoke volumes. She opened the door, fixed me with a frosty frown, tossed Eddie's motion in my face, then spun around and walked over to a chair by the window. She fell into it and waited.

I read it. His suspicions were vague, and some of the details were salaciously off base, but Eddie's query was inclusive enough that I was in big trouble. In a nutshell, he wanted to know if I was in any way involved in the flight of his two key witnesses. That was broad. That was too broad to wiggle out of.

The truth was I'd probably crossed some line. I hadn't meant to. I'd been unintentionally drawn much deeper into the CIA's counterespionage activities than I'd expected, and along the way, I'd become a player.

"Well?" Katherine asked, once I'd digested the motion.

"Well, well," I evasively replied. I could feel my face redden. I hoped my bruises and scabs kept it hidden.

The room got colder. "Do we have a problem here?"

"We could," I admitted.

"Tell me about it," she demanded. She had the right to know.

But I couldn't sate her highly warranted curiosity. Everything involved in the Bales-Choi case was classified. If I told her a word and suddenly journalists started showing up on Mercer's doorstep, I'd be looking at prison time.

I said, "I can't."

She looked quite angry. "The hell you can't, Drummond. You're my co-counsel. You work for me on this case. I have every right to know what you've been doing."

"All the more reason I can't. If I share my knowledge with you, I'll infect you. You'll be just as much at risk as I am of being disqualified."

That wasn't what she wanted to hear, but it was true. If I informed her what I'd learned about Bales and Choi by working with the CIA and the KCIA, she'd share in the fruits of my efforts.

Right now, everybody on the defense team partook of the common suspicion that the Itaewon precinct was rotten. They also shared the unproven conjecture that Choi and Bales were fixing cases and framing our client. Their motive, though, was still a mystery. Maybe it was anti-Americanism, like I'd suggested in one strategy review. Maybe it was antigay hysteria, like Allie had suggested. Maybe they were taking money or trying to drive up their conviction rates. Maybe they were just a couple of homicidal, sadistic maniacs out to create havoc and have a good time.

I was the only one who knew their real motive, and that put me in a box. I couldn't disclose that motive in court, and with Eddie's motion I couldn't even hint at it to Katherine without subjecting her to the same risk of disqualification.

But like I already said, that wasn't what she wanted to hear.

"Are you admitting involvement in implicating activities?"

"I'm not admitting anything."

We traded cold fish eyes for a long-drawn-out moment.

Then Katherine stiffly said, "We have an appointment to meet with Carruthers and Golden in one hour."

And I said, "Forget about it. I'll have a private conversation with Carruthers. One way or another I'll get it resolved."

"Be that as it may. Do I need to prepare a consent for substitution of counsel?"

"It's probably not a bad idea," I was unhappily forced to admit.

I awkwardly continued. "There's one or two really good lawyers here on the peninsula. I know a guy down in Pusan. He's a crackerjack. You'd like him. If you want, I'll make some calls, see if he's free."

While I was still babbling, she stood up and walked over to her desk. She turned her back on me and picked up some papers that she started to read through. "Call me with the name by three this afternoon so I can submit the consent before close of business. Now, please leave."

I was being summarily dismissed.

I didn't move, while she tried to pretend I was already gone. I knew she was mad about this legal thing, but I'm not a completely clueless oaf. That phone call to my room early that morning was butting its ugly head into this.

But just like this legal imbroglio, I couldn't admit my real relationship with Carol Kim. I couldn't very well say, "Hey look, she was a CIA agent and the two of us were busy breaking up the biggest spy ring in our country's history." Even if she believed me, Mercer would have my balls.

What I should've done was let it drop. I should've sneaked out with my tail between my legs. But for some funny reason, I didn't want to.

I shuffled my feet and coughed. "Hey, about this morning . . ."

At first she didn't answer, like she hadn't heard me speak.

Not until it was apparent I wasn't just going to slink away did she murmur, "What about this morning?"

"You called my room around five."

"Did I?" she asked, motionless.

"It wasn't what you think."

She still had her back turned and was reading through her papers. "I didn't think anything. I don't even remember calling."

"Come on. I was in the shower. A woman answered," I filled in the blanks, unnecessarily of course. But a hurt woman can play games, and you just have to march along with the flow. That's a primary rule of life.

"Umhumm," she mumbled, her voice rising on that "humm" part, like, How could it possibly have been anything different from what she thought?

"Katherine, the woman was a business colleague. It was a uh, a business meeting."

Her back was still turned, and I'm a perceptive guy, so I took that as a poor harbinger. Maybe I should've explained this some other way. That "business" word was the type of adjective that can be open to nasty misinterpretation. After all, what kind of business is conducted in a hotel room at five in the morning?

I said, "Sure, it sounds a little odd that I was taking a shower with a woman in my room. I can see where you might get the wrong impression. But I'd been up all night. I needed a shower."

"Get out," she mumbled.

That being "up all night" phrase, I suddenly realized, was another ambiguous choice on my part. Maybe I should have specified I was *awake* all night. Maybe I shouldn't have said anything.

"Look, I, uh—"

She spun around and pointed her tiny hand at the door. "I said get out. I mean get out."

Her face had icicles hanging off it.

I left.

And I did the only other thing I could. I walked to the judge's office. I told his long-nosed secretary I needed to see him in private, and she haughtily ordered me to sit and wait. So I sat and waited.

Finally she pushed her snooty nose in the air and told me to go in.

The office was dark again and I wondered if that had anything to do with his moods. You know, like bright on a cheery day; dark when he was in the mood to kill somebody.

I stuck my head in and said, "Good morning, Your Honor. I need to have a private word with you."

He said, "Come in and have a seat."

I fell into the chair across from his desk, and a huge explosion of air escaped from my lungs. If you think I was nervous, you're right. Confessing in a dark, screened-off booth to a faceless Catholic priest whose job it is to forgive you, well, that's one thing. Confessing to the hanging judge, eye-to-eye, in the privacy of his chambers, that's another damned thing altogether. I was reminded of that old drill sergeant's warning that God doesn't get to exact his punishments till the Army's done with you.

He examined my face. "Drummond, you look even worse than you did yesterday. You've got to stop burning the candle at both ends. Get some sleep, boy."

I was beginning to get tired of everybody I saw these days telling me I looked like crap. It can start to wear on you.

Anyway, I said, "I think I've got a problem. Carlson gave me a copy of Golden's motion."

He held up a big, beefy hand. "We shouldn't be discussing this without the two lead attorneys present. The motion has been filed."

I gave him a pinched grin. "I know all that. Can we have another of those mano-to-mano chats?"

He leaned back into his big chair, and I'd like to say he looked receptive, or at least amused. He didn't.

So I launched in anyway. "I'm talking theoretically here. Suppose you had an attorney involved in a criminal case. Then all of a sudden, it started to look like an espionage case. Suppose that attorney was approached by a very secret American agency and asked to share some knowledge. Is that crossing a boundary?"

His expression began to change. He leaned forward in his chair and the lines on his face deepened. All the lines—the ones on his forehead, around his lips, even the ones next to his ears.

"The sharing of knowledge of itself does not violate any legal ethics. As long as you don't breach attorney-client privilege."

"Nope, no breaches in that regard. But say things got a little deeper. Say people start getting murdered. The lawyer decides he has to do more than merely provide information."

"If he can help stop the killings, he has a moral imperative to do that. He has to help."

"Yes, but before he knows it, he's helping that secret government agency hunt down spies. And it happens that two of those spies are actually key government witnesses."

To say I had Carruthers's attention would be an understatement. His head was canted at an odd angle like he was experiencing difficulty breathing.

"Bales and Choi?" he asked.

"Please, Your Honor," I reminded him. "We're only talking theories right now."

"Okay. Theoretically, that could pose serious problems. How much did this attorney learn in the course of this effort?"

I inadvertently sighed. "He learned a lot. He learned that the two witnesses were at the center of a massive spy ring. He even helped chase them off."

"So he learned things relevant to the case?"

"A great deal. He developed a reasonable theory that his client was framed by this spy ring. The problem is, even if he could prove it—which he can't—he still can't introduce anything into direct evidence. This is all still theoretical, of course, but that secret government agency warned him there's a lid on all information."

Carruthers was shaking his big head back and forth and rolling his eyes. "Has this mythical attorney shared any of this knowledge with his co-counsels? Any at all?"

"No sir. There have been firewalls. Because the attorney was involved in classified matters, and his co-counsels are all civilians, he's kept them completely in the dark."

"Holy shit," Carruthers said. And frankly, I couldn't have said it better myself.

"Anyway," I continued, "the prosecutor has now submitted a motion for discovery that would force our mythical counselor to admit he gained pertinent knowledge by working with a key government agency. It's obviously knowledge he can't share with the prosecution."

Carruthers snorted once or twice, pushed himself up from the chair, fell back down, then ran his stubby fingers across his eyes and forehead. He stared at his desk a long time. I stared at the floor and didn't say anything, either. I'd said enough already.

He finally concluded, "Our theoretical attorney must recuse himself."

"The problem with that," I said, "is that it would severely penalize his client. The law is intended to be fair, and it would be criminally unfair."

"Be that as it may, our attorney has relevant knowledge unfairly gained. If, through remarkable willpower, he did not employ that knowledge in court, the effect would be the same as though he had recused himself. He would still be denying his client the value of what he'd learned."

"True," I admitted.

"And if he did exploit that knowledge—if I even suspected he was exploiting that knowledge—I would have to declare a mistrial and seek to have him disbarred."

I miserably said, "I'll have my letter on your desk before noon."

"Good. That would be the proper thing to do. And I am hereby announcing a judge's restraining order that under no conditions are you to have any further contact with Miss Carlson and her team. If I find out you've been within a hundred yards of each other, I'll be forced to declare a mistrial, and I'll personally appoint the new counsel for Whitehall. Is that clear?"

I said, "Yes, Your Honor. Could you please notify Carlson?"

He nodded.

"And can you tell her I recommend Captain Kip Goins as my substitute?"

I stood up and started to make my way to the door.

"Drummond," Carruthers said.

I looked over my shoulder. "Yes sir."

"I'm sorry it turned out this way. I truly am. I was actually looking forward to having you in my court. I don't know why, but I had the sense it was going to be very entertaining."

"Well, some other day, maybe."

He nodded and I left. I couldn't remember feeling more downtrodden or frustrated. I had a client I knew was innocent, a co-counsel whose affection and trust I'd lost, and I'd just spent two of the hardest, most painful weeks of my life for nothing.

CHAPTER
43
★ ★ ★

It took three minutes to type the letter. All it said was "I, Major Sean Drummond, request to be recused from the case of Captain Thomas Whitehall."

Nothing dramatic or elegant because, frankly, the law frowns on anything that smacks of passion or lavishness. I scrawled my signature at the bottom, and then called Imelda and had her send up one of her assistants to deliver it. The moment she was gone, I fell into bed.

It's amazing how quickly I was out. You'd think I'd roil around on the sheets and agonize over my situation, but I was too exhausted. I was in a coma about thirty seconds after my head hit the pillow. And I slept like a log.

At least, until the phone rang. This was at 6:00 P.M., maybe seven hours after I went out. I lifted it up and heard the voice of Major General Clapper, the chief of the JAG Corps.

"Drummond, that you?" he asked.

"Hello, General, it's me," I replied, of course recognizing his voice.

"I just got word that you were recused."

"Uh . . . yeah," I mumbled, still hazy.

"Do you want to tell me about it?"

"No, General. It'll have to wait till I get back to Washington. That or we'll have to talk on a secure line."

"Okay, we'll wait. When can you get back here?"

"As soon as you tell me to be there, although a day or two of grace would be sorely appreciated. I, uh, I got a little beat-up, and shot, too, and I haven't gotten much sleep the past four or five days."

He said, "Hell, it's Friday anyway. Can you be out of there Sunday night?"

"I'll make the reservation tonight."

There was a long pause, then, "Sean?"

"Yes sir?"

"I got a long message about you from General Spears."

This was the last thing I needed. On top of everything, now the theater commander was sending hate mail to my boss. I saw what was left of my career flash by. Let me tell you, it was a very brief flash.

Clapper said, "He said you performed brilliantly, and that the nation owes you a huge debt. I don't know what you did out there, but you should feel proud."

If I could only have gotten my breath back, I'd have said, "Ah shucks, it was nothing, really."

But Clapper didn't wait to hear anything. He said he'd see me Monday in his office and hung up.

I got up and called room service and told them send up a rare steak, some potatoes, and a bottle of wine. I couldn't remember the last time I'd treated myself to an evening of quiet relaxation, and in my wallowing self-pity, I was convinced I deserved it.

I took a long, hot shower and shaved, and when I walked out, the room service kid was knocking on the door. I took my tray, paid him, and settled down in front of the TV set.

I flipped it on, ate, watched CNN spill through its thirty-minute roundup, watched it do its thirty-minute roundup again, and realized that nothing dramatic had changed in the world in the past hour. For want of anything else to watch, I flipped to a Korean channel.

It can be fun watching a foreign newscaster move his or her lips even when you don't have a clue what they're saying. You stare at the picture that flashes up behind them, or at the short news clip, and you try to imagine the narration. It's like buying cartoons with all the pictures, only there are no captions inside the bubbles. You get to invent those yourself.

First I watched a story that showed a bunch of babies stuffed in cribs in a big room that was probably an orphanage. In all likelihood the real story was some scandal about mistreated, neglected orphans, but I wasn't in the mood for that.

I imagined the newscaster saying, "Today Bill Gates, the American capitalist, announced he is giving an inheritance of one billion dollars to each of these babies. The line of people who've rushed to the doors of the orphanage to seek a child to adopt stretches all the way to China. The airports and seaports are crowded with more prospective parents coming from around the world to get their child."

That's a nice story with a happy ending, right?

Next came a news clip of a bunch of gloomy-looking striking workers wearing white masks over their faces, all sitting down in front of a big, thirty-chimneyed plant. Then it cut to an attractive young female reporter holding a microphone in front of her mouth.

This one? Probably she was talking about how these workers were struggling to get a dollar-an-hour increase so they could feed their families, and the plant executives were bringing in cops and scabs to teach them a lesson.

That just wouldn't do. I imagined her saying, "The chairman of Lipto Motors today agreed with his striking workers that it was shameful he should be making two hundred million dollars a year. He therefore offered to take all his personal wealth, as well as that of all other company executives, and place it in a large pool to be distributed among the workers who actually make the cars."

I'm not a socialist, but I liked that ending.

The next clip was live, and it showed the American Secretary of State walking from a big black car with two U.S. flags flying off the front, through two lines of South Korean soldiers in spanky-looking dress uniforms, and into the side entrance of the South Korean Blue House, which, if you don't know, is their version of the American White House. And right next to the man himself was my old buddy Arthur Brandewaite, chatting him up and trying to look natty and consequential for the cameras.

The newscaster started moving his lips, only I wasn't paying attention. I hadn't realized the Secretary of State was still here. I thought he'd done the normal butterfly routine of flying in for consultations, then a news conference or two, then off to the next trouble spot. I mean, how long can big diplomats yammer on about some court case or even a massacre? Don't they run out of things to say? Plus, if you stay in one place for a day or two, pretty soon there's gonna be a disaster somewhere else in the world that completely eclipses this one, and off you go.

Next flashed up a picture of an American naval officer with four gold captain's stripes on his sleeve. There were some Hangul stick figures underneath his picture, probably the dates of his life. I surmised this was Harry Elmore and the media had been fed some phony story about his death, like maybe he was slain in a burglary gone wrong. Harry wasn't a bad-looking guy. The photo was recent because of his captain's stripes. There he was, sincere-looking blue eyes, a strong chin, a mouth that looked like it used to smile a lot.

Who would've thought? The poor bastard didn't even have an important job. Why would Choi be interested in him? A protocol officer? I'm an expert on the American military, and until Spears mentioned that Elmore sometimes snuck into important briefings, I never would've imagined he had access to anything the least bit sensitive or important. Hell, Spears himself didn't picture it until he was forced to think about it.

How did Choi know? Did Bales tell him? How in the hell could some lowly warrant officer who worked in CID know that angle, when even Elmore's own four-star boss didn't appreciate how much access his man had?

That's when it hit me. It was the one thing we'd overlooked.

I leaned over and dialed the number Buzz Mercer gave me so I wouldn't have to go through General Spears's henchman anymore.

Mercer's droll voice answered, "Yes?"

"It's me, Drummond. I need to see you right away."

I could hear him sigh. "Drummond, it's late and I'm exhausted. Can't it wait?"

I said, "Yeah, sure, I guess it could. If you're willing to let Choi and his goons kill the Secretary of State right here in your backyard."

CHAPTER
44
⭐ ⭐ ⭐

The problem was, we didn't know who or what we were looking for. We didn't really even know if he, or she, or they, would be there. Worse, I was the only one even remotely confident anybody would be there.

I think Mercer and Carol Kim were simply humoring me because I'd been so forceful and insistent. Or maybe they figured I'd been right on too many other things to ignore. When your horse wins the first two of the trifecta, you have a tendency to bet on it again.

So there we were with five of Buzz's spook buddies, wandering through the crowd outside the Blue House, trying hopelessly to see if we could detect anybody who didn't look like he or she should be there.

The problem was that *nobody* looked like they should be there. Or *everybody* looked like they should be there. Take your pick.

Some of them were Korean government bureaucrats who were there because the Korean president's staff ordered them to come and make the Secretary of State feel like he was so damned popular people would stay out on the streets late at night to catch sight of him. And there were gazillions of reporters. Since the Whitehall trial was postponed, most of them were there to convince their networks or newspapers or magazines they were still finding honest ways to earn their pay. Then there were the genuinely curious idiots whose lives were so dull they'd go anywhere and wait forever to catch a fleeting glimpse of a real-life celebrity.

One of those curious idiots was about six foot three and had spiky hair, which you couldn't miss because she towered over most of the crowd. I was surprised to see Allie mixed in with the rest of them, because she'd never struck me as the stargazing type. Maybe she'd just been passing by and decided to see what the commotion was about.

The Secretary of State was inside having dinner with the president of South Korea because the Secretary was scheduled to depart Korea the next morning. According to what Buzz had found out, they were supposed to finish their dinner at 9:15, then the Secretary of State was supposed to be driven by motorcade to the house of Minister of Defense Lee Jung Kim. There he would express condolences and apologies on behalf of the President of the United States, and all the American people, over the tragic death of Lee's son.

None of this was particularly difficult information to come by, since his final day's schedule had been published in the South Korean newspapers. See, the Secretary of State wanted the South Korean people to know what he was doing. He wanted cameras and newspeople cluttered at his every stop. He wanted the world to see the third highest official in the executive branch dining amicably with the South Korean president on his final day, as though a serious breach in relations had been miraculously healed. He wanted the South Korean people to see him make the very Asian gesture of stopping by to apologize and pay respects to the bereaved mother and father.

The only problem was that when he and his security detail had planned and publicized that schedule, they were unaware the alliance's protocol officer was owned by North Korea.

That, I'd finally concluded, was why Choi wanted Harry Elmore in his stable. Elmore had access to the plans that involved VIP visits. He knew what the security arrangements were. He was one of the two or three guys who controlled access to VIPs. His office printed the passes, and took the requests, and decided who would and who wouldn't get within spitting distance of the high and mighty. Even if the event was controlled by the State Department, all Harry had to do was call his counterpart, the protocol officer at the embassy, and tell him he needed two dozen passes. I'm sure they talked all the time. They probably horse-traded back and forth like Belgian gem merchants.

"Hey, Harry, I hear the Dallas Cowboys Cheerleaders are coming over for a military morale visit. Think you could slide me thirty tickets under the table?" "Hey, no problem, Bill, but listen, I've got twenty Korean buddies climbing all over my ass because they want to be seen in the proximity of the American Secretary of State. How about passes for that?"

Buzz had several guys sitting in a room right now combing over the lists of those who'd gotten passes to be inside the ropes. We knew it was hopeless. Whoever Choi sent to do the dirty deed would either use a false name or a name we wouldn't recognize anyway.

Thus, we were reduced to what we were doing. Mercer had one of his guys inform the head of the Secretary's security detail what we suspected, and the rest of us were combing through the crowd, looking for familiar faces or suspicious activities.

Part of the problem was these were North Koreans we were talking about. The same guys who walk around with poison pellets hidden in their teeth. Professional security people will tell you that any assassin willing to end his or her own life has something like a 90 percent chance of success. It's generally true, too. Remember Lincoln's assassination? President Garfield's? Bobby Kennedy's? John Lennon's? Those all involved assassins crazy or willing enough to get close, to trade their chances of escape and survival to get their target.

Anyway, we finally ran into Carol and found a spot where we could overwatch the crowd and put our heads together.

Carol's eyes roamed the crowd. "I'm bothered by something."

"What?" her boss asked.

"Why would the North Koreans kill the American Secretary of State?"

I said, "Good question. Why would they?"

Mercer said, "Yeah. It would be too stupid for words. Even if it didn't cause a war, we'd never pull another soldier off Korean soil until North Korea was a distant memory. That's the last thing they'd want."

Sometimes, even when you're not trying, you come to a moment of truth. It just hits you in the face.

The assassin or assassins would have to be somebody you'd never connect to North Korea. But if a South Korean murdered the Secretary of State, the alliance really would be a trashheap.

And wouldn't you know, just at that moment a large crowd of protesters came streaming around a street corner, headed our way. They were yelling and hollering and moving fast. They were carrying banners, and most of them were wearing white medical masks the way a lot of Asians do to protect their lungs from smog, or to screen their faces from being ID'ed by cops when they're ready to rumble.

It was ten after nine. The dinner was supposed to be over in five minutes. The protesters had obviously planned their arrival to coincide with the Secretary of State's departure from the Blue House. They wanted all those television cameras and reporters to see that the symbolic, everything's-been-healed meal was a farce, that the South Korean people were still furiously angry over the death of Lee No Tae and wanted the lawless American troops off their soil.

On the other hand, it was a known fact that North Korean agents and sympathizers had thoroughly penetrated South Korea's student and labor movements and could spark a protest or riot pretty much at will.

I looked at Buzz Mercer and he looked at me, and we exchanged a telepathic aw-shit. Somewhere in that crowd of protesters were probably one or two people with passes to get past the police lines.

CHAPTER
45
⭐ ⭐ ⭐

The Secretary of State chose that moment to stride purposefully out the entrance of the Blue House and begin walking between the ceremonial files of soldiers toward his car.

Whoever planned this thing had an exquisite sense of timing, not to mention a thorough knowledge of South Korean crowd-control methods. Because there'd been no application to the city authorities for this protest, only a small contingent of blue-suited crowd-control troops were on hand.

A platoon, thirty or so men, was loitering by a gray bus. They weren't expecting trouble, so they didn't have on their riot gear. Most were hunched over small stoves, cooking rice or noodles and preparing to eat.

Maybe ten uniformed policemen were present—a token force—because the folks crowded around the Blue House were all supposed to be friendly. Then there was the honor guard whose job it was to make a snazzy cordon for the Secretary of State to pass through on his way to the car. They had rifles, but it was doubtful those had ammunition.

The thing that became instantly apparent was that nobody had planned for this. There was no central, controlling authority capable of organizing an orderly response to the unfolding situation. I could see the leader of the blue-suited troops screaming at his men to get their riot gear on and get in line, even as he was yelling into a radio, probably calling for reinforcements. It was a hopeless gesture. Nobody could get here in time.

The army guard did what ceremonial troops normally do. They stayed stiffly in their cordon and held their rifles at the salute position for the distinguished man walking between them.

Suddenly the crowd of rioters lunged forward and began running pell-mell down the block toward the Blue House. They hurtled straight into the crowd of peaceful gatherers and reporters, shoving people aside and carrying others along with their speed and mass. They were yelling and screaming and waving their placards and protest signs in the air. At the same instant, the small group of kids in blue suits rushed out to meet them. They carried their helmets and shields and batons in their hands, in a breathtakingly valiant effort to throw themselves between the crowd and the diplomatic party.

The Secretary's security detail had a split second to decide. They could turn the Secretary around and shove him back inside the Blue House. Or they could push him forward, toward the bulletproof black sedan waiting at the curb. The car door was being held open by a South Korean soldier. The car was closer.

It did look like the best choice at the time. They literally lifted him off his feet, and began carrying him forward, when suddenly the natty-looking soldier holding the car door flew forward and the door slammed shut. The soldier lay flat on the ground, like he'd been nailed on the back of the skull with a blackjack, or, considering this was Asia, a nunchaku.

At moments like this, a fraction of a second means everything. And I'll give the Secretary's security guys credit. They instantly threw him on the ground and two of them piled themselves on top of him, while the other two drew their pistols and turned about and faced the crowd. They instinctively recognized the situation was out of control, and we had warned them there was a grave risk, so they weren't taking any chances.

Buzz Mercer and I were running toward the Secretary of State when we heard the first loud bang, even over the noise of the crowd, and one of the Secretary's security men flew backward with a big spray of blood spewing from his head. Then *Bang!* The other standing security guard grabbed his gut, sank to his knees, and fell over.

Then *Bang! Bang! Bang!*—three more shots were fired. But by this time, Carol and I were there. So were seven or eight South Korean uniformed policemen with their pistols drawn.

You sometimes wonder about the difference two seconds would make. Or what would've happened if Clapper hadn't called and woken me up. Or if I hadn't been so bored that I'd been channel-surfing through Korean newscasts. Things would've turned out quite differently, because I was probably the only guy in the crowd who would've recognized him and the threat he posed.

He was holding up his police shield and pointing his pistol, and you could've sworn he had every right to be there, that he was just doing his job. He even had the proper security pass pinned to his lapel.

Choi Lee Min, experienced policeman that he was, blended right in with the other cops.

I ended up right next to him. I looked at him, and he turned his head and saw me, and there was one of those shocked milliseconds that seem to last forever.

Then he spun his body to shoot me, and despite all those years of hand-to-hand training I'd had in the outfit, I knew in that instant I didn't stand a chance. I saw the pistol aimed at my stomach and I instinctively knew that no matter how fast I moved, it wouldn't be fast enough.

But before he could pull the trigger a hand crashed down on his forearm and knocked the weapon loose. It landed on the cement at his feet and we both turned to see who'd smacked him. Allie stood right next to him, glaring at his face.

Choi's eyes turned to the ground; just as he started to bend over to retrieve his pistol, Allie threw her stiffened fingers straight into his throat. An explosion of pain must have raced through his synapses. She'd hit him hard. She'd meant to. She'd driven his Adam's apple right into his larynx, like a nail jabbed into a balloon.

His head drove forward and a sickening gurgling, choking sound came from his mouth. He buckled to his knees and his hands flew to his throat, trying to get some air into his lungs.

I threw myself down on the ground and scrambled around for his pistol. In one way, that proved to be the right thing to do. But in another way, it wasn't.

Because here's what happened: I looked up just in time to see a Korean rioter pushing his way through the crowd. In his hand I saw a black metal ball that an experienced soldier like me would recognize immediately as a hand grenade.

He was so close that even with my awful marksmanship I couldn't miss. I didn't even think. I just picked up the pistol and shot him. Right in the forehead. And since I was firing up from the ground, the bullet lifted him off his feet and sent him flying backward.

Then there were two loud booms. The first was not nearly as noisy as the second. In fact, it was hardly more than a quick pop. I mean, it sounded loud to me, but that first one was only a pistol shot. The second boom was the one that got everybody's attention. It was so loud it was deafening. That was the hand grenade going off in the middle of the crowd.

Here's what they figured out later. Choi had gotten his security pass from Harry Elmore. He'd used that pass to get past the barriers and blend in with the other Korean cops. None of the other cops remembered him being there throughout the evening, so he probably hadn't risked showing his face until right before the assassination was supposed to go down. He was there to run interference and see that everything went down right.

It was probably Choi who used his pistol butt to clobber the Korean soldier at the Secretary of State's car door, and then slam the door closed in front of him.

The protester was armed with a grenade because that was the weapon of choice for their plan. Say Choi hadn't been able to get the car door slammed in the Secretary's face, then he would've been shoved into the backseat by his guards. But the car wasn't going anywhere, because protesters were cluttered in front of it, and even an American Secretary of State, oddly enough, isn't allowed to run over a dozen or so foreigners inside their own country. Therefore his car would've been stranded by the curb and the protester would've flung the armed hand grenade underneath it. Now, here's a fact: Bulletproof cars aren't invulnerable to large explosions on their undersides. That's where the gas tank is located. Also, the undersides of those behemoths don't have all that thick armor plating. There would likely have been a huge explosion.

But Choi did get the car door closed. So he prepared the way for the second contingency. The Secretary's security detail, if they ever saw Choi, assumed he was on their side. He was holding up his police shield as he shot the security guards and cleared the way for the kid with the grenade to jump on top of the Secretary and blow them both to pieces. Ballistic tests proved that the bullets that killed three of the Secretary's security detail came from Choi's pistol.

As it was, the suicide bomber killed another four people and wounded nine more. It was lucky for the Secretary that I'd fired my shot up from the ground, because that sent the bomber flying backward into the crowd and made the grenade roll backward out of his hand, so some other hapless souls ended up absorbing the explosion and shrapnel meant for him.

As for the suicide bomber, he was a senior at Kwangju University about 120 miles south of Seoul. He was as South Korean as they come. He was born and raised in the city of Kwangju, the capital city of a South Korean province that was known as a virulent hotbed of antigovernment and anti-American sentiments. Twenty-two years before, his father, as well as many other citizens of Kwangju, had been killed by South Korean troops who were brutally suppressing a huge revolt in the city. Korean lore had it that the troops who went into the city to suppress the revolt were there at the behest and encouragement of the American military command. It wasn't true, because they had actually been sent in by an angry, ambitious military dictator, who afterward distorted the facts to deflect the blame away from himself. But the myth persisted. The kid had been very active in campus antigovernment groups. He was known around the school as a hothead and a fanatical anti-American.

He was the perfect cutout. Which was exactly why Choi picked him. Had he killed the Secretary of State, and had Choi simply vanished back into the crowd and made his escape, it would've looked like a South Korean extremist had assassinated a key American government official right on the steps of South Korea's presidential palace.

The kid had probably never met Choi. He probably never even knew he was working for the North Koreans. Most likely he was recruited by someone in the campus movement, was told what to do, was provided with the hand grenade, and his hatred drove him on from there. On the outside chance he survived to be interrogated, the world still would've been convinced the Secretary of State was murdered by an angry South Korean. And it would've been true.

And Lord knows what would have happened to the already egregiously wounded alliance after that.

As for Choi, he never made his getaway. He choked to death right where Allie chopped him. You think about life and its many coincidences. Allie's being at the Blue House, and her having the presence of mind to rush to the point of confrontation, knock the gun away, and kill Choi, was simply amazing. It was what you might call an act of God, to let Allie be his hand of retribution. They found Choi there when they were cleaning up the bodies, his eyes bulging out of their sockets, blood still dribbling out of his throat onto the cement. I had no regrets about that.

What I had regrets about was the South Korean cop who saw me pick up a pistol and shoot someone. That was that first popping sound I told you about. That was the bullet that entered my back next to my lower spine and pinned me to the concrete like a grounded fish.

That was the one that turned out the lights inside my head.

CHAPTER
46
★ ★ ★

See if you can guess the first face I saw when I came to?

It was déjà vu all over again, as they say. Doc Bridges and I were right back where we were the last time I saw him. I was flat on my back in a hospital bed, inside the same room even, and he was standing beside the bed taking my pulse and making some notes on a clipboard. I'll bet it was even the same clipboard.

I said something like, "Oh Christ," and he chuckled.

Then he said, "Hey, you're a hero again."

He held a newspaper in front of my face. It was the *Herald Tribune*. The boldface title line was "The Unlucky Hero."

Some cynical reporter had gotten a real gas out of the fact that the guy who saved the life of the Secretary of State, and maybe the whole alliance, was shot by a Korean cop for his troubles.

Where was the outrage?, I asked myself.

Doc Bridges took the newspaper away, then held a finger in front of my eyes and we did the "follow this with your pupils" routine again.

In a very clinical tone, he said, "The bullet passed within millimeters of your spine. You're lucky."

"How lucky?"

He was reading something off a chart. "It missed your spine, didn't it?"

"I guess."

"I could see you've been shot before, so you know the drill. You'll be in a wheelchair for a while, then you'll use a cane. But after some physical therapy, you'll be almost normal."

I suppose I should've been relieved, but if you've ever spent any time in physical therapy, you know that's not something you eagerly anticipate. And Army hospitals are to physical therapy what Nazi death camps were to racial harmony in Europe.

I groaned. "*Almost* normal? What's that mean?"

He chuckled to himself. "You weren't exactly normal in the first place. I'm not a miracle worker. Don't expect me to turn out improved products."

This is another of those old jokes doctors find funny. No wonder the hospital staff kept this guy hidden at the rear of the hospital, as far from humanity as they could get him.

He put the clipboard on its hook and said, "There's another lady who's been waiting outside for you. In fact, she's the one who made me come in here and wake you up. I tried telling her you need your rest, and she said she knew what you needed better than I do."

"What's she look like?" I asked.

He shrugged.

"What's that mean?" I asked.

"She's been giving me hell since you got here. She told me if I lost you, she'd break my neck. She meant it, too. Very frightening."

He spun around and walked out. A moment later the door slammed back open and in stomped the living typhoon herself: the one and only Imelda Pepperfield.

She looked at me, then huffed and puffed a couple of times.

I said, "You know you're not supposed to be here?"

"'Course I know that."

I tried to frown, but I smiled.

"It hurt?" she asked.

"Not a bit," I candidly admitted. "I think I've got enough drugs pumping through my veins, you could reach over and rip off one of my arms and I wouldn't feel a thing."

She nodded a few times, then she said, "You done damned good, Major."

Now, if you know anything about Imelda Pepperfield, you know praise coming from her lips is like water pouring from a rock. In other words, it don't happen often. And when it does, don't act shy or aw-shucksy. Relish the moment.

I was beaming like a little idiot, and she actually reached over and patted me on the head. I was like a cat getting its back stroked by a proud master.

She scooched her butt onto the side of my bed. "You been re-cused," she said, confirming what I already knew.

"There were some conflicts," I replied, obviously unable to ex-plain what had really happened, even to Imelda. She, unlike me, was still a member of Katherine's staff, so I couldn't risk compro-mising her.

"Trial starts tomorrow," she told me.

"You mean today's Monday already?"

"Uh-huh. You were so drugged up, you slept through Saturday and Sunday."

I stared at the far wall, and whatever satisfaction I felt about being a hero and all that suddenly evaporated.

She said, "I went and visited with Cap'n Whitehall."

"Really?"

"Seems somebody got him addicted to hamburgers and beer, so he was havin' withdrawal."

Katherine had told her about that, I figured. I could just imag-ine Imelda with Whitehall's goonish keeper. She probably didn't even have to bribe him with a bottle of Johnnie Walker Blue. She probably told him that as long as he let her through with her con-traband, she'd promise not to rip his ears off.

Anyway, I said, "So what'd you think?"

She sucked in her lips and seemed to chew on them a moment. "That boy's got his mind set. He gets convicted, he's gonna find a way to kill hisself. He had that look in his eye. That's what I think."

"Yeah," I replied, since I'd already reached the same conclusion. One thing I'd learned about Whitehall was he was one of those people who, if they told you they were going to do something, they'd do it. I doubted he'd even wait for an appeals process.

I said, "So what do you think his chances are?"

"I wouldn't wanna be in his shoes. That Eddie Golden, he's ruthless."

"You know Fast Eddie?" I asked, surprised.

"Hadda work for him once or twice."

"You did? You've never mentioned it."

The Army has a small pool of senior legal specialists, and they rotate around depending on trial needs. It shouldn't come as any surprise that Imelda ended up on Eddie's team once or twice. No wonder she'd withdrawn into the corner when we questioned Jackson and Moran about whether they were beaten.

Her face got this distasteful look, which on Imelda, frankly, looked like somebody had poured acid down her throat.

"Wasn't anything I was proud of. He don't have scruples. Truth don't mean nothin' to him, just winnin'."

"Well, he's up against Katherine, and they don't get any better than her. Trust me. She's going to give Eddie a run for his money."

Imelda didn't respond to that.

So I said, "Did you get my substitute yet?"

"Cap'n Kip Goins. Got here yesterday mornin'. The judge arranged it."

"Kip's a good man. He's also done two murder trials, so he'll know what he's doing."

She didn't respond to that, either.

I thought I knew what might be going on. Imelda and I had been together a long time. After years of trying cases together, we'd developed a special bond. But there's more. Imelda was like a talisman to me. She was that rabbit's foot a paratrooper kisses just before he goes out the door.

I might be kidding myself here, but maybe Imelda was thinking of me the same way.

"Look, you'll get 'em through this. Don't let Golden pull any fast ones on Katherine. Keep her on her toes."

Imelda nodded, but I didn't get the impression she felt good about this.

Then Bridges stuck his head in and said I needed to get my beauty rest. Imelda jumped off the bed and made her way slowly and reluctantly toward the door. As soon as she was gone, I pushed the buzzer beside my bed, and a nurse who looked like she could bench five hundred pounds came rushing in.

I said, "I need a phone."

She started to argue, but I gave her a look that would sizzle steaks and reminded her I was a major in the United States Army. I told her I better see the back of her muscle-bound ass going out the door for a phone.

The second she got it hooked up, I dialed Buzz Mercer's number. For once he actually sounded happy to hear it was me. He'd better sound happy—damned happy. I'd saved his bacon.

I said, "I need you to come over here right away."

Well, what could he say to that? Gee, Drummond, old buddy, I know you nearly gave your life and saved the alliance and all, and you saved my career, but I've got some paperwork I'm behind on.

If he said anything but yes, I'd find some way to get out of that bed and go kill him.

Twenty minutes later there was a light knock, then his little butch-cutted head peeked inside.

I said, "Come in, please."

He wasn't alone. Carol was with him. They found two chairs over in the corner and pulled them up against my bed. Then Buzz reached over and shook my hand. Gently, of course, because there were several IVs sticking in my arm.

I said, "I'll bet your bosses back in Washington are tickled pink with you two."

Buzz grinned from ear to ear. "Let's just say I'm pretty sure I'll make it to retirement. And Carol here has been submitted for the Gold Medal."

That Gold Medal thing is the secret award they give to spooks when they do real good. Nobody in the public knows about it,

which if you think about it, doesn't make it much of an award. But
hey, spooks are a little different from the rest of us.

Also, although Buzz didn't mention it, it was a reasonable assumption that if his subordinate was getting a Gold Medal, well
then, he probably was, too. He was too much the fifties kind of guy
to mention it.

With gushing insincerity, I said, "Congratulations to you both.
You deserve whatever honors a proud nation can bestow upon
you."

Which was my backhanded way of reminding them they owed
me the world. They get the Gold Medal and I get a bullet in the
back.

Carol, the poor girl, was taking my phony praise seriously. She
was blushing and looking down at the ground with embarrassment. Not Buzz. Like I've already mentioned, he doesn't miss much.

"What can I do for you?" he asked, cutting through the bull.

Well, I always like a man who comes straight to the point. "I've
got a former client rotting in a Korean prison. He's innocent, only
there's no way on earth his lawyers are able to prove that."

Buzz ran a hand across those little bristles of hair on his head.
"Drummond, I already told you, I can't let any of this out."

"Why not? It's over, isn't it?"

"Over? We picked up four more traitors this morning."

"Four more?" I asked.

"That's right. And of the first eight, we've confirmed that six
were working for the North Koreans. Christ, we can't let this out
of the bag. Not now. It would be a disaster."

"Why? It'll have to get out eventually. It always does, Buzz. Why
not get it out in time to help an innocent man?"

He was stubbornly shaking his head. "First we've got to do a
damage assessment. That'll take weeks, maybe months. This was serious shit here, Drummond. These guys may have given away the
whole store. The command needs time to make changes to its war
plan, write a new aircraft targeting plan, shift some units around,
improve port and airfield security. You don't tell the bad guys you

know how much they know until you've made the right preparations. That's counterespionage 101."

I tried to rise up and lean toward him, but I suddenly discovered my overdrugged body was ignoring my central nervous system. Huffing and puffing with frustration, I said, "Look, damn it, can't we come to a reasonable accommodation here?"

"I'm willing to listen."

"What if we can handle this in a closed, classified hearing?"

"Can you do that?"

"It's up to the judge. Of course I'll have to tell him what it's about."

He stroked his chin. "Can he be trusted?"

"Of course."

"Would it make a difference?"

"I hope so. He can make rulings based on what we present. Of course, the prosecutor has to be present as well. It's unorthodox, I guess, but judges pull lawyers into chambers all the time to make off-line rulings on critical issues. And they're always privy to evidence the jury never sees."

I wasn't sure how Mercer was going to come down. He wasn't committing. He wasn't saying no. He was pondering.

I said, "So I'll bet you two end up going to the White House and getting a pat on the back from the man himself. Doesn't the CIA give monetary awards, too? I'll bet you get enough that you don't have to worry about making your rent payments for a few years. You probably have a house in McLean, right, Buzz? I mean, all you Agency guys like to build nests next to the big building, right? I'll bet it's killing you having to handle that mortgage while you're over—"

"God damn it, Drummond, all right. Enough already. We'll try it."

"One other thing?"

"What's that?"

"We're going to want to hear what Bales's wife told you when she broke. A videotaped testimony would be fine. Just make sure you've got a chain of evidence on it."

He looked at me from under his eyebrows. "Who said she broke?"

"Buzz, no offense to your professional competence, but how else did you find out there were four more traitors?"

He rolled his eyes. For a minute I could swear he actually liked me. But probably I was only kidding myself. Spooks don't have feelings.

CHAPTER
47

★ ★ ★

I felt deeply honored about the way it got set up. On Tuesday morning at eight, the trial kicked off as scheduled. The next two days, Katherine and Eddie fenced back and forth over board members. As voir dire processes go, it was one of the bloodiest skirmishes in military court history.

See, military law doesn't have the exact same challenge procedures as federal law, but close enough. As long as Katherine could show that a potential board member had an axe to grind against gays, she could get them disqualified. Eddie's job was harder, because you can't disqualify a member just because they *don't* have an axe to grind against gays. Eddie had to show they believed gays were a persecuted minority who deserved to be in the Army, whose lifestyle was perfectly normal, even admirable, who were vulnerable victims of military witch hunts and were often framed for crimes they didn't commit. It wasn't like a lot of Army people were going admit they felt that way.

As a result, the mayhem was done by Katherine. She was winnowing out the antigay bigots and seeking ten men or women who were either fair-minded or equivocal about homosexuality. The infantry guys on the board got massacred. She knocked off eight that I could count. Three female officers actually made the final list, which was considerably better than how I thought it would turn out. Females, as Imelda had observed, tend to be less judgmental on sexual issues—well, excepting bigamy or adultery. If you've got a client accused of either of those offenses, the last thing you want's a female jurist.

Katherine performed superbly.

How did I know this? Because for once the military opened the trial to the press. There were even TV cameras in the courtroom, and to the best of my knowledge that's unheard of in military trials. But given the rabid public interest in this case, and that all of Korea was interested in the outcome, a closed court would've been a disaster. To preserve the alliance, the Army had to discard its traditional cloaked process.

On the morning of the third day, Eddie got up and made his opening statement. The TV cameras were rolling and he was positively preening. This was the moment he had waited for all his life. He paced back and forth, spoke completely extemporaneously, and went on for exactly thirty minutes. He really did bear an uncanny resemblance to a youthful Robert Redford. And the camera picked that up.

I hated to, but I had to give him credit. He was brilliant. He was brief and he was passionate. He resisted the impulse to hog the limelight and I'm sure it killed him. He emphasized again and again the sheer, disgusting ugliness of the crime. He reminded everybody that the accused was a West Point graduate, an experienced officer, a man who had done his duties in every other way, but was a callous, brutal murderer nonetheless.

This was a sly preemptive strike on his part, since it was evident Katherine was going to emphasize that her client was a highly accomplished officer, with a prestigious professional pedigree, and thus was unlikely to have committed the lowly acts he was accused of.

Eddie had also somehow learned about Whitehall's boxing career. He spent a few moments dwelling on that theme as well, noting how the blows inflicted on Lee's body were described by the pathologist as particularly fierce and forceful, the kind that could be rendered only by a powerful, trained fighter.

Eddie kept subtly reminding the board of the homosexual nature of the crime, playing to whatever residue of subtle prejudice they possessed. He was masterful.

Then he reared up on his hind legs and outdid himself. He told the board and faces behind the TV cameras to put themselves in Lee No Tae's shoes. Imagine you're twenty-one years old, highly intelligent, handsome, the child of loving parents, a young man with a brilliant future ahead of you. Imagine you've just been invited by an American officer to his private quarters for a party. You feel honored, and you happily accept. You like Americans. You trust Americans and you look up to American officers. So you go. The Americans get drunk and you get the first inklings you've made a serious mistake. Then—Eddie paused for theatrical effect—then you're being held down, you're fighting and you're kicking and you're struggling, and the most horrifying things are being done to your body. Two of them restrain you, while the third exploits you. They're drunk and they're using you in the most vile ways to satisfy their unnatural lusts. You scream in pain, but they muffle you. You beg them to stop and they laugh. Then a belt is thrown around your neck, and you feel it tightening, and . . .

Eddie paused there. He gazed into the faces of the board. He affected a bottomless, soulful sadness. He stared down at the floor and shook his head, as though he couldn't go on, as though the necrophilia was too sickening, as though the revulsion and horror of it was simply too much. Then he bravely gulped and looked back up at the ten faces in the jury box. He placed his hands on the railing, worked up a courageously stern expression, leaned toward the board, and very quietly said, "You are American officers. You will know before this trial ends the terrible damage Thomas Whitehall has done to our profession, to our reputations, to our ashamed nation. Show the world . . . Show Lee No Tae's family . . . Show the people of South Korea that ours is a profession of honor. Wipe away the terrible stain that has occurred. Show that we know how to deal with the man seated at the defense table. Show the world . . . Well, you know what to show them. You know your duty."

Then he spun around and returned to the prosecution table, an angry, pouncing eagerness to his walk, as though he could not wait to expunge this blot from the reputation of his profession.

Frankly, to my eyes it was a bit overdone, and it was more of a closing argument than an opener, but that only showed how supremely confident Eddie was. He'd hit all the right notes. He'd never once mentioned Whitehall's rank, as though Tommy no longer deserved the honored appellation. He'd stressed how deeply Whitehall had shamed the profession of arms, because military officers are the most institutional creatures there are, and Eddie was stoking their furnaces, exhorting them to remember the disgrace Tommy had brought on them. Plus, the defense counsel was a civilian. He was trying to distance her from the board.

But if Eddie was good in front of a camera, Katherine was simply spectacular. You knew the instant you watched her approach the jury box that you were seeing the difference between a hometown player and a Broadway star. He just didn't have her experience or her instinctive gift for theatrics. Besides, Eddie was too proud of his own good looks. He moved like a peacock. Katherine moved like a graceful, gorgeous swan who'd never owned a mirror because she didn't need one. She stood perfectly still for a long, telling moment to allow the camera to focus just on her. And what the world saw was a petite, unadorned, plainly dressed woman with the face of an angel. My eyes were fixed on her face, and it suddenly struck me: She looked just like those statues of the Virgin Mary you see in churches. There was such a simple, essential purity to her that it actually made my heart ache.

Looking at her, the question you were forced to ask was, How could a woman such as this ever defend a murderer, a rapist, a defiler of corpses?

Then she began. And I could see immediately why OGMM employed her as their heavy hitter. She emitted a fierce energy in the court. She glowed with conviction. She wasn't shrill or wordy or choppy. Her words flowed, a human volcano emitting a stream of white-hot lava that gracefully curled down its slopes.

She spoke for two minutes, then she ordered the board to look at her client. Ten heads immediately turned. Even the cameras shifted to focus on Tommy Whitehall, sitting stiffly erect in his Army greens. And that's when I literally lost my breath. Why I hadn't figured it out before, I don't know, but as they say, the camera doesn't lie. As I looked at Tommy's face on that TV screen it hit me like a fist. I suddenly knew. I finally understood.

I wanted to scream. If I could have, I would have leaped out of that hospital bed and run straight over to the courtroom. I would've rushed up and pulled Katherine Carlson into my arms. I would've kissed her and comforted her, and begged her forgiveness.

Then the cameras and my own attention returned to Katherine. Perhaps it was my newfound knowledge, but she looked sadder than any human being I'd ever seen. She was admitting to the board that Eddie Golden was going to present one of the most compelling prosecution cases the world had ever heard. Every piece of evidence, every witness, every word out of Eddie's lips was going to make it impossible to believe that *Captain* Whitehall didn't commit the crimes of which he was accused.

There was a reason for this, she announced. *Captain* Whitehall was framed. She might not be able to prove this. She admitted this very forthrightly, because she had no intention of lying or misleading the board. The people who'd framed her client had made no mistakes. They'd left no implicating evidence. They'd thought it through and acted deliberately and skillfully. They'd done an astonishingly clever job of pinning it on her client. Nor was it difficult to do. Just a few simple steps was all it took.

Katherine warned them: As you listen to the prosecutor's case, as you hear his witnesses, as you view his evidence, remember that you're looking at the fabric of a murder committed by somebody else and blamed on *Captain* Whitehall. Put yourself in *Captain* Whitehall's shoes. Don't put yourself in Eddie Golden's shoes, because he's the biggest fool in this courtroom. He's been gulled, cuckolded, misled. He's the real murderer's best ally. Remember that with every word that spews from his mouth: He's already been fooled.

Considering the circumstances, Katherine's opener was about as good as they come. Fast Eddie, though, was seated at his table, unsuccessfully fighting a smug smile. Katherine had given the signal that all experienced attorneys know how to interpret. She'd admitted in her opening statement she couldn't defeat the state's case. So she'd done the only other reasonable thing you could do. She'd tried to get the board to imagine a conspiracy—not to ignore the witnesses or the evidence, but to see them as proof of the framer's skill. She couldn't undermine the evidence, so she was attacking the credibility of the presenter.

A nice touch, but I knew Eddie. He was going to cut her to shreds.

Katherine went back to her table, then the judge asked both attorneys to approach the bench. At this point the station cut to a commercial, but I knew what was happening.

When the broadcast resumed, the court was breaking up and the correspondent announced that Judge Carruthers had declared a recess for the rest of the day. Eddie and Katherine were collecting their papers from their respective tables. Katherine was smiling as she walked from the bench, which I found curious. But I guess she was just relieved to have another day to try to figure some new approach, to discover some breakthrough or create some new surprise for Eddie.

I flipped off the TV and tried to nap. I was going to need some sleep to pull this off.

About three hours later, they began arriving. First came a pair of MPs who peeked inside my room, then backed out and posted themselves outside my door.

Then Buzz and Carol showed up. Then two technicians lugged in a TV set and a VCR and a big camcorder on a tripod. Then the court bailiff entered. Then Eddie arrived looking miffed and sulky. Then came Captain Kip Goins, Katherine's substitute military co-counsel, who was representing his lead counsel because classified materials were going to be discussed. Finally, when everything was ready, Colonel Carruthers arrived in full dress greens. It was the first time I'd seen him with all his ribbons and regalia, and the first time I realized he was a former infantryman himself. I knew this because there was a Combat Infantryman's Badge on his breast, and a Ranger tab, and two Purple Hearts, and a Silver Star. No wonder he was such a hardass. With all due respect, of course.

A small metal desk had been set up on the far side of the room, and frankly Carruthers looked comical as he struggled to cram his huge frame behind that tiny thing. It's worth noting, though, that nobody giggled or showed the slightest sign of amusement.

While everybody was facing the judge, the door opened again and an elderly Korean man slipped in the back and took a seat by the door. It was Minister of Defense Lee. I'd made sure he was invited, although until this moment I wasn't sure he was going to come.

Carruthers opened with a fierce glower and explanation that this was a highly unusual procedure that was essential for the pursuit of justice. He pointed at the camcorder and informed us that the proceedings would be taped and preserved in the event of a subsequent appeal. The proceeding would be treated as though we were in the courtroom. He informed us we'd be hearing classified testimony, and if a single word uttered in this room leaked out, there'd be another court-martial, and he'd personally chair it, and it wouldn't be pretty.

Such was the judge's manner that even Buzz Mercer gulped.

Then Carruthers pulled a wooden mallet out of a pocket and slammed his little desk two or three times.

Mercer was asked to move to a chair in front of the judge's desk, where he was sworn in by the bailiff. The judge asked him a few introductory questions, like who was he, and what was his job, and what was his involvement with this case.

Eddie was seated in the corner of the room, and I kept my eyes on him, while his own kept wandering warily over to me. I could see he was curious, even nervous, about my role. I wasn't here as an attorney, since I'd already recused myself. Nor was I a witness. I was here as a specially appointed military assistant to Judge Barry Carruthers.

We'd even sent a frantic query to the military's review court in

Alexandria, Virginia, about our intentions, and they'd responded that they'd never heard of anything like this being done before, but as I was a sworn officer of the court, there didn't seem to be anything in the Uniform Code of Military Justice that precluded it. You can only have one judge in a criminal trial, but what law says he can't have an assistant?

Since nothing about to be discussed had been made available through pretrial discovery to either side, or even to the judge, this really was an unprecedented thing. On the other hand, both Carruthers and I had worked in the SPECAT court, where extraordinary things were done as a matter of course to protect the country's security.

Anyway, once Mercer had told everybody who he was, and about his involvement in this case, the judge turned the proceeding over to his specially appointed assistant. That meant he turned it over to me.

I said, "Mr. Mercer, could you please explain to the court the trail of events that led to your discovery that Chief Warrant Officer Michael Bales and Chief Inspector Choi Lee Min were operating as agents of North Korea?"

I thought Eddie was going to have a heart attack right on the spot. He started to stand up, and I'm sure he was on the verge of protesting, but Carruthers banged his mallet twice, hard, and Eddie fell quietly back into his chair.

I helped guide Buzz through everything. At key points, I made him slow down and explain how some particular deduction was made, or I made him provide more detailed explanations of some twist or turn in the investigation. It only got awkward when he kept bringing my name into it, which happened to be fairly often, as you might imagine. But again, I wasn't here as an attorney but as a member of the judge's staff, so there was nothing prejudicial about it.

It took about an hour to get it all out, and frankly every soul in that room, even Eddie, was completely mesmerized. The men and women in this room were hearing the intricate, blow-by-blow details of the largest counterespionage case in U.S. history. The public wasn't even yet aware it'd happened.

When Buzz was done, there was this odd moment you wouldn't exactly call a stunned silence. It was more like a bunch of people seated around a room staring at a bombshell that had just crashed through the ceiling, a not-yet-exploded one that you could hear ticking away. There was a communal reluctance to move, or breathe, or speak.

Then Eddie recovered his wits. "Your Honor," he called out in an irritated voice, "do I get to examine the witness?"

"Of course," Carruthers announced. "But this is a courtroom, so defense precedes."

Poor Kip was frozen in his seat. I could see his eyes darting around as he wondered what he could possibly ask the CIA station chief who'd just fingered two of the prosecution's witnesses as North Korean spies.

Finally he just shook his head. "I'll reserve till cross-examination."

That was actually a pretty smart move on Kip's part. Let Golden take his best shots, then see what damage needed to be repaired.

Eddie stood up and paced around trying to look lawyerly. I wanted to remind him there were no TV cameras in this room, so just cut the bullshit. He eventually stopped of his own accord right in front of Buzz.

He somehow managed to make himself looked amused. "Uh, Mr. Mercer, I'm sorry. That was a very, very entertaining story, but I didn't really hear you present any evidence that either Michael Bales or Choi Lee Min are agents of North Korea."

Buzz said, "No, I guess I didn't."

"I didn't think you did," Eddie said, instantly agreeable. "What I heard was a wildly circumstantial story that could have two dozen different entirely plausible explanations. You're a trained intelligence officer, aren't you? Assumptions can be very dangerous in your line of work. Don't you agree?"

Buzz was scratching his head and nodding. "Absolutely, Major. One of the most dangerous mistakes you can make."

"And Michael Bales is not here and is therefore unable to defend himself, right?"

"That's true," Buzz said. "Just seems to have dropped off the face of the earth."

"And Choi's dead, isn't he?"

"He is indeed dead," Buzz said with all-too-apparent satisfaction. "Major Drummond's co-counsel killed him."

"So you're asking us to take on face value that they were agents of North Korea. Isn't that true?"

"No, I wouldn't say that. I'd—"

There's a lawyer's dictum that you never, ever ask a potentially antagonistic witness a question you don't already know the answer to. Eddie had done his best to avoid it, slickly using his first four or five questions to feel out what Mercer had, to narrow down the odds, but in the end he'd stepped blindly off the cliff. He'd violated that dictum. And he knew it.

But he wasn't known as Fast Eddie for nothing.

"That's all I have," he quickly interrupted.

Buzz's lips were still parted, and he looked ready to say something more—he obviously wanted to—so Eddie leaned toward him and fixed him with a perfectly evil stare. "I said that's all I have, Mr. Mercer."

Then Eddie stomped over to his seat. The only problem was, he'd already committed legal suicide.

Carruthers looked at Kip. "Do you have any questions?"

Maybe Kip would've gotten around to asking it anyway, but Eddie had just opened the doorway for him, so Kip stood up and smiled, and stepped right through.

"Let me start, Mr. Mercer, by congratulating you. As a soldier and an American, I'm deeply impressed by the service you've rendered."

"Thank you, Captain." Buzz nodded, playing his role to the hilt.

Then Kip looked over at me. "And you, too, Major Drummond. You're a real hero."

I mumbled, "Thank you."

Kip grinned and then turned back to Mercer. "Now, I know you're a very busy man, so I have only one subject of inquiry."

"Yes?"

"Do you have any direct evidence that Michael Bales or Choi Lee Min were agents of North Korea?"

"In fact, I do."

"And where is this evidence?"

"Actually," Buzz said, pointing at the TV screen, "I brought along a videotape. We interrogated Mrs. Michael Bales, who also was an intelligence agent employed by North Korea."

"Can we see that tape?" Kip quite naturally asked.

"That's why I brought it."

CHAPTER

48

★ ★ ★

Eddie was screaming, "Objection! Objection!" loud enough I thought he'd give himself a hernia. I wished he would. I'd love to see him crumple to the floor in a ball of excruciating pain.

The two technicians ignored him and shifted the TV so everybody could see it, and then began preloading a black videocassette. Carruthers looked over at Golden.

"What is it?"

"If this is evidence from Bales's wife, it's inadmissible. A wife may not be compelled to testify against her husband."

"If it was compelled," Carruthers said. Then he glanced over at Mercer. "Was it?"

Buzz shrugged. "In a manner of speaking. They didn't let her sleep for five days."

Kip stood up. "Actually, I think Major Golden is confused. The testimony is not against the accused, Thomas Whitehall. It concerns a key prosecution witness."

Carruthers scratched his head a moment. "The point may still be relevant. Compelled testimony from the wife of a witness could enjoy the same protections."

Then I popped up. "May I help clarify a point for the court?"

Golden glowered, but Carruthers nodded.

I said, "Mr. Mercer, could we have the full name of the woman on the tape?"

Buzz jovially said, "The name on her military dependent ID card is Jin May Bales."

"Is that her real name?"

"Nope. Her real name's Lee Chin Moon."

"Where's she from?"

"The papers she filed with American military authorities say she was born in Chicago, Illinois, and came here in 1995."

"Was that factual?"

"Nope. Lee Chin Moon never set foot in the United States. She spent her whole life in a special camp in North Korea, at least until a submarine landed her off the east coast of the Republic of Korea."

"Are you saying everything she reported to the military authorities when she and Bales applied for marriage was false?"

Buzz chuckled, then matter-of-factly said, "Very nearly. Except for the block she stamped that identified her as a female. She is in fact a female. I'll attest to that."

"And how would you describe their marriage?"

"It wasn't a marriage. It was her cover. She was actually the controller for Choi and Bales. She was sent down here to run their operation when it was determined to be an intelligence gold mine."

"I'm sorry, why'd they send her down here?"

"To run this whole operation."

Even I had to shake my head at that one. "She was in charge of this?"

"Yep. They gave her a legend as Choi's sister, then made it foolproof by having her marry Bales. A pretty slick solution, if you think about it. She's living right on an American base as an officer's wife, she's controlling the man she lives with, and Choi gets to stop by and visit his 'sister' as often as he wants. And nobody's suspicious."

At this point we could have become embroiled in one of those lengthy arguments that you often see in bigamy contests about whether a marriage is still legal even if one of the participants used a false name—but really, what would be the point?

Eddie was squirming and trying to come up with something to

object to, but I guess he finally realized he'd only make an utter fool of himself. I wanted to see him try anyway.

Carruthers said, "Play the tape," and Eddie kept his mouth shut.

Minister Lee himself reached up and turned out the lights.

The TV screen flickered as the tape cued, then a picture popped up of a woman seated on a white chair in the middle of a white room. A wool blanket had been thrown over her body to cover her nakedness.

She looked filthy and exhausted, and her hair hung down in oily straggles. She was still breathtakingly beautiful.

For about thirty seconds, there were some exchanges between her and a man who was hidden from the camera. They were speaking in Korean, so I didn't understand what they were saying, but her voice and her demeanor were pleading, and the man's voice was sharp, overbearing, harsh.

She finally hung her head in resignation and allowed it to bob up and down in an exhausted nodding motion.

The man said, "Describe your relationship to Michael Bales."

He made her go through everything Buzz Mercer just told us, only it was infinitely more compelling to hear it from the lips of this woman taped into a chair. Carol Kim had been right. Her English was excellent, right down to the midwestern twang. But it should be. Like Choi, before coming south she'd spent her whole life in that special camp that Kim, the KCIA man, had mentioned, being taught English by former American POWs.

Then came questions about her responsibilities, and it turned out her role in the conspiracy included controlling the traitors Bales and Choi caught inside their net. In fits and starts, and often speaking haltingly, she said she told her traitors what information her masters in North Korea wanted, she collected their products, and on market days she went downtown and dropped them off with a contact who sped them up north.

Then came the part we were awaiting.

"How was Michael Bales enlisted?"

She stared at the floor. She seemed to be having trouble recalling it, maybe because she was exhausted, or maybe because she didn't want to get Bales confused with all the other Americans they'd entrapped.

Then she said, "This happened months before I arrived. Bales went to Itaewon one night to the King Mae Bar. He drank heavily and went upstairs with a prostitute. Bales likes . . . well, he likes rough sex. We had problems with him even after he was recruited. That night, though, Bales beat the whore as he screwed her . . ." She drew a few quick breaths like she needed oxygen to keep talking. "He drove her nose bone into her brain. She hemorrhaged and died. Choi came to investigate. Bales immediately identified himself as a police officer and Choi recognized how valuable he could be."

"So they struck a bargain?" the unseen questioner asked.

"Yes . . . a . . . a bargain."

"It was that simple?"

She nodded.

"Then what?"

"Who cares about the death of a whore? Who complains if her killer is never found? Her pimp? Choi wrote in the criminal file that Bales was there as an investigator, rather than a suspect. After two months he closed the case as unsolvable."

"Didn't you worry that Bales might flee or go back on the bargain?"

"There were always second files. I sent them north for safety. I could get them if . . . well, if I needed them."

"What did Bales do for you?"

Her chin fell on her chest, but her eyeballs looked up and stared at her questioner. "I'm tired . . . uh, ask me later."

The questioner screamed something at her in Korean, and while I had no idea what he said, she obviously did, and it brought her chin right off her chest.

The questioner said, "Now, answer the question. What did Bales do for you?"

Her head rolled backward, like she was trying to get blood flowing in her brain. "The first year . . . background checks on targets. He could access military personnel and FBI files. That was helpful."

"Anything else?"

"After a few years, he helped with entrapments. Choi would call him when he found a target. Bales would . . . he would help persuade them. The Americans, they became worried when he arrived. He would help pressure them."

"Did you give him money?"

"Some money. We sent it to a foreign account. It was not important to him, though."

"Why?" the interrogator asked.

Her chin fell on her chest again, but this time she kept talking, although her voice was trailing off. "He is very egotistical. Choi arranged to make him look like a super-detective." She then chuckled to herself, like it was a big joke only she got. "Very funny, really. Bales's superiors began relying on him to handle most of the cases committed off base. And when Bales's tours ended, they were eager to see his time extended in Korea."

"Tell us about the American Keith Merritt."

"No," she said, her voice becoming very weak. "It is time to sleep . . . You promised."

The screen suddenly went dark, but the sound was still on and you could hear the noise of footsteps, then four loud whacks, and the woman yelping from pain. Then the picture returned. Her cheeks were red, and she was staring at her interpreter with a mixture of resentment and anger.

The interpreter barked something in Korean and she nodded her head.

She said, "He came here weeks before the rest of them. He was nosing around. He interviewed Bales two days after he arrived, so we began watching him. Then, uh, later, he and Carlson . . . later they returned to interview Bales together . . . He was handed a glass of water. Bales took fingerprints off it. He sent them to the FBI. He wasn't an attorney. He was a private detective."

"Who tried to kill him?"

"Other people handled it. Two agents from Inchon. We didn't want to risk having any of our people identified."

"Why?"

"At first he focused his efforts on trying to prove Lee was a homosexual. Later, he suspected Whitehall was framed. But he had no facts." She stopped and stared at the floor a moment. "Still . . . we began to worry. Would he start looking at Bales and Choi?"

"How did you learn this? Did you bug his room, too?"

"No, only Whitehall's apartment in the months before his arrest. Melborne was a detective. We thought, maybe . . . he knew how to check. We used other means to eavesdrop on him."

Her head slumped forward again. We saw the interrogator's back move toward her, and then he shook her a few times, harshly enough that her head flopped back and forth. She seemed to come back to consciousness.

She said, "We overheard Merritt discussing his suspicions with Carlson, Whitehall's lawyer."

"And how did Melborne arrive at that suspicion?"

"He was guessing. But it was too close."

"So you lured him to Itaewon?"

"Choi thought of it. One of our people called Merritt and said they needed to talk. Melborne was told to walk down the street and shop. Our man told him he had seen his picture in the paper. They would meet and talk."

There was a brief pause and I wondered about Melborne's discussion with Katherine about a frame-up. How come Katherine never mentioned those suspicions to me? Was that why she'd told us to employ a frame defense?

Then before I could think any further about it, the unseen voice said, "Tell us about Whitehall."

Again she hung her head, as though she needed to work to recall the details. Considering that she probably hadn't slept in five or six days, I was amazed she could do anything except babble and drool.

Then the camera went dark again, and there were the sounds of more slaps and yelps, then her whimpering and saying something in Korean that sounded like begging, then the interrogator's voice sounding harsh and uncompromising.

The woman came into focus again. "We learned of Whitehall's

BRIAN HAIG

affair with Lee four . . . maybe five months ago. They thought they were discreet. The fools. When an apartment is rented to an American, the landlord must report it to the precinct."

"Is that how Choi knew?"

"He always watched for that. Usually the Americans are seeking a place to keep their mistresses, to conduct affairs."

"Why didn't you try to recruit Whitehall?"

She looked directly into the camera. "He was too unimportant. He held only a minor position on base. I directed Choi to have some assistants see what Whitehall was doing."

"And you discovered Lee No Tae?"

She nodded. "Two, sometimes four times a week they would meet in the apartment. Eventually, we bugged it."

"Whose idea was it to murder Lee No Tae?"

For a brief millisecond, you could see a spark of her earlier defiance. Or maybe it was pride.

"I ordered it."

"Why?"

"Isn't it obvious? To drive the Americans off Korean soil."

"Why that night?"

"They were about to separate. It would be our last chance."

I inadvertently turned and looked to the back of the room where Minister Lee was seated. His eyes were on the television screen. His arms were crossed and his face was expressionless. I didn't even want to imagine what he was feeling.

"How did you get inside the apartment?"

"We didn't."

"You didn't?"

"Lee always awoke at three-thirty to go back onto base. Privates have to be present when their sergeants go through the barracks to awaken the soldiers. Otherwise he would've gotten into trouble."

"So he was killed outside the apartment?"

The camera focused on her a moment until it was evident she was sound asleep. Her chin was back on her chest and you could tell by the way her breasts were moving that she was in la-la land.

The film went through the dark-again-whack-ouch-whack-ouch-whack-ouch routine, then there were more words in Korean, then her face came back on the screen.

"We killed him in the stairwell. Lee put up a fight. He even struck Choi several times. Finally, though, the men held him. They beat him for a while. He had to appear roughed up."

"How was he killed?"

"Choi pulled his . . . uh, belt out of his pants and strangled him." She paused and her lip curled upward, ever so slightly. "It turned out, when Lee dressed, he took the wrong belt. It was Whitehall's. Lucky," she mumbled.

The interrogator said something sharp, like he didn't think there was anything the least bit happy about any of this. She stared back at him, her face completely exhausted, but something in her eyes let you know she thought she'd won one here.

The questioner said, "How did you get him back into the apartment?"

This time I already knew the answer before she gave it.

"A key to the apartment . . . in Lee's pocket. Whitehall gave it to him, months before. Choi used it then, then, uh, laid his body next to Whitehall's. The door had an automatic lock. It relocked when they closed it."

"How did you make it appear the body had been raped?"

"Choi brought along a . . . ?" she suddenly appeared perplexed, then said some word in Korean.

"A dildo," the hidden voice translated for her.

She nodded. "They inserted it and left it in his body for twenty minutes. Choi has investigated many sex crimes. This was his idea. It was a nice touch."

This time when I turned back around and stole a look at Minister Lee, he was staring down at the floor and there were tears rolling down his cheeks. I felt a shudder of pain for him. One of the few facts about this case I'd been able to establish on my own was how much he and his wife loved their son. No parent should have a child murdered. Worse, no parent should ever be forced to listen to one of the murderers recount the tawdry details of the crime.

The questioner asked, "Then Choi returned to the precinct?"
She shook her head.

"Where, then?" the man yelled. "Where did he go?"

"Home. He waited there for the call. Bales waited with me."

"You mean Bales was there?"

"Of course. He enjoys these things. As I told you, he is a sadist."

Then the hidden questioner and some other hidden male voice exchanged a few words in Korean, and the screen went dark.

It took the minister a few seconds to turn the light back on. When I turned around to look at him, his back was just going out the door.

The rest of the room was silent. Eddie was slumped over in his chair looking like death warmed over. That's one of the many things I don't like about that bastard. He really didn't give a damn that a man had been brutally murdered, or that an innocent man had been framed. He was feeling despondent that he wasn't going to win this case.

Carruthers surveyed the psychic carnage in the room, then asked everybody to leave except the two opposing lawyers and me. It took nearly a minute for the rest of them to clear out, until all that was left were raw emotions, one judge, and three lawyers.

CHAPTER
49
⭐ ⭐ ⭐

The other three gathered around my bed like a coven of witches. Eddie had a sourpuss, Kip's face was elated, and mine was, well, pained. As happy as I was to finally have the facts on the table, I was closer to the victims of this case than anyone else in this room, and I'd been sickened to hear that coldhearted bitch talk about murdering a young kid and destroying the lives of countless other people.

She and her buddies ran a meat market.

Carruthers's face simply looked grim and purposeful.

Kip said, "The murder, rape, and necrophilia charges have to be dropped."

For a brief second, Eddie looked like he was going to have a heart attack, but I gave him a positively murderous look, and, to tell you the truth, even though I was lying in bed, and I still had a big hole in my back, if he'd tried to raise an objection I might very well have climbed out of bed and gone over and knocked his pretty lips right through the back of his head.

Carruthers said, "I agree. They're dropped."

Then I asked, "What about the rest of it?"

The judge had his nostrils pinched between his forefinger and thumb. "That, I don't know about. Nor do I have the latitude to decide. The preponderance of evidence suggests there was homosexual activity between an officer and some enlisted soldiers. That's not a minor offense."

I thought about saying something, but I had nothing to add Carruthers didn't already know, so I kept my mouth shut.

Carruthers said, "Not a word from any of you on any of this until I announce my decision." Then he formally recessed the court, such as it was. A moment later the technicians returned to collect the TV and VCR and the camcorder that had been running this whole time.

Before I knew it, I had my hospital room back. I thought about everything that just happened, and my eyes closed and I floated off to sleep. The thing about being seriously wounded and drugged to the gills is that you don't realize how very little exertion it takes to sap every bit of your energy.

I was awakened about four hours later by Doc Bridges, who rushed in with three frantic-looking nurses and started running around, straightening up the room, smoothing my sheets, and changing my hospital garb into something starchier and spankier-looking. Doc Bridges even had on a neatly pressed and completely spotless white lab coat, and his hair was neatly combed—well, as neatly combed as he could make it, meaning he looked like a porcupine.

If there'd been a paintbrush and bucket of lime green paint around, I'll bet they would've slapped a fresh coat on the walls. As an experienced Army guy, I recognized the drill. Somebody important was about to come visit, and the hospital commander had ordered Bridges to get me and my room looking presentable, toute suite, as they say in the ranks.

Then the door flew open and General Spears and Acting Ambassador Brandewaite and Minister of Defense Lee walked in. General Spears hooked a finger in the direction of the door and Doc Bridges and his nurses nearly left a smoke trail, they moved out so fast.

I was struggling to sit up in bed. Spears said, "Stay the way you are, Drummond."

I said, "Yes sir," which wasn't witty or bright but fit the occasion.

The three of them then gathered around and stared down at me. If you think I was apprehensive, you've got that right. Here were three of the warlords of Korea and here was little old me with a hole in my back so if things got bad I couldn't even get up and run away.

I had no idea what they wanted, but I wasn't betting it was good. I'd just blown the lid off the Lee No Tae case and thrown a terrible dilemma into their collective laps. I'd proven the minister's kid was gay, despite a thousand warnings by a thousand people that this was utterly taboo. I gulped a few times and looked at their collective faces.

Finally, Brandewaite stroked his handsome chin and said, "We seem to have a most incredible situation on our hands."

"Indeed we do," Spears agreed. "But sometimes, in the midst of tragedy, you find opportunity."

"That's right," Brandewaite said.

This might almost have been funny if I'd had even the slightest idea what they were talking about.

Brandewaite said, "Drummond, this afternoon we've been in contact with the White House and the president of Korea."

I nodded like I understood, which I didn't.

But before he could say another word, Minister Lee stepped forward. "Please. Let me handle this. I'd like a private moment with Major Drummond."

Spears and Brandewaite both nodded respectfully, then stepped out of the room.

"Major Drummond," the minister said, "I want you to know something."

"Yes sir."

"My wife and I, we . . . we loved our son very much."

He had to stop for a moment, because it was evident he was having difficulty. He took a few heavy breaths, then said, "I am not ashamed of No. You understand that."

"Yes, Mr. Minister."

"He struggled against what he was. He wanted us to be proud of him. And we *were* proud of him. Always. It was not his fault, what he was."

"No sir."

"We knew, of course. We knew our son loved men. Children cannot hide such things from parents."

I'd already suspected this. I'd suspected it from the moment the three of us had entered No's bedroom together. When the minister had opened his lips and struggled to say something, I'd thought he might have been on the verge of admitting he knew his son was gay.

Why hadn't he admitted it? I think because he felt he owed the gift of silence to his son's memory. Koreans are funny that way. Despite the fact that they're the most Christian nation in Asia, they still worship and honor their dead ancestors. They even have this big national holiday called Chusok, where they all go like lemmings to graveyards around the country to honor their dead forefathers and foremothers, or whatever.

I couldn't imagine the agony he and his wife had been through. And I suppose that accounted for why he'd bent over backward to be fair to Whitehall. I think he'd suspected from the beginning Whitehall hadn't done it. I think he hoped his son wouldn't hook up with a man who would do such terrible things to him. I think he wanted us to prove Tommy was innocent. I think he wanted us to find the real killers. Maybe I was kidding myself, but that's what I thought. That's what I'd thought ever since I'd left him and his wife in their house.

He put his hand on my arm. "I've asked the president of South Korea to order the release of Captain Whitehall. And I've asked General Spears to drop all charges."

A big breath of air poured out of my mouth.

"I am not trying to hide my son's relationship with Whitehall. Not any longer. But it's best for both our nations if we simply say my son was murdered by the North Koreans, and Whitehall was framed, just as your protesters were murdered by the North Koreans. It would be best for our alliance."

I wanted to say something meaningful, something to take away his pain, to make this easier for him.

But all I could get out was, "It's true, Mr. Minister. Your son was murdered by the North Koreans."

He nodded his head in the knowing way some very wise old people have, and he gently patted my arm and left.

Then General Spears and Brandewaite came back in. They stood beside my bed for a long moment. Brandewaite said, "I just want you to know, Drummond, that I bear no hard feelings toward you over all of this."

I wasn't exactly sure I heard that right. I mean, the last time I checked, I was the one who was supposed to have hard feelings against him. But I guess that's what it takes to be a diplomat. Always distort the facts to your own advantage. Or is that a lawyer? Whatever.

Even General Spears seemed to catch the idiocy of it, because he waited till Brandewaite had his back turned and was headed toward the door before he rolled his eyes, and then he did this little jerky motion with his right hand that most folks would interpret to be a fairly disrespectful gesture.

Once Brandewaite was gone, the general reached into his pocket and withdrew a medal with a fancy ribbon on it. He placed it on the bed right beside me. "The President asked me to give you this. He said to tell you that the nation is very proud and appreciative of your efforts."

I glanced at the medal for a moment, and he seemed to be at a loss for words. He finally squeezed my arm. "Sean, nobody's more proud of what you just accomplished than me, but as far as the world is concerned, this whole thing never happened. There was an assassination attempt and you saved the Secretary's life, but the true facts will never be known."

I nodded like it made no difference to me, and really I guess it didn't.

Then he paused for a moment before he said, "Son, most people would think a little piece of ribbon doesn't seem like much for what you did, but in our profession it's everything."

Then he spun around and walked out and left me fingering the tiny medal he'd left me. I stared at it, and damn if it didn't look just like the Distinguished Service Cross, the second highest award for heroism.

But maybe I was just imagining all that happened. I was doped up to the max, and I'd been beaten, stabbed, and shot, then shot again—and the mind does play funny tricks.

CHAPTER
50
★ ★ ★

The physical therapy was every bit as wicked as I had dreaded it would be. They actually transported me back to Walter Reed Army Medical Center on a medevac plane, keeping me happily doped up till we got there. Then the nazis at Walter Reed got their first look at me, took the drugs away, and my life turned into pure hell.

The Army's idea of medicine can be summed up by that old maxim "Spare the rod and spoil the child." Phrased another way, "If you let a knife get dull, it takes a lot longer to resharpen than one kept sharp."

If you want to hear more of these inane sayings, I could go on, because in my six-week stay at Walter Reed I heard about two million of them from the sadists who made me get up every morning and make my own bed, who brought me Jell-O and actually made me eat it, and thousands of other unspeakable things. My personal favorite was the 250-pound female nurse who showed up on my third day, deadly intent on rolling me over and giving me an enema. I put up one hell of a fight. I swear I did. But alas, I lost.

On my sixth night, an official State Department courier showed up with a handwritten note from the Secretary of State himself, thanking me for saving his life and inviting me to stop by for a private dinner after I got out of the hospital. I thought about sending back a note saying I was pretty busy and wasn't sure I could make it. That lasted about a nanosecond. Like I'd ever turn down a free meal. And besides, I was dying to share my views about the world with the Secretary; and since I'd saved his life, he'd have to sit and politely listen. How often does life offer you a chance like that?

A few days later, I got a very nice note from Tommy Whitehall, thanking me profusely for everything I did. I can't say we'd gotten to know each other well, and the circumstances of our relationship were certainly awkward, if that's the right word to use. I did like him, though. And I thought he was a damned fine officer, too. If I were still an infantry officer, and I was getting ready to go into battle, I'd love to have a guy like Tommy on my flank.

A few days after that, I got an equally nice note from Allie saying she really enjoyed working with me and hoped I was feeling better. She actually gave me her address and phone number in case I ever needed anything. And I decided that maybe my first order of business once I got out of this hellhole was to go look her up and take her to dinner. I mean, she's not the type I usually take to dinner, since she's a little tall for me, and there's that spiky hair, and I knew we'd draw some odd stares, but when you get right down to it, the honor and pleasure would be all mine.

Maria and Allie and Whitehall, and everything else about this case, had certainly forced me to do a lot of hard thinking about whether gays should be allowed to serve openly in the ranks. On the face of it, why not? Is this country really so rich in patriots that it can afford to turn down any Americans who volunteer to spend a few precious years of their lives in its service? And hey, do you ever hear anyone bitching about collecting taxes from gays who admit they're gays? Right.

On the other hand, I'm just not sure us heteros can handle it. Maybe it's our problem and not theirs. But it's still a problem.

Imelda dropped by a few times. She brought my mail and a bottle of castor oil she insisted would cure all ills. She can be fusty and old-fashioned that way. The third time, she sat beside my bed and heckled me to quit faking it and get my ass back to work. She'd never admit it, but I knew she missed having me around.

And what *about* Imelda? Is she really gay? Nah, I don't think so.

I figured she was just trying to force some fresh air into my closed mind. If you really know Imelda, you know she's not above a little playacting when it serves her. Like when she came by to see me in my hospital room that last time in Korea. She wasn't checking on my health. She was there to get the doctor to wake me up, then guilt me into exerting one last breath of effort for Tommy Whitehall. See, Imelda's that way. She does whatever it takes to get the job done. She's old Army right down to her OD green undershorts. And if you think Katherine's devious, Imelda could kick her ass at chess any day.

Then one day I watched on TV as the defense minister of North Korea paid a visit to the South Koreans, and every spinmeister on every talk show began yabbering about the surprisingly sudden breakthrough in relations between these two implacable foes. They called it a miracle, but it wasn't any miracle.

I mean, North Korea's lonely and broke and has millions of starving and unhappy people, and no matter how stubborn it is, any idiot can tell the clock's running out on their future. What I figured was, Choi's plot was a last-ditch attempt to have it their way. And had it worked, North Korea's defense minister might still be visiting South Korea, only in a slightly different capacity—at the head of his three-million-man army. Of course, there were no guarantees it wouldn't eventually end up that way, but the chances were suddenly much smaller.

On the second day of the fourth week, just when I thought I'd go crazy with boredom, I got my first glimpse of hope and salvation. She came waltzing into my room, wearing her usual pinstriped pantsuit with a bulging shopping bag under her arm. She didn't say anything at first. Instead she grabbed a chair, went over and closed the door, then she actually propped the chair underneath the knob so nobody could peek in.

I sat up in bed and shyly hiked the sheets around my chest.

She walked over and fell onto the edge of my bed. "Hello, Attila."

I smiled. "Hey, Moonbeam."

She smiled back. "Wait'll you see what I brought you."

She reached into the bag and withdrew guess what? A magnum-size bottle of Johnnie Walker Blue. No kidding, it was the biggest damned bottle I'd ever seen, and it was filled with that glorious, throat-searing golden liquid. It must've cost at least five or six hundred dollars, I figured. I rubbed my eyes and stared at it.

"Go ahead," she told me, prodding the bottle in my direction. "I couldn't afford it on my salary, but OGMM decided you deserved to be compensated for your out-of-pocket expenses."

"Gee, I don't know," I said. "I mean, the Army's got these fairly stiff regulations against accepting a gift that costs over fifty dollars. And from an organization like OGMM, to boot." Then I yanked the bottle out of her hand. "Of course, when it's compensation for legitimate expenses, I'm sure that's a different thing."

I swiftly screwed off the top and took a long gulp. My eyes actually glazed over and my throat felt like it was on fire.

"Where's Tommy?" I asked when I could finally speak again.

"He's home, on leave."

"Uh-huh. He going to stay in or get out?"

"He hasn't made up his mind. He has some bitterness. And he knows that if he stays, he'll be under a microscope."

"Yeah, tough decision. I guess he's talking it over with your mom and dad, huh?"

It isn't often that you surprise Katherine Carlson, but I got her on that one. I mean, I really got her. Her head reeled back and her mouth hung open.

"You knew he was my brother?"

"Hell yeah. The whole time," I assured her.

"Liar."

I shrugged. Of course, I should've known it when Ernie, Whitehall's old cadet roomie, told me about that picture Tommy kept on his desk. That had to be a photograph of his sister. Or I should've seen the family resemblance any of those times we were together in those cells. I didn't, though. Not until I saw them both through the camera's eyes.

"Why didn't you tell me?"

"I couldn't."

"Why not? Maybe I would've been more sensitive. Maybe I wouldn't have stuffed my foot in my mouth so many times."

"You? Sensitive? God, Drummond, give me a break."

"Try me."

"Okay, I was respecting an old oath."

"Tell me about it."

"When Thomas left for West Point, he made the whole family swear we'd stay away from him."

"Why? Was he ashamed?"

"Maybe a bit, but we didn't take offense. What we all decided was that he was actually ashamed of the Army, that it could be so closed-minded. The Army wouldn't have approved of us."

"Because your parents are hippies?"

"Certainly that. But when Thomas got older he really didn't approve of their life, either. It just wasn't for him. Remember that old TV series *Family Ties*?"

"What? Tommy was Michael J. Fox?"

She chuckled. "To a tee. Everybody in the commune was mystified by him. The rest of us were dressed in hand-me-downs, but Thomas always wore pressed pants and shined shoes. Whenever we played cowboys and Indians, the rest of us would fight to be the oppressed Indians, but Thomas always wanted to be the cavalry officer. Why do you think I call him Thomas, instead of Tom or Tommy? He insisted on it. He was just different."

"And maybe he was worried about the fact you work for OGMM?"

"That, too."

I nodded because she had a point. As much as I love the Army, it's a pretty one-way organization. It's famous for being one-way. Conformity and uniformity are almost synonymous with the word "Army." Alternative lifestyles just aren't real appreciated by the green machine.

I said, "That why you do it? That why you specialize in military gay cases?"

"It might be part of it. You didn't think I was doing it because I was gay, did you?"

"Hell no," I lied.

She smiled and chuckled because she knew I was lying.

I said, "So you decided to dedicate your life to crusade for your brother? Do I have that right?"

"Only partly. I love Thomas very much and I'm very proud of him. I don't like the Army, but I can't understand why this country won't approve of him leading troops into battle. Him, and a few hundred thousand more just like him. I might've chosen this field anyway, but having my brother as an inspiration made it more personal."

"And you figured, what? That if anybody ever knew the two of you were brother and sister, what with your work for OGMM, you might expose his sexuality?"

"That thought had crossed both our minds."

"You still could've told me."

"No, I couldn't. It was even more critical to keep it private after he was arrested. If a court-martial board knew I was his sister, they would've discounted my advocacy as blind allegiance."

She was right about that, obviously.

I said, "What about Whitehall? How'd he get that name?"

"Well, Carlson was the name of the commune where I was born, right? See if you can guess the name of the nearest town."

"Let me see. Was it Smithsville?"

She punched me on the chin. As a trained lawyer my skills of deduction are razor-sharp.

I took another long sip to work up my nerve. I'd been anxiously waiting four weeks to clear this up. Finally I said, "Hey, about that morning."

"What morning?"

"Christ, are we gonna go through this again?"

"Okay, about that morning . . ."

"That really was business. I swear it was. I was just trying to get your brother off."

I probably could've said that any of ten other ways, but hey, a little spur in her conscience wasn't going to hurt anything, right?

She looked me right in the eye and evaded the entire subject.

"So have you heard anything about Bales? Or did he just disappear into the night?"

"Nah, they caught him," I told her.

"Really?"

"Yeah. He was actually hiding out somewhere in the Philippines, using a false passport. But it seems he beat up a prostitute, and when the cops arrested him they notified the American embassy, and voilà."

"How'd you hear that?"

"You wouldn't believe me if I told you."

"Try me."

"Okay. The second he got taken into custody he said he wanted a lawyer. You'll never guess who he asked for."

She started laughing.

And I said, "No, really. The chief of the JAG Corps himself called to ask if I'd take his case."

"And did you say no?"

"What do you think I said?"

She smirked.

"I told him I'll think about it."

Her nose crinkled in this really cute way. Then she looked down at her watch, and she stood up and bent over and kissed me. Right in the middle of the forehead. A gushless, grandmother's peck. Ouch.

Then she straightened back up and smiled at me very curiously.

She said, "You know, Sean, you really did a good job. And I'm not just saying that. There were moments when Allie and I really doubted you'd break this case, but you came through. I really was ready to cut a deal to buy us some more time."

If she only knew the half of it. But I could never tell her about that other half, so instead I just blushed and said, "Yeah, well . . ."

Her smile broadened. "No, really, we couldn't have done it without you. Or Buzz Mercer, either. As much as I despise the CIA, they sure pulled through on this one. Be sure to pass on to him how deeply appreciative we are."

And in that instant, my mouth just fell open.

I gagged and stammered once or twice, and tried to force some air through my throat, but before I could say anything she shrugged and thumped a hand on her forehead and said, "Oh, right, of course. No need to remind me. Carol Kim, too. She certainly deserves some credit."

I sputtered out, "How'd you . . . uh? Oh my God. The bugs? Those were yours?"

She nodded. "Don't lose it on me now, Attila. We bugged your predecessor's room too. That's how we discovered he was leaking information to Spears's legal adviser, which was actually why I fired him. As I told you before, you really have no idea how your side plays. When I asked for you, I certainly hoped I could trust you, but under the circumstances I had to be sure."

And suddenly little pieces began falling into place.

Her grin broadened. "I don't mean to rub it in, but we even bugged your hospital room. God, that little court scene was riveting. Tell me, what was the look on Golden's face when Mercer finished his testimony?"

I knew what she was up to. She was trying to evade my explosion. I yelled, "My hospital room? You bugged my goddamned hospital room?"

She nodded.

"But how?"

"How what?"

"Don't give me that crap! How in the hell did you bug my hospital room?"

"Well, I didn't do it personally. Captain Bridges handled that. He's a full, dues-paying member of OGMM, you know."

I guess I looked pretty angry, because I was starting to lunge forward and say something when she reached down and put a finger on my lips.

"Look, before you get all worked up, just remember—if we hadn't been listening, we wouldn't have heard you call Mercer about the attempt at the Blue House, and Allie wouldn't have been there to keep Choi from shooting you."

And in that instant I suddenly realized how thoroughly Katherine Carlson had deceived me from the very beginning. She'd known everything I was up to. She'd manipulated and exploited me like a dumb mackerel on the end of her fishing line.

No wonder she hadn't insisted on a change of venue when I'd discovered the bugs. It isn't like her to give in so easily. Why hadn't I been more suspicious about that? But they were her bugs. And after I'd ripped them out, and then run to her, she'd faked her little tantrum, then allowed herself to be talked out of it, then simply had them replaced.

But what about Imelda? Wasn't she supposed to be having my room swept every day? Hell, she'd assured me two or three times that my room was clear. Then it hit me. She was in on it. And that probably meant I was wrong, that she also must be a member of . . . oh my God, OGMM.

I tried to think through all the ramifications and odd angles, but it was simply too vast and complicated to begin to contemplate. I'd been dancing in Katherine's web from the beginning.

She'd known about the North Koreans. She'd known everything I'd discovered about the Itaewon station, even as I discovered it.

Which of course meant she'd known there'd been nothing romantic between Carol Kim and me, too. But she'd played it like a Broadway star, kissing and kicking and prodding me along at all the right moments.

And then another piece fell into place. I suddenly understood why she'd been so desperate to get the charges for committing homosexual acts and consorting with enlisted troops dropped. Of all the charges against her brother, those were far and away the least serious. So why those two? Because she knew her brother hadn't murdered Lee, because he was her brother. Because she'd tracked my progress, and she'd overheard me getting closer and closer, and she'd figured that I'd eventually find out who actually murdered Lee, so she wanted to get her brother cleared of the only two charges that would stick regardless, the two crimes he'd actually committed.

All in all, it was staggeringly brilliant. I felt so profoundly stupid and used I almost sank through the mattress.

But why hadn't she told me Melborne was a detective, or about his suspicions? Or that Whitehall was her brother? I mean, what was the harm?

And then I understood everything. Or nearly everything. Maybe her brother was in on it, too. Maybe Tommy Whitehall had deliberately held back from me, forcing me to come up to speed, forcing me to dig deeply into things I never would've checked if he and Katherine had just sat me down and told me everything they knew from the start. Tommy had waited until I was completely flummoxed and at a dead end before he told me about that key he'd given Lee.

See, Katherine knows me too well. I mean, this wasn't just about trust, although that was no doubt part of it. She just knew how senselessly and remorselessly competitive I can be. She knew how hard I'd work to beat her out, to vie for her client's loyalty, to prove I was a better legal brawler, a more thorough investigator, a tougher litigator. She knew I'd kill myself to get ahead of her. And I very nearly did. She set it up perfectly.

Or maybe that wasn't it at all. Maybe she went to all these great lengths just to put me in my place, to show me she really was better than me.

Or maybe it was none of that, because if there was one thing she'd taught me, it was that I'd never really know what was in that beautiful, brilliant head of hers. The woman was a walking enigma on stilts.

I was still shaking my head in shock as she walked over and pulled the chair away from the door.

I said, "Hey? Why'd you put that chair against the door?"

She returned the chair to its place beside my bed. "I don't know. I just did."

She was pulling her bag over her shoulder and running a hand through that gorgeous hair of hers.

I said, "Y'know, someday they're gonna let me outta this place."

"Not if they do a psychiatric on you, Attila."

"Yeah, maybe. But you know, I still have some vacation time built up. See, the last time I tried to take one, somebody ruined it."

She put a finger on her lower lip and I swear to God, it was the most enchanting thing I'd ever seen. "So go to Bermuda. I hear they have Swedish stewardesses running all over the place."

"Nah, that's just what they tell the tourists. All they really got is burned-out secretaries with big puffy hairdos and Bronx twangs."

She nodded, like, Yeah, that's what she'd heard, too.

"Well, Attila, I hate to run, but I have to be in court in one hour."

I guess I looked dispirited, or bewildered, or maybe suicidal. She studied my face a moment, then bent over and kissed me again. And right on the lips this time. Maybe it was only what you'd call a pity kiss, or maybe it was a full-blown conquest kiss, but like I said before, I'll take it any way I can get it.

Then she walked out the door and was gone.

The truth was I knew damned well why she put that chair against the door. Of course, you have to know Katherine to really understand it. I mean, she knew before she even walked in the room that I was sexually comatose.

That chair thing, that was a teaser.

Or maybe it was a rain check, a signal that as soon as I got out of this place, I could put a chair against *her* door.

Not that I was sure it would ever work. She really is the most conniving, deceitful attorney I've ever met—you've got to believe me about that. The woman wasn't first in the class for nothing.